The Paris Secret

Karen Swan was previously a fashion editor and lives
in East Sussex with her husband and three children.

Visit Karen's website at www.karenswan.com or
you can find her author page on Facebook
or follow her on Twitter @KarenSwan1

Also by Karen Swan

Players
Prima Donna
Christmas at Tiffany's
The Perfect Present
Christmas at Claridge's
The Summer Without You
Christmas in the Snow
Summer at Tiffany's
Christmas on Primrose Hill

The PARIS SECRET

KAREN SWAN

MACMILLAN

First published 2016 by Macmillan
an imprint of Pan Macmillan
20 New Wharf Road, London N1 9RR
Associated companies throughout the world
www.panmacmillan.com

ISBN 978-1-4472-8029-3

1 3 5 7 9 8 6 4 2

A CIP catalogue record for this book is available from the British Library.

Typeset by Ellipsis Digital Limited, Glasgow
Printed and bound by CPI Group (UK) Ltd, Croydon, CR0 4YY

Visit **www.panmacmillan.com** to read more about all our books
and to buy them. You will also find features, author interviews and
news of any author events, and you can sign up for e-newsletters
so that you're always first to hear about our new releases.

For Aunty Flora
The original and best Bad Influence

Prologue

Paris, July 2016

Clouds bearded the moon and the horizon was still inky, with every one of the world-famous lights turned off, save for the beacon at the top of the distinctive tower that distinguished the famous city even in the dark. The two men moved unseen on the mansard roofs, keeping their heads below the ridge line, bodies curled inwards like autumn leaves, their stealthy footsteps no more than the mere padding of cats to the sleeping inhabitants of the apartments below.

Catching sight of their mark on the other side of the street, they stopped and crouched between the dormers, their eyes counting down the number of windows echoed in the matching buildings across the street. In silence, they spooled out the rope, the carabiners clipped on their harnesses clattering together like chimes as they moved – sure-footed, pulses up – and anchored themselves to the chimney stack.

The first man stepped over the edge, feeling that familiar rush as gravity exerted its might and the rope tightened; he paused for a second, checking that everything would hold, before dropping down below the roofline, pushing off from the wall with his feet every few metres.

The other man followed and within a minute, they were there – the dust-screened windows which had first caught their attention, every bit as obscured, close up, as they had hoped. The Juliet balcony outside it was shallow, wide enough only for a potted rose, but it was sufficient for a foothold and they swung their legs over the intricate balustrade. Standing with their feet parallel to the wall, they could angle their body weight in to the building and each of them cupped his hands around his face, trying to peer past the obfuscated glass. But it was like trying to see through smoke.

In the distance, a siren sounded and both men stiffened, their reflexes sharp as they tracked which direction it was coming from – and where it was heading to.

Not here. That was all they needed to know.

They resumed their efforts to get in, gloved hands on the doors. There was no handle on the outside and the inner, left-facing, door didn't budge, but the outer one rattled lightly, showing it was loose. Loose enough, anyway. These doors were old – the wood rotting, the single-glazing so thin they could crack it with a sneeze. But even that wouldn't be necessary. The first man had bent his knees and, his eye level with the latch, could clearly see the thin metal arm of an old-fashioned hook that was the only thing keeping the outside out. He grabbed his knife from his back pocket and jemmying it into the gap, quickly flicked it upwards. The hook swung up, round and back, knocking lightly against itself.

They were in. It was that easy – a sharp eye, a rope and a knife.

The doors were stiff with neglect, the hinges protesting

with loud creaks as they were forced back, but open they did and both men stepped onto the parquet floor. They twisted their head-torches on and, unclipping themselves from the ropes, began to move silently through the empty rooms.

The air was so stale it almost had a physical texture to it and they couldn't help but cough, even though the need for silence was paramount. That wasn't all they disturbed – their footsteps on the dusty floor recorded their path through the apartment like tracks in the snow, but who would ever see? It was obvious no one apart from them knew this place was still here. It was hidden in plain sight, the neighbours' apathy no doubt perpetuating the secret, everyone working on the assumption that it belonged to someone else; that it was someone else's problem. You couldn't just *lose* an apartment, after all; couldn't forget you owned it.

But someone had.

The first man stopped in the kitchen. A single chair lay on its side on the floor, a dresser stood bare, its hooks like curled, arthritic fingers with nothing to hold. There wasn't a pot or a pan, a bucket or mop. The place had been stripped.

Disappointed, they walked further down the hall, their twin beams of light crossing over each other like duelling swords in the blackness as they continued to search.

Both men stopped at the threshold to the bedroom. An iron bedstead was pushed against the back wall but that wasn't what quickened their pulses. A large wooden crate stood at the end, the lid splintered from where it had been levered off, a crowbar still on the bed slats.

They hurried over, the first man squinting as he read a small sheet of paper stapled to the inside. The handwritten script had faded in the sun but there was a company name and oval logo on the top and it looked like some kind of pro-forma docket.

Behind him, the second man tripped over something on the floor and lurched heavily into the end of the bed. He swore and looked back irritably, picking up the offending article. He had thought it just a rag, but on closer inspection saw it was a child's toy – a cloth duck comforter, its stuffed head bald from overuse, the terry towelling fabric bleached with age and thick with dust. The man immediately sneezed, letting it drop to the floor again.

So much for silence, his companion thought. They might as well just hold a party and invite the neighbours.

'Holy shit,' he whispered, shining a light into the crate as he stared in.

The second man hurried over, his torch too flooding the dark cavity with light.

Both men stared, open-mouthed, at what was inside. It was more than they could have dreamed of.

'Quick. Let's get her out.'

Chapter One

Wiltshire, England, August 2016

Summertime had England in its grip. The heatwave baking the Continent had finally hit British shores and the nation was revelling in its signature jubilant mood that was always unzipped any time the mercury nudged the thirties – deck-chairs dotted the parks, freckles multiplied, children played in fountains and residential streets reverberated to the slap of flip-flops on bare feet.

Not that Flora Sykes could see or hear any of this. Her parents' back garden – eight acres in the Wiltshire country-side – was bordered by high beech hedges and carpeted in camomile lawns, and she had been blissfully face down and unconscious on the lounger by the pool since arriving, a cool three hours after she'd stepped off the plane. Her big brother Freddie was still nowhere to be seen, sleeping like a student; her father was on the golf course; and her mother, swatting away Flora's half-hearted, exhausted offers to help, was efficiently plunging langoustines into boiling water, apparently unmoved by the creatures' Nemo-like attempts to escape by wriggling the plastic bags they were held in across the worktops.

Flora had intended to read. One of her New Year's

resolutions involving working less and playing more had been to read everything on last year's Man Booker longlist, but by March that had been amended to reading the short-list and now she would just be grateful to get through this first book that she'd bought in January and was still only a third of the way through. The problem was adrenalin. Her life was ruled by it – long, intense, work-around-the-clock bursts, followed by crashes into oblivion – and it left precious little time or energy for pastimes like reading.

This week had been a case in point. She had woken up in Palm Beach on Monday, Chicago on Wednesday, and had squeezed in a meeting and drinks party in Manhattan yesterday, before darting to JFK in her cocktail dress for the red-eye to Heathrow.

'Cup of tea, darling?' Her mother's voice, distant, sounded in her ear. She heard the chink of china on limestone. 'And you need to put some more lotion on. Your shoulders are beginning to go pink.'

A warm hand touched her skin, testing across her shoulders for proof. Flora raised her head, a cloud of butter-blonde hair falling over her face. 'Huh?' she groaned.

'Oh, darling, I worry about you. All this jet lag plays havoc with your system.'

Flora flipped her hair back and tried to push up into a sitting position. Her mother was swinging her legs onto the lounger next to her, a copy of *The Lady* on her lap and a matching tea in her hands. Her straw hat threw shade over a face that was still beautiful, even in her late fifties.

Flora fiddled with the straps of her Liberty-print cotton bikini – not great for swimming in but she had no intention of getting wet; well, assuming Freddie didn't chuck her in – and reached for the tea. The steam pinked her already sleep-flushed face as she drowsily watched the electric-blue dragonflies skimming the water's surface, swallows swooping in the clear skies above.

'You work too hard. It's not good for you.'

'I know but I can't step back at the moment. I need to keep bringing in new clients – it's what Angus hired me for. I can relax a bit come Christmas.'

'*Christmas?* Darling, you'll be long dead by then. It's only August. Frankly, I'm worried you won't see out the day.'

'Well, of course you are, you're always worried. You'd worry about not having anything to worry about,' Flora smiled. 'When's Daddy getting back?'

Her mother glanced across, eyebrows hitched and a sceptical expression in her blue eyes. 'I said lunch was twelve-thirty – so one.'

'And when *is* lunch?'

'Two.'

Flora chuckled. Her father's tardiness was legendary. He had been late to his own wedding (burst tyre on the Aston), the hospital when Freddie was born (traffic in Mayfair), the hospital when she was born (the dog got lost in Hyde Park and the ambulance couldn't wait) and his brother's funeral (the high street closed for the farmers' market in Marlborough). The only things he had never, ever been late for – not once in forty years – were his auctions. He had been chief auctioneer at Christie's throughout the late eighties until fairly recently when he'd retired; the auctions were known as lively, rambunctious affairs more akin to shooting parties and he had been feted for his witty commentaries which whipped up both mood and appetite and meant that, more often than not, he brought the hammer down on record prices.

But lunch, they all knew, could wait. No doubt he would still be hacking divots into the sixteenth green at twelve-thirty, in spite of his very best intentions to obey his adored wife.

'Freddie's sleeping late,' Flora observed, catching sight of the time as she sipped her tea. It was twelve-fifteen already, although her body was telling her it was dawn.

'. . . Yes. He is.'

Flora tipped her head back against the teak and looked across at her mother. 'What?'

'Nothing.'

'Mummy, I know that tone. What is it?'

Her mother glanced over but Flora could tell she didn't really see her. 'He's very thin.'

'He's always thin.'

'Well, he's lost a lot of weight then. I don't think he's eating properly.'

'I can almost guarantee it,' Flora said with a groan, extending a leg to examine her pedicure. Three weeks in and it was holding up well. 'This is the man who uses the possibility of scurvy as justification for buying multi-packs of Frazzles, remember.'

But her mother didn't laugh as she looked over the stretch of springy lawns. 'I think something's wrong.'

Flora chortled. 'You *always* think something's wrong.' If her father was perpetually late, her mother was perpetually worried. Then she caught sight of her mother's expression. 'Mummy, the only thing that's wrong is he's missing Aggie, I bet. He's finally realized what a whopping great mistake he made finishing with her, that's all.' She dropped her foot back down and, closing her eyes, enjoyed the feeling of the sun beating down on her skin. 'Aggie's the best thing that ever happened to him.'

'Apparently she's already going out with someone new.'

Flora opened one eye. 'Who told you that?'

'I do have my own contacts you know, darling. Coffee mornings weren't invented by your generation.' A pained expression flitted over her mother's face. 'Silly boy.'

Flora shifted position onto her side, tucking her knees in tight. 'Listen, she might make him sit up and beg for a bit, but there's no question she'll take him back.'

Her mother's lips pressed together as they always did when she was concerned. Flora recognized it from the day of her Maths Common Entrance exam, the day her father took his helicopter-licence test, the day Freddie announced he was running the Marathon des Sables . . . 'I hope you're right.'

They fell quiet, only the sound of pages being turned interrupting the symphony of bees working in the hydrangea bushes, blackbirds singing from the oak tree and Bolly, their labrador's, tail thumping sporadically on the tiles whenever Flora dropped her hand down to stroke his coat as he lay in the shade beneath her lounger.

Her mother closed the magazine and turned to face her, trying to seem brighter. 'So, tell me *your* news – and I don't mean work. Are you seeing anyone at the moment?'

Flora cast a sideways glance at her mother without moving her head. She suppressed a sigh. 'No. No time.'

Her mother too suppressed a sigh. 'Darling, you have to make time. How can you ever expect to meet someone if you spend your life in vaults and warehouses and galleries and on planes?'

'I meet plenty of people, Mummy. Just none who are . . .' She searched for the right word.

'Special?'

'I was going to say "different", but yes, same thing I guess.'

'Different from what?'

Flora shrugged, even though she knew perfectly well. She met hundreds of men in her line of work – dealers, gallery owners, collectors, art historians, specialist repairers, not to mention clients though of course she'd never consider crossing the line and dating one of them – but they invariably boiled down to two types. Men like her boss, Angus: bespoke-suited, ex-public school educated, elitist and cliquey. Or her father: erudite, eccentric, larger than life but hopeless with anything practical, absent and vague on the mundanities of daily life. She wanted someone with a bit of 'edge'.

'It's just you're such a beautiful girl. I can't understand why you haven't been snapped up already.'

'I'm not a pot of yoghurt!' Flora laughed. 'I don't have a best-before date.'

'Now that's naive, darling. Of course you do. All women do.'

Flora allowed the sigh to escape her this time. She wished her mother would let this subject drop. 'Look, Mum – I'm perfectly happy with my life the way it is. It'll happen when it happens. You can't go looking for it.'

They fell into a silent truce, both of them watching a couple of blackbirds hopping on the lawn and pecking for worms. Flora knew she didn't need to hold Bolly back as she would once have done – he was too arthritic to care these days, preferring to snooze in the shade.

'So is the slaughter in the kitchen concluded?' Flora asked, changing the subject.

'Perfectly boiled and pink and warm,' her mother said with satisfaction. She was as elegant a cook as she was a dresser. 'And I've done your brother's favourite cheesecake for pudding.'

'Oh good, that'll get him out of bed then. I'm beginning to think we might have to plant a small explosive device outside his bedroom door.'

Her mother chuckled even as she winced, just as a crunch of wheels on the gravel made them twist and turn to see Flora's father flying up the drive, the cream top down on his XK8, his perfectly white hair cresting in the wind as the sound of Fleetwood Mac poured into the slipstream behind him.

'I don't believe it!' Flora exclaimed in astonishment. 'He's actually on time.'

'Yes, but still driving like he's late.' Her mother tutted as she swung her legs off the sunbed and slid her pedicured feet into her white leather slides. 'Honestly, he'll have the heads off my delphiniums! Who does he think he is? Stirling Moss?' She sighed, taking Flora's empty teacup from her hands and walking across the lawn to her husband, happy to have something else to worry about.

Within the half-hour, the morning's quiet slumber had been pulled from the house like a dust sheet off a chair and Radio 4 was blaring out as her father emerged ruddy-cheeked and ravenous from the shower, the floor still scattered with pin-hole templates of mud from his golf shoes.

'Hi, Daddy.' Flora smiled as her father caught sight of her

11

sitting sideways on the worktop, her feet in the sink – a favourite resting position when at home, ever since the time she'd fallen in nettles when she was eight and her mother had cooled her burning, itching feet in iced water. She braced herself for the exuberant kiss that he'd plant on the centre of her forehead, a hand clasped over each of her ears so that the world was temporarily muffled, as though underwater. 'Good round?'

Her words brought pain, it appeared, as his wide smile faded and he slapped a hand across his own forehead. 'Terrible! Bloody awful!' he moaned. 'I'd have played better hitting the damn ball with a hoover! I don't know what's wrong with me.'

'I'll tell you what's wrong with you,' her mother said, snipping a fresh sprig of rosemary from the window box, her eyes on a squirrel digging for acorns rather too close to the lobelias for her liking. She rapped on the window smartly, sending it skittering back up the nearest oak. 'That extra glass of Maury last night, that's what.'

There followed an aghast silence.

'But darling, we were having figs!' her father protested as soon as he'd recovered, agog that it could even be considered that they might be eaten without the Maury's accompanying top notes of pomegranate molasses.

'You know what I'm saying,' her mother replied, turning back to them both but pinning her husband with an expression of reproach. He tried to catch her for a kiss as she pulled the olive bread from the Aga, her slim arms swamped in the oven gloves. 'The Pouilly-Fumé was perfectly sufficient.' She handed him the tray of rosemary-sprinkled bread in lieu of the kiss. 'Put that on the table for me, please.'

Flora giggled as her father – sporting a particularly

colourful ensemble of cherry-pink shorts and a grass-green polo shirt – shuffled away, disconsolate at his wife's insistence on worrying about the state of his liver. Between his speeding, his wine consumption and the state of the kitchen floor, he was well and truly in the doghouse. 'Poor Daddy.'

Her mother was heaping the warm, shelled langoustines onto the club salad, and Flora, spotting her chance, stole a slice of avocado. Her mother automatically went to reprimand her with a slap on the wrist, then thought better of it and handed Flora another slice herself. 'You need feeding up. Now call your brother, will you, please?' she said, lifting the laden serving plate. 'Then bring through those napkins and the flowers.'

'Yes, sir!' Flora saluted, clicking her heels in the sink and grinning as her mother walked away with a sigh and a shake of her head.

'Honestly.'

Flora jumped down from the worktop and went and stood at the bottom of the stairs in the hall. 'Hey! Ratfink!' she hollered as loudly as she could. 'Lunch in the garden now or I'm sending in the army!'

'If I'd wanted to let the neighbours know we were eating, I'd have invited them over,' her mother said wryly as Flora trotted out into the garden a moment later and set down the oyster-pink linen napkins and a milk jug filled with freshly cut white sweet peas.

'Bet he's up now though,' Flora grinned, sidling into the chair beside her father and tearing off a chunk of the still-warm bread.

Her father reluctantly poured the lime soda which his wife was trying to sell to him as an equally refreshing alternative to a champagne spritzer and she took a sip and closed her eyes, feeling the condensation running down the chilled glass onto her hand, the drowsy throb of the midday sun like a pulse on her skin. She didn't need to open them again to know her brother was finally crossing the grass. Yes, she'd heard the creak on the bottom stair, heard the French door knock against the wall, but she'd always been able to detect when he was nearby – hence his nickname for her, Bat Ears, which had morphed over the years into Batty. There were just under two years between them but they had been inseparable from the moment her mother had brought her home from the hospital, with Freddie climbing into her cot each night and sharing his favourite toy. He'd looked out for her in the school playground on her first day and helped her on her paper-round on Sundays (at her father's insistence they earn their own money) when the supplements meant the papers were too heavy for her to carry; he'd promised not to tell their mum when the butterfly tattoo she got on her hip became infected; he'd threatened to beat up any of his friends who tried to hit on her and had vetted those boys she did date, more fiercely than their father had.

'In your own time, Ratty,' she grinned, lazily opening her eyes and pinning him with a grin. 'We'll just starve to death out here while you— holy shit!'

'Flossie! Language!' her mother scolded.

But Flora couldn't take her eyes off her brother – her lanky, rangy, sandy, mop-haired brother still covered in the boyish freckles they'd once tried to count by joining them up with permanent marker. But the lopsided smile that had got him off numerous detentions had clearly slid off him somewhere along the M4, along with eight kilos.

He pointed a finger straight at her as she literally jumped

to attention. 'Don't start! You look *minging*,' he said. 'Seriously, sis, lay off the pies.'

She wanted to laugh. It was his usual joke, normally received with great hilarity, but she noticed that no one was laughing today. 'What the hell's happened to you?' she asked, her eyes trying to persuade him to seriousness.

'Flora, lang—' her mother said again, but from the corner of her eye, Flora saw her father's hand shoot forward and quieten her.

He shrugged. 'Nothing. Chill.'

'But you're so thin!' she cried, almost laughing at the irony that he was trying to pretend everything was fine.

'Pot. Kettle. Black,' he replied, flopping artfully into the spare chair and taking a glug of lime soda. He pulled a face and scowled at the glass, then cast a sceptical look at his father who could only shrug in reply.

'Mum, tell him,' Flora ordered.

'I have, darling, and I told you too,' she replied, heaping an extra-large helping of salad onto his plate. 'Why do you think I ordered an extra kilo of langoustines?'

Freddie seemed to pale at the sight of it, his fork inert in his hand.

'You look properly shocking,' Flora said, putting her elbows on the table and staring him right in the eye, refusing to let it drop. She knew her brother better than anyone. 'For real. What's going on?'

He opened his mouth to respond, but unlike the food that he couldn't seem to put in it, the words by contrast couldn't seem to get out. He just shrugged.

A long silence opened up into which concern rushed. They were all definitely worried now. Freddie might not be able to eat but he could always, *always* talk. Flora watched him, her mind racing. Had he heard that Aggie was dating again? Had it knocked him more than they had anticipated?

But there was no time even to ask. The sudden scraping of his chair on the flagstones made them all jump.

'I can't do this,' he mumbled.

'Freddie?' their father enquired, concern stripping his voice of its usual humour, as Freddie strode back towards the house, his arms swinging too high, too wildly.

The rest of the family stared at one another – shocked, alarmed, shaken.

'You two are close. Has he said *anything* to you?' her mother asked in a low voice, her elbows on the table. 'Anything at all that could explain this?'

Flora shook her head, still looking into the space he had just travelled through, as though he'd torn through the fabric of the air and left it hanging in rags behind him.

'I'm going after him,' her father said, throwing down his napkin on the table, but Flora put her hand on his forearm and stopped him.

'No, let me,' she insisted.

She stood and ran into the shaded house, the old floorboards creaking beneath her weight, branches of the jasmine trailing in through the open windows, honeysuckle blossoms nodding behind the glass, her fingers sliding over the bumpy walls as she took the stairs two at a time. She put her head in at his bedroom door but she already knew she wouldn't find him in there, and instead continued up the staircase to the attic room at the top. It was decorated in a turquoise Toile de Jouy paper, heavy gingham curtains hanging at the small windows and a broken clock tossed on the bed, forgotten. It had once been the au pair's room but the two of them had been undeterred by that, forever sneaking past whichever sleeping German or Swedish girl was there at the time, en route to their secret hiding place.

She stopped by the wall and opened the small hatch built halfway up it, which they had been strictly forbidden from ever opening when they were young. She crawled through, emerging moments later onto the flat section of roof, a hidden valley obscured from sight of the garden by the slopes of all the gable ends. Freddie didn't look surprised to see her as she scooted over to him, keeping low out of habit.

They used to sunbathe up here, and sneakily learned to smoke too, although Freddie had drawn the line at them drinking up here – alcohol and heights weren't a good idea.

'Tell me what's wrong,' she said quietly, sitting against him. Usually they leaned back, pressing themselves against the roof tiles either to feel the sun on their faces or to watch the moon, but today he was hunched forward like a curled-up beetle, his elbows on his knees, his head dropped low.

'Can't.' He shook his head.

She clasped his arm as his words confirmed her worst fear that she wasn't imagining this, it wasn't her mother's overblown anxiety that something was wrong. It really, truly was. 'Whatever it is, I'm on your side. You know I am.'

He shook his head, staring at her sidelong. 'You won't be. Not this time.'

'Freddie, there is literally nothing that you could say that would ever make me doubt you. You're my big brother. I adore you.'

He dropped his head down, squeezing his hands together so tightly, his knuckles blanched white. She winced on his behalf.

'Is it why you wanted us all to be here this weekend?'
She had had to move heaven and earth to bring her diary
into alignment with his unusual request that they all gather
here.

'I thought I could do it. I thought I could tell you all.
I thought it was the right thing to do . . .'

'You can,' she whispered. 'It is.'

'No. I can't.'

'Why not?'

'Because I was watching you all down there and you're
the same as you've always been. You so perfect and sarcastic and sweet, Dad so bluff, Mum making everything
beautiful and worrying about nothing.' He paused. 'Only
now she really has got something to worry about. I've
ruined it.'

'Ruined what?'

'Us – our family. And I can't bear to see the looks in your
eyes when I tell you.'

It was her turn to fall quiet, her eyes scouring his face
as he pulled away again, his emotions pleating inwards as
though hiding from her gaze. 'What have you done, Freddie?
You have to tell me.' Her grip tightened on his arm. 'You
know we're not getting down from here until you do.'

He took a juddering breath. 'It's not true. You have to
believe me.'

'And I will, I promise. I already do.'

'You don't know what it is yet.'

'No. But I know you. I support *you*. I love *you*.'

He nodded and dropped his head down, letting the tears
come first. And then, finally, the words.

Chapter Two

London, one week later

The auction room was packed, with every seat taken and people standing in a crowd at the back. Everyone was talking and laughing loudly, catalogues in hand and eyes skippy as they evaluated who was here – and more importantly who wasn't – and the deep banks of Sotheby's staff manning the phone and internet bids.

Flora shifted position in her seat, the bidding paddle obscured in her lap by the soft folds of her pink silk skirt. She made a point of never getting involved with this presale gossip and conjecture. It might be good for networking but she didn't like to bring attention to herself when she wanted to clinch a sale; there was something to be said for understatement, a light touch. And besides, in her opinion, networking was always far more effective with a good dress and a cocktail in one's hand.

She waited patiently while the Peter Doig oil painting was wheeled out by gloved porters and the room regrouped. The Warhol *Marilyn (Reversal)*, and the reason she was here, was up next but that wasn't why her boss Angus was texting her every third minute. She ignored his latest update through the traffic as it buzzed in her bag. If he was so anxious to see what happened with the Bacon triptych, then he should learn not to fly in for the London Evening Sale on a New York flight that only landed forty minutes before the auction started. She exhaled her irritation quietly. She didn't understand his constant need for chaos and action. Her boss thrived on adrenalin rushes and perpetual near-misses, as though a result was only validated by a dramatic narrative around it.

A man with florid cheeks and a red tie imprinted with monkeys balancing on teacups – Hermès, then – caught her eye, wordlessly communicating his question down the aisle with hitched-up eyebrows and a glance at the empty seat – the only one in the room – beside her. She shook her head sympathetically but firmly and, tapping at her watchless wrist, rolled her eyes. The man got the point, his mouth settling into an irritated line, and returned to the back of the room.

Flora brushed her blonde hair off her shoulders and fanned herself lightly with the paddle. It was a close night, the sky already blooming into a bruise as she had hopped out of the cab earlier, and thunder was forecast. She hoped she could get home before that happened. She hadn't had time to collect her jacket from the office in her haste to get here from an overrun appointment and she didn't fancy being caught in a downpour in this white silk shirt and her strappy red suede heels.

The door behind the auctioneer opened and the tension in the room tightened again, like cloth being pulled across a loom, as the Warhol screen print was wheeled out. Flora remained impassive, even though she felt the same quickening that made others gasp, murmur, smile. Unlike the bright rainbow colours of the better-known Marilyn screen prints which had been owned by stars almost as famous as the subject, this reversal was dark and brooding, a subversion of the disco-happy original: smoky black with smudges of neon pink, the negative of a film photograph, it was perfect for her clients, a young Russian couple who had swapped Moscow for Mayfair. She had worked carefully with them for the past eighteen months, building their bent for bold colour into a fledgling contemporary art collection that was already worth more than £11 million. She had taken them to the Fine Art Fairs in Maastricht and Palm Beach, closed on private deals for them at Chatsworth and in Dubai, and successfully bid in auctions in New York, Zurich and Los Angeles. Tonight, if she got it for the right price, the Warhol would fill the remaining blank wall above the bed in the master suite. The client's wife had already instructed her decorators to repaint the room in gold leaf in anticipation of its arrival.

The auctioneer, Giles, whom Flora knew from a (very) brief fling at university – dubious taste in pants, predilection for spanking – shuffled his papers and raised his head. The room fell into a hush again and Flora set to work.

'Ladies and gentlemen, we come now to lot twelve: one pink-and-black Marilyn print from the *Reversal* series, by Andy Warhol. Executed 1979 to 1986, the year before his untimely death. This is an acrylic and silkscreen ink on canvas.' As he intoned venerably, his voice ringing crisp as a bell through the suspended crowd, Flora tried not to recall the sobbing messages he'd left on her phone when she'd finished with him. 'Unframed . . .'

Flora listened like a teacher's pet, even though she already knew what was coming next. She had fully examined the provenance and condition reports and was unperturbed by the hairline craquelure at the pull margins.

She was so absorbed that it took her a moment to realize Angus had taken his seat beside her, his tight strawberry blonde curls damp with sweat, round cheeks rosy, panting slightly as though he'd actually sprinted here from the airport. He had barely made it in time and she could see he was stressed, his favourite thing to be.

'How's it going?' he stage-whispered, loosening his tie slightly as the bidding started up.

'Fine.' She kept her eyes on the auctioneer, her back straight as she kept track – without moving her head – of who was throwing their hat in the ring, clocking who was sitting with whom, representing whom, who was staying silent and still, who had turned down the corners of their catalogues to this lot, circled it with fountain-pen ink . . . It was no coincidence that she was an exceptional high-stakes poker player.

'I thought—'

'Don't talk,' she murmured, her eyes sticking on a man in a grey suit in the opposite corner, sitting angled in his chair, one arm slung across the back of it. He had placed an early bid but then fallen quiet; she could tell from his body language, though, that he wasn't out of the game yet.

She didn't recognize him. He wasn't a dealer, trader or collector that she was aware of and the fine-art world was a small one. Since graduating from St Andrews with her degree in history of fine art six years earlier, Flora had worked in various roles at Phillips, Christie's and the Saatchi Gallery before joining Angus's eponymous agency, Beaumont's Fine Art Agents, last year as a junior partner; as such, she was exceptionally well connected. She could put a name to nearly every face in this room and had sipped Manhattans at one time or another with most of them.

'Sorry. Sorry, you do your thing,' Angus whispered, sitting back and raking his fingers through his curls, as though loosening them.

The phones were busy too. Flora watched the Sotheby's staff, looking for who was talking most to their clients. Anyone who needed 'talking up' would be out early; it was the quiet ones she was interested in. She calculated there were two serious buyers there.

The guy in the grey suit was still sitting in his almost louche position but the sinews in his neck kept twitching and she could see the tension in his hands as he tried to keep from raising them, to get back in the game.

Flora looked again at the phone bank. They were down to one there, the paddles in the air growing fewer as the numbers increased and the painting steadily slipped out of reach of the majority, like a yacht that had loosed her moorings and was heading for the horizon.

The auctioneer was looking round the room, the phone bidder now alone in the ring.

Flora looked at the grey-suited guy just as he nodded his head. Back in the game.

Satisfied by her accurate prediction, she let the two of them play for a bit. The estimate had been set between £1.2 and £1.8 million but they were at £1.92 million now and the pace of the sale had slowed down, with longer pauses between the bids. The bidder in the room was nearing his limit; Flora could tell from the way he spread his shoulders wide and forward, trying to release the tension in his neck. He was looking round the room more, too, checking no one else was coming in. He hadn't spotted her – or if he had, he hadn't considered her a threat.

Which was a mistake. This was why Angus had hired her. When it came to the saleroom, she had a fine pedigree for winning, but she was regimented too, never overspending her clients' money. That was for amateurs.

She tossed her head lightly, feeling warm and relaxed, sensing that her moment was approaching. She sat straighter, her fingers clutching the paddle in readiness. They were at £2.1 million now, which was clearly not a number either bidder was comfortable with. She wasn't thrilled with it herself – every increment over £2 million cut into potential growth profit, but the research she had undertaken in readiness for today had taken into account expansion in the contemporary market as well as global factors such as the Chinese economic slowdown, and she was happy to go to £2.3 million max, having estimated a minimum 2 per cent growth in the next five years, 8 per cent in the next ten. Even at that it would be a good return, a sound investment. Worth it. She was paid to make that judgement call.

Giles was pointing at Grey Suit now, his gavel in the air. He was scanning the room but with no real conviction of another bid.

'Two point one five,' he called. 'Going once . . . going twice . . .'

She flashed her paddle, bringing an audible gasp from the people sitting immediately in the vicinity who already had their hands poised to clap. Giles's auctioneer's eyebrows shot to the top of his head as he saw her, his arm already raised above his head in anticipation of dramatically swooping down and concluding the sale.

'I have two point two!' he cried, in disbelief as much as happiness.

Grey Suit swivelled in his seat, his languid pose completely banished as he looked to see who was gazumping him at this last moment. Flora didn't move a hair.

Grey Suit's arm shot up – angrily, defiantly.

'Two point two five.' Giles looked back at Flora and she nodded again. 'Two point three.' He looked across at Grey Suit.

'Two point five!' the man shouted, with an imperial flourish of his hand.

There was another collective gasp, murmurs of appreciation, some chuckles. The gauntlet had been thrown.

Flora tutted and sat back, shaking her head. She was out. She wouldn't breach her ceiling.

Grey Suit smirked and faced the front again, clapping himself as the gavel came down a few moments later and the prize was his.

'Oh, bad luck, Flora,' Angus murmured as the crowd cogitated.

'Not really. Christie's Palm Beach have got the Elizabeth Taylor next month. I wasn't happy about going over two anyway. He's paid way over the odds, typical amateur getting carried away. Are you staying for the Bacon?'

'I can't believe you're not,' he said, shifting his legs as she stood up and made to pass.

'Dinner plans.'

'Date?'

'Something like that. See you tomorrow. I'll be in late. I'm having breakfast at the Wolseley with the new head of Old Masters at Phillips.'

'Have fun,' Angus called after her as she politely made her way down the row, past all the angled legs.

'Which one – dinner or breakfast?'

'Both!'

She smiled, reaching the aisle at the same time as Grey Suit. She held out her hand for him to shake.

'Congratulations,' she smiled. 'It's a wonderful piece.'

'I think so,' he said with a triumphant smirk.

They began to walk towards the back. Flora needed to return her paddle; Grey Suit needed to pay.

'It's a shame you couldn't stretch to it,' he said, motioning for her to go ahead as they squeezed past those people still coming in, hoping to see – or bid for – the Bacon. 'It was just getting interesting.'

Flora resisted the urge to roll her eyes. He clearly wasn't a professional – dealer, agent . . .

'Well, I was never going to go to those numbers. Two point three was my limit. You must have really wanted it,' she said, reaching the registration desk and handing over her paddle with a smile.

'Two point *three*?' Grey Suit echoed, his bombast deflated, realizing that his braggadocio in making such an aggressive counter-strike had cost him an unnecessary £150,000. If he had only waited one more bid, not felt so emasculated by being almost outbid by – heaven forefend – a younger woman.

Ouch. Flora winced as she saw him process the hit. 'As I said, though, it's a superb work. You'll make money on it,' she smiled, turning to leave. 'Eventually.'

She left Grey Suit gawping after her, counting the cost of his pride, as she pushed through the doors and went to get her bags. The place was only getting busier as people

squeezed past her into the already crammed space – collectors, gallerists, restorers, agents, back-office personnel, even
the bar staff: the Bacon triptych was coming up next and the
real action of the night was about to commence; the starting
bid alone was a princely £12.5 million.

She was just handing over her ticket when Angus came
rushing up. 'Thank God I caught you,' he panted, his face
alive with delight.

'What's wrong?' she asked patiently, an eyebrow arched
and knowing something dramatic must have happened for
him to be standing here with her. Bidding had just started
on the Bacon and he'd flown in from New York especially to
witness it.

He shook his head. 'Something more important's come
up.'

'What could possibly be more important than Bacon?' she
smiled. He was so easy to tease.

'I'm afraid you're going to have to cancel your breakfast
meeting and anything else you've got booked for the rest of
the week. We need to be in Paris, first thing in the morning.'

'Why?'

He turned the phone towards her so that she could see
the message on the screen. 'This.'

Chapter Three

Paris

They were on the Rue de Rivoli by quarter to ten and settled in the salon of the Vermeil family's palatial Haussmann town house nine minutes after that. Angus paced by the windows, checking his emails for something to do, as Flora took a mental inventory of the impressive artworks hanging on the walls.

She was admiring a Canaletto when the tall panelled door was opened and Madame Vermeil walked in. Flora rose to her feet, grateful for the tiny weights sewn into the hem of her navy Valentino dress which pulled out creases and kept her looking fresh, even after a dawn start and three-hour journey. She hoped, though, as she took in Madame Vermeil's classic quilted Chanel ballerinas, that the Rockstud flats weren't too much.

Angus strode towards their hostess with his worn-in smile, hand outstretched to clasp hers and press it to his lips. 'Lilian, you look rapturously well.'

Madame Vermeil's greeting in return was every bit as warm. The private-client sphere of fine art fostered close relationships which, if handled well, stretched over generations with the grander families. Flora could tell from

Angus's greeting alone that this was one such bond. On the train over he had handed her a file briefing her on the family's background – Swiss ancestry, fortune made in telecoms, big charity players, even bigger political contacts. Jacques Vermeil, her husband, was an eminent cardiologist.

'Allow me to introduce my new associate, Flora Sykes. I stole her away from Saatchi to head up our European operations.'

'Sykes,' Madame Vermeil murmured thoughtfully, swinging her gaze onto Flora's still form.

'Indeed. You may know Flora's father – Hugh Sykes, former chairman of LAPADA and before that—'

'Chief auctioneer at Christie's,' Madame Vermeil finished for him. 'But of course. I was in the room when he sold the *Sunflowers* for – twenty-five million pounds, was it?'

'Twenty-four point seven five, yes,' Flora nodded. She knew the number by heart even though she hadn't even been born then. The story of her father roaring up the drive in his E-Type, gravel spraying the lupins, before bounding into the house and straight down to the cellar where he grabbed the bottle of Puligny-Montrachet and drank it in the rose garden with her mother and the gardener, was so ingrained, both she and Freddie felt they had been there themselves.

'The atmosphere in the room that day, I have never forgotten it. People literally could not breathe,' said Madame Vermeil, her hands clasping her throat, 'as the numbers they went up and up and up. There had never been anything like it before that.'

'I know,' Flora smiled. 'My mother says my father's feet didn't touch the ground for a month afterwards.'

Madame Vermeil regarded her closely. Though surely in

her late fifties, she was a tall, undernourished woman with prominent bone structure and short, coiffed ash-blonde hair, her grey-blue eyes quick as darting fishes. She had the BCBG Parisian look down pat too – narrow navy trousers that finished just above defined ankles, a dove-grey matt satin blouse and a thread of pearls resting at the base of her throat. 'So then, you have joined the family business. Art is in your blood.'

'Yes, I think it was pretty much considered a foregone conclusion the day I used a Limoges dinner service to have a tea party with my dolls. Besides, I'm not sure my father would ever have spoken to me again if I'd gone into law.'

'That was something you considered?'

'For a while.'

Madame Vermeil looked across at Angus. 'Brains as well as beauty – you chose wisely, Angus.'

'Don't think I don't know it,' he laughed. 'I've barely had to pay for a lunch in the last three months – the phone's ringing off the hook with people wanting to take *us* out, I wonder why.'

Madame Vermeil laughed lightly and the sound was like sunlight bouncing off crystal. 'Flora, please call me Lilian. Come, you must sit,' she said, placing a small yellowed envelope on a side table and moving towards the ice-blue velvet sofa, her Chanel flats silent on the corn-yellow silk rug.

Flora and Angus sat together on the opposite sofa, abundant blooms of fondant-pink peonies frothing from urns beside them and the honeyed morning light spilling through the floor-to-ceiling windows, draping over the furniture like bolts of liquid silk.

'You must forgive me for not being here to greet you. I

was in discussion with Monsieur Travers, our notary. You can imagine, this has all been a great surprise to us. It is not every day that you learn you have a property that has been completely forgotten, *non*?'

'Indeed,' Angus agreed warmly. 'I was at the Bacon sale last night when I received your text and everything else faded into insignificance. In fact, I still don't know what it sold for.' He looked at Flora quizzically.

'Twenty-seven million,' she replied.

Angus gave a laugh and a shrug as he turned back to his client. 'Who knew? Who cares? The possibility for what may be discovered in *your* home is far more exciting.'

Madame Vermeil nodded. 'Well, you are the only person who knows, outside of the family. We would not want there to be any publicity concerning it, not least because Jacques' mother has not taken the news with the same delight. In fact, she is positively displeased.' She looked across at Flora. 'Angus has told you the details of what has happened?'

'Yes. I've never heard of such a thing. It really hasn't been opened in seventy-three years?'

Madame Vermeil shrugged. 'We knew nothing of it until we received the letter. Our notary Monsieur Travers, who has been forced to come back early from his holiday to deal with this, has been obliged to confirm that he has the deeds to the property, but there is seemingly a codicil on my father-in-law's will which insisted it should not be disclosed until after both his *and* Jacques' mother's deaths. Well, my father-in-law died during the war, of course, when Jacques was just a small boy, but his mother is alive and living in Antibes.'

'So technically speaking, you aren't supposed to know about it yet?' Angus murmured.

'Exactly so. This is why Magda is so upset about it. She

feels it has contravened François – her husband's – final wishes.'

'So your mother-in-law knew about the property?' Angus asked.

Lilian paused, making a tiny clicking sound with her tongue on the roof of her mouth. 'Yes. I believe she did. Unfortunately, she is quite insistent that *we* are not to visit the apartment.'

Flora bit her lip thoughtfully, wondering why Madame Vermeil's parents-in-law wanted the house to remain hidden until after their deaths. What were they going to find in there?

Madame Vermeil reached out to the small envelope on the side table and opened it, pulling out a large, old key. 'Monsieur Travers just gave me this.' She held it up for Angus to take. 'I'm afraid you will have to go without me. My mother-in-law may be very old, but she is still a strong woman.' A smile came into her cool eyes. 'Even now, I would not dare to defy her.'

Angus stared at the key before taking it. 'Forgive me for pressing, Lilian, but if your father-in-law's will stipulated the apartment should remain a secret until after his and your mother-in-law's deaths, but your mother-in-law is still alive, surely the wishes of the codicil still stand? I just want to establish that we are following due process, you understand. If we should find anything of value inside the property, we would not want there to be any sort of accusation that you came to it unlawfully.'

Madame Vermeil smiled. 'I appreciate your diligence, Angus, but Monsieur Travers has assured me that the law is on our side. Our hand has been forced. The property was broken into and a letter forwarded on to us, informing us of its existence. The bonds of the codicil are worthless now that we know about it. Besides, there are practicalities to consider and we must be realistic. My dear mother-in-law celebrates her centenary next year. One has to presume this would have been revealed to us anyway in the next few years, at the very most.' She arched an eyebrow ever so slightly, suggesting it probably would be – she wished it to be – sooner than that and Flora deduced that the relationship between the two women was not a close one.

'Do you mind my asking – who sent you the letter?' Flora asked, leaning forwards slightly, fascinated. As a child, she had devoured all of Agatha Christie's novels and if Angus had a bent for melodrama, she had a similar leaning for mysteries.

'The people who broke in,' Madame Vermeil replied, throwing her hands out in the air in equal surprise.

'And they sent you a letter?' Flora couldn't disguise her astonishment. 'They broke in and sent you a *letter*?'

Madame Vermeil nodded again. 'I know. *Incroyable, non?*'

Flora couldn't stop her mouth from hanging open. 'Well, what did it say? "Did you know you own this apartment?"'

Madame Vermeil laughed. 'Pretty much, yes.'

Angus looked rather more pained. 'Has anything been stolen, do you know? If these people were rooting around . . .'

There was a pause and the previous moment's levity dissipated. 'This we do not know and may never know,' Madame Vermeil replied more solemnly. 'We have no idea what is in there – if anything. How could we? It has remained hidden from us for all these years.'

Angus groaned. 'It would be too awful for it to have lain untouched all that time, only to be looted of its most important treasures a week before you're enlightened about it.' He raked a hand through his hair but Flora could see her boss already attaching himself to this dramatic irony.

Madame Vermeil stretched her back elegantly in her own particular way. 'If it is any consolation, I myself do not believe there can be anything of much value in there. My father-in-law was an astute man. He had to be, to build a fortune like this.' She indicated the lavish room with a flick of her eyes. 'Art was his entire world. He would not have left any great treasure locked up and hidden from view, mouldering in the dark.'

Beside Flora, Angus wilted at the logic, though the smile remained on his face. Was this just going to be a rifle through some upmarket bric-a-brac?

'Oh dear, Angus, I do hope I have not raised your hopes too much in summoning you over from London,' Madame Vermeil continued, her knowing eyes on her agent.

'Not in the least. We are eager to assist in any way we can,' he replied smoothly, smacking his palms lightly on his thighs. 'We'll simply inventory what we find, *if* we find anything, and then come back to you on the next steps – be it packing and redelivery, or valuing for a sale should you wish.'

'I do hope the apartment is not empty.' Madame Vermeil laughed suddenly, clapping her hands together and resting her chin on her fingertips. 'Wouldn't that just be too awful? All our hopes denied.'

It was rather harder for Angus to smile through that prospect. On the train over he'd been like a child on Christmas Eve, wondering what treasures they might find inside this hidden apartment of such a grand family. Flora had seen the business accounts in April. She well knew he'd overstretched himself with the new Tribeca space for the company's New York headquarters; the business overdraft now more than £200,000. He needed this project to deliver on its promise of a long-lost haul and the commission that would come from dealing with it. 'Me too, Lilian. Me too.'

Madame Vermeil lent them her driver to shuttle them over to the apartment. It was in the Montparnasse district in the 14th arrondissement, and the roads were blessedly free-flowing in the mid-morning sun, many of the capital's families having already fled the city's intense summer heat for the breezier climes of the Midi and Alpes-Maritimes regions.

Flora checked her make-up in her Chanel compact as they sped across the Place de la Concorde towards the river.

'I still can't believe the apartment stood untouched for all that time,' she said, eyes alert to the slight pinch in her cheeks that came from last night's late dinner date. (Nice but . . . well, nice.) 'You'd think *someone* would have noticed that no one ever went in or out of it.'

'People are busy,' Angus said, without looking up from his iPhone. 'They mind their own business, particularly in the smarter districts. And there's a lot of overseas owners. Most people don't own – they rent here – and the landlords like long lets with minimal hassle from their tenants. A mate of mine had to get his *parents* to act as guarantors for a lease and he's thirty-eight!'

'Yes, but nothing at all – in seventy-three years? Come on.'

Angus shrugged.

'If nothing else, you'd imagine there must have been plumbing leaks from neighbours – or what about needing to read electricity meters? Or calculate rates?'

Angus paused and considered this. 'I doubt it has any electricity. If it was abandoned in the war and no one ever sought to get it reconnected, the electricity board is hardly going to go looking for it.'

'And the rates?' she persisted stubbornly.

Angus looked back at her, bemused. 'Well, the apartment clearly hasn't been extended or altered in that time so I guess everything would have just gradually gone up with inflation. Lilian said it had all been set up by her father-in-law for the payments to be paid quarterly via the notary.'

'But they said nothing to the family all that time? It's weird!'

'No. They were just doing their duty,' Angus shrugged. 'They're not paid to pass comment.'

Flora looked back out of the window. They had crossed the river, and the wide boulevards and bountiful banks of flowers planted in strict formations along the Jardins des Tuileries had been replaced by labyrinthine streets that looped and twisted back on themselves, modest fountains or stand-alone trees populating tiny, dusty squares, metal grilles pushed back against shop walls. The roads narrowed to become one-way only and racks of bikes and scooters littered the kerbs.

She looked on with interest and a foreigner's eyes. The properties here now commanded handsome prices but the area had only become really fashionable from the 1950s onwards; and for all its bohemian charm, the 14th was a far cry from the opulence of the Napoleonic Haussmann boulevards and town houses in the 16th district where the family now lived.

Their circumstances had clearly changed for the better in the intervening years, she thought as the car drew up outside a building where the render had long since been blackened. A cascade of decorative Juliet balconies scaled the wall, one at every window, but only a couple boasted tended window boxes on them and the paint on the bottle-green main door was dull and split.

Even as she looked up from the street, she could see that the dust on some of the windows was as thick as a net curtain. Flora glanced around at the neighbouring properties as she climbed out – at the bike on one balcony, washing on a collapsible airer on another – those apartments across the street only six metres away and the inhabitants surely able to peer in. Had they really never been curious about the complete absence of life in those rooms? Never questioned the eerie stillness, quietness, darkness that shrouded the apartment at all times?

Angus, eager to reassure himself against Madame Vermeil's worry that their trip had been wasted, thrust the key into the communal door lock and bounded up the stairs two at a time, Flora's footsteps a light staccato on the wooden treads behind him. They stopped on the fourth floor outside Apartment 8, the bronze figure on the door dull with age and neglect. Flora bit her lip, suddenly apprehensive. It felt odd to be standing on the threshold of a shuttered apartment that wasn't theirs, to be the first people through and the family themselves denied.

Angus swore quietly under his breath as the key refused to move in the rusted lock; it took two hands to force it to turn and then his shoulder to the door to push back against the hip-height pile of fliers and post that had accumulated behind it. He squeezed in, telling Flora to wait until he could clear it out of the way and open the door, unimpeded.

A minute, several, dragged past. What was he doing in there?

'Angus? Is everything OK?' she called, pushing her face through the gap.

When finally he opened the door a moment later, his cheeks were florid with high excitement. 'Sorry, I . . . Well, you'll see. Come in.' He opened the door wider and darkness spilled out like a cloud of bats. Flora stared into the gloom, Angus's sharp-suited silhouette already retreating from her and disappearing into the shadows. 'I'll just check everything's clear,' he called over his shoulder like some TV cop.

She stood rooted to the spot. It was as though the packers had already arrived – pictures were stacked in rows on the floor, twelve, eighteen deep; leather-bound books piled high in leaning towers, and that was just in the hall. She followed Angus, stepping carefully around the collapsed mountain of post, her fingers tripping over the stacked paintings as she wove slowly past – was that a Matisse? – all the while coughing lightly as the stale air sank in her lungs, eyes automatically scouring for treasure: she saw a Napoleon convex mirror, round and topped with eagle motifs. Several hundred euros maybe. Nice but no cigar.

She did a quick estimate – there must be fifty, eighty, paintings in the hallway alone.

A door to the right was already open. Angus must have glanced in; from the sound of his footsteps on the stripped floors, he was tearing through the apartment for a quick look-see before settling in for a more detailed survey.

She peered in, aware of a powdery odour – more books, piles of them, some on the floor, the red and green cloth covers faded to mere tints, the corners fraying and pulling back like shed skin. Swagged curtains in burgundy silk hung as limp as broken bones, the rail coming away from the wall in one corner so that light escaped around the side; papers scattered across a desk.

She looked around the room, trying to see what *wasn't* there – her eyes searching for lighter stains on the walls where paintings which might once have hung had now been removed, their absence delineated and marked out. But there was nothing amiss. Shelves laden with books entirely covered two of the walls, the windows a third, and the fourth wall was decorated with an Empire-print wallpaper that had begun to peel in the top corners. A couple of small watercolours of agricultural scenes hung on wire from the picture rails.

She heard the sound of something being scraped across the floors further along; Angus was clearly investigating. She quickly took a few snaps on her phone camera and walked out of the room, back into the hall.

A door in the wall revealed a small cloakroom – there were coats hanging on a rack, some shoes on the floor, and a black fedora on a shelf, the dimple of the finger-pinch almost white with dust. She reached out to touch the sleeve of an opera coat – crushed rose-pink velvet and bordered with a gold brocade; beside it, a woman's brown tweed belted coat with leather buttons; beside that, a man's dark grey Crombie coat, one single black hair on the collar.

She walked on, stopping in the doorway of the kitchen. Copper pans, long since oxidized to green, sat nesting one inside the other on a shelf; tea towels, stained and limp, hung from the rail of a grey gas stove with an enamel splashback; a rubber hot-water bottle dangled from a hook, its pleated gills cracked with age. A dainty gold-rimmed tea service with hand-painted burgundy-and-black roses was arranged neatly on a wooden dresser, one teacup missing and a large chip on the side of the milk jug. The handle of a mesh sieve was pushed behind, and held in place by, a copper pipe that ran down the wall; a wooden clothes airer was strung up to the ceiling on blackened rope; there was a well-worn butcher's block still faintly stained; and a coal scuttle stood half full by a boiler, a misting of coal dust on the wall beside it.

Flora opened the narrow door in the darkest corner of the room, opposite the tall window that faced onto a patch of concrete and the back of the building behind, her eyes watering at the release of the sharp odour trapped within. The larder: she scanned rows of Kilner jars of pickled fruit and vegetables, a thick scummy skin of mould furring the tops of the liquid; a dish of lard; white enamel jars with *Sucre* and *Farine* written on them in red; tins of condensed milk; sachets of what she thought were powdered eggs . . . She closed the door again, the odour beginning to catch in the back of her throat.

She walked back out to the hall and towards the large room opposite, stopping in the doorway as she surveyed it in wonder. It was a tableau from another time – grey velvet curtains and pelmets dressed the windows, the walls were lined with duck-egg flocked wallpaper, an elaborate marble fireplace was topped with an ornate gilded mirror which was as stippled with age spots as an old man's hand. But it was the stuffed ostrich Flora couldn't help staring at – it was seven feet tall on spindled legs, and its glassy eyes and open beak gave the impression it was laughing, as though amused by the ivory satin bed-jacket draped insouciantly over its feathered back. Her eyes wandered obediently, professionally, to the finer details of the room: the crystal chandelier, blackamoor lamps, gold candlesticks, Aubusson rug, but it was the ostrich to which they kept returning – it invested the room with whimsy and glamour, bringing to her ear the sounds of long-faded laughter and conversation, the tinkle of crystal and jewels, the crackle of a fire and the sinuous sliding of silk. She could feel the lives that had once pulsed here, the social gaiety that must have been enjoyed in this very room before the horrors of war and then the enduring silence afterwards. She walked over and reached out a hand to touch the bird's plumage—

'Flora!' Angus's voice was muffled but she caught the tone of it, the slice of excitement. 'In here.'

'Coming.' Her hand dropped down and she crossed the hall into the dining room, a carmine-red salon with twelve chairs pushed around a large rectangular table and dressed with a jacquard cloth. The tabletop was strewn with scattered *objets* and ornaments – a pair of china swans, Lalique crystal figurines, burnished silverware, balloon decanters . . . Angus was waiting for her, his feet hidden from view by the sheer number of boxes on the floor, and holding in his arms a large framed portrait of a young girl.

'Stream of consciousness, tell me what you think. What do you see?'

Flora frowned in concentration, taking in the rose tint on the girl's cheeks, the paleness of her grey eyes, the high sash of her silk dress and the precise undulations of her bonnet. She saw the formal pose – the girl's body turned slightly away, a closed parasol in her hand – and the stately manse in the background, horses nosing the grass, with softly whipped, sun-tinted clouds in the summer sky, hints of

41

cadmium yellow. 'It looks like Faucheux to me,' she said with a breath of amazement.

'Exactly.'

Faucheux had not been a prolific artist, dying of syphilis when he was only twenty-five, but he had already painted for some of France's noblest families by the time of his death in 1811 and almost all his works were held in private collections.

'God, when was the last time a Faucheux came onto the open market?' she mused as Angus turned the painting around and propped it on a chair by the wall so that they could both look at it. 'It was the fifties, wasn't it?'

'Something like that. I do know for a fact only two others have been sold since the artist's death.'

Flora felt a spike of excitement. The painting was a good size, handsome, and the rarity factor meant there would be significant buzz around it. 'What do you think for the reserve?'

Angus tapped his chin, eyes screwed tight. 'Two hundred and fifty?'

She nodded. 'I agree. I can think of four buyers off the bat who'd be interested.'

'And I've got some contacts in the States who I know would sit up and beg for this.'

Flora felt her breath quicken. She looked around the room. Even apart from the pieces littering the table, there must be another five dozen paintings stacked in piles against the walls. The sheer volume of art and artefacts was staggering. There was far more, surely, than could ever have been hung on the walls here; the apartment was not grand or built on the lofty scale of the Haussmann town houses. What were they all doing here?

'What else have you found?' she asked, wandering over to the nearest lot and beginning to flick through them.

'A lot of modernism, actually,' Angus said, watching as she held up an accomplished pastel of a river view. 'I've found a few Picasso sketches, a couple of Cézannes, Matisse, Dalí . . . Nothing standout or important but signed, nonetheless.'

'Gosh,' she murmured, remembering the Canaletto in Madame Vermeil's drawing room. 'Think we'll get much for the ostrich?' she smiled, crouching on her slim haunches and flicking carefully through the next batch of paintings.

He chuckled. 'Unbelievable, isn't it?' he murmured, picking through the contents of a different box. 'Another world.'

She scanned the batch carefully before sighing and folding her arms over her knees. 'Anywhere else to check?'

'Just the bedroom back there. I haven't looked in yet. Didn't make it past this bounty. Be my guest.'

Flora slipped from the room and into the bedroom. Like the drawing room, it stood as a memorial to a bygone age; there were no paintings stacked along the walls in here or sculptures on the bed. It was the colour of coral and champagne, with a rosewood dressing table and stool, a mahogany wardrobe and a small (by today's standards) double bed.

Again, Flora cast a critical eye over the room like a detective at a crime scene. What could she tell from it? That Monsieur Vermeil's mother had had long dark hair according to the hairbrush set on the dressing table, walked in a cloud of perfume thanks to the cut-crystal spray bottle beside it, and set her face with a swansdown puff. She had been a woman of some means – if not quite the extravagant wealth they enjoyed now – and if the silver brocade gown still draped on a mannequin was anything to go by, a woman of fashion too.

On the floor were her shoes – some feathered, others robed in velvet and satin – and a large crocodile-skin trunk was pushed against the wall. Flora lifted the half-closed lid, jumping back, startled, as a moth fluttered out, its crêpe wings stretching in the new space.

The windows rattled lightly in the breeze, the iron hook-lock only just doing its job. Flora walked over and, after a brief struggle, released the catch. The air inside the entire apartment was stuffy and stale, and she was beginning to feel cloistered, overwhelmed somehow. She closed her eyes with relief as the fresh day blew in.

Leaning on the pretty balcony, she looked out. In the apartment opposite, one floor down, a girl in her twenties was lying on a bed in just her underwear, headphones on and her foot tapping as she watched something on her iPad. She was oblivious to Flora's stare, just as she'd been oblivious to this treasure trove staring her in the face. On the street below, a small van was trying to get past a guy on a moped who was talking on his mobile; a couple of women with ripped jeans and white sneakers swung their bags as they headed for the river.

Flora turned back into the room, astonished by the difference in light quality now that everything wasn't filtered through a gauze of dust, and in the fraction of the moment it took to raise her head, she caught something of the original lustre of the coral curtains, the satin thread on the champagne counterpane glistening like a fish slipping through the water.

There was something else too, barely visible – it could almost have been confused for a trick of the light – a thin slip of white peeping out from the mattress, like a pocket handkerchief in a gentleman's jacket. She walked over and, lifting the mattress just enough to release the weight, pulled free a letter.

Flora felt her curiosity swell, and then her disappointment as she saw it was written in German. Her knowledge of that began and ended with the basic manners of *Danke* and *Guten Tag*. She could only make out that the name signed at the end matched the one typeset in grey ink at the top – *Birgita Bergurren* – and that it had been written on 14 October 1940. The paper had darkened with age to a nicotine tint and there were a few faint coil shapes of rust which must have come from the bed springs. It was so old and so delicate, it was a wonder the letter had survived this long, especially given its precarious hiding place.

Flora looked back under the mattress, checking for other letters or perhaps the envelope to say where it had come from, but there was nothing. She stared again at the paper – it was crinkled, as though it had been crushed in a fist before being smoothed open again. Was that simply the effect of being hidden under a mattress on which people had slept and turned and made love? Or perhaps something in the letter had upset the reader? A lover's quarrel?

Why had it been hidden there?

She had to know, not least because it might contain some vital information for the family. If it was important enough to hide, then it must be important, full stop. She folded the letter and slipped it carefully into her pocket. Angus would know someone who could translate it for them.

She straightened the mattress, just as – further down the hall – she heard him dragging something across the floor. 'Flora!' he called. 'I need a hand!'

'Coming,' she replied, noticing how her footsteps in the dust traced her path round the room like a deer's in the snow.

Angus was standing beside a painting he'd propped up on a chair, one hand on his hip, the other on the frame. It was large, but more than that – arrestingly beautiful, showing a woman sitting on a garden bench in a long, vibrant yellow dress, her dark hair caught in swags, her face in profile as a parasol kept her in the shade. Indistinct blooms in lilac and rose clustered behind and a navy ribbon clasped her throat.

Flora stopped in her tracks as she absorbed the deftness of touch with the sable brush, the interplay of shadow and light, the exquisite mastery of texture and form. It was a masterpiece, of that there was no doubt, and she didn't need to read the name in the bottom right to know who had rendered it.

'Go on, say it,' Angus beamed, looking as pleased as punch, closing his eyes. 'I want to hear those words said out loud.'

Flora crossed her arms and smiled at him. Always so dramatic. 'Why, Angus,' she exclaimed wryly, playing along, excited herself. That overdraft was about to be paid off. 'You appear to be holding a Renoir.'

Chapter Four

The moon was high in the sky before Flora put her key in the lock of the vast oak door and stepped into the inner courtyard. Judging by the number of Vespas and bikes propped around the honey-coloured walls, everyone in the building was home – even those who'd been out for the evening. Her travel bag clattered noisily over the scrubbed cobbles as she walked towards the apartments at the far end, her eyes too weary to notice the night-blossoming jasmine climbing the walls, her mind too distracted to hear the distant music that tumbled down into the space and filled it like coloured vapour.

She entered the building code and trudged up the stone stairs, half-hoping that her friends would have retired to bed, leaving her free to march straight to the spare bedroom – hers, by long-standing agreement, whenever she was in the city – and conk out on top of the bed, fully dressed, teeth unbrushed, whatever. She couldn't remember when she'd last felt so tired and yet she wasn't convinced she'd be able to sleep either, her entire nervous system feeling wired from the day's strange and magnificent discoveries.

Angus had left hours ago now, jumping onto the 13.13 Eurostar and heading straight back to London, his entire head glowing magenta with excitement, and she wondered how he had got on with his enquiries at the Art Loss Register, the ALR. It was the absolute first step on this path; nothing else could be decided without the feedback from those records and their wildest hopes and dreams would be dashed in an instant if the Renoir (and the Faucheux, although it wasn't quite in the same bracket) was registered as lost or stolen. The authorities – perhaps from several countries – would immediately become involved and put intense pressure on their clients to explain how it had come to be in their possession. A Renoir – especially one of this size and beauty – was a world-class fine-art treasure and precious few were left in private collections; most had been sold to museums worldwide. It was a once-in-a-lifetime discovery and the person who had left it in the apartment, positioned away from the others in a separate crate in the dining room, must have known its importance.

Of course, if Angus reported back with good news, then the next imperative would be to ascertain its authenticity; although it was signed, extensive tests would still need to be run, and provenance was paramount to explain how it had ended up here, locked in a forlorn, abandoned apartment with lawyers holding the keys and its existence deliberately kept secret for seventy-plus years.

They couldn't afford any delays. The new activity in the apartment meant word was bound to get out quickly amongst the neighbours and the sheer scale and value of the recovered haul – if glimpsed or suggested – would become a honeypot, not to the common-or-garden burglar or thief, but the organized crime gangs that traded fine art as collateral in their shady dealings.

Angus had left her with instructions to compile a preliminary inventory – numbers, lists of artists, rough estimates and potential values – before he returned for their meeting scheduled with the family tomorrow afternoon, but she had barely been able to lock the door on it all this evening. Her instinct to call the security firm they worked with, to come out and protect the premises, at least until tomorrow when Angus returned with news and a plan of action, was still ringing loud and clear in her head, but he had been insistent that doing nothing was the best protection. It had survived over seventy years locked up. It could last another night. The less activity around the apartment, the better.

A strip of light escaped under the door of Apartment E and she opened it with the spare key she'd been given, peering down the long bone-white hall. The door to Bruno and Ines's bedroom was ajar, top notes of a tagine – Ines's signature dish – still lingering in the air, the soft strum of an out-of-sight guitar telling her that her friends were still awake.

She glanced at her watch – a gift from her father when she'd landed her first job at Christie's and growing increasingly important to her as all her friends and colleagues switched to finding out the time from their phones and iPads – and saw it was 1.30 a.m. She sagged in the doorway and looked yearningly at her own bedroom door. The light was on in there too, meaning Ines had received her text and was expecting her.

The two women had met in their gap years backpacking around Asia, and in a classic case of opposites attracting, had instantly become firm friends. If Flora was everyone's perfect Head Girl, Ines had been the rebel, the cool girl who knew all the gossip and didn't care what anyone thought; Flora found Ines's curious mix of bohemian languor and international polish, hewn from years at top-notch Swiss school Aiglon, absolutely irresistible and they had made a pact that Flora would live with her friend whenever she was in the city.

Wishing she could take a running jump towards the bed, she instead dropped her bag and walked down the hallway, past the giant discs covered with turquoise feathers on the walls, her shoes clip-clopping on the old parquet floor. An open bottle of tequila was sitting on the polished concrete worktop in the kitchen and, from experience, she knew to pour herself a shot before heading out to the roof terrace.

Ines saw her before Flora's eyes could adjust to the darkness – the flickering Moroccan tea lights throwing out about as much light as they did heat – and she reached for Flora with outstretched arms and a scatter of throaty laughter. 'You are here!'

'Sorry I'm late,' Flora replied with characteristic understatement as she walked towards her friend, who was sitting sideways in a fringed linen hammock, and leaned over to kiss her cheeks. Camellia perfume embraced her as much as Ines's slim brown arms, her riotous and untameable coal-black hair flapping like a pirates' flag in the night breeze. 'I hope you didn't wait for me.'

'Not likely!' Ines laughed, indicating for Flora to squeeze in next to her. 'There would have been mutiny on the ship.'

'Hello, boys.' Flora blew air-kisses at Bruno, sitting on the low wall, and Stefan, sprawled in a Missoni chair; Bruno caught his with an extravagant flourish; Stefan merely nodded, his eyes still, the index finger of one hand rubbing across his mouth as he watched her. They'd had a one-night dalliance a year ago that had left her satisfied and him wanting more.

'Are you hungry?' Ines asked, affectionately squeezing her thigh. 'There's some left, I think.'

'Thanks but –' Flora waved the offer away and held up her shot glass briefly before downing it with a smack of her lips. That would have to pass as dinner for tonight.

Ines tutted. 'No wonder you are skinny.'

'So tell us, Flora,' Bruno said, picking up his guitar and propping one foot on Stefan's chair. 'What brings you back to Paris?' He strummed a chord and looked up at her, his dark eyes crinkling at the corners, his smile all the brighter for the beard surrounding it, his washed-out shorts almost falling off his narrow hips. 'And what – or *who* – has been keeping you up so late?'

Flora smiled enigmatically. 'Oh, you know me – people to see, places to be.'

'Ah,' he grinned. 'So it's someone famous then. Or powerful. Perhaps both?'

Flora shrugged off his teases. 'It's not a secret.' It was true – it wasn't. The Vermeils hadn't requested anonymity. They rarely bought or sold, and most of Angus's work for them, till now, had been curation and preservation management; perhaps they felt that kept them sufficiently below the parapet – unlike the newly minted Russians and Chinese splashing their cash at the auctions? Either way, a request for anonymity hadn't been specified. 'Although you've probably never heard of them. They are *very* private.'

'Try us,' Stefan said, a challenge in his eyes; as the European editor-at-large of *Vanity Fair*, there wasn't anyone he didn't know and Flora was hoping he could add a bit of colour and perspective. Angus's background notes had been formal and dry: principal client, Jacques Vermeil, now seventy-five; only child of Magda and François Vermeil;

married late to Lilian, fifty-nine; two kids, Xavier, twenty-seven, and Natascha, twenty-one . . .

'The Vermeils?'

Bruno snorted as though she'd said something funny. He held a hand up by way of apology.

Ines shot him a look. 'Ignore Bruno,' she said with an expression of stretched patience before inclining her head to rest it on Flora's shoulder, her long legs looking brown as they swung in the candlelight.

'What's so funny?' Flora asked lightly.

'The idea that they are private,' Stefan smirked. 'Jacques and Lilian Vermeil have just funded the extension at the Opéra and she sits on so many charity boards, you would think she was applying for sainthood.' He paused. 'Not that that's likely with their kids.'

'Their kids?'

'They're out of control. The parents keep it out of the papers – God knows how, but they do – but everybody knows they're cokeheads. Xavier thinks he is God's gift and Natascha's a party girl.'

Flora jogged Ines. 'Is this true?'

'I'm afraid so. She's got a real bad-ass reputation – sleeps with anyone, hasn't eaten for three years, just lives on Diet Coke and jelly babies. I know people who know her and they say she's seen and done it all. She's already bored with the world.' She inspected a teal nail carefully, arched an eyebrow. 'Someone who knows these things told me she OD'd on cocaine and the lead singer of a *very* famous band she was partying with had to give her an Adrenalin shot direct to the heart.'

'Straight from *Pulp Fiction*?' Stefan asked, scepticism lacing his words.

'*Exactement*,' Ines said firmly. 'And you're not allowed to use that, by the way. It is off the record.' She pointed a stern foot at him.

Bruno snorted again, setting down his guitar and getting a pack of rolling papers out of his pocket. 'These rich kids . . . Always it is the same. Too much money – it fucks you up,' he muttered, shaking his head.

'Well, some of us did OK,' Ines said shortly. As the sole heiress to a boutique-hotel empire she was the embodiment of everything that Bruno – wrong side of the tracks, fifth of eight kids, left home at sixteen – railed against. But with the heart of a hippy, she was also his soulmate and it was only occasionally that they found themselves caught in the cross-fire of their conflicting childhood politics.

He blew her a kiss – apologetic, whimsical – but their eyes lingered and Flora looked away from the private promises that were communicated between them. They had been together now for four years – moving in together within a weekend of meeting at a party in Ibiza – and were not just settled in any old pedestrian relationship but a sex-on-the-stairs and breathless-abandonment *coup de foudre* that Ines couldn't understand wasn't contagious.

Flora smiled. Was it any wonder she enjoyed hanging out with these guys so much? Their divergent backgrounds, sharp moralities and burning ambitions were refreshing to her and such a break from the circles she moved in professionally.

'Keep away from them. They're trouble,' Stefan said shortly, throwing his hands behind his head and fixing her with a sharp stare.

'I doubt I'll be privy to any such histrionics in the course of curating their fine-art collection,' Flora said ironically.

'Stefan's just bitter because he's lost more than one girl to Xavier Vermeil. Isn't that right, Stefan?' Ines laughed.

'It has nothing to do with that,' Stefan replied testily.

'So what, then?'

'They're unprofessional and spoilt. They think the world revolves around them.'

'Oh God,' Ines groaned. 'You're not still going on about that photo shoot, are you? Let it drop!'

'They pissed off a lot of people that day, not just me. Busy people. Important people.'

Flora dangled her leg idly. 'Rewind a bit, please. What happened?'

'They pulled out of an article we were running,' Stefan said, flexing his foot.

'On them?'

'And others. The title was "Young Guns, the hip new scions of old dynasties".'

'Oh, hey, I remember that. *You* were in it,' Flora smiled, lazily digging Ines in the ribs with her elbow.

'Only because I was doing my friend here a favour,' Ines shrugged. 'My father was furious with me.'

'Excuse me – I was doing *you* the favour,' Stefan replied lightly, earning himself a tatty linen Chanel espadrille that went flying through the air towards his head as Ines swore under her breath in French. 'You know yourself how much attention that article got. It made your business.'

It was true that Ines's eponymous erotic-lingerie label had mushroomed from a modest hand-sewn sideline, using leftover lace and ribbons from the Chanel atelier (the head of couture was a friend of her parents) into a cult brand with a flagship store in the Marais. Gaggles of Asian tourists and fashion students already made pilgrimages just to

Instagram the boutique which was justly notorious for the handmade Belgian white lace stretched taut across the windows, hiding and revealing what was inside at the same time: alpaca fur rugs on the floors in the changing rooms and velvet on the walls. There was usually at least one paparazzo lurking on a Vespa nearby, ready to snap the latest celebrity or society darling on her way out with a smile on her lips and a bag in her hand.

'Please,' Ines said with a roll of her eyes but gently nudging Flora with her arm. Stefan was successful and very good-looking with cropped, almost shaven, hair and a tide of stubble. He was forever appearing on his own magazine's pages, photographed stepping out with models and actresses in borrowed couture, but he was humourlessly ambitious and that made him an easy target to his old friends. 'The company is following my business plan perfectly. It was just coincidence that the article came out at the same time.'

Flora knew there was no business plan. Ines was not the type of woman to bother with anything as grey as that; she lived by instinct and passionate conviction.

But Stefan took the bait. 'Ines, it was our biggest-selling issue of the last three years and the feature syndicated to thirty-six countries.'

'So? The women coming to my store bring word-of-mouth recommendations from their friends,' Ines teased him.

'You pretend—'

'OK, OK, kids,' Flora interrupted. It was too late for one-upmanship. 'Why did it matter so much if they pulled out of that article?'

'Everything was set up for the shoot, dozens of people

waiting – Annie Leibovitz, for Chrissakes! – and then after three hours of waiting, they cancel? *Vraiment?* Who do they think they are? The Casiraghis?'

A glint of devilment glittered in Ines's eyes. 'Well, Xavier does have the same luck with women. And they're almost as rich.'

Stefan shrugged but with stiff shoulders, reaching out to take the roll-up offered to him by Bruno.

Flora remained quiet, leaning her head back and staring up at the velvet sky as Bruno began to strum again, Stefan's intermittent smoke trail drifting into her line of sight. They were about to become a whole lot richer, those heirs. More damaged, too? It seemed hard to reconcile Madame Vermeil's cultivated refinement with the stories being shared here.

Idly, she mused on their reactions if they were to hear about the long-locked apartment opened today after a sleep of over seventy years. She could imagine Bruno's – he would sneer at the profligacy of owning so many properties that it was even possible to forget about one. Stefan would jump on the family's surprisingly, and hitherto-unknown, modest background; how had they risen so high, so fast? he would wonder.

But as she closed her eyes, sleep beginning to snap at her heels like a nervy dog, that wasn't where her thoughts snagged. An apartment with over two hundred valuable paintings and artworks stored within it, deliberately locked up and left to the dust? It wasn't *how* the situation could have come to pass that bothered her, it was *why*.

The cool breath of night made her shiver. She assumed it was that.

Chapter Five

She was back in the dust by dawn. As predicted, she had barely slept, creeping from her artfully tumbled linen sheets before five to occupy the abandoned apartment and keep watch over the priceless treasures. The floorboards had creaked beneath her feet as she'd let herself in, the large key solid and weighty in her palm as she'd checked all the rooms, anxious as a mother with her newborn, hoping that the people in the apartment below wouldn't be disturbed by the unusual movements above. Of course, she knew she would be little use against anyone intent on gaining access but it made her feel better to be there anyway, offering some sort of resistance.

The street was still in shadow, the sun not yet high enough in the sky to illuminate the apartment, and the room slumbered on in hooded gloom. Without any electricity supply, there were no lights, nothing to see by – funnily enough, she didn't travel with a supply of candles – so she had spent almost an hour stretched out on the faded velvet chaise longue in the bedroom, waiting for the light and just staring at the Renoir. It had felt like keeping vigil. Later today, the picture would be moved to an atmospherically controlled environment where it would be tested for damage and decay and the delicate process of cleaning would begin.

It would, in all likelihood, eventually be sold to a leading museum where guards would flank the long marble halls and tourists would stand behind red ropes to gaze at it, but Flora alone would have had the privilege of enjoying it in the intimacy of a domestic setting, this totem of timeless majesty propped up on a rumpled and sagging bed.

She wished her father could have been in here with her. It was because of him that she had fallen in love with art in the first place, holding on to his hand as he walked her through long galleries to show her just one painting or one sculpture, to sit on a bench with her and stare at it for an hour, sometimes playing I Spy with the canvas, other times challenging her to think of twenty different shades of green or blue or yellow.

Yes, he would love this. Art had always been their shared game. When she had been barely five, she had tucked herself into the hollow of his podium, wanting to play hide-and-seek, staring at his highly polished shoes as she heard his voice rebound throughout the room, his trousers flapping faster and faster at his calves as he pointed to one bidder, then another, as excitable as a conductor lost in the music.

And now she was on a treasure hunt, a world-class quest to return a fine-art masterpiece to the public eye. But she wasn't a child any more and this wasn't a game. And when the first spot of sun appeared on the wall, a finger of light pointing her to her duties, she rose to her feet, walked out into the hall and with her camera and her clipboard, she set to work.

First, she had to count. It took over an hour just to walk through the apartment and tally up the numbers of fine-art treasures in the space. In total, there were 203 paintings; 57

sculptures; 316 artefacts (including candlesticks, perfume bottles, lamps, ornaments, jewellery dishes) and 1 ostrich, whom she had taken to calling Gertie as she worked. (Where the name had come from, she had no idea. It just seemed to fit.)

Next, she had begun to classify the pieces in order of value, and therefore importance, identifying them via a system of coloured sticky dots with red as the most esteemed, moving through orange, yellow, green and finally to blue for the minor pieces. According to her notes, there were two reds (the large Renoir which she double-dotted, and the Faucheux), 14 orange (some very charming but of minor importance, small sketch oils, lithographs and drawings by Matisse, Dalí and Pissarro amongst others), 266 yellow and the rest a mix of green and blue. She used a different room to 'store' each category – she left the Renoir on the bed and put the Faucheux beside it; everything with an orange dot stayed in the dining room, those with yellow were moved over to the drawing room, greens to the study and blues in the kitchen. After she had moved each piece, she numbered and photographed it extensively – front, back, sides.

Finally, as lunchtime approached after already seven hours' work, she began subdividing the dotted lists into schools – modernist, Impressionist, cubist, surrealist and so on – and then artists. Her pulse was quickening with every name she wrote and as she moved a Renoir sketch into the dining room (only experience told her who the artist was, for he never signed his sketches), another storm of dust swirled around her and she launched into a new sneezing fit. Her eyes were beginning to stream and as she saw the dust patches blackening on her knees she realized that her white boyfriend jeans, pulled on in the dark, had been a mistake.

She sighed, weary and famished, setting down her work files and reaching for her bag. She needed something to eat. Art could only sustain her for so long.

With her anxiety levels peaking again – it felt so wrong to leave it all – she turned the old lock on the door and left the treasures alone and unguarded, stepping out into the street. The sun was gentle on her face as she crossed the road, out of the shadows, an easterly breeze keeping the temperature down. Marching quickly, she watched her own shadow, lost in thought as questions clattered against each other in her head. What news would Angus have from the ALR? He must be in transit for she hadn't been able to get hold of him all morning. What were the Vermeils going to do when she reported back to them – keep or sell? Had anyone in the neighbouring apartments heard the sounds or noticed the new activity in this one? She hoped to God not. Until they had moved the most valuable pieces or got the security guards installed, she couldn't relax. This was on her watch.

Her stomach growled – had she eaten dinner last night? She couldn't remember. She crossed the street, heading towards a small pedestrianized square, a church with a leaded dome facing her; passing a dry cleaner's and a *tabac*, an Italian restaurant and a shoe shop seemingly catering to the over-fifties. She wasn't going to be fussy – usually she tried to be gluten-free but today she'd take the first café or *boulangerie* she came to, buying whatever she could take away.

In the event, she found a sushi bar first and dived in, emerging four minutes later with a box of *maki*. She ordered a coffee to go from the café next door, just so she could use the loo, before hurriedly retracing her steps. She knew Angus was right – that after over seventy years' obscurity, another night and day wouldn't make a difference – but she couldn't relax knowing that a significant, long-lost Renoir and Faucheux were just sitting there, propped on the bed, awaiting her return.

Her phone rang and she pulled it hurriedly from her bag. Angus?

'Freddie?' she asked, her voice instantly tinged with anxiety. 'What's wrong? Is everything OK?'

There was a brief pause. 'Mum? Mum? Is that you?'

'Oh, ha ha!'

He chuckled lightly. 'You deserved that.'

'Yes, all right,' she said, rolling her eyes. She pressed one hand to her ear to try to drown out the background drone of traffic. She could just imagine him now, noise-reducing headphones clamped round his neck, a coffee in one hand. As an assistant director, he was climbing steadily towards the top of the tree in the British film industry and she knew he was currently filming some adventure movie with a hefty dose of irony at Elstree Studios. No one at work knew yet and he was insisting on continuing to live his life as normal, at least for as long as he could. 'Innocent until proven guilty, right?' he'd said bravely, as they'd all huddled around him that Saturday afternoon in the shaded house.

'Really, though – how are you?' she asked. They hadn't spoken for several days; at his insistence, he just wanted to try to keep everything as it always had been.

There was another pause. 'Knackered.'

'You do sound tired.'

'Well, that's probably more to do with the fact that Troy

was waging war with our resident bike snatchers again last night.'

'They haven't nicked another one, have they?'

'I hope not but I didn't stick my head out to see. It'd be the fifth this year if they did, though.'

'But surely he locks them up properly?'

'Course he does, but I think they enjoy taunting him as much as anything. I mean, I know his bikes are seriously hardcore but no one else's seem to get nicked. He reckons it's personal.'

'Poor guy.'

'Poor them, you mean. If he ever gets his hands on them, he'll be six feet two of sheer Aussie rage.'

'Ha! He's a neighbour you'd better keep on the right side of, then.'

'Yeah.'

They fell into an easy silence, both thinking about the same thing.

She was the first to break it. 'And how are things otherwise? Are you sleeping OK?'

He made a non-committal sound that she took to mean 'no'.

'But you're eating, yes?'

'Yes.' Which also meant 'no'.

'Any word back from the CPS?'

'Not yet.'

'I promise you, they won't press charges,' she said fiercely. 'It's too tenuous. They'd never be able to prove beyond reasonable doubt.'

'Maybe. Maybe not.'

They fell quiet again.

'. . . You still in Paris?'

'Yep.'

'Coming back soon?'

'I can come back any time you need me to,' she said quickly. 'You just say the word and I'll be there, Freds. I'm three hours away.'

'I know, that's not what I . . . It's not what I meant. I was only calling to check in with you. Just give me a bell when you're next back in London town, OK?'

'Sure.'

'Thanks, Batty. Love you.'

'Backatcha, Ratfink.'

He hung up and she pushed open the front door, trudging up the stairs and letting herself into the apartment again. Everything was exactly as she'd left it twenty minutes earlier – the dust still spinning through the air from all her re-arrangements, the artworks now organized in tidy groupings in every room. She checked in on Gertie but then made her way straight to the bedroom where she opened the French doors which looked onto the street – present-day Paris pushed its way into the preserved apartment once again and released the past's hold on it. She sat on the small balcony, her back against the wall, her legs propped up on the railings, and began to eat her lunch, twiddling the chopsticks between her fingers as she thought about her beleaguered brother.

The apartment wasn't high enough for her to see over the neighbouring rooftops to the horizon and she was forced to look down for a view – the street was seemingly a quiet one as hardly anyone was about, just a young couple walking at an idle pace, holding brown grocery bags in their arms as they chatted.

Flora watched as they drew closer and then stopped

outside the building opposite, the woman leaning back to balance the bags against her torso as she reached into her boyfriend's shorts for the keys. They disappeared from sight a moment later, the wooden door closing behind them with a slam.

Flora deliberated between a salmon *nigiri* and a tuna *maki*, finally choosing the salmon on account of its prettier colour. When she looked up again, the couple had reappeared in the apartment directly opposite, one level down, and she realized that although she couldn't see their faces because of the lowered blind, this woman was the same one she'd seen lying on the bed, listening to music, the previous afternoon. It was odd to have this dual-aspect perspective on her life: the public and private sides.

Flora watched intermittently – more interested in her lunch – as the woman shrugged off her T-shirt and stepped out of her jean shorts, laying the clothes on the bed and padding out of sight in her underwear.

The man was in the room too – only his feet visible at first, although he slowly came into view, walking around the bed whilst reading something on his phone. Only when he sank onto the side of the bed, texting a message on his phone, a loop of orange rope peeping out from the divan by his feet, could she see his face.

What did he use the rope for? she wondered, starting on the tuna *maki* roll and watching dispassionately. Was he a climber perhaps? He had an athletic build, she supposed, her mind distracted, her eyes drawn to every car that rolled down the street, looking for Angus. He'd be back any minute now, surely? The man in the apartment opposite tossed the phone on the bed and walked over to the French doors. He was stocky but very muscular, his calf muscles well defined below his khaki shorts. He stepped into the sun, leaning on his elbows as he looked down at the street below. A cat was prowling the pavement, and as a trio of men in shirts and ties were talking and walking quickly, one of the men forced was onto the road and the other had to step round the cat which immediately shot away in fright, sheltering under the hulk of a parked car.

Then he looked up.

Flora stopped eating as she saw him stiffen. The way he stared at her – so shocked – she knew immediately that he knew no one was ever seen here; that her presence meant the apartment had been opened. She watched him crane his neck, could see his features pleat together as he squinted, trying to get a better look. She got to her feet and scrambled away from the window, closing the French doors behind her, shutting him out so that only his building was reflected back to him. But it was a pointless gesture. She had been seen. The neglected apartment reclaimed at long last. The past was stirring and shaking off the dust. The neighbours would soon know, then the city, until finally, when the sale was announced, the entire world. After seventy-three years of silence, the secret was finally slipping out.

Chapter Six

Angus was in his best suit and favourite Lanvin tie – that alone had told Flora it was good news, although he'd said precious little himself and had been glued to his phone ever since he'd arrived. He had been frustratingly elusive all day, not responding to her emails and merely texting her from the train instructing her to meet him at the Vermeils' at three o'clock, as though oblivious to the fact that she'd barely slept or eaten from nerves in the twenty-four hours since they'd unlocked that old door.

They were waiting in the same room as before, Flora setting up the Renoir and Faucheux on easels, and shrouding them with spare sheets which she'd found, saved from the worst of the dust, in the bedroom cupboard. It was hardly museum-quality protection, especially given that she'd travelled over with them by cab. Yet again, she had considered booking the security firm they normally used to send a private car for her to transport the paintings, but it would have had blacked-out windows and a driver and escort and she was worried that would attract far too much attention – she was already concerned enough by the curiosity of the man across the street and had spent the rest of the afternoon darting to the windows to check if he'd still been looking (twice, he had). She didn't want it to appear as though anything of significant value was coming out of, or worse, being left in, the apartment. She was barely consoled by the fact that the most valuable paintings were in her possession.

The door swung open and Madame Vermeil stood before them again, serene and elegant in a powder-pink linen shift dress and baroque pearls. Two men followed after her, one tanned, lean and lofty at what must be nudging six feet four and the other almost comically short. The shorter man was carrying an attaché case; he had wire-framed glasses pushed up his nose, and grey hair rimming his head, leaving a bald pate. The tall man was wearing a pale sand-coloured linen suit and brown moccasins, and Flora caught a flash of a Breguet watch that told her he was the client's husband and not the lawyer.

'Lilian, Jacques,' Angus confirmed, greeting them both with a confident smile. Lilian visibly relaxed at the sight of it. '*Monsieur.*'

'Angus, Flora,' Madame Vermeil smiled, shaking Flora's hand and motioning towards the tall man a step behind her. 'My husband, Jacques, and our notary, Monsieur Travers.'

'How do you do?' Flora said to them all. She looked remarkably more polished than she felt, having almost jumped from the moving cab as she'd asked him to stop at Ines's apartment en route, so that she could dash in (a painting under each arm) and change. She hadn't dared leave the apartment beforehand – not now she'd been spotted – and she had changed into her baby-blue culottes, Miu Miu block heels and white cotton blouse in record time.

They all took their seats, Angus choosing to remain standing. Flora crossed her ankles, knowing her moment was coming.

'Well, it's been an eventful twenty-four hours,' Angus began, clasping his hands together. 'Flora's been working for almost all of them.'

'It is just as well then we don't pay you by the hour,' Jacques Vermeil said with a smile, looking across at Flora and prompting a laugh from the group. Angus's notes had mentioned that he was an eminent cardiologist, retired now of course, and he wore the suavity that characterized most men in this elite tier – his movements both few and unhurried, an air of bemusement mixed with boredom just behind his eyes and lips. Flora guessed women loved him.

'Well, you'd certainly be able to afford it,' Angus continued, dipping his head. 'There were quite a few surprises awaiting us in there.'

'Had our kindly intruders damaged anything?' Lilian asked, a sombre expression on her features.

Angus shook his head. 'On the contrary, from what we could see, there was no sign of any previous entry whatsoever. The door was locked and very stiff with a pile of post still in place behind the door, the windows were closed, and there were no footprints or hand marks in the dust. If you didn't know for a fact someone had been in there, I would have said no one had.' He shrugged.

'It was all very odd. There was no obvious sign of theft either,' Flora added. 'Quite apart from the additional surprises awaiting us, the actual furnishings of the apartment were still intact – the pictures were still on the walls, desks and chairs in place, all the shelves filled with books. Either they didn't realize the significance of what they'd stumbled into and mistook it all for dusty junk, or they've taken something specific, in which case, short of finding an inventory somewhere, we'll probably never know what that was.'

'Dusty junk?' Jacques Vermeil echoed quizzically, as though something had been lost in translation.

Flora went to reply but Angus cleared his throat and she stayed quiet. 'Indeed. When we entered the apartment, there were literally hundreds of paintings stacked against the walls, many in the hall itself but mainly in the dining room. The sheer volume of pieces in there could have persuaded them that none of it had any value. Else, why would the owners have left it?'

There was a pause.

'And *is* any of it valuable?' Jacques asked.

'See for yourself.' Angus's eyes brightened as, with a flourish, he pulled the first cloth down to reveal the Faucheux. Madame Vermeil gave a small gasp and leaned forward in her chair, her eyes expertly reading the painting, understanding its nuances and symbolism.

'*Mon Dieu,*' she whispered. 'She is beautiful.'

'And rare,' Angus added. 'The artist Faucheux died just as he hit his prime. The last time one of his works came to open market was in 1951 in Berlin. Almost all his known catalogue is in private collections. Only a handful of museums worldwide boast a Faucheux.' He held up his fingers on one hand and began counting. 'The Prado in Madrid, the Guggenheim Bilbao, the Uffizi in Florence and the Courtauld in London.'

Just four museums. Jacques Vermeil's eyebrows shot up his tanned forehead. 'So if we chose to sell . . .'

'You would in all likelihood find yourself with a bidding war from some of the biggest institutions in the fine-art world, not to mention the most serious private collectors who would like to add his name to their catalogues.'

'How pleasing,' Jacques replied coolly after a moment.

'This is a particularly fine work,' Angus said, looking back at the painting. 'I think it would attract a lot of interest.'

'How is its condition?' Madame Vermeil asked, getting up to inspect the painting more closely. She pointed a manicured nail at the top-left corner where the craquelure was heavily crazed. 'The colour is dulled. It has hardly been stored in an ideal environment.'

'Not ideal, no,' Angus conceded. 'But looking at the positives, the apartment was sealed and watertight and being on the fourth floor helped – there was no mould or damp that we detected. Obviously humidity would have changed throughout the year as the space wasn't climate-controlled but all things considered, not a disaster. If we're lucky, I think a clean and some minor cosmetic work on the varnish will be all that's required.'

'I think we're already lucky,' Jacques said in a softly amused voice as his wife sat down again.

'Actually, you're *even* luckier,' Angus said, smiling broadly as he walked over to the other easel. He waited for a moment, enjoying the drama and his audience's tense anticipation, building up the suspense before he whisked the shroud away.

It took the Vermeils only a moment to recognize what was before them, Renoir's exquisite light touch alone, the dashes of vermilion red and cobalt blues, shouting out his name. Madame Vermeil was on her feet again, her hands to her mouth, as she approached the painting with almost holy reverence, her eyes roaming the painting with expert analysis once more. 'It will need to be verified,' she said firmly, as though the shock had frightened her.

'Of course,' Angus agreed. 'It's signed, thank heavens.

Flora and I have examined it closely and it looks right to our eyes but of course, we'll need an expert opinion, no question – I've already put a call in with the Musée Renoir in Cagnes. A sticker on the back says it's titled *Yellow Dress, Sitting* but we'll need to check it's listed in the *catalogue raisonné*, of course, and then we'll start on the provenance right away. I think you'll agree it's right to begin by working on these two totemic paintings first. I went back to London to personally check the records at the ALR and I am very pleased to be able to confirm that neither painting is registered as either stolen or missing.'

'Well, of course not,' Madame Vermeil said sharply. 'Why would they be, if they are in our apartment?'

Angus was unruffled. 'I'm not implying anything, Lilian – it's merely a formality, the first step in due diligence any time an artwork of this importance re-emerges on the market. If for any reason the paintings were registered with the ALR, they'd be rendered instantly worthless – you wouldn't be able to sell them and within hours of me logging the search, the authorities would be breathing down your necks. It is my job to make sure you are not put in that position.'

Lilian smiled, mollified. 'Do you hear that, Monsieur Travers?' she asked the silent notary sitting to her and Jacques' right. 'Mr Beaumont works in our interests, not against them.'

Flora was surprised by the caustic comment and caught the poor man pressing his shoulders down from his ears. He murmured something in French, which Flora translated as 'merely following orders'.

Angus cleared his throat politely. 'Clearly, you need time to gather your thoughts and consider whether or not you want to keep the Renoir, but you should know there's an important Impressionist sale happening at Christie's next month. The catalogue isn't out yet so exact details aren't confirmed, but from what I've heard on the grapevine, there are some very intriguing paintings going in, including some high-profile Pissarros and a Manet. It'll attract a lot of attention and some serious buyers – those on the inside track are expecting records to be broken. Blood will be up and there's no doubt in my mind that a painting of this calibre, in that sale, would achieve a very good price indeed.'

Flora smiled, staying silent, knowing exactly why Angus was pushing for a sale – if the painting was sold, the agency would take a cool 1.7 per cent commission of total sale value, a significant leapfrog over their research, inventory and curation fees.

'How good?' Jacques enquired coolly.

'At your common or garden sale, this would fetch an easy six million pounds. At that one, you could be upwards of nine, even ten.' Angus smiled. The numbers were intoxicating. He looked punch drunk. 'But that's just something for you to consider. No pressure, clearly. It's your call. The deadline for submissions is in the next couple of weeks – I'd need to ascertain when, exactly – but if you are interested in selling it, we'd need to act quickly to get it in on time. There'd be a *lot* of work to do.' He rubbed his hands together, pleased. 'Anyway, that's the end of my song and dance. Now Flora is going to present you with a rundown of everything else we found.'

Flora stood, holding her iPad in the crook of her right arm and clicking on the Apple remote in her left. An image of the cluttered hallway, taken as they'd first entered the apartment, was beamed onto the collapsible white screen that they used for mobile meetings such as this.

'Well, this is how everything looked when we first walked in,' she began. 'As you can see, it's a very haphazard jumble of artworks –' she clicked onto the next image, this time of the study and the towers of antique books – 'and artefacts . . .'

Madame Vermeil's hands tightened in her lap, a frown creasing her brow, as she looked from the screen to Monsieur Travers. 'And you knew about all this?'

The lawyer appeared to suppress a sigh. 'We did not, Madame Vermeil. Only that there was a property, not what was inside it,' he replied with impressive neutrality.

'Someone must have known. Your father.'

'If he did, he is – as you know – long dead, Madame.'

Madame Vermeil turned away from him with a look of distaste.

Flora hesitated, not sure whether to continue. '. . . Anyway, there was no classification system, no filing at all, really. Everything was set down almost as though it had been placed there in a rush.'

'Well, there was a war going on,' Jacques said, that half-smile on his lips as he watched her.

'Of course,' she said with a tip of her head. 'So I've done a preliminary inventory. In total, there are two hundred and three paintings of which sixteen, including the Renoir and Faucheux, are significant. The collection includes some Picasso sketches, small oil sketches by Manet, Matisse and Cézanne – so, the modernists predominantly. In addition, there are three hundred and sixteen artefacts by which I mean candlesticks, sculptures and the like.'

Whilst she had been talking, she had been flicking

through the images on the white screen, giving almost a guided tour through the apartment. The Vermeils were riveted, Madame Vermeil looking on in dismay when they got to Gertie.

'How extraordinary,' Madame Vermeil murmured, her eyes pinned to the boudoir jacket draped over the giant bird's plumage. 'To see the home your parents lived in before the war, *cher*, exactly as it was when they were there.'

Flora wanted to ask whether Jacques' mother had given any further detail as to why she didn't want them seeing the apartment but she kept quiet, merely flicking through the hundreds of photos she had taken, trying to give the clients an understanding of exactly what had been found.

'Clearly, there's a huge amount of work to be done – everything will need to be moved to secure premises where we can begin proper classifications so that you can see exactly what you've got, the condition it's in and what restoration work may be required, insurance valuations, sale estimates . . .'

Madame Vermeil sat back on the silk sofa, looking momentarily overwhelmed.

'Well, I think we'll want to sell most of it, won't we?' she said. 'It's not like we really need anything else.' She gestured vaguely to the pristine perfection of the room they were sitting in.

'Don't you think that's a decision my mother should make?' Jacques asked her, a smile on his mouth but a glint of coldness in his voice. 'She is not dead yet, remember. Technically, all this is hers.'

'Of course, *cher*,' Lilian conceded with a vague toss of the hand. 'I am merely trying to avoid clutter.'

Clutter? Flora almost fell off the chair.

'But you're right. Certain pieces may suit very well in Antibes and of course the children need things for the walls in their homes too,' his wife continued, staring back at the screen. 'Even if they do barely ever set foot in them.'

'*Bien sûr.*' Jacques caught Flora's eye and though he didn't roll his eyes at her, something in his expression implied it. She looked away quickly.

'You have done a superb job. It is a wonderful start,' Lilian Vermeil said with a clap of her hands, signalling that the meeting was at a close and rising to her Chanel-clad feet. Angus walked towards her. 'We would have been quite overwhelmed to have walked into such chaos. It was *absolument* the right thing to call you in.'

'Well, you're at the beginning of a very exciting journey, Lilian, and we're honoured to walk it with you. I'm afraid I've got to shoot off to the airport – I'm heading back to New York tonight – but Flora will be staying here for as long as it takes to get everything shipshape and Bristol fashion for you.'

Flora looked at him in surprise. She was? It was news to her. She specialized in bringing in new business and going for the kill in the saleroom. Research wasn't her strength.

'You are testing my English,' Madame Vermeil laughed, placing a hand on his arm. 'But we are grateful you have overseen this yourself.'

'Personal service is what we're about, Lilian.' Angus turned back to Flora. 'Can I give you a lift?'

'Don't worry,' she replied. 'I've arranged for the security firm to come at four to deliver these to the vault so I'll just pack up and wait, and then catch a cab.'

'Our driver is free,' Madame Vermeil offered. 'He'd be happy to take you wherever you need to go.'

Over her shoulder, Angus shrugged his approval. 'That would be great, thank you,' she nodded.

'I'll send him round. He will wait at the front for you.'

'We'll speak tomorrow and you can give me the updates,' Angus said, clicking his fingers and pointing at Flora by way of a goodbye.

'Sure.'

'Come, we will walk you out,' Madame Vermeil said, as Monsieur Travers opened the door and the group of three filed out. The old notary nodded his head at Flora and left the room.

She sighed, exhaustion breaking over her as the adrenalin from the meeting began to subside. Bruno was out at a competition tonight – as a pro-skateboarder, he worked odd hours – and Ines had promised a quiet night in for them both. Flora wanted to be in bed by nine.

She threw the dust cloths over the paintings again and began to disassemble the white screen. Voices drifted and dissipated through the open door. Somewhere another door slammed.

Footsteps in the hall made her look up and she saw the butler escorting two security guards towards her. Early! 'Ah, excellent,' she smiled, pleased to see they were carrying the wooden crates and packing materials she had ordered too.

It didn't take her long to protect the paintings, wrapping each one first in acid-free tissue paper and then bubble wrap, taking particular care with the more vulnerable corners, before sliding them into the wooden boxes which were nailed shut. She filled in the pro-forma documents, identifying each artwork as the responsibility of the agency, signed on many dotted lines and then watched as they were carried away, incognito. She would sleep well tonight knowing those pieces were in a secure – and insured – location at last.

Her phone buzzed – it was Ines asking if she fancied chicken for dinner. Flora's stomach growled at the mere suggestion. A snackbox of sushi as the only sustenance in twenty-four hours wasn't anywhere near good enough and her fingers almost trembled as she started to text back her agreement.

The butler appeared again.

'Votre voiture, mam'selle.'

'Ah, oui. Merci.'

With a last glance around the room, the collapsible white screen now telescoped and under her arm, she followed him out into the mirrored hall, her high heels sounding out her presence on the marble floors. Little wonder Madame Vermeil seemingly preferred to wear flats – she could move without being tracked.

He opened the front door and held it for her. *'Mam'selle,'* he murmured, motioning to the sleek, glossy chauffeur-driven Mercedes parked directly outside.

'Merci,' she nodded, skipping down the steps.

The driver climbed out and opened the door for her, taking the white board and putting it into the boot. She slid onto the vanilla-coloured leather seats and resumed texting again, the loud *YES* to the chicken question halfway across the screen when the car door was suddenly flung open and a flurry of limbs and coconut-scented hair fell in.

There was an alarmed pause.

'Hey!' the young woman beamed suddenly, her smile slightly too big, too sudden.

In the corner of her eye, Flora could see the driver twisting back in his seat, trying to see what was happening.

'Who are you?'

'I . . . I'm Flora Sykes. I work for Beaumont Fine Art Agency. Madame Vermeil has lent me this car to go home,' she said in tangled, anxious French.

The young woman was openly looking Flora up and down, taking in her edgy trousers, Lalique crystal cabochon ring, sold-out-everywhere shoes. There was a long pause. '. . . Fine art?' she asked finally.

'That's right.'

She angled her legs towards Flora's, suddenly a lot more friendly. 'So then you are working on the lost apartment.'

Flora hesitated. It was fairly obvious to her who this must be, but she couldn't make assumptions. Her work for the family was confidential. 'Sorry, you are . . . ?'

It was the wrong thing to have asked.

'Natascha,' she replied, letting the word drop from her lips as though it were an insult. 'Pascal! *Allez!*' And she uttered an address Flora had never heard of to the driver.

The car began to move.

'Uh, hang on,' Flora said quickly. 'Listen, this is your car. You obviously need it. I'll jump out and catch a cab.'

'*Non.*' Natascha stared back at her with her father's rich brown eyes but her mother's coolness.

'No?' Flora echoed. She gave a nervous laugh, sure that her French – usually perfect – was letting her down and the young woman had misunderstood. 'Listen, you don't understand. I have to go. There's someplace I have to be. If we can just stop the car,' she said more carefully.

'*Non.*' Natascha stared out of the window. She took after her father with her deep-set eyes, slightly hooked nose and olive skin, and was handsome rather than beautiful, but Flora could see there was something magnetic about her –

probably down to the self-confidence that she suspected strayed too often into obnoxiousness and arrogance. Her legs were coltish and tanned in black denim hot pants, a blue denim shirt tucked in but the buttons almost entirely undone, revealing a non-wired black mesh bra underneath; a Chanel Boy bag lay on the seat beside her. A braid was tightly plaited just under the front section of her hair.

'Look, I don't know what you think you're doing or if you've confused me with someone else but—'

Natascha looked back sharply at Flora. 'I need you.'

'Me? *You* need *me*?'

Natascha nodded. 'You work for my family, don't you?'

'Well, yes, but—'

'So then I need your help.'

There was another pause as Flora tried to take all this in.

'And what is it you think I can do for you?' she asked, almost laughing at the absurdity of her being kidnapped in broad daylight from one of the ritziest streets in Paris.

'You will see when we get there.' And Natascha took her phone from her bag and made a call, speaking to someone in a low, hurried voice.

Flora stared at her in open-mouthed disbelief. Seriously? Now she was ignoring her? Client or not, Flora found her indignation rising as they navigated the city streets.

Within minutes, they were pulling up outside a baroque building, brass plaques screwed into the wall.

'Follow me,' Natascha ordered, jumping out and sweeping into the building as though she owned it, which – who knew? – perhaps she did.

Flora followed behind, confusion making her compliant as she tried to work out what was going on and exactly how cross she ought to be.

Natascha was holding the lift for her but she ignored Flora's question, again asking where they were and why, as they travelled up two floors. Natascha strode out the second the doors pinged open again. The girl behind the reception desk sprang to standing and was already shaking her head apologetically by the time Flora joined them all of three seconds later.

'Well, then, where is his assistant?' Natascha was asking furiously.

The receptionist nodded her head and quickly escorted them through an open-plan room populated by people in sober suits to an office at the back of the building. Flora had no idea where they were – an accountant's? an undertaker's? – but she knew that she and Natascha, in their preppy culottes and trashy hot pants respectively, made an odd couple.

Natascha was shown into an office (Flora being told by her to 'stay outside', as though she were the dog) where a young man – mid-twenties, Flora guessed – was working at a screen. Just like the receptionist, he jumped up deferentially and offered Natascha a seat, some coffee, but she just shook her head, speaking to him and holding out her hand as though she was expecting to be given something.

The man looked embarrassed and Natascha's hand dropped down, her agitation increasing as he spoke. Flora, watching through the glass, couldn't decipher the conversation – she couldn't hear a thing and certainly couldn't lip-read French – when suddenly Natascha turned and motioned to her through the glass, telling her to come in. Flora complied again, too bewildered not to.

'Tell him who you are,' she commanded.

Flora looked between Natascha and the man. 'Uh . . . I'm

Flora Sykes, Head of European Operations for Beaumont Fine Art Agency,' she said tentatively, offering a hand.

The young man shook it warily. He looked harassed – much like her, actually. 'Claude Descalier.'

'You see?' Natascha said. 'I don't see why you have a problem. She just had the meeting with your boss and my parents. This is all completely authorized.'

What was?

'Do I need to point it out to you that your firm has represented my family for almost eighty years now? Your boss is like a brother to my father. Why do you insist on acting as though there are secrets? Unless you have something to hide?'

The young man, his skin now almost grey, looked between them both before turning and walking towards a painting on the back wall. He pushed down on the right-hand side of the frame and the entire thing swung back, as on a hinge, revealing a safe. He entered a code and, opening the door, returned a moment later with a long white envelope which he handed to Natascha.

'Thank you,' she said, taking it from him and stuffing it into her bag. She laughed. 'You can stop looking so scared, you know. You have done nothing wrong.'

Flora looked at him, expecting an explanation at least – what had been in that envelope and why had Flora been required to be present to get it? – but Natascha had left the room again and was already halfway across the office.

'You are going with her, *non*?' the man told, rather than asked, Flora, hurrying her along with an urgent tone as he saw her standing motionless. 'You must go.'

He almost pushed her out the door and she had to jog to catch up with Natascha who was already back at the lift.

Only as the doors closed and she looked back did Flora catch sight of the name of the company etched in gold across the front of the reception desk. The receptionist had a smile frozen to her face that Flora had no doubt would fall off the moment the doors closed.

'Natascha, what did that man just give you?' she asked, her voice rising an octave.

'What concern is that of yours?'

'Well, given that you just used my name and presence to get hold of it, I would say quite a lot, actually.'

The lift doors pinged open and they walked back out and into the waiting car again.

'*Natascha?*' Flora persisted, more stridently this time. Professional courtesy would only last for so long. 'You've just barged into your family's notary's and somehow used me to get something you wanted. What was it?'

Natascha glanced up at her. 'It is no big deal. He just gave me the spare keys to the apartment.' And she quickly fired off the now-familiar address to Pascal who silently nodded and pulled out into the traffic.

'But you can't do that! You're not supposed to go there!' Flora cried. 'Your grandmother has specifically barred you from doing so – she has the legal prerogative to do that.'

'*Non*, she forbade my mother – not me, not my brother.' Natascha sounded bored again. 'Why shouldn't I go, anyway? It belongs to our family.'

Flora didn't know what to say. She had no idea of the specifics of Magda Vermeil's diktats to her family or the legalities of the codicil. She was just a fine-arts specialist, there to record, preserve and classify what they found. 'Listen, the scene is sensitive at the moment. There are a lot of valuable artworks just lying on the floor.'

'Which is why I'm taking you with me. You can make sure I don't do any damage. Be my witness, in case I need it.' A hint of a sneer curled her lip.

'Look, the fewer people going in there the better. If you want to see the paintings, of course, you can – but in a protective environment. Once we've moved everything to—'

'I want to see my grandparents' home, my heritage,' Natascha said unconvincingly. Flora suspected the only heritage Natascha cared about was her trust fund.

'But—'

Natascha stopped Flora in her tracks by holding up her hand, inches from Flora's face. 'Stop talking now.'

Flora stared at her in disbelief but Natascha was already oblivious, pressing Buy Now on the Net-A-Porter app for a punky orange-striped Fendi fur jacket from the pre-fall collection. Flora turned away in a fit of anger, her cheeks flaming with humiliation. But Natascha was oblivious – 5,000 euros and six minutes later, they pulled up outside the apartment and she ripped the keys from the envelope before bounding out of the car like an excited puppy.

'Coming?' she asked disingenuously, as Flora remained where she was in the car.

'No!' Flora pointedly turned the other cheek but she could see Natascha shrug in the window's reflection and disappear into the building.

Flora managed to hold her ground for all of twelve seconds before she followed. It was more than she could bear to think of Natascha bulldozing through the apartment – supposedly in search of her heritage – and potentially damaging the artworks within. This was still her watch, at least until the security company moved the rest of the contents into proper storage tomorrow.

She could hear Natascha climbing the stairs on the storey above her; fitness didn't seem to be her thing, unless running to the fridge for more vodka counted as exercise in her world.

Flora, ascending the stairs two at a time, caught up with her on the third floor. Or rather, she saw Natascha disappear into an apartment on the third floor, her long legs scissoring out of sight down a long, dark, dusty hall.

What?

She braked to a stop. No. How? This wasn't right.

But the door was open, Natascha out of sight.

'Natascha?' she called after her. 'You can't go in there.'

No reply.

'Natascha! Get back out here now!'

Silence.

'For God's sake,' Flora muttered, taking a single step over the threshold, as though afraid to follow, her hand tracing the number 6 on the open front door, her fingers finding the key in the lock . . .

Wait, what? The key fit? It was the key for this door?

She could hear Natascha's footsteps on the stripped floors as she barged from room to room. 'Natascha!'

Slowly, she began to walk down the hall, sure she must be tripping. This made no sense. She doubted her own mind. Was *she* the one mistaken? She stared back at the door – at the brass 6 – and then back down the empty hall; she passed bare rooms, thick with dust and nothing else. She found Natascha in the bedroom at the front of the building. A wooden bedstead – no mattress – stood in the room, beside a crate.

'Is that *it*?' Natascha demanded, her hands on her hips.

Almost as though in slow motion, Flora looked at the

painting lying face up on the slats of the bedstead. What was going on? Was this some kind of game? She walked towards the bed, noticing a toy on the floor beside the crate.

But that wasn't what she was interested in. Her eyes were almost immediately drawn back to the solitary painting lying on the bones of the bed. Its beauty was luminous and all the more startling for being found here, alone – a portrait of a woman, Edwardian period, her green eyes shaped like pear-cut emeralds, her russet hair twisted and fashioned into an intricate topknot, the exquisitely rendered silk of her peacock-blue dress modulating through teal to turquoise to sea-green, with top notes of gold flecks. On one elegant hand was a gold signet ring, on the other a ruby, the vermilion scratch shocking against the creaminess of her skin, like blood in the snow.

Flora's eyes flicked to the bottom corners, looking for a signature, but there wasn't one that she could see and she turned it over and checked the back – nothing. No gallery sticker or dealer name, no exhibition number, no clue to reveal who this woman was, nor who had immortalized her. Immediately Flora knew this rendered the painting almost worthless on the open market but she wasn't sure she'd ever seen a more beautiful portrait.

'You said there were hundreds of paintings here!' Natascha shouted, dragging her from her immersive thoughts. 'I heard you. I stood behind the door and I heard you!'

But Flora wasn't interested in Natascha's confession. All her concentration was folded inwards as her brain tried to process what her eyes were showing her. It wasn't just that the apartment was almost entirely empty . . . 'I don't understand. You had a key?'

'Don't try and play the innocent with me! What have you done with them?'

'Done with what?'

'My family's paintings! Where have you hidden them?'

'I haven't hidden anything!'

'Then explain to me where are the *hundreds* of paintings in my grandparents' apartment,' Natascha said sarcastically, holding her arms out wide and indicating the empty space. 'What have you done? Where are they?'

Flora blinked back, understanding precious little more than Natascha did. But without saying a word, she unfurled her index finger and pointed to the ceiling.

Chapter Seven

Flora stood by the front door, refusing to play ball. She wouldn't be part of this; she wouldn't be Natascha's tour guide. It wasn't as though she knew what the hell was going on anyway. She couldn't make sense of what had just happened: another key, another apartment, another painting?

Her finger traced the brass figure *8* on the door as Natascha prowled the rooms, sated now by the haul – her heritage – before her, idly flicking through the stacked paintings like someone at a retro vinyl store.

Her face upon first entering the apartment had been a picture itself – for a girl born into a life of mirrored hallways and twenty-foot ceilings, it had been a shock for her to see the reality of her grandparents' early lifestyle: dark wood panelling, stripped pine floors, low ceilings. They had been by no means poor but it was a far cry from the rarefied echelons the family inhabited now. If Natascha felt dismay, however, she didn't show it, instead laughing at everything – the ragged silk curtains, the fusty coats in the cupboard, the pickle jars in the larder.

Only when she nonchalantly went to light a cigarette in the hall was Flora forced to abandon her post and act, snatching it away from her and sending up prayers of relief that the Renoir and Faucheux were already in safekeeping, far away from this spoilt girl's pithy curiosity.

'You can't smoke in here,' she cried, scarcely able to believe anyone could be so stupid, her eyes falling to a stack of canvases – now flicked to the floor – in the dining room over Natascha's shoulder. 'And don't touch anything,' she said testily as Natascha walked off again with a careless shrug. Didn't the girl have any clue about the value of these pieces? Their fragility after over seventy years in seclusion?

Flora was replacing the canvases against the wall when she heard Natascha's throaty screech of delight come from the drawing room and knew that she had found Gertie.

'Flora!' Natascha called, her tone almost friendly, as though she'd completely forgotten that she'd driven Flora across the city against her will, made her complicit in (possibly illegally) gaining access to the property, held a hand up to her face to silence her. 'Look at this!'

Flora walked in and almost fainted on the spot. Natascha was sitting astride the ostrich, her long, bare legs wrapped around the bird's neck as though she were Miley Cyrus on a wrecking ball. 'Now this I've got to have!' she shrieked, wiggling her shoulders and throwing her head back. 'My mother will detest it!'

'Get off it, Natascha,' she said firmly. Though she herself was only six years older than Natascha, she felt as though she had to be mother. This girl was like a toddler, with no sense of boundaries.

'Why?'

Why? Flora wanted to scream. Had there ever been a more stupid question? 'Because your parents have entrusted the care and safekeeping of everything in this apartment to the agency, and until we have signed it all off, the ostrich is strictly off limits. So I'll say it again – get off the ostrich.'

'*Non,*' Natascha said defiantly, a bead of light dancing in her eyes. She lived to defy, it seemed.

Flora sighed, marched across the room and stood in front of her, hands planted firmly – and warningly – on her hips. 'Natascha, get off Gertie. I mean it.'

'Gertie? Who is Gertie?' Natascha asked, baffled.

Flora coloured up. 'I meant the ostrich.'

'You have given it a name?'

'Of course not. Don't be so ridiculous. Gertie is an English slang word for ostrich.'

A moment pulsed in silence as the two women stared at each other.

'No, it isn't!' Natascha cried, bursting out laughing.

Flora felt the red thread of her temper snap. 'I said, get off her!' she cried back, grabbing Natascha's nearest arm and pulling it away hard, so that the girl lost her balance and fell sideways. Unfortunately, her legs remained tightly gripped round the bird's neck and Gertie toppled with her, onto her.

Natascha began shouting and swearing furiously in French but she wouldn't let go of the bird, even now, her legs gripping it even tighter.

'I said, let go!' Flora shouted, pulling at her arms. 'You'll break her!'

'Get off me!' Natascha cried, beginning to scream as though she was being murdered.

'Then let go!'

'What the fuck is going on?'

The voice made them both jump, stop and turn. At the sight of the man standing in the doorway, Natascha went limp and stopped struggling. For a moment, Flora thought it was the neighbour from the apartment across the street, but this man was taller, leaner, with shaggy black hair and deep-set grey eyes, a squared-off chin and bevelled cheek-bones. He looked like a Viking and Flora felt herself go limp too, albeit seemingly for a very different reason.

'Xav!' Natascha cried, beginning to struggle again and saying something that to Flora's ear was incomprehensible (though in fact she felt she'd lost the power of speech, full stop, not just her command of the French language). Flora stepped back as Xavier crossed the room and effortlessly lifted the stuffed bird off his sister, freeing her.

Natascha scrambled to her feet, dishevelled and furious. Flora had no idea what she was saying to him; she felt the rug had been pulled out from under her again. Two shocks in ten minutes was not what she needed on three hours' sleep and only a sushi snack. She took another step back, away from the two of them, feeling distinctly outnumbered.

Xavier turned to look at her. 'You are from the fine-art agency.' It wasn't so much a question as a statement.

'Yes, that's right,' she said quietly, trying to regain some dignity, pushing her hair back from her face and checking her buttons – some of them had been ripped off in the fracas and she tried to hold her blouse together.

'And you have told my sister here that you are in charge of this collection?'

'That's correct.'

'So then why was the door to the apartment wide open? Anyone could have walked in here.' He gestured with one arm towards the cone of light pooling in the hall.

Flora stared back at him in horror. She had left her post. Left the apartment wide open. He was right – anyone could have just walked in; he had, after all. 'I – I – it wasn't my fault. She was about to start smoking in here. I had no choice but to stop her.'

She looked across at Natascha, only to find the girl doing exactly, defiantly that – *again*!

'No!' Flora shouted, lunging forward and swatting the cigarette out of Natascha's pout. 'How many times do I have to tell you? You cannot smoke in here!' she cried, just as Natascha swung an arm and hit Flora smack in the face.

Flora gasped, her hand flying to her cheek, before the red mist descended and she slapped her back. Harder.

It was Natascha's turn to gasp but before she could retaliate – again – Xavier stepped between them both. Natascha instead slapped Xavier on the arm as though this was some sort of attack command.

Flora retreated a step.

'Stop it! Both of you!' he demanded.

Both women fell silent, breathless and pumped, their hair and eyes wild, cheeks furiously red and marked with the other's handprints, their shirts torn.

'Apologize to my sister,' Xavier demanded, glowering down at Flora.

She stared back at him, hardly able to believe he was serious, knowing it was futile to expect anything different. What was it Ines had said? Cokehead? Playboy? She took in his pale blue crumpled linen shirt, barely buttoned up like his sister's (well, hers too now) and the tails hanging out, beige cargo shorts, suede moccasins. At first glance, he didn't look like a society player, a multimillionaire's scion, but she had a sharp eye from years of working closely with the super-rich and she knew the shoes were Prada, the shirt Zegna, the watch on his wrist a top-of-the-range Breitling.

'Go to hell.' The words were out before she even knew they were hers. She almost jumped at the sound of them. Had she really just said that to her clients' son?

Something mercurial darted through his eyes, like silver fish in a dark pool, and she knew she'd crossed a line from which there was no turning back. None of this was her fault, but she wasn't helping herself now either; it was as though she had stepped outside herself in their presence and become someone wild. Feral.

She felt her breath hitch as his glare blackened – surprise hardening into contempt. As the only girl and the baby of her family, she had grown up adored and yes, indulged. Throughout school and university she had always found it easy to make friends and keep them, boys and then men fell for her readily and she understood, without ever consciously considering it, that she was universally admired. So to encounter animosity as naked as this running through this man's eyes was an unpleasant rarity. What would it yield by tomorrow? Revenge? She could well imagine what form it would take.

'Do you want to try that again?' he asked, folding his arms, seemingly growing an inch.

Flora tossed her head back, barely able to recognize herself. It was all over now anyway. 'Why? Didn't you hear me the first time?'

Oh God! What was she *doing*? But she couldn't stop herself. She felt almost possessed by defiance. And she strode out of the apartment, her heels ringing on the wooden floor, her heart leaping in her chest. She had just got herself fired. Spectacularly so! The consolation that she would never have to see Xavier Vermeil or his sister again was scant indeed.

*

Ines giggled at her own joke and swung the hammock a bit harder. The sky was a smoky red above them, the wall of bamboo shoots on the far side of the roof terrace bending gently in the breeze, a flock of starlings swooping and pitching above the rooftops before turning as one like a page, and heading for the fiery river. It was a stunning sunset and Flora, lying beside her, tried to enjoy the moment, drowsy from a full tummy, her hand weighted with an almost-empty wine glass, but her mind was agitated and nervy, and Ines's voice kept fading from her ear as she replayed over and over this afternoon's showdown.

'Hey, you want to hear some gossip?' Ines asked, bringing her back to the present.

'Always.'

'Guess who came into the boutique today?'

'Can't.' Flora took another sip of her rosé.

'Lucia Cantarello.'

Flora hesitated, waiting for the punchline. What was so interesting – or unusual – about a model buying lingerie?

'She was buying for her girlfriend.'

Flora frowned. She was vaguely aware that the model was engaged to some Russian billionaire. 'Who's the lucky girl?' she asked dutifully but she was already falling back into her memories again – Natascha's palm at her face; Xavier's entitled arrogance as he'd stared down at her . . .

'Flor?'

'Huh? What . . . ?'

'It is a scandal, *non*?' Ines asked, a conspiratorial smile on her face as she cupped the bottom of her wine glass.

She tried to rally, get back into the conversation. 'It's a mess. And what's worse, I bet that's exactly what she loves about it – the drama and chaos.'

'Well, to be honest, there is a lot to be said for high passion,' Ines said with a wink.

'What? Screaming fights and crying all night? No, thanks. I can't think of anything worse, all the *drama*.'

Ines patted her arm, a bemused grin on her lips. 'I hope that when love finds you, it will be as straightforward as you expect.'

'Why wouldn't it be? It's perfectly simple – you love someone or you don't. There's no grey area.'

'Love is *completely* grey! There are no absolutes, no certainties. Sometimes love cannot be stopped even when it is wrong. And what if you end up falling for someone you don't *want* to love?'

Flora looked at her as though she was mad. 'Well, you just wouldn't.'

'Why not? How could you stop it? Sometimes the chemistry is just too much. Look at me and Bruno. Everything is opposite – our parents, our childhoods, our jobs, our dreams.'

'That's different. You're the classic Yin/Yang, Opposites Attract story – you two are made for each other, everyone can see that.'

'Not everyone. Lots of people think he's with me for my money.'

'They won't now he's got that contract with Hawk. He's hitting the big league and it's without any help from you – no contacts, no loans.'

'I hope you're right,' Ines sighed. 'He's really nervous about the showcase tonight.'

'He always is, but he'll smash it.'

The sky was darkening rapidly now and although the breeze was picking up, it was still warm. Flora sensed that thunderstorms were on the way. They drifted into silence again, Ines's legs kicking out like a swimmer's, keeping the hammock swaying. Flora heard her hair rustle against the fabric sling as she turned to face her.

'Flo, are you OK? You're so quiet tonight.'

Flora bit her lip. 'Actually, no. I think I just lost my job.'

Ines gasped. 'But how?'

Flora grimaced, hiding her face with her hands. She didn't even know where to start with it all – no one came out of it well. 'I may have slightly slapped Natascha Vermeil in the face.'

Ines almost fell backwards out of the hammock. 'You did *what*?' she screeched, clearly delighted. 'Do you have any idea how many people want to do that to that girl? People will be lining up to shake you by the hand.'

'She hit me first!' Flora tried to justify, before blowing out through her cheeks. 'Oh Christ, what was I thinking? She's my clients' daughter! I don't even know what happened to me. I just . . . lost it with them.'

'Them?'

'The brother was there too. I told him to go to hell.'

'Oh. My. God,' Ines screeched, gripping her arm so tightly, she was sure it would bruise. 'Tell me *everything*.'

Flora slumped further in the hammock and told her.

'. . . So the Poison Princess was sitting on the *ostrich*?' Ines repeated, when she'd finished.

Flora nodded.

'And the Dark Prince walked in when you were fighting with her?'

Flora tried to smile at her friend's dramatic names, but she couldn't. They were too true. Ines was silent and after a few moments, Flora looked across at her, anxious at the horror she'd see in her friend's eyes.

Only, it wasn't horror that she saw. Ines was sitting beside her with one hand clapped over her mouth, tears streaming from her eyes as she tried to stifle her laughter.

'It's not funny!'

'Oh, but it is!' Ines wailed, letting the hand drop and clutching her sides instead.

Flora waited, unamused, as Ines recovered herself. 'You don't understand. I'm going to get *fired*, Ines. The second Angus touches down in New York and gets my messages—' She checked her watch again. Angus would be landing in five and a half hours from now.

'No, you won't,' Ines said definitively.

'I will. They'll say I assaulted her and insulted him. And I did!'

'*Pah!* You think it will be the first time the parents have heard such stories from those two? That is *nothing* compared to what they usually deal with.'

'Ines, they are my clients. I'm employed by the family – it's only reasonable to expect that I would behave in a professional manner.'

'Did they behave reasonably with you? Was Natascha reasonable when she drove off with you in the car?'

'Well, no, but—'

'And when she stuck her hand in your face?'

'Well no, but—'

'And how about when she deliberately defied you and then hit you? First.'

Flora shook her head. 'Well, there's no excuse for how I spoke to Xavier.'

'He was completely unreasonable expecting you to apologize.'

'He was defending his sister.'

'Hey! Whose side are you on?' Ines jogged her with her elbow. '. . . Or maybe I should not be surprised. Passions always run high around him.'

Flora's eyebrows shot up. 'Excuse me?'

'Well, you've got to admit he is handsome, *non*?'

'No, I don't!'

'*Non?* You don't think so?'

'You *do*? The man's an arrogant, self-entitled, spoilt egomaniac who clearly thinks the world owes him and his sister a living.'

'I know! But that doesn't mean he's not completely gorgeous.'

'He's an arse.'

Nonplussed, Ines gave up with her tease and rolled forward to reach for the bottle of rosé, refilling both their glasses. 'Well, I am sure you are making worse of it than it is. Besides, they are not your only clients. Angus needs you more than he needs them.'

'Two days ago I might have agreed with you, but if he had to choose now, he'd choose them. The Vermeils are suddenly much more valuable to him, not just in terms of commission but exposure too. Once the news about this job gets out, it's going to be picked up in papers *all* across the world, trust me.'

Ines rolled on the hammock so that she was facing inwards to Flora. 'Why will it be in papers all over the world?'

'Because the family owns an apartment that's been

locked up since the war. No one knew anything about it until three days ago.'

Ines's mouth dropped open. 'You are joking me?'

'Nope. It's a complete time capsule. That's why they've called us in.'

'Oh my God, what did you find in there?' she asked intently. 'No dead bodies, I hope.'

Flora pulled a face. 'No, but it was stuffed to the rafters with paintings, ornaments, you name it. And Gertie the ostrich of course. That's where we had the fight.'

'I don't believe it,' Ines murmured.

'Nor could we. Nor could *they*, to be honest. We presented them with the inventory today. There's hundreds of pieces in there.'

'What are they going to do with it all?'

Flora shrugged. 'Sell it, probably.'

'I can't believe they forgot they had an entire apartment. God, don't let Bruno hear about it!'

'Actually, two apartments. It turns out they own the apartment downstairs too – although that one was pretty much empty. The only things in it are a bed and a painting. Here, have a look.' She brought up a photo of the portrait on her phone.

'Wow!' Ines murmured. 'I love the colour of that dress. It would look so great in a bra.'

Flora chuckled, pocketing the phone again.

'So, they forgot about *two* apartments. How careless.' Ines tucked her legs into her chest, curling up like a hedgehog, and Flora automatically took over swinging the hammock with her foot.

'The weird thing is, I get the impression the family

doesn't know there are two apartments. I mean, they will now of course – Natascha's hardly likely to keep shtum – but it wasn't mentioned in our meeting yesterday. They only ever talked about one.' She wrinkled her nose. 'Don't you think that's odd?'

'Mmmm.' Ines thought for a moment. 'But you said one was empty, right?'

Flora nodded.

'Well, if you were called in to assess the art inside, there wouldn't have been any point discussing the one *without* any art in it, would there?'

'It had the portrait in it.'

'Yeah. Just one painting. Not worth mentioning.'

'I guess.' Flora sighed and they swung in easy silence for a few moments. 'Did I mention there was a codicil in the grandfather's will saying no one in the family was to even know about the apartment until his wife dies?'

'No! Is she dead?'

'Nope, alive and well and living in Antibes apparently. And she's forbidden them all from going to the apartment.'

'Oh!' Ines said, catching on. 'So *that's* why they called you in – you're their "eyes".'

'Exactly.'

Ines chewed her inner cheek thoughtfully. 'Well, that explains why Natascha kidnapped you. As soon as she's told she can't do something, you can bet it's all she wants to do.'

She knew her friend was right. Natascha had admitted she had been listening at the door; she would have heard that Flora was leaving separately, alone and in the family's own car; and she would have known that she needed Flora

– as one of the only two people authorized to enter the property – to help her get the key. Little had she realized she'd gone about it the hard way. Flora had had her own copy of the key in her bag. If only Natascha had thought to ask and not grab . . .

Flora watched as a raven landed on a chimney stack and began cleaning its ruffled feathers, her mind still on the key. She was certain the assistant had thought he was giving her the spare, as though there was only one apartment.

She remembered something suddenly. 'Oh! I nearly forgot . . . Wait there.'

Flora wriggled out of the hammock and ran over the roof terrace into the apartment. A moment later she returned with the letter in her hand. 'I found it in the apartment yesterday. I meant to give it to Angus but I forgot.'

Ines looked at the tatty sheet. 'It's in German.'

'I know,' Flora nodded, climbing back into the hammock again. 'Can you read it?'

Ines cast her eye over it. 'Not well. It's not Swiss German, anyway, which is about the *only* thing I learnt at that school.'

Flora shrugged. 'Whatever you can tell me would help.'

Ines blew out through her cheeks. 'OK, well, here we go,' she said, her eyes travelling over the page. 'It's sent from Amsterdam, in October 1940.'

'Ooh,' Flora said, resting her cheek on Ines's shoulder.

'"... Dearest Sister, thank you for your nice words. Edmund and I are both . . . *faring* well, in spite of the increasing . . . scarcity of food. It has been one hundred and twenty days now since the Germans occupied the city and I think we cannot pretend any longer that the situation is a peaceful one, or even civilized. There have been rumours that the

Germans are deliberately blockading supplies but I do not believe this myself. It is too much to believe they would resort to these tactics, starving us like dogs. Isn't it?"'

Ines cocked a sad eyebrow at Flora before continuing to read.

'"I pray things are easier with you. I wish you were here. I feel, even as hard as things are here, they must surely be better than Paris. I think I could bear it so much more to have you here with me. We could walk, like we always used to as girls. You could talk to me too, confide in me all your cares. I was . . . dismayed to read your unhappiness in your last letter and spent many nights . . . fretting about you, not just about your most recent loss – for which I cried for you, sister, truly I did – but also your worries for your marriage. If you will permit, I will speak frankly – your husband is still the man you married. He always has been a *bon viveur* who loves the limelight; indeed, was it not his vitality that drew you to him first? It is no surprise to me that his vanity has grown with his success – perhaps it was even to be expected. Every man has his pride and Daddy didn't make it easy for him asking for your hand, so now that he has both money and power, of course women laugh more easily in his company. But does this mean his love for you has dimmed? On the contrary, I am certain that much of his flamboyance can be attributed to a desire to provide a better life for you. He is an ambitious man, simply playing the game. Just remember – he plays it for you.

'"My advice to you is simple – turn the other cheek when he comes in late from the opera, ignore the scent of perfume on his coat, put out his meals with your best smile and ensure he visits you nightly. You can be sure he will settle down once he has a family. Take it from me, fatherhood sobers the flightiest of men. Write soon. Your loving sister always, Birgita.'"

Ines folded the letter with pursed lips. 'Having a baby to save a marriage?' she tutted. 'Thank God I am a modern woman. They would have had me shot for insubordination to my husband, I can tell you,' she cackled.

'Hmm,' Flora smiled wanly, putting the letter back in her pocket and feeling slightly disappointed. She had hoped the fact that the letter had been hidden under the bed had meant it might concern more specific secrets – such as why an apartment full of treasure had been locked up and left for over seventy years.

'Do you think Angus has got my messages yet?' she asked, biting her lip anxiously. 'Maybe there's Wi-Fi on his plane.'

'Well, you've only sent seven hundred so far. You'd better send another just in case.' Ines took one look at Flora's stricken face. 'I'm joking! Hey, listen, you need to relax. Remember we've got the Hermès party tomorrow night. They always serve the best champagne.'

'Sure,' Flora replied distractedly, clearly not hearing a word.

Ines jogged her with her arm. 'We're going to Île de Ré this weekend. I can't stay in the city in this heat. You should come.'

Flora turned her head to look at her. 'Thanks, but if Angus fires me, I'll have to go back to London, and if by some freak miracle he doesn't, I'll probably need to make it up to him and work through.'

'Really? Stefan's coming.'

Flora arched an eyebrow. 'And you're mentioning that because . . . ?'

'I'm just saying,' Ines shrugged carelessly. 'You two rub along nicely together, that's all.'

'He's a friend. That's it.'

Ines smirked – she knew full well that the two of them had hooked up once before – but Flora swiped her lightly on the arm.

'I'm telling you, that's all we are. Friends.'

Ines shrugged again. 'OK. I just thought you could do with a bit of fun. All work and no play . . .'

'Excuse me! I am *not* dull,' Flora pouted. 'We can't all be having sex on the stairs, you know.'

But Ines didn't reply. She simply squeezed Flora's hand as they swung in the hammock and watched the stars begin to stud the night sky.

Chapter Eight

Paris sparkled in the sun, golden statues glinting on the bridges, the river below gleaming as boats laden with tourists passed up and down on well-worn routes that would have long since carved out gorges on dry land. Flora walked past them with the unseeing eyes and briskness of a local, oblivious to the heavy-headed swaying of the plane tree canopies or the amusing sight of a couple of policemen on rollerblades, drinking frappés. She didn't care that the Eiffel Tower had suddenly come into view in a gap between the buildings as she walked down the street, nor was she moved by the sight of a *Sale* sign outside the Caravane store. She had forgotten all about the blister that had been threatening to form on her heel with these new shoes; she had forgotten about the macaroons she had intended to pick up as a farewell gift for Ines on her way past this afternoon.

Angus still hadn't rung and she was so distracted with nerves that she was scarcely conscious of where she was and why. In the absence of a call, she had bullishly decided to continue as normal. If he was ruminating on whether or not to fire her, he might be appeased if she achieved something productive today.

And so she had. This morning's appointment at Bernheim-

104

Jeune (the recognized authority on Renoir's official works) had been wearing and time-consuming, but ultimately successful. She had sifted through every page of Renoir's *catalogue raisonné* – no mean feat for an artist who had produced more than 4,000 works of art during his lifetime – but she had eventually found the image of the Vermeils' picture. It was officially called *Yellow Dress, Sitting*, as per the sticker on the back, but not only that; it had a companion piece: *Yellow Dress, Walking*.

She had taken photographs and details of both entries, and with a brisk handshake had left, eager to get back to the office and feed the details into the various databases that could get their search well and truly off the ground.

The Paris office wasn't anywhere near as splashy as the New York headquarters, a vast converted warehouse in Tribeca with a newly purchased Pollock in the reception area; nor did it match the muted old-school splendour of the London base in Mayfair where their European operations were based and which she now headed up. Rather, it was a lone outpost in the Marais which Angus had rented for his fleeting visits through the capital, just a single room above an old *papeterie*, with little in it apart from a Napoleon desk, a chair, a plug socket and a view into the nail bar opposite.

She let herself in and without even opening the windows – and it was stiflingly hot in there – logged on to the Getty Provenance Index, her eyes flickering every few seconds up to the huge former stationmaster's clock which she had bought at Clignancourt flea market.

Ten minutes till New York opened. She and Angus always touched base at 9 a.m. his time. He might have ignored her messages last night but he couldn't avoid her for much longer now. If he was planning on firing her, he was going to have to do it to her face and she didn't intend to make it easy for him. In the space of the twenty-four hours since he'd left, yes, she'd had a fracas with the clients' daughter but she had also established that their prize Renoir was officially recognized in the *catalogue raisonné* and she had a title and date for it. If she could just establish the chain of ownership, or provenance, from the artist through to the Vermeils, before he called . . .

Her fingers flitted over the keypad, her eyes scanning the screen quickly, dispassionately, as the information uploaded. She wrote down the pertinent details: *Yellow Dress, Sitting* had been painted in 1908 and sold to Renoir's renowned dealer Ambroise Vollard in May that same year. It was sold in London in 1910 to a man called Fritz Haas who kept it until his death, when it was sold by his daughter in 1943 to—

Flora stopped scribbling as she saw the next name to acquire it: Franz Von Taschelt. She knew the name; any decent industry professional would. Von Taschelt had been a prominent dealer of modernism in Paris, with a successful gallery on Place Valhubert. But when the Nazis occupied Paris, Von Taschelt had collaborated with them, becoming complicit in systematically plundering wealthy Jewish families' private collections in which sales were forced and their assets seized. The worst part of it all? He was Jewish himself.

The fact that there wasn't a name below his on the Provenance Index worried her –Von Taschelt was rightly reviled for what he'd done and even all these years later, the mere mention of his name inspired contempt in those who knew of such things. Factor in that the Vermeils were an influential family with a high philanthropic profile, and it would be terrible PR for them if it transpired they had bought it from him – no doubt for a song. There had been practically no art market in Europe during the war and the Third Reich's crackdown on what they considered to be modernist 'degenerate' art meant works by Dalí, Cézanne, Picasso and the like were almost unsaleable. The opposite had been true in North America, by contrast, with many of the most venerable institutions buying the grand-master and modernist stocks that the Nazis didn't want, via the regime's small network of six dealers who were authorized to trade on this free market, with all proceeds going straight from the art to the Third Reich's armaments programme. There had even been a bureau dedicated to these wartime 'deals' – the ERR, the Einsatzstab Reichsleiter Rosenberg; to maintain an appearance of legality, its purported goal was to 'safeguard the works' belonging to wealthy Jews but no one was fooled by that and this plundering of art had been declared a war crime in the Nuremberg Trials immediately following the end of the war. It was art history's darkest hour and Flora wasn't pleased to see that her clients had been brushed by it.

She dropped her head in her hands. Her remarkable run had come to a juddering halt. This was not what Angus would want to hear; she needed to establish how the Vermeils had come to be in possession of the painting and whether or not Von Taschelt had sold it on to them directly, or to someone else in between . . .

The FaceTime dial tone suddenly rang out.

She was out of time.

She checked the clock again. Ten past nine in the morning in New York.

'Angus,' she smiled, her voice full of a lightness she didn't feel, as his image suddenly beamed onto the screen. He didn't look happy.

He ran his hands over his face. 'You actually *slapped* her?'

As an opening gambit, it wasn't promising.

'She hit me first,' Flora replied quietly. 'If that makes any difference.'

'No! Not really!'

She inhaled slowly and watched as he paced the office – so much bigger and brighter than hers. She could see a new Anne Magill oil above the desk, his silver Montblanc pen strewn over some papers.

'You realize you almost gave me a goddam heart attack when I got off the plane last night and saw your messages? All twelve of them.'

'Sorry. I just . . . I wanted you to hear it from me first. It was a crazy situation. I didn't want her to make it sound worse than it was.'

'You mean it's possible to *get* any worse after kidnapping and assault?' He raked his hands through his hair. 'Christ almighty, I mean, they're our single-biggest clients right now.'

'I know.'

'If we get this entire collection to sale, do you realize what it'll do to our bottom line this year?'

'I can imagine.'

'Imagine harder. It's more than we could have dreamed of. Not to mention the exposure we'll get once the press gets wind of it, and they will – you can be sure of that.'

Flora closed her eyes. And if they got wind of the fight between her and Natascha . . . ? Her position here was untenable, she saw that now. It didn't matter what she brought to the table on the Renoir, he couldn't hold on to her in these circumstances. The agency had too much to lose.

'Angus, I understand your position. I know I've put you in an impossible situation. I'll resign my post with immediate effect. Just please don't fire me—'

'*Fire you?* What, are you kidding me?' Angus looked furious now.

'But I thought—'

'You should be so lucky as to think I'm going to fire you. We've got a ton of work to do and I need you on the ground over there.'

Flora stared back at him in astonishment. 'But what about the Vermeils?'

He shrugged. 'What about them? Lilian and Jacques haven't been in contact. I've been waiting for a call but if they haven't been in touch by now then as far as I'm concerned, nothing's happened. It's business as usual.'

'But surely . . .' Flora was flabbergasted. She'd barely slept for worrying about the fight and . . . what? Natascha and Xavier hadn't even mentioned it? They were going to let it fly?

Angus lowered his voice. 'Listen, I didn't like to say anything before, but Xavier and Natascha don't exactly have the best reputations. I'm not sure their word counts for much with most people, including their parents. Although that's strictly off the record.'

'. . . OK.' She was dumbfounded.

He looked back at her sternly again. 'But that doesn't mean *I'm* letting you off the hook, Flora. It is not OK to go round slugging the clients, especially those with priceless Renoirs in their possession.'

'Angus, I assure you, nothing like this has ever happened before, nor ever will again. It was a complete freak thing. You can trust me.'

He blinked down the screen at her, taking in the bags under her eyes and her wan pallor. It must be clear to him that she'd been beating herself up over it.

'Yes, well, you're just lucky they're French. If it had happened over here, you'd have been hauled up on assault charges.'

'Understood,' she nodded. Christ, like her parents needed *that* right now.

'Right, well, that's the end of today's lecture. Make it up to me. Give me some good news,' he said, perching on the edge of the desk again and folding his arms over his chest. Flora thought he looked even more relieved than she did.

'OK . . . uh . . . well, the good news is the Renoir is in the *cat rais*. As we thought, it is called *Yellow Dress, Sitting* and guess what? It has a companion. *Yellow Dress, Walking*.'

Angus looked pleased by this. 'Interesting.'

'I thought so,' she said, relaxing a little. 'Now, the paintings were painted over the winter of 1908, and sold by Renoir to his dealer Ambroise Vollard in May, who in turn sold both in 1910 to a man called Fritz Haas. He kept them till 1943.' She bit her lip. 'But here comes the bad bit – that year his daughter sold our Renoir to Franz Von Taschelt.'

She watched as Angus's expression changed. '. . . Please tell me there's more.'

'I'm afraid not,' she replied. 'The Getty site doesn't have anything registered for it after that sale in 1943.'

There was a long pause. 'So how the hell did it get into the Vermeils' apartment?' Angus asked eventually.

'I don't know yet, but I'll find out. I'm only just back from Bernheim-Jeune.'

He rubbed his face in his hands again. 'Jesus. Of all the places for the trail to run cold.' He looked up again. 'You do realize this throws the Vermeils' ownership into doubt? It doesn't matter if they bought from him in good faith. Practically all his deals were covers for asset-stripping rich Jews.'

'I know. But you've already checked the ALR and there aren't any heirs placing a claim to it, so that's got to be something – the transaction *could* have been genuine.'

Angus looked sceptical. 'We definitely need to get this provenance sewn up. The Resistance flooded the market with good-quality fakes to dupe the Germans as it was. If we can't show a step-perfect paper trail, all bets are off. The painting's authenticity will be thrown into doubt if we go to market saying it was found in an abandoned apartment and our clients can't explain how they came by it.'

'Well, if there was one thing the Nazis were meticulous about, it was keeping their books – they made a big show of recording all the bills of sale to conceal the forced nature of the transactions, so there'll be something written down somewhere,' she said reassuringly. 'It may take a while but I'll find it. I'll speak to the family again and try to find out what other paperwork they've got from the father.'

Huh,' Angus snorted. 'After all this time? Good luck. François Vermeil's been dead over seventy years.'

'Maybe the notaries have a ledger listing everything that was in the apartment, or a receipt of sale? You never know,' she said, determined to sound optimistic.

Angus looked somewhat mollified. 'OK, well, I don't care how you get it – you have to turn in the goods on this, Flora. The buck does not stop with Von Taschelt, you hear me? Under no circumstances does the trail stop with that Nazi. The family would never sell if that connection had to be made public.'

In which case, bang went their commission and up went the overdraft. 'Don't worry, I'll find out how it came into the Vermeils' possession.'

'You know, it might be worth trying to find the owners of the companion piece,' Angus said thoughtfully. 'If it's still with the same family, they might know something – like why one of the pair was sold to Von Taschelt.'

'Everyone needs money in a war.'

'Hmmm, 1943 you said?'

'That's right.'

'That's the same year the Vermeils shut up the apartment, meaning they must have bought it off him almost immediately,' he murmured. Then he brightened suddenly. 'In which case, Von Taschelt may have acted just as a broker between the two parties, you know – flipped it? So there'd be a reasonable chance the Haas heirs know what happened next. If a painting as important as that was in the family for . . . what, thirty-odd years, and they held on to the other one, they're bound to have kept tabs on it. They could well know something about that sale.' He got up from the corner of the desk he had perched on and walked round to his chair. 'What did you say the other one was called?'

'*Yellow Dress, Walking*.'

She watched as he tapped on his keyboard for a moment, no doubt in the Getty Provenance archives too. He looked back at her triumphantly a moment later. 'Don't bloody believe it,' he winked. 'A New York address!'

'Brilliant,' she nodded, not quite as convinced as he was that this would make a material difference to their search.

Did it matter *why* one of the Renoirs had been sold? The fact was, it had left the Haas family and ended up with another. It was the second part of that equation they needed to answer.

'Right, leave that with me. I'll make contact at this end and get a meeting set up pronto.'

'OK.' She leaned forwards, getting ready to disconnect. 'And I'll come back to you as soon as I know anything more on the provenance for ours.'

'OK, I've got to run. I've a meeting with Rory Mortlake at Christie's in fifteen.' He looked at her, as if noticing her for the first time. 'And get a decent sleep, Flora. You look tired.'

She tried to rally. 'Me? No, I'm fine.'

He was quiet for a moment. 'Hmmm . . . well, keep me posted.'

'Sure thing.' The screen went black and she slumped back in the chair, dropping her head on her folded arms for a minute. He was right, she was exhausted but this was no time to let up. She'd been *that* close to getting fired.

She tabbed back in to the Getty site. 'So if Von Taschelt was the last recorded owner . . .' she murmured to herself. 'Then, if I do a search under dealers . . .'

Her eyes scanned the information that came up.

1934–1938: Blumka Von Taschelt Gallery, Innere Stadt district, Vienna, specializing in French Impressionism and post-Impressionism.

1938–1943: Galerie Von Taschelt, Place Valhubert, Paris. Specialists in surrealism, modernism, cubism, Impressionism, post-Impressionism.

1944–Current day: Attlee & Bergurren, Saint-Paul-de-Vence, specializing in twentieth-century modernism. Gallery maintains fragmentary historic records for Galerie Von Taschelt: picture stock books, sale books, property received, correspondence, clippings, exhibition catalogues.

'Bingo.' Flora sat back in her chair, swinging it lightly on the pivot. It was that easy. If only Angus had given her a few more minutes . . . The details of Von Taschett's sale of the Renoir would be in those historic ledgers. The answer she needed was in the South of France.

She smiled. She was back on top.

Chapter Nine

Ines was waiting for her by the scooter when she finally exited the building four hours later.

'Your bell doesn't ring,' Ines muttered, a cigarette dangling from her mouth as Flora grabbed the spare helmet from the back.

'I hope that's not a euphemism for my sex life,' Flora quipped.

Ines cackled with laughter, grinding her cigarette into the ground and hopping astride the bike. 'You're in a good mood today.'

'I've had a good day,' Flora smiled, fastening the chin strap.

'He didn't fire you then?'

'Dodged a bullet this time.'

'Didn't I tell you?' Ines winked. 'They are so much badder than a catfight, those two. I bet they have completely forgotten already.'

Flora clasped her hands around her friend's waist, feeling discomfited by the thought. She hadn't been able to forget either of them so easily; in fact, her mind kept replaying events every time she fell into a daydream – Natascha's viciousness, the sudden appearance of Xavier at the door.

There was no question of riding astride the scooter in her

narrow olive-green skirt, so she sat side-saddle, her arms around Ines's waist and her friend's curly black hair tickling her face as they zipped through the traffic. The city was drowsy from the midsummer heat and the roads were quiet, Ines languidly manoeuvring the bike along the boulevards, boys whistling at them each time they stopped at the lights.

They were there in just a few minutes, stopping at the junction where Rue du Faubourg Saint-Honoré meets Rue Boissy d'Anglas. Flora slid off the seat, Ines dismounting with a careless leg thrown high like a gymnast's as she shook her hair out of the helmet, her Isabel Marant minidress perfectly pitched for the city heat.

Ines handed her a stiff ivory invitation and they were waved through the multi-storeyed Hermès flagship building by the security guards. They stepped into the mirrored private lift and both women set to checking their appearances – Ines backcombing the roots of her hair with her fingers, Flora fiddling with the collar of her white shirt.

She fanned her neck. 'Damn, it's hot. I should have gone home first and changed. This shirt is wilting. I look grim.'

'You look gorgeous. You always look gorgeous. Anyway, for once, no one will be looking at you.' The doors had opened and Ines winked at her as she walked out. 'Just wait till you see this.'

Flora followed, scarcely able to believe what she was seeing. She had anticipated the rooftop being a stone affair with tasteful lighting and maybe some artfully arranged plant pots. She hadn't counted on a perfect lawn banked with beds of jasmine; apple and pear trees heavy with fruit; magnolia branches spreading like splayed hands above the crowd and casting dappled shade onto the lawn; balustraded pathways squaring the perimeter of the space and keeping the garden back and hidden from view from the streets below; charming country-house *treillage* laddering the walls. It was a pocket Eden in the heart of the capital.

'Paris's secret garden,' Ines said in an excited whisper. 'Only a very few people know it is even here. This is VVVIP, baby.'

They each took a whisper-fine crystal flute of champagne from a tray and stepped seamlessly into the chic crowd. White was clearly the new black; almost everyone was wearing it, bolts of white linen accented with flashes of grass-green or red, but mainly Hermès' trademark orange – be it the ribbons on neat panamas or orange H-slide sandals, *'collier de chien'* studded cuffs or double-strap Kelly watches.

Flora relaxed, realizing she blended in better than she had anticipated, and let Ines direct the conversation as her eyes drifted over the bucolic scene, feeling almost assaulted by the intense fragrance that showered down like a burst storm cloud above their select grouping. She half-expected to see bluebirds in the trees, or at least snow-white doves, and for a moment it felt possible to forget the ugliness, the black fog that had crept without sound or warning around the periphery of her life and was creeping ever closer . . .

Ines had made eye contact with an old acquaintance, who was now gliding over as though on castors, and introduced them both. 'Flora, Claudia.' They had known each other at Aiglon College in Switzerland and the woman boasted the distinctive polish of the international rich – chiselled bones and tight skin, swept-back bronde hair, a putty-coloured *shahtoosh* draped over one shoulder. Her BCBG look was in startling contrast to Ines's rebellious 'bohemian princess' vibe – did Claudia know that Ines sold cupless bras for a living? Flora was sure she would look scandalized by the idea – and Flora listened with feigned interest as they discussed a mutual friend's wedding in Toulouse, forcing herself to laugh politely at the requisite intervals.

Other people joined them – a man who knew Claudia's husband from INSEAD, a friend of Ines's cousin, then a contact of Stefan based in Boston, a gallerist from Berlin – and their group divided and then subdivided again, Flora becoming detached from Ines as her own small cluster organically revolved around the lawn in a conversational waltz so that within forty minutes, and by the time a gentleman in buff linen clapped his hands for attention, she had spoken to at least half the guests there.

'Ladies and gentlemen,' he began in a French accent that was refined even to her ear. 'Thank you for joining us here tonight, to celebrate the launch of a project that is very close to our hearts . . .'

Flora absent-mindedly smoothed her skirt over her hips, trying mentally to count how many of her business cards she had handed out this evening. Angus was going to love her – coming here had proved to be a networker's dream and it was like shooting fish in a barrel whenever her line of work became the topic of discussion, everyone on this rarefied patch of lawn being cultured, rich and interested in art.

'. . . Our little garden here remains one of the best-kept secrets in the city and it is our great pleasure to be able to share it with you all tonight. Of course, it did not always look as magnificent as this. The garden itself was originally planted during the Nazi Occupation when food supplies were scarce and self-sufficiency became vital. We grew potatoes, beans, carrots here—'

Some people tittered, amused by the thought of potatoes on this roof. Others nodded their heads sombrely at the atrocity that had necessitated it.

'Only when the crisis had passed could we turn our minds to beauty once more and these very trees casting dappled shade on us this evening were planted then. I consider myself one of the most fortunate men in all of Paris to be able to take my lunch here and sit in quiet solitude, surrounded throughout the year by the delicate scents of jasmine, magnolia, pear and—'

The sound of a glass smashing on the stone floor made everyone turn in surprise, all seeming equally shocked that the pastoral perfection of the setting could be undermined in any way, but the offender – a woman – was obscured from clear view by the splay of camellia leaves, and their host continued talking after only the barest of hesitations. Accidents happened, after all, and it wouldn't do to make a fuss.

'Of course, we realize that it is simply not possible to open the gardens to the public but an idea began to form that a new *parfum*, inspired by this very garden, could make its experience accessible to all—'

'Get your hands off me!'

This time the silence that followed was heavy and protracted, everyone leaning and craning to see who, *who*, was sabotaging this pristine moment. The culprits were standing on the elevated pathway that created a border between the garden's lush verdancy and the hard, stone encroachment of the city it sat in; Flora craned her neck to see flashes of bare flesh moving behind the leaves, hear voices being

119

lowered to whispered hisses, the stinging sound of skin slapping skin.

An audible gasp whistled round the space before a man suddenly emerged, one cheek noticeably redder than the other beneath his shades. He tried to hide his face as he strode down the three steps to the lawn, murmuring an apology of sorts to the hosts before he pushed through the crowd and disappeared into the lift. Flora, looking around to see Ines's reaction, only just caught sight of the back of another man who was running up the steps opposite and disappeared behind the same shrubbery.

A low murmur of disapproving exchanges rose up like a bee swarm and Flora felt Ines's warm hand on her arm, her excited breath in her ear.

'My God, you know who that was, don't you?' she whispered, her eyes too on the woman still hiding behind the bush.

'Should I?'

'The Interior Minister.'

'Oh. That's awkward.'

'It will be if the woman behind there turns out not to be his wife,' Ines murmured, loving the scandal. 'Come on, come on – she can't stay there all night.'

As if agreeing the same, the mysterious woman began to move, the pin-tap of her heels sounding out on the path, and moments later there was a collective tut as Natascha Vermeil, rail-thin and conspicuous in a short red playsuit, emerged with a defiant sneer.

'Oh, why am I not surprised?' Ines asked rhetorically.

'What are you all looking at?' Natascha demanded, staring everyone back down even though no one could tear their gaze from her mascara-clotted eyes and the smear of lipstick against her jaw, which had been unsuccessfully rubbed out. Her brother was only two steps behind her, muttering something beneath his breath as he took her by the elbow and steered her down the steps, Natascha continuing her tirade. 'Huh? I asked you?' she sneered, suddenly lunging forwards, pushing her face against that of a woman who had to recoil to get away. 'You think you're better than me?'

'. . . she drunk?' Flora heard someone murmur.

'High, more like,' another voice returned.

'This is what they do. They're like a double act,' Ines continued murmuring to Flora. 'Every time I've ever been in the same place as them, something like this happens. They're addicted to the chaos, I reckon.'

Xavier, looking even angrier as he heard the dissent, whipped his own glare up to meet the crowd, defying them to crow their taunts and show their disgust to his face. Flora watched, thunderstruck, as the siblings' gazes swung over them all like a spotlight. And then he spotted her. He stopped walking, the astonishment plain as day on his face to see *her, here*. Flora didn't doubt he was wondering how she'd been invited – the guest list being small, select and very French – but there was no time for him to ponder it. In the next instant, Natascha, troubled by her brother's sudden freeze, had spotted her too. 'You!' she cried, pointing at Flora.

Xavier was startled back into the moment and he gripped Natascha tighter around the arm, herding her straight to the lifts. 'We're leaving.'

'No! I'm not standing for that!' Natascha argued, vehemently trying to wrestle her way free. 'Did you see the way she was looking at me? At us, Xav? Did you *see* her—?'

Xavier said nothing but Flora could see he was struggling to contain her. The crowd parted for them like a sea, open expressions of disdain and even contempt on their faces, as Xavier pushed through.

'. . . Like she thinks she's better than us!'

Flora felt her cheeks flame to have been drawn into their scene. Ines's hand squeezed her shoulder.

The lift doors were already open, a security guard waiting politely to escort them downstairs and off the premises, but even as the doors closed, Natascha could still be heard shouting, swearing, screaming.

The garden was suddenly buzzing with excited conversation.

'That was odd,' Flora muttered under her breath, aware of the guests staring at her now and intrigued as to why she'd been singled out. She wondered what they'd say if she told them it had started with a fight over an ostrich.

'Well,' Ines said brightly as the party reset itself. 'Maybe you haven't been forgotten after all.'

'I don't care,' Flora lied, feeling shaken. 'She isn't important to me.'

'It wasn't *her* I was talking about,' Ines said, sipping her drink and looking at Flora from beneath curled lashes. 'What did you do to make him look at you like that?'

'Like what?'

'Well, he looked like he wanted to either kill you or . . .'

But their host was clapping his hands again. The buzz died down and a new mood of subdued restraint – so elegant and appropriate in the wake of those raffish Vermeils – blanketed them all, and whatever Ines had been intending to say was lost in the excitement of top notes, heritage and floral bouquets.

Chapter Ten

'. . . So you see, a gap such as this in the provenance can cause very real problems in terms of both valuation and ability to sell. It is imperative that we are able to establish how the painting came to be in your parents-in-law's apartment. There must be, somewhere, a receipt or a bill of sale – something that shows from whom your family purchased it,' Flora smiled.

She was pleased that she had managed to get through the conversation without mentioning Von Taschelt by name. She was also pleased to have made the mid-morning post; She had spoken to the gallery in Saint-Paul-de-Vence yesterday afternoon but they were old school, insisting on her request being put in writing, and although she'd branded the letter with her red *URGENT* stamp, she had a feeling it wasn't going to be a speedy process, hence her meeting here now. Whatever she could do to expedite the provenance research, she'd do. 'Perhaps if I could speak to your mother-in-law? She might remember a conversation or a name—'

'That is impossible, I am afraid,' Lilian said firmly, cutting her off. 'As I said before, my husband's mother is very displeased about this business. She feels we have gone against her husband's wishes and she refuses to have any part in it.' Lilian looked briefly at her ringed hands, a pearl bracelet clasped around one narrow wrist.

'Well, in which case, might the notaries have anything we could examine? They may well have been entrusted with the paperwork for such a valuable artwork.'

'You would have to ask them.'

'I'm afraid they won't release any information to me, *madame*, not without your explicit permission.'

'Oh, I see.' Lilian nodded. 'I will contact Monsieur Travers and ask him to give you full disclosure.'

'Thank you.' Flora took another sip of her tea. A thought occurred to her. 'Oh, another thing that could help – are there any photographs?'

'Excuse me?'

'Does your mother-in-law have any photograph albums from early in her marriage, something that may show the painting hanging on the apartment walls? That can often be helpful in the absence of paperwork. It's not conclusive, of course – it doesn't mean what's seen hanging on the wall was authentic – but it can help build the case.'

'There are no photographs that I have ever seen. In fact, I'm not sure there's anything from before Jacques was born – no wedding photographs, no baby photographs. When his parents fled Paris during the war, they had to leave everything behind.' She gave a small smile at the irony. 'As you know.'

Flora was quiet for a moment. If everything had been left behind in the apartment and now *they* had everything that was in there . . . 'So then perhaps the evidence is still in the apartment,' she murmured, feeling a tiny flutter of hope. She remembered the library, the walls lined with shelves and thick, leather-bound books; she remembered the way her eyes had flicked over them uninterestedly, more intent on discovering lost art treasures than exploring the personal history of the family who had lived there – but she should have known: when you're dealing with art at this level, they're one and the same, inextricably linked.

'I should go over there now,' she said, replacing her cup on its saucer.

Lilian rose and led her to the door. They walked through the mirrored hall together. 'Well, thank you for coming. It is so fascinating to see how the project is unfolding.'

The butler was already at the front door, hand poised to open it at precisely the right moment.

'I'll keep you informed of how I get on. And you're sure you don't mind asking Monsieur Travers to give me full disclosure?' It didn't hurt to remind her.

'*Bien sûr*. We are all working towards the same goal.'

The two women shook hands and the butler opened the door.

'*Merci*,' Flora smiled, glancing at him politely as she stepped out – and was immediately sent flying by a slight, but seemingly furious, woman rushing into the house. She cried out, feeling herself begin to fall back but a pair of hands caught her and righted her to standing again. It all happened so quickly, it might not have happened at all, except that when she looked up, disorientated and grateful, she found she was looking up into the impassive face of Xavier Vermeil. In a flash, last night's events rushed through her mind as she remembered his anger, humiliation, embarrassment, defiance – all aimed at her.

Except, standing here, it appeared he didn't have time to retrieve that special contempt, for it wasn't disgust that she saw in his eyes – not this time – and when in the next instant he released her, wordlessly sidestepping around her and disappearing into the building too, she could have sworn a sudden polar wind barrelled down the boulevard.

'Xavier!' his mother barked. '*Pardon*,' she said after a moment, looking embarrassed when he didn't come back.

'It's quite all right,' Flora said quickly, smoothing her hair primly and hoping she didn't look as ruffled as she felt. 'I . . . I should have looked where I was going.'

'That was my son Xavier and his girlfriend. They are always arguing.' She tutted. 'Too passionate, that is the problem.'

'Oh.' She wasn't quite sure what to say to that. She had the opposite problem herself. 'Well, goodbye. I'll be in touch.'

Flora walked down the steps onto the pavement and looked up and down the street for a cab. She could see one with its light on, further up the road, but it was caught by roadworks and indicating left.

No, no, no! She needed to get on.

She waved her arm in the air, trying to get the driver's attention, but he didn't appear to have seen her. She waved again, giving a little jump too, but her dress was just a bit too short and full-skirted for that, she realized, when a man wolf-whistled as he drove past.

There was nothing else for it. Putting her thumb and forefinger in her mouth as Freddie had taught her to when she was eleven, she gave an almighty whistle that screamed up the street. The driver heard, sticking his head out of the window, and she waved her arm at him again. This time, he saw her and gave her a wave back, turning off the indicator.

Flora breathed a sigh of relief, just as she heard someone laugh. She turned but there was no one there on the street.

She looked back up at the Vermeils' imposing town house. All of the windows were open on the upper levels but this side of the street was in shadow and she couldn't see into the tall, deep rooms. She bit her lip – had someone in there seen her whistle like a barrow-boy? (Freddie had said if she couldn't be a boy, she could at least behave like one.)

The cab pulled up alongside her and she gave the driver the address in Montparnasse before hurriedly jumping in the back. She looked up at the house again as they pulled away and for a second she thought she saw a dark figure half-hidden at the window. But she couldn't be sure and within a minute, the cab had rounded the corner and she was back in the Paris light.

Walking back into the apartment, now that it had been emptied of the artworks and decorative antiques, was a strange experience. Flora could tell that life had invaded the space in the intervening days since she and Angus had first stepped in. It was as though the very molecules in the air had shifted position and resettled at a different density – it felt easier to see, to breathe, and the floor looked like a patchwork rug now that the paintings had been removed, the boards chequered with the large, bright areas that had been protected from the dust for so long.

She did a quick recce of the apartment. Nothing had been touched in the kitchen as there had been no art haul in there; the dining room looked strangely naked now that the table and chairs – bare of their loot – were left standing at odd angles and isolated from one another in the middle of the room, as though a game of musical chairs had been interrupted, the children scattered in hidden corners. To her relief, Gertie was still there and, after a quick check, it seemed she was undamaged from Natascha's joyride.

Flora turned and stood beside the bird for a moment, one hand on its back, staring at the doorway, remembering Natasha's almost violent defiance, her outrageous behaviour verging on the manic; and by contrast, her brother's brooding silence, his black look and contemptuous scorn.

She shook him from her thoughts and walked through to the library, stopping in the doorway, her eyes scanning the walls lined with books. Flora walked in, trying to read the titles on the spines but they were faded from where the sun had hit. Most were French but some appeared to be in English and German too and she glossed over them quickly, not sure exactly what she was looking for. She pulled a couple from the shelves, flicking open pages that were sticky with spider's webs, the curled husks of long-dead beetles punctuating the wooden runs.

She turned her attention to the desk and sat carefully on the chair, checking it first for loose joints. The room looked different from her seated position and she could see how it might once have felt to work from there – the street view from the window on her left; the dramatic, showy curtains that set a socially ambitious tone as guests entered the apartment, the insulation of all the books making the space feel sequestered and private. Her hands rested on the smooth desk, swirls and knots in the wood grain as beautiful as if they'd been painted in—

She frowned suddenly. Hadn't there been papers on here when she and Angus had first come in? Or was she imagining that?

She shook her head, unable to remember, and began

opening the drawers instead, finding yet more evidence of lost worlds – ink pots and a silver fountain pen; pencils that had been sharpened to a point by a knife; a pamphlet for a carol service in the Sacré-Coeur, December 1939; a single cufflink; a silver cigar cutter; a lighter fashioned from horn. A small gold travel clock had stopped at 11.23. But on which day, she wondered, and which year? When had the life in this place ground to a halt even as a war raged outside the windows?

She moved to the first drawer further down, surprised to find it almost entirely empty. But it hadn't been. She squinted, noticing the telltale rim of dust in the corner of the drawer which indicated that something had been sitting in it until recently. Very recently.

She checked the other drawers but it was a repeated pattern – dusty outlines where files or papers had sat untouched for so many years, now conspicuous by their new absence. Flora sat back in the chair, bothered by the discovery, knowing her hunch was right about the papers on top of the desk, as well as those in it. Had it been something in *here* that the initial intruders had been searching for all along? Had she and Angus been so anxious to protect and safeguard the artworks that they'd missed the real target for the break-in?

After all, something had been off with that story from the start – it had rankled with her even if it hadn't with Angus or the Vermeils, but she didn't believe that people would go to the trouble of breaking in to an abandoned apartment and then, without touching a thing, simply *notify* the family of its existence. It was especially difficult to believe that they had somehow overlooked the intrinsic fortune tied up in the haul of artworks scattered around the place. No, it only made sense if it wasn't the artworks they were after, but something in these drawers . . .

But what? And who? And most of all – why?

Either the desk was exceptionally large or Monsieur Travers was far smaller than she had recalled; regardless, there was no mistaking the distance or difference of perspectives between them. The notary's demeanour throughout this meeting had been cool, to say the least, and Flora was beginning to feel it would be easier to gain access to the legal documentation for *his* house than the Montparnasse apartment.

'Madame Vermeil assured me she would arrange this with you, *monsieur*.'

Monsieur Travers merely cocked his head to the side slightly, as though he couldn't quite understand what she was saying.

'All I require is access to the instructions that were left to you by her husband's father regarding the apartment.'

He cocked his head to the other side.

'It would also be helpful,' she continued, 'to see if there were any letters or correspondence in which Monsieur Vermeil's father revealed or detailed any purchases he might have made, before he closed up the apartment and left the city.'

There was a long silence but when he spoke, it was with the air of his patience having been stretched very thin. 'There are no letters between Monsieur Vermeil's father and my own, *mam'selle*. My father was a notary, not a penpal. He had only the deeds to the apartment and the codicil which specified the apartment should not be touched or opened before the death of his wife. That is all.'

'Apartments,' she said, correcting him. But his error piqued her interest. 'Which reminds me – why wasn't it mentioned in the initial meeting that there were two apartments?'

'I did not think it necessary. The purpose of that meeting was to authorize you to enter the property and conduct an evaluation of the contents inside. There is nothing in the second apartment, therefore we did not need to discuss it.'

'Except there was something in there – a painting.'

Monsieur Travers looked at her, unblinking, before pushing his glasses up his nose and looking away again, moving a few papers around on his desk, keeping his hands busy. 'Well, I did not know that, but I'm sure it is of no consequence. What is one more painting, given the hundreds found upstairs?'

'But why were there two apartments? Why have two properties in the same building? It's very odd.'

'Not at all. The Vermeils are a wealthy family. They own many properties.'

'Not back then they weren't – at least, not to the degree they are now. And the *quatorzième* wasn't a prosperous neighbourhood back then. It seems unlikely that if you could afford to buy multiple properties, you would buy another in the same building. You'd upgrade surely? Buy somewhere bigger, somewhere more fashionable?'

'I'm not sure what you're trying to imply, *mam'selle*.'

'I'm not trying to imply anything, I'm trying to understand. Why was the apartment upstairs bursting at the seams with artworks and the one downstairs empty, save for one?'

Monsieur Travers gave a Gallic shrug. 'That I cannot answer. I am only the notary.'

More like the gatekeeper, Flora thought, watching him closely. What had she learned from him today? Precisely nothing. She took a moment to consider. 'Do you have the deeds for Apartment six?'

'Apartment six?' he repeated.

'The apartment downstairs,' she replied briskly. He was just playing games, wasting her time. 'The one we've just been talking about.'

He inhaled and held the breath. 'Oh. Yes, of course,' he replied finally. 'Would you like to see them? I would have to ask for them to be retrieved from storage, if you can wait. It should only take an hour or two.'

Flora blinked, knowing exactly what he was doing, wanting to call his bluff and have them search, but in truth she didn't see how property deeds were going to be helpful in her search for provenance. It wasn't the ownership of the apartment that was in question but that of the paintings. She shook her head. 'But I'd like to see the codicil, please.'

Monsieur Travers flicked through the thin file of papers before him and handed it to her.

'*This* is the codicil?' she asked in surprise, flapping the torn piece of paper in the air. It had been ripped from a larger sheaf, the writing written on a slope and very hurried. Even the two signatures at the bottom were illegible.

Monsieur Travers nodded patiently.

'It doesn't look like a legal and binding document to me.'

'It was written in difficult circumstances, during the war, you recall. I agree, it would not necessarily stand up if contested in court but . . .' He shrugged. 'It never has been contested, so it stands. Monsieur Vermeil and my father had worked together for many years. It was my father's true belief that the instructions written therein were Monsieur

Vermeil's most deeply held wishes, and he acted according to that belief.'

'And what were his wishes exactly?' She frowned, trying to read the elaborate script. 'Apart from no one entering the apartment before his and Magda's deaths, I mean?'

'Just that.'

She frowned deeper. 'Is this in *German*?' She looked up.

'It is.'

'But I don't read German.'

'I'm sorry to hear that.'

'Do *you* speak German?'

'No.'

Flora glowered at him. The man was maddening. 'Then I'd like a copy of this, please, so that I can get it translated.'

Monsieur Travers looked apologetic. 'For that, I would require Monsieur Vermeil's express written permission.'

'But Madame Vermeil has already authorized you to give me full disclosure.'

'It would need to be Monsieur Vermeil. I am sorry.'

He was not, and they both knew it.

She stared at the unintelligible directive in her hand, knowing this was another dead end. She didn't need to be able to read German to know it said no one was to enter the property before François' and Magda's deaths. Lilian Vermeil had already told her that.

She pushed the scrap of paper back towards him with a sigh. 'Well, can you tell me how the family came to know about the existence of the apartments, if not from you?'

'A note was sent to our offices by the intruders – I was on vacation at the time and it was forwarded on by a junior associate. He felt obliged to act promptly and notify the clients that this new asset had come to light as he felt there was a suggestion of a threat in its tone.'

She leaned forward. 'What kind of a threat?'

Travers pulled out a photocopy of a letter from the pile of papers. The writing was neat, small, as though care had been taken with it.

She translated it from the French: *Be careful what you leave lying around. Finders can be keepers.* Attached to it was a photograph of the apartment taken at night, shot from the street, the road sign visible in the corner.

'Squatters?'

'That is what my associate assumed. He was unaware of the codicil or else he never would have forwarded it without checking with me first.'

She turned the paper over. 'Which apartment are they referring to – six or eight? They could have been in either. Or both, surely?'

'It was Apartment Eight.'

'Because . . . ?'

Monsieur Travers suppressed a sigh. Just. 'Because the envelope the letter came in was addressed, "To the owners of Apartment Eight", care of this company.'

'That's a very specific thing for you to know, given that you said you didn't see the letter yourself.'

'My associate made a grave error acting without full authority but he made photocopies of the documents before he sent them on. Be assured I interrogated him fully on the matter on my return and there is now nothing I do not know about it. It is my job to notice the details.' He stared at her. 'Forgive me, *mam'selle*, but I sense you are trying to . . . trick me in some way. We are on the same side, are we not?'

'Yes, of course.' She sighed, feeling defeated.

'I do not understand what all these questions about the legal papers of the apartment and the intricacies of the anonymous letter have to do with *your* job of making an inventory of the artworks?'

Flora stared at him, wondering if she could trust him. He was right, after all – they were on the same side. 'What I'm looking for, Monsieur Travers, is paperwork that can show how all those paintings came to be in Monsieur Vermeil's possession. Without provenance, those artworks can't realize their full market value. In fact, without it, they're pretty much unsaleable – no reputable auction house or dealer would touch them – and it appears that some papers, which may or may not have been relevant to this research, have recently been taken from the desk in the study in Apartment Eight.'

Travers frowned. 'Oh, I see.'

'I was rather hoping you were going to tell me the intruders had broken into the apartment *downstairs* – it would make a lot more sense of things. It just seems odd to me that whoever broke into Apartment Eight would steal some papers and not the small fortune in fine art sitting a few metres away.'

'I agree. That does sound odd. Do you know what these papers were, that are missing?'

'I have no idea. All I know is the drawers are now empty. They may have held vital evidence for my research, or they may not, but whatever was in them was important to someone – even more important than the paintings.'

Travers looked troubled by this. 'I'm sorry I cannot be of more help.'

She gathered her bag and rose to her feet. 'It was a long shot, anyway.'

'Your job is an interesting one, *mam'selle*,' he said, walking her to the door. 'You have to be almost a detective, no?'

'Well, a better one than me,' she replied, shaking his hand. 'Right now I'm not sure I could find my way out of a paper bag.'

She was climbing into a taxi to head back to the office, wondering if three o'clock on a Friday afternoon counted as the weekend yet, when her phone rang.

'I've got a name,' Angus shouted down the line and Flora wondered if he was in a lift, for the connection kept rattling and hissing between them.

'A name for what?' she shouted back.

'The Renoir companion. Last-known owner. It's a chap called – have you got a pen?'

'That's a funny name,' Flora quipped, prompting sarcastic laughter down the line as she clamped the phone to her ear and rifled in her bag. 'Just a sec . . . Right, go on.'

'OK. It's a chap called Noah Haas.'

'Noah Haas,' Flora repeated as she wrote it down. 'And what did he say?'

'Nothing yet. He's a New Yorker but guess what?'

'What?'

'He's the only guy in Manhattan *not* spending his summer in the Hamptons.'

'So where is he then?' But even as she asked the question, she had an inkling of what he was going to say next. Paris.

'Vienna. I need you to go over there.'

'*Vienna?* But Angus, I'm up to my eyes over here!'

'And? Any joy? Did you speak to Lilian?'

She sighed. 'Yes and her mother-in-law won't talk to us and there's no family records from before the war. They lost

136

everything. I've just spoken to the family lawyers and they have nothing helpful to add either. But one thing I did find out yesterday – the historic records for Von Taschelt's Paris gallery are now held in another gallery in Provence. I put a call in with them this morning asking for details of sales of any Renoirs made from 1943 onwards but they've insisted I send a *letter*, can you believe it, as everything's archived.'

'Jesus. How long's that going to take?'

'Piece of string, isn't it? But I marked it as urgent. I'll chase them up on Monday.'

'Well then, that's even more reason why you need to go to Vienna. We can't afford to wait around – if we want to get the Renoir in for that sale next month, we need to get this tied up. Haas could know something that gives us crucial information about his family's sale to Von Taschelt, and in turn the Vermeils.'

Flora sighed. She knew he was right; they couldn't just sit around hoping for good news, they had to check every lead. Travers was right too; she did have to be something of a detective. 'Fine. I'll fly out in the next few days.'

'Already done. You're on the seven-fifty out of Charles de Gaulle tomorrow morning. Haas is expecting you at one p.m. I've texted the address.'

She slapped a hand over her forehead. That meant a 5 a.m. start, *on a Saturday*, and she was out tonight (not that she was in any position to start quibbling over details like that right now). Would she ever get any rest?

'I've gotta go, but call me when you're out, OK?' And he hung up.

Flora sighed and stared out of the window, Paris flashing past her eyes in a blur. Much like her life.

Chapter Eleven

'I don't know how you can watch!' Flora groaned, covering her eyes with her hands.

Ines patted her leg. 'Faith,' she smiled, her beer bottle clasped loosely in her hand as she watched her boyfriend twist in the air, two metres above them.

The skate park was rammed, hip-hop blaring from the sound system, the day-glo colours of the graffiti sprayed on the walls and sides of the ramps tinged an acid yellow under the spotlights. From the other side of the space, the wall where they were sitting overlooking the vert ramp appeared to be fringed with legs, heads bobbing to the dub-step as the riders shredded before them.

Tonight was a pro showcase and Hawk competition, and Bruno, as Hawk's new star signing and home-grown Paris boy, was the local hero. It wasn't just the riders risking injury on the course either; the photographers too seemed to have a death wish, swarming between the jumps and leaning over the edges in the split seconds after the skaters sped past, all wanting the perfect, 'most rad' shot.

Bruno was soaring again, his hands clutching the board to his feet as he performed a perfect 360-degree aerial turn, landing backwards and zooming straight down the nigh-on vertical ramp and back up the other side.

Ines laughed and drummed her heels loudly on the wall. 'He did that for me! I love goofy foot. He knows it's my favourite,' she shrieked, before cupping her mouth with her hands and whooping for him.

Flora turned to Stefan sitting beside her. 'Do *you* love goofy foot?' she asked wryly, taking a swig of her beer.

He looked up at her from his iPad. 'I don't know what the hell it means.'

'Riding with the wrong foot forwards.'

'Oh.' He frowned. 'I thought that was fakie.'

'No. Fakie's riding backwards.'

'Agh, shit, forwards, backwards, I dunno. It's all crazy to me.' He shot her a rare smile.

She glanced down at his iPad. 'What are you looking at, anyway?'

'An idea for a feature that we're working on. I'm just checking out a few websites for the visuals.'

'You're working at a skate competition?' she asked. 'Oh, come on, Stefan! Even I've switched off!'

He shrugged. 'Yeah, but we just had to pull a piece last minute and we need a filler, quickly. I've got a call in with New York at midnight. We go to the printers at six in the morning and I need something we can use fast.'

'So what are you thinking? Skateboarding's the new yoga? Graffiti is the new wallpaper?'

'Urban explorers.'

'Urban *what*? What are they looking for? Lost polar bears on the Champs-Élysées?'

He laughed. 'Yeah, you'd think! Actually, it's an underground movement. They find old abandoned and disused spaces in cities – so, like, closed-down metro stations or derelict gas works.'

'*Why?*'

He shrugged. 'They're explorers but not all frontiers are new. Going back to the past can be like stepping into a new world. Past lives, past stories . . . They never know what they're going to come across.'

'How brilliant!' Flora said sarcastically. 'Oh look, a bunch of old pipes!' She sipped her beer again and watched as another rider kickflipped past them.

'Hey, don't be such a cynic,' he said, flicking the screen quickly. 'I think they're on to something. There's so much that we don't see in cities, especially up high or underground . . .'

She remembered the Hermès garden. Xavier Vermeil.

Another rash of irritation prickled her skin and she shivered, trying to shake the thought of him off her. 'Yeah, but what do they do when they get there? I mean, are they like squatters? Do they occupy these buildings they find?'

'Of course not. The journey is the destination, right? They're just finding old treasures and trying to return them to the city but there's no guarantee of success. Some nights they can't get in, others they get busted. Other times it's a wasted trip because there's nothing to find.'

'So much fun, so little time,' she sighed, sarcasm tainting every word.

'Hey, what's up with you tonight? You OK?'

'Of course I am,' she replied, a little too quickly. 'Why wouldn't I be?'

He shrugged, his eyes skipping over her suspiciously, as though her secret was a black stain he could see. 'I dunno. You just seem tetchy.'

She looked away with a tut, blankly watching a rider do a flip three metres above their heads, but her mind was on

Freddie again – wondering what he was doing right now, and with whom. Was he alone, or out with friends? How many of them knew? How many of them would still be friends when it all came out? The thoughts made her feel jittery and she tried to force calm on her body, but her nervous system felt wired, her brain working too fast as the adrenalin began to bite. The truth was that she was far from fine. She'd woken up twice last night, each time believing the charges had been dismissed and feeling crushed when she'd realized that the nightmare was in the waking, not the sleeping.

'. . . Anyway, some of the hippest architects in the city are looking at these spaces for redevelopment.'

'What? You mean decommissioned metro tunnels as flats?' she scoffed.

'Not flats, no,' he said patiently. 'But restaurants, swimming pools . . . Here, look at this,' Stefan said, sliding his iPad over his lap for her to see some photos. 'That's the old Rothschild chateau in Parc de Boulogne. It's been abandoned since the war. If that was done up, I bet you wouldn't mind living there.'

'Well now, that's different. I'm born to chateaux,' she shrugged.

His eyes fell to her wry smile. 'Yeah.' He looked back at the screen. 'OK, how about this place?' he asked, clicking on a vast underground tunnel of vaulted concrete. 'An old detonator store.'

'No windows?' She arched an eyebrow. 'You know how to live.'

'But check out those high ceilings! Or what about this one?' he asked, holding up the tablet to show a desolate red-brick mill with blown-out windows, the masonry scarred black from a fire.

'Talk about Bleak House,' she grimaced. 'Honestly, I still don't get why anyone would want to go into these places. They must be nutjobs.'

'Those nutjobs –' the word sounded funny in his French accent – 'are professionals from all walks of life, people who see there is more to a city than just shop windows.'

'Do you know them? These explorers, I mean.'

'Only my friend. They explore in small numbers and post online anonymously. They have to – the police would have them for trespassing otherwise.' He clicked on a new link and laughed. 'Ah, now an asylum!' he nodded. 'I can see you in there. Large white space, padded walls, bars at the windows . . . every mod con!'

Flora grinned as she joshed him with her elbow. 'Stop it.'

'No? Too edgy? You want something more bourgeois? . . . Oh, wait . . . wait . . . I got it. Home Sweet Home, right?' He showed her the screen again.

Flora felt the smile slide off her face.

'*No?* Man, I thought I nailed it there!'

But Flora couldn't laugh or smile or talk. She could only stare at the image of the painting, on the bed, in the empty room.

'How did you get that?' she demanded, taking the tablet from him.

Stefan blinked. 'Duh, you know how. You just watched me. You swipe side to side on the screen . . .' He grinned, as though she were stupid.

'No, I mean where did you get this picture from? I have to know, Stefan. It's important.'

Stefan frowned, realizing she was serious, seeing the joke

had ended. 'Flora, you know I can't tell you that. What does it matter, anyway?'

'Because it does.'

Stefan glanced back at the photo of the empty apartment. 'Do you know something about this place?'

'*I* can't tell *you* that!' she replied testily, digging in her heels. 'You're not the only one with confidentiality issues.'

It was Stefan's turn to look irritated. 'Fine,' he said after a moment. 'All I can tell you about it is my friend. His name's Antoine and he does stills photography for us occasionally. He was shooting a story last week and had almost got busted on an expedition at some old munitions factory in St Denis the night before – that's how we got chatting about it.'

'Did *he* go inside that apartment?'

'Flora, I don't know—'

'Would he have sent a letter to the owners?'

'*A letter?*' Stefan repeated incredulously. 'What for?'

'Notifying them of its dilapidation. Is that something they do?'

He shrugged hopelessly. 'I-I dunno. Maybe. He said they see themselves as sort of eco warriors.'

'Where does he live, your friend?'

'Uh . . . Montparnasse somewhere, I think – I'd have to check.'

Montparnasse?

Flora blinked as she suddenly remembered the man in the apartment opposite, the climbing rope on the floor beneath the bed . . . his visible interest when he'd seen her on the balcony. A hobby in urban exploring might make you vigilant to abandoned buildings and then sudden activity, especially if it was right across the road from where you lived . . .

Stefan clicked his fingers in front of her, getting her attention. 'Now your turn. What do you know about that place?'

Flora hesitated. 'It belongs to some clients, that's all.' She tried to keep her tone light, dismissive.

'What could *you* possibly be doing for clients there?' Stefan asked incredulously. 'The place is empty.'

'We're cataloguing the collection.'

Stefan laughed, his eyes on the single painting on the lone bed. 'Hell of a collection.'

Flora turned towards Stefan, not interested in his sarcasm. 'Are these pictures on a specific website?'

'I don't know,' he shrugged. 'I told Antoine it sounded interesting and he sent through this selection for me to look at. That's it. He's said I can go out with them on their next trip. You want me to ask him?'

Flora shook her head. She didn't want to alert anyone else to this. It was bad enough the apartment had been found by these 'urban explorers'. If they found out to whom it belonged, there was no doubt the press would be interested and any kind of publicity would be toxic right now.

She flicked back through the images, trying to find others – were there any of the upstairs apartment? Had they found anything else? Had they removed anything? But there was nothing more than those couple of photos of Apartment 6 and it all looked, to her eye, exactly as she had seen it that day with Natascha.

Still, it rankled with her that it was Apartment 6 these urban explorers had found. Travers had told her the intruders had broken into Apartment 8, upstairs, but what were the chances that these urban explorers were separate from the intruders in Number 8? What were the chances of two break-ins and no apparent thefts, seemingly only weeks apart, for the first time in over seventy years?

Furthermore, she and Angus had been the first people in Apartment 8, of that she was certain. No one else could have walked through the property and, now that she thought about it, Angus's were the only footprints she had seen in the thick carpet of dust.

Flora frowned at the implications. In spite of what Travers had said, the intruders *must* have broken into Number 6. It was the more logical conclusion. It was also the very apartment the notaries had had the keys for and failed to disclose. But if she was right, if Number 6 was the only apartment that had been broken into – then why was Travers lying about it? And what was he trying to hide?

Chapter Twelve

'Miss Sykes, welcome to the City of Dreams,' Noah Haas said in a soft American accent, reaching out a hand as she stepped over the stone threshold. He was casually dressed in jeans and an Oxford shirt but he exuded the low-key sophistication that comes from a life of privilege.

'Mr Haas,' she smiled, shaking his hand back. 'It's so good of you to agree to meet with me at such short notice.'

'Not at all. I was intrigued when I got the call from your colleague,' Noah replied, leading her through to a wide open-plan area with neat cubed sofas that could have accommodated twelve people, expensively distressed silk rugs whose patterns were woven to fade into obsolescence, glimmering underfoot. They were on the top floor of a modern apartment building in Lerchenfeld, a fashionable district of Vienna although not one of the grandest, and it boasted latticed glass walls that swept up and over into the roof, flooding the space with light. Her eyes were automatically drawn to the magnificent view and the traditional wedding-cake apartments opposite. 'Can I get you a drink?' he enquired from the kitchen – divided from the living area by a not-full-height marble wall – and holding up two small espresso cups.

'Lovely,' she replied, walking back towards him. 'What a stunning apartment.'

'Thank you. I preferred having somewhere with more light when I came over.'

'Yes, Angus said you live in New York?'

'That's right. I grew up there but we always spent the summers here when I was growing up.'

'Do you come back often?'

'Every summer. It's good to escape Manhattan in the heat if at all possible. You ever been there?'

'Oh yes, frequently,' she smiled, accepting the coffee as he handed it to her. 'Our head office is based over there and of course, I'm always flying around going to sales or searching out specific pieces for clients.'

'It sounds like a fascinating job you do, Miss Sykes.'

'Thank you. I enjoy it. And please call me Flora.'

'Flora. Ditto, Noah.'

She smiled and took a sip of coffee. 'So what is it you do?' she asked, always open to the possibility of procuring a new client. Her success in bringing in new accounts was partly what had brought her to Angus's attention in the first place.

'Nothing so exciting, I'm afraid. Asset management.'

'Oh, I'm sure it has its moments.'

He laughed lightly, his eyes flickering over her quickly before he too drank some coffee. 'Tell me, do you always dress to match your paintings?'

'Excuse me?' she asked, before looking down and seeing that she had put on a yellow dress: it was just above knee length and had cutaway sleeves that bared her shoulders, but it was a yellow dress nonetheless. 'Oh my goodness, I hadn't even clocked that!' she laughed, before quipping,

'But yes, you're quite right, I love getting into character. You should see me when I'm selling a Gaugin.'

'Well now, I think I'd like to,' he replied, smiling as he watched her.

Flora's laughter faded – she'd been referring to the sarongs and flowers of Gaugin's island women, but they were very often topless too and she detected a top note of something more than professional interest. She smiled politely, taking another sip of her coffee. A small silence bloomed and Noah shifted position at the worktop.

'Would you like to see the painting? You've travelled so far to see it.'

'I'd love to, although I'm working in Paris at the moment so the journey wasn't too bad.'

'Really?' he asked, leading her across the cavernous space towards a door in the far wall. 'Do you like it there?'

'Yes. I have friends in the city so it's rather like a home-from-home. I probably live there three to four months of the year now.'

'And where is home-home for you?'

She faltered, although she kept the smile on her face. She wanted to say Little Foxes, Wiltshire but her most recent memory of the place now was that of the devastated faces of her family and it had overwritten in a flash the years of laughter around the kitchen table, bombing in the swimming pool, playing German Spotlight in the garden, the prickle of Christmas-tree needles on her and Freddie's backs as they hid on Christmas Eve wanting to 'catch' Santa, their father reading the paper in his chair in the snug, the sound of *The Archers* blaring from the radio as their mother hauled the rib of beef from the Aga . . . 'London,' she said simply.

'Knew it. I love that city. I have a flat in Albany. Do you know it?'

'Absolutely.'

'It's just in here,' he said, opening the door and leading her into a bedroom, immaculately made up in smoke-grey with ivory accents. 'I would have moved it off the wall for you to see out here, but I'm afraid it's hard-wired to the alarm. We'd have armed police surrounding the building in two minutes.'

'Of course.' Flora's mouth dropped open as she immediately saw the Renoir hanging opposite the bed. The vibrancy of the woman's dress was arresting against the bedroom's dark matte walls, the glow of her pale skin telling of wealth, the shy tilt of her head suggesting feminine power, the rustle of her skirts as she brushed against the flowers almost audible in the silence of this stranger's room as Flora absorbed its narrative power.

'It's beautiful,' she whispered, walking closer, automatically scanning the canvas for signs of damage or disrepair, anything that might affect a valuation price, but it was pristine, in far better condition than the Vermeils' piece, which was currently being professionally cleaned. Flora was transfixed by the vividity of colour and she estimated that the layers of dust that had settled over it had muted the palette of the Vermeils' painting by 30 to 40 per cent.

'Isn't it?' Noah answered. 'I always say it's the most beautiful thing in my life.'

Flora glanced across at him, detecting ambiguity in his voice again. He was staring at her and he smiled before looking back at the painting.

'So you inherited this?' she asked, walking back towards him.

'From my mother, yes, but it was bought originally by my great-grandfather. As I told your colleague on the plane, he owned both pieces in the set and when he died, my great-aunt inherited one, my grandfather the other.'

'Wow,' she smiled. 'That's some inheritance.'

'Yes, it is.' He watched her gaze at the painting for a moment, seeming pleased by her reaction. 'Tell me, are you here because your clients are looking to buy my Renoir – or sell theirs?'

Flora was taken aback by the directness of the question but she hid it with a smile. 'That would be getting ahead of ourselves. At the moment, we're merely establishing provenance.'

He gave her a knowing look. 'Oh, I see. So then I assume you're having problems tracing it beyond the dealer Franz Von Taschelt too?'

Flora looked at him coolly. 'That's right.'

'And you're here because you're hoping I might know something about who he sold it on to, and when.'

'I am. We don't think Von Taschelt held on to it for long. In fact, according to the dates we've got, we think he flipped it – sold it on – immediately. We thought your family might have retained an interest.'

'You thought right. I've been trying to locate the painting for a number of years – ever since I inherited this one, in fact.' He put one hand in his pocket.

Flora masked a ripple of impatience. *His* interest in the painting was irrelevant. 'And historically? Did your grandfather know what happened to the other one after it was sold?'

'Sadly not. He was in America by then. I'm sure you know that a lot of Von Taschelt's records were destroyed during the war? All sorts of documentation was lost due to fires, bombing, looting . . .'

'Yes,' she lied, wondering whether *he* knew that Galerie Von Taschelt's historic documents were stored at the Attlee & Bergurren Gallery in Saint-Paul. 'It's a frustrating process.'

Haas continued watching her, his gaze on her profile. 'Are you allowed to tell me who your clients are?'

'Sadly not,' she demurred, keeping her eyes on the painting.

'I'd like to meet them. It would be worth their while. I'd make them a serious offer.'

She nodded, glancing over at him. 'Well, I'll certainly pass that on to them but as I said, it's too early to think about anything beyond provenance at this point.'

He gave a small laugh, bemused by her polished rebuffs. 'You *really* can't tell me who they are? Not a small clue?'

She laughed too. 'I'm afraid not. Not yet, anyway.' She smiled. She had learned long ago that a smile could disarm most people. 'So tell me, do you have a full provenance for *this* painting?' she asked, changing the subject.

Noah Haas wasn't fooled but his eyes skipped over her with interest. 'Yes.'

Another smile, broader. 'Do you think I could see it?'

He paused, then nodded. 'Of course.'

They walked out of the bedroom and back into the vast living area where the sun was resting on the floor in gigantic puddles and the giant black TV screen was animated by the city's reflection. Flora followed him to the far wall which had been clad ceiling-to-floor and wall-to-wall in black wooden shelves. Some of them had been partitioned off, resulting in individually spotlit cubby-holes with various bronze sculptures inside and she clocked a couple of black-and-white photographs, seemingly of Noah as a boy with his parents. No other children – was he an only child?

The book titles she couldn't decipher, since they were in German, but she logged a couple of author names – Donna Tartt, Philip Roth, E. L. James—

What?

She couldn't help but give a little snort of amusement at the sight of it.

'What?' Noah asked, pulling a box file from an invisible drawer than ran along the base of the unit, and straightening up.

'Nothing,' she replied. 'Just a frog in my throat.'

But Noah, unconvinced, looked back to where she must have been staring and after a moment, he chuckled too. 'Oh. That. My girlfriend. Well, ex-girlfriend.' He glanced at her. 'Don't worry, I haven't read it.'

'Oh. No. I didn't assume . . .'

'Have you?'

The question took her by surprise. 'What?'

'Have you read it?'

'Oh God, no. No.'

He watched her protest too much and laughed, taking the box file over to the dining table which looked as though it seated sixteen. She could only imagine the size of the dinner parties he must hold here. How many friends did this man have?

She looked at him more closely as he opened up the file. He was certainly attractive – not as urbane or hipster as Stefan, nor as raffish as Xavier Vermeil (not that she thought about what *he* looked like – she didn't know why he'd even popped into her mind), but he had deep-set blue eyes and a prominent brow that gave a strong masculine impression. He wasn't overly tall but he was in good shape – she thought he looked like a rackets man – and she could imagine he was competitive; judging by the top-spec apartment, a minimalist, possibly a control freak too. Late thirties, perhaps?

He glanced up as if aware of her scrutiny, catching her staring at him, and she gave a smile.

He smiled back as though amused. 'Right,' he said, flicking past some red inner card files. She caught a glimpse of the names written on some of the tabs: *Bank*; *Cars*; *Charities*; *Gold* . . . 'OK,' he murmured, lifting out one tabbed *Art*.

He opened it and Flora had to force herself not to reach forward and handle the papers herself. Many of them were yellowed with age, feint lines grown almost indistinct over time, ink mellowing to shadows on the page. She saw that most of the paperwork had been arranged into slim piles, fastened with paper clips and a fly-sheet on the front with the artist's name. They were seemingly arranged alphabetically and as he flicked through – *Angrand, Bazille, Derain* – she knew she couldn't leave here without giving him her card. There was a prize private collection here and if not here, in this apartment – she let her eyes wander the space again, finding what she guessed to be a Seurat on one wall – then certainly somewhere in his possession. New York? Angus would have to make a visit when Noah returned to the city next month.

'Right, Auguste Renoir,' he said, pulling the sheaf from the file and unclipping the fastening, spreading the papers over the table.

This time Flora did reach forward, seeing an ink copy of the ledger detailing the sale from the artist to his dealer Ambroise Vollard dated May 1908.

She put it down carefully and reached for the next papers on the table – one, a black-and-white photograph showing both Renoirs hanging together as part of a galleried display on a drawing-room wall, the other a photocopy of a black-and-white photograph in a magazine that clearly showed *Yellow Dress, Walking*, exhibited in a gallery somewhere. She read the small print.

'Grafton Galleries?' she asked, looking at him in surprise. 'It was shown in the Manet and post-Impressionist exhibition in 1910?'

Noah looked impressed. 'You know your stuff, Miss Sykes.'

'Flora,' she corrected him, pleased he was impressed. 'And I wouldn't be very good at my job if I didn't know these things.'

'Well, Vollard lent both paintings for the exhibition and they were sold, as a consequence, to my great-grandfather Fritz, who was in London on business at the time,' he said, picking up a fragile handwritten receipt that showed: *'Lady walking, yellow dress', 1908, Auguste Renoir. To Fritz Haas, 10th November 1910 £38.*

'Do you know why your great-aunt sold her Renoir?' she asked.

'Yes.'

Flora waited a moment, glancing up at him when he didn't reply immediately.

'It was the Second World War and they needed money. Flight tax.'

'She was Jewish?'

He nodded.

'Did they escape?'

He shook his head. 'My great-uncle had some connections

which bought them time but they refused to leave Austria, their homeland. They didn't see it was hopeless until it was too late.'

'I'm so sorry,' she murmured.

Noah nodded, grateful for her sympathy, and she carefully replaced the receipt on the pile and examined the others, trying not to feel a growing disappointment with the step-perfect provenance laid out before her. Everything here was original, every paper transaction that had been recorded over the past hundred years to bring the painting from Auguste Renoir's own studio to this contemporary penthouse apartment in Vienna, was in this file.

She, meanwhile, was stuck with a dusty apartment and a Nazi. Contrary to Angus's wild hopes, there was nothing here that could help them with the search for filling the hole in their paper trail. There had been a war raging, the family trying to flee for their lives and Noah's grandfather was already safe in America – of course he wouldn't have known to whom Von Taschelt had sold the painting or when. It hadn't been anyone's immediate priority at the time.

And she couldn't ask Noah if he knew anything about Jacques Vermeil's father François or his link with Franz Von Taschelt – not without identifying the Vermeils as the current possessors, and with both such a shaky claim to ownership at the moment and Von Taschelt's notoriety for forcing sales, she didn't dare risk opening up any counter-claims.

This had been a wasted trip.

'Does this help you with your search?' he asked, as if reading her mind while she carefully sifted through the papers in a neat file.

She glanced at him apologetically. 'Sadly not. We have provenance up until the same point as you found, but I'm sure you don't need me to tell you there's a gap where the final sale should be. We're looking for something that can tell us when and where the painting was sold on after 1943 and when and how it came into our clients' possession.'

'Which is going to be tricky when you're smack bang in the middle of the war,' he said carefully. 'You know, I'd still be interested in buying, even without a full provenance. That painting was in my family's ownership for many years. I'd just like to put the pair back together again.' He shrugged, as though doing her a favour. 'No one else has the same emotional investment in this as my family. I'd be prepared to accept it under terms most others wouldn't.'

Flora smiled, knowing full well this wasn't a favour. He'd spotted an opportunity to get it at a knock-down price. Maybe his offer wouldn't be so 'serious' after all. 'You're very generous. I will be sure to pass that on to my clients,' she smiled. 'And it's been so kind of you to try to help us. We really appreciate it.'

He looked irked by her faultless rebuff but was too polite to say so. 'It's no problem. I've done my own share of art-history research over the years for our family collection. I find it fascinating. It's almost a hobby for me.'

'Well, you're very lucky,' she said. 'And if ever you should want to—'

She had been about to offer her professional services, the business card already in her hand, but her eyes had snagged on the black-and-white photograph now on the top of the pile of papers. She had only glanced at it previously, a woman sitting centre stage on a chaise in evening dress, the two Renoirs clearly visible and prominent on the wall behind her. But not only that . . .

Flora's mouth opened in surprise as questions flooded her mind. It couldn't be the same painting of course – that was with the Vermeils in Paris. She had seen it with her own eyes just a few days ago . . . . And yet why was there a photograph of it in a file here, along with the other artworks supposedly in Noah Haas's collection?

'Everything OK?' Noah asked, seeing the sudden intensity on her face.

'Uh . . . yes,' she said, struggling to recover, unable to tear her eyes away from the photograph.

He glanced down at it, trying to identify the source of her discomfiture. 'Oh. That's my great-aunt Natalya, my grandfather's sister,' he said, pointing to the woman in the photo. 'You can see the Renoirs behind her there, on the wall. I keep this as further evidence of our family's ownership of the title. The more documentation, the better with these things.'

'Absolutely,' Flora murmured, not in the least bit interested in the Renoirs now. 'She was very beautiful, your great-aunt.'

'Yes, she was,' he agreed. 'A great beauty by all accounts. In fact, she had her portrait painted by a very fashionable artist when she was just eighteen. You can just see it over her left shoulder.'

'That's her?' Flora asked as he pointed out the very portrait that had just caught her attention. She pretended to be surprised, taking full opportunity to scrutinize the woman in both the photo and the portrait. Her head was reeling. The woman in the portrait was his great-aunt?

'Yes, although she looks quite different in this photo. She's thirty-two here and fashions had changed from when she was painted – war was coming.'

'Of course.' Her voice was a whisper, alarm bells sounding in her mind. Something wasn't right. Coincidences like this didn't happen. 'Do you still have it? The portrait, I mean.'

She knew he didn't, of course, but she wanted to know what he knew.

'Sadly not, though, again, I've been trying to trace it for years. I have a similar file to this one, *full* of photos and papers, but no painting at the end to show for it all.' He shuffled the papers back into the folder and replaced it – in alphabetical order – in the box file. 'As I said, it's quite a hobby.'

'Can you tell me anything about the painting? Perhaps I could help?'

'Maybe you could,' he said consideringly, a thoughtful smile beginning to play on his lips. 'How about I tell you over dinner?'

'Sorry?' She was wrong-footed by the question. She hadn't anticipated it. At least, not *now* she hadn't, too distracted by the sudden appearance of the portrait.

He smiled. 'Would you like to go for dinner? Tonight?'

'Oh.' She met his gaze and could see quite clearly his interest in her, in spite of – or perhaps because of – the age gap. Could he see her interest in him too? Could he tell that it wasn't the same kind? She swallowed, her mind racing. She had to know what he knew about this portrait that was currently in her care. Why did she have it and he didn't? Had François Vermeil known Noah's great-aunt? Were the two families connected by more than the matching Renoirs?

She had to tread carefully. This man had information she needed but he wasn't obliged to help her; he didn't need to tell her a single thing about it. She had arrived here looking for answers and was leaving with only more questions. 'I'm afraid I make it a policy not to go for dinner with my clients.'

'But I'm not your client,' he replied, quick as a flash. 'Besides, where's the harm? I'll trade you a story for your company and some good wine,' he said, walking her slowly towards the door.

'OK,' she smiled, stopping and offering him her hand. 'It's a deal.'

He grinned as he took her hand in his. 'No, Miss Sykes. It's a date.'

Chapter Thirteen

Vienna glittered like an electrical circuit board, the city's grand imperial palaces and baroque museums laced with thousands of lights, their verdigris roofs obscured by the darkness for now, the Danube silkily winding its way out to sea.

Flora stood on the small balcony that gave over the busy streets, watching the trams gliding past in an electric whoosh, shoppers and office workers below making their way home from another hot, dusty day. She stared down, already dressed and primped and trying to drum up some kind of appetite for tonight. She had spent the afternoon shopping – she hadn't packed for dinner at one of the best restaurants in the city – finally settling on a Saint Laurent black silk tuxedo and a simple pair of Gianvito Rossi heels.

She pressed redial on the phone and tried Freddie's number again. He had called her earlier when she'd been on the plane. She couldn't bear it, the irony. The one time her phone was switched off! He hadn't left a message of course and that had only worried her more. She couldn't help it. She felt the physical distance between them more keenly from this city, perhaps because it was her first time here and she felt disorientated and small. She had always wanted to visit Vienna. It was Europe's cultural capital, once home to radical thinkers like Sigmund Freud, great artists like Egon Schiele and Klimt. When she was a little girl, her father had thrilled her with stories of the cascading fountains at the Belvedere Palace and the 850-year-old tower of St Stephen's cathedral which had, for centuries, been the tallest building in Europe. For years she had promised herself she would visit and see all these things when she finally had the opportunity, but now that she did, would she? How could she value art and beauty when there was no regard for the truth? When her family was being dismantled with lies?

'Batty.'

'. . . *F-Freds?*' she stammered, taken aback that he'd picked up.

'No need to sound so stunned,' he quipped. 'You did call me.'

'Yes, but . . . you never pick up!' she cried, turning her back on the city to focus on his voice.

'Law of averages means I will sometimes.' It was a typically pithy response. She tried to take it as a good sign.

'How are you?'

'Fine.'

'Really?'

'I'm fine.'

'You don't sound fine. Are you eating? Even your voice sounds thin.'

'Have you been talking to Mum?'

'Not since I left England. Why?'

'Nothing.'

'Freds! What would she tell me? Why did you ring?'

There was a pause at the other end of the line. '. . . Work's found out.'

She bit her lip, squeezing her eyes shut as she heard the tremor marble his voice. 'But how? Who would've said? I mean, who would—'

'It wasn't anyone. It was circumstance. We've finished the scenes at Elstree and we're moving to location now. Morocco . . .' He sighed. 'Except I can't. Bail conditions – I can't leave the country. The police have got my passport.'

'Oh shit,' she whispered.

'Yeah. The one time we're ahead of schedule . . .'

It was intended as another wisecrack but he couldn't deliver it and she didn't care. She raked her hands through her hair, her mind whirring. Then she sank down into a ball behind the balustrade, crouching on her high heels, her elbows resting on her knees. 'So . . . so what happened? What did they say?'

She heard him take in a deep breath. 'That I'm suspended on full pay, pending the outcome of the court case.'

'Right.'

'But . . . well, that's probably bullshit. I don't know if I'll be able to go back, regardless of the verdict. Mud sticks, right?'

'No, it doesn't,' she said defiantly. 'It washes off. All of this is going to go away, I promise you.'

There was a pause. Then: 'You're sweet, Bats.'

She closed her eyes. She didn't want to be sweet. She wanted to be right. 'Where are Mum and Dad anyway? They never pick up when I call home.'

'No. They've moved back into the flat for the foreseeable.'

'Well, that's great!' she said, trying to sound cheery. Their parents' first home together, a pied-à-terre in Cadogan

Gardens, was only a ten-minute bus ride from Freddie's place in Fulham.

'Is it? Bolly's walking along the pavements like a man in heels. And you should see Dad's face when he has to poo-pick after him. They're not used to city living any more. They shouldn't be here – it's only adding to the stress for them. They should be at home.'

'So should you.'

'I'm better here. Normal's good.'

'Freds, I'm serious – are you eating?'

'You're kidding, right? Every time I get back to the flat, there's another pot of chilli in the fridge or a pie in the oven or the ironing's been done. It's like I've got elves.'

Flora chuckled, grateful for both her mother's fussiness and this hint of her brother's old humour. He'd never had to try too hard to make people smile, laugh, like him. If she had breezed through life thus far, popular and well liked, Freddie had blasted through, universally loved. People were drawn to him – old, young, male, female – and she was so proud to call him her brother; to have a blood claim on someone like him felt special and rare.

There was a natural pause and she inhaled deeply, gathering courage. 'Freddie, look, I know you said you don't want anyone outside the family knowing but . . . I really think you should speak to Aggie. She *is* family. You guys were together for six years. You broke up a month ago. You can't pretend—'

'I'm not pretending anything! But she's not in my life any more,' Freddie said, his voice suddenly brittle and hard. 'I don't want her getting involved with this. She's better off . . . she's better off staying out of it.'

'But she still loves you. I know she does.'

'She's moved on.' His voice was flat.

'Because she's been on a few dates? Don't be daft! She wanted to marry you, Freds. The week before you guys broke up, she told me she thought you were going to propose.'

There was a long silence.

'She still loves you,' she said, emboldened. 'I just know that if you told her, she'd be there for you. It'll be so much worse if she hears it from someone else. I mean, what if she reads it in the papers? Wouldn't you be—'

'Enough!' His voice was a general's roar, stunning her into silence. Freddie never raised his voice. He was Mr Mild. 'We're not talking about her any more, do you understand? I don't want to hear her name. No exceptions. It's over. And if you call her, if you tell her anything, I swear I'll never speak to you again either.'

Flora couldn't reply. She'd never heard him so angry, she'd never encountered this rage in him before.

His voice cracked. 'I'm sorry. I'm sorry, Flora, but that's just how it has to be. Look, I'll call you soon, OK?'

And he hung up, leaving her alone in the City of Dreams, trapped in a nightmare.

'You look beautiful.'

Noah's eyes, bluer than she'd recalled, gazed at her across the table. She smiled her thanks but didn't believe a word of it. Reception had called up to her room only minutes after Freddie had hung up on her and – shocked, frustrated, despairing – she hadn't had time for her colour to go down.

Not that she cared about how she looked.

All she'd wanted to do was have a hot shower, curl up in

a towel and go to sleep for a week but she couldn't; she was here, working again, a fake smile plastered on her face and she felt rushed, stretched, spasmodic, feral. She didn't quite trust herself; she wasn't sure she could be relied upon to make small talk all night, to care about art when her family life was in ruins, to eat with a stranger when she needed the company of friends.

She closed her eyes momentarily, wishing she was back in Paris. Ines would know what to do.

Noah was still staring at her when she opened her eyes again and she took another sip of wine. 'Sorry.'

'Tired?'

'A little.'

'I know how you feel. I have to travel a lot in my line of work too.' His hand hovered at the base of his glass. 'Listen, if you'd rather not do this—'

'No. Not at all,' she said quickly, remembering herself. Even the company of a stranger was better than being alone in that hotel room right now. 'I'm so happy to be here. I can't believe you were able to get a table at such short notice.'

He looked pleased. 'Well, my family has been coming for many years. They're usually able to oblige me.'

Flora smiled, noticing how good he looked in his indigo hopsack suit that was so lean it seemed to leave no room for a wallet or mobile phone in the pockets.

She fiddled with her glass too, glancing around at the other diners – all finely dressed and bedecked in summer jewels, white tablecloths hanging to the floor on the round tables, tobacco-smoked mirrors lining the walls and reflecting their images like shadows.

'Actually, my great-grandparents were patrons here

when it first opened in 1907,' he continued, filling the silence.

'Really?' She feigned interest, willing herself to get into the game.

'Yes.' He paused for a moment. 'And my great-aunt sang here for a season. You remember? It was her portrait you were interested in earlier.'

'Oh, yes. What was her name?'

'Natalya Spiegel; Haas before she married.'

She lifted her glass slowly, trying not to look too interested whilst simultaneously absorbing every last detail. 'And who painted the portrait, do you know?'

'An artist called Gustav Huber.'

Flora swallowed the wine and frowned. 'Huber? I've not come across him before.'

Noah blinked, studying her concentration and the way she wrinkled her brow. 'No. By all accounts he came to art late, picking up a brush in his late thirties and finding he had a talent for it. He only painted Natalya and a few other society figures before he was commissioned. He died on the Eastern Front.'

'What a terrible waste. It looks like he had a great talent.'

'I agree.'

She replaced her glass on the table. 'And you said your family doesn't have the portrait any more.'

'That's right. Again, it was sold by my great-aunt during the war.' He hesitated. 'Well, I say sold. What I really mean is stolen – signed away with a Nazi's gun pointed at her head.' The bitterness in his voice was palpable and Flora sat in silence as he reached for the wine and took a sip; she knew exactly where this conversation was heading. He caught sight of her subdued expression. 'Sorry. I . . .

I shouldn't get onto the subject. It doesn't make for good manners or polite conversation.'

'No, I understand,' Flora said quickly. 'The Nazis' looting of fine art is an issue that still plagues the industry today. It's a complex and painful path to navigate with no easy answers.' She looked down, knowing she'd given him a stock professional response to a highly personal revelation, panicking as she found herself bound by client confidentiality on the one hand and basic human compassion on the other.

He looked at her. 'Did you lose any family in the war?'

'My grandfather was a Halifax bomber pilot. He survived. Somehow.'

'Well, that's good to hear.' He paused. 'My family weren't so lucky. They were double-crossed and sent to their deaths.' His words were hard, thrown out there like grenades.

Flora didn't know what to say. '. . . Double-crossed?'

'Yes. They made a deal to break up and sell their estate in exchange for safe passage to Switzerland. Three days later, expecting their passes for the border, they were packed by the SS on a one-way train to Dachau.' He took another gulp of his drink.

'Oh my God,' Flora gasped. 'I'm so sorry.'

'Almost my entire family wiped out in a stroke – my great-aunt, her husband and their four children.'

Flora covered her mouth – knowing the theory of the horrors and coming face to face with them were two entirely different things. Four children? 'I don't know what to say,' she whispered.

Noah inhaled and shook his head, his tone apologetic. 'There's nothing to say. Sadly this is a story shared by millions of people. Like I told you earlier, my grandfather –

Natalya's brother – had already emigrated to America before the outbreak of war, otherwise I guess I wouldn't be sitting here now either. My grandfather never forgave himself for not making his sister go too – it affected the rest of his life. Survivor's guilt.' He glanced at Flora's aghast expression and dropped his head a little. 'I'm sorry, forgive me. As I said, it doesn't make for good conversation.'

'No, I . . . it's so sad.' She let a beat pass as the waiter came over with the menus. '. . . Do you know who owns it now? The portrait, I mean.' She was sure he must be able to hear the lies coming from her mouth, to see the duplicity in her eyes.

'Yes and no.'

He didn't elaborate and she gave a hesitant laugh. 'I'm confused.'

'I know to whom it was last sold, back in 1943 – the guy who double-crossed them, the same guy who bought your Renoir.' Flora swallowed, not remotely surprised. All roads, it seemed, led back to Von Taschelt. 'But he died the same year himself, leaving no apparent heirs. I have no idea where or with whom it is now. Like the Renoir, it's vanished. No trace.' He cast her a look. 'Of course, if the Renoir's showed up with your clients, perhaps you have the portrait too?'

Flora's mouth dropped open and he laughed. 'I'm just messing with you.'

'Oh!' She swallowed, so sure he'd been able to see the truth in her face. 'Well . . .' she said, trying to recover. 'If ever . . . if ever you should want—'

His hand reached across the table and clasped hers. 'Is this where you offer me your services and try to find it for me?' he asked, his voice lower suddenly. 'Because if what you said earlier is true, about not dating your clients, then I'm really not feeling incentivized to become one of them.'

Flora felt the floor drop an inch. 'I . . . I . . .' she stammered, feeling the blood rush up her cheeks like a tide as he held her stare, his pupils opening like black tulips, his cards on the table now.

For the second time in as many minutes, she didn't know what to say.

'Are you hungry?' he asked, his thumb pressing slightly on the veins on her inner wrist, feeling how her pulse raced.

She shook her head. Between the argument with Freddie and this conversation, she had been well and truly robbed of her appetite. 'No, not really,' she admitted.

'Want to get out of here?'

He stared at her, unafraid of the silence his question brought, unafraid of the rejection she might yet give, unafraid of everything. He was bold, brave, vital, here.

'Yes,' she whispered, even as he raised his arm to get the bill.

The moon fell in great sabre-flashes of lambent light across the dark glossed floor, the cadmium yellow of the painted dress glowing like a miniature sun on the opposite wall. She couldn't take her eyes off it. It had felt as though another person had been in the room with them, its presence so fully fleshed and defined.

Beside her, Noah slept and she wondered again at the events that had led to them lying here together. There were so many reasons why, ordinarily, it would never have happened – she wasn't looking for this, he wasn't her type, she was here to work . . . Good reasons, all of them. But events of the past few weeks had converged inside her to create a perfect storm of insecurity and lies, tipping her off-balance just enough to send her running for the escape he offered, if only for a night.

She watched the slow rise and fall of his chest, his skin tanned and dark beneath light sweeps of hair, his muscles relaxed, mouth parted slightly. He had been a skilled lover and she had clung to him, hungry and grateful for the hiatus he brought as she allowed her body to take over from her mind for a while. How long had it been since she'd shared a bed with someone? Two months? Nearly three? Too long, anyway, for a young single woman, that was for sure. Was it any wonder Ines kept trying to get her to give things another go with Stefan?

She stared at the Renoir, knowing precisely what a privilege it was to even stand in a room and be witness to it, much less to sleep there. There wasn't much else to look at, anyway, possibly for that very reason. What else could compete? There wasn't anything more to see in there than she had clocked on her fleeting, polite visit this afternoon. (Had it really only been this afternoon that she'd first come here? She'd had no inkling then that she'd be sleeping here the same night.) The wardrobes were flush and push-touch; the shimmery silk rug, delicious to the touch of her bare feet, a plain grey rising to silver; the stovepipe-dark walls free of a single fingerprint. There were no chests of drawers or radiators to break up the lines of the room, no other photographs or even a cufflink tray to betray human occupancy of the almost gallery-like space. There was just the painting, the bed and them.

She lay there a while longer, listening to the sound of his slow, sleeping breaths, her legs beginning to twitch as she replayed in her mind the conversation with Freddie. He wouldn't really cut her off. Would he? She had no doubt her instincts were right about Aggie. If she only knew what was happening . . . But could she take the risk?

She jerked suddenly, a bolt of anger barrelling through her that they were even in this position – hiding from friends, living with secrets and lies. Noah stirred slightly, shifting onto his side, away from her. Flora lay still for a moment, restless, heart pounding, before she silently lifted the duvet off her and got up. She couldn't lie here next to him.

She padded over the rug, slipping on a cotton dressing gown that had been hanging on the hook in the bathroom. It swamped her and she rolled back the sleeves, tiptoeing out of the bedroom and into the vast acreage of the main living area.

At the kitchen sink, she ran herself a glass of water – it took several minutes of pushing against dummy walls before she located the glasses. As she sipped the water, she dispassionately surveyed the trail of clothes that stretched along the floor, these traces of passion marring the otherwise pristine minimalism of the apartment. She winced and looked away, walking over to the windows and looking down on Vienna as it slept. There wasn't a light on in any of the opposing apartment blocks and the trams were still at last. It was after three in the morning – 'the witching hour', her father had always said – and she felt as though she was the only person in Europe awake right now.

She turned away from the peaceful scene, gazing back into the apartment, her eyes scanning it with an outsider's scrutiny. She took in the expensive Italian sofa, the Seurat above the fireplace, the marble wall, the industrial kitchen, the bank of impressive books and sculptures making a considered statement about the refined cultural tastes of the owner of the apartment – *Fifty Shades of Grey* notwithstanding.

It felt wrong being here. She knew she ought to go to bed, try to sleep and then make a polite but hasty retreat in the morning. If she could escape before he suggested breakfast, she'd be doing well—

Her eyes fell to the drawer, the almost-invisible drawer that lined the bottom of the bookcase like a plinth. Instantly, her mind went back to work. The portrait.

There was a file in there, he'd told her that, detailing the provenance of the portrait with the same meticulous attention to detail as he'd compiled on the Renoir. Yes, at the restaurant he'd given her the name of the artist and the name of the subject, both of which would be helpful in establishing the title and kicking off that provenance research. On the other hand, if the information was all just sitting there, already collated . . .

She looked over to the bedroom door. It remained ajar, not a sound suggesting Noah had stirred or noticed her missing. Quickly she put down her glass and scurried to the drawer, pushing on it and pulling out the box file. Inside, she looked for the red folder tabbed *Art*. Then she flicked the sub-files for the artist Gustav Huber.

She found it quickly thanks to his alphabetized system and, kneeling on the floor, her eyes darting every few seconds towards the bedroom, she hurriedly took off the paper clip. Topmost was a colour photocopy of the painting and stapled to it, the same photo she'd seen in the Renoir file earlier.

She put the photos down and looked at the next sheet of paper. To her surprise it wasn't a receipt or copy of a ledger but a letter – she scanned it quickly but as it was in German she was unable to understand anything it said, only that it was addressed to Herr Haas and signed Gustav Huber. There were no numerals that she could make out suggesting a transfer of money between them, not unless it was written in longhand. Had it been a gift, perhaps? Or was this just an acceptance of the commission? A chase for payment maybe? There were so many possibilities and yet again she was locked out of understanding what they might be.

Remembering her phone in her bag, she thought she could photograph the letter and get someone else to translate it later, but it was in the bedroom, beside the bed. Dare she go in there and risk waking Noah? She couldn't afford to leave this paperwork lying around in case he did wake up.

Frustrated, she set it aside and studied the final sheet. It was an original copy of a ledger, the ink now bleeding rusty yellow onto the paper, that familiar trademark oval around the letter-heading at the top of the page and she took in the dates, that dreaded name again.

But she felt the hairs rise on the backs of her arms as a sudden sound – the one she'd feared – in the bedroom caught her attention. She heard the creak of the bed, the rustle of the duvet being thrown back. With a gasp, she shuffled the papers into a neat pile and paper-clipped them together, but there wasn't time to find the exact spot in the alphabetized order and she slid them randomly into the red file before placing it in the box file and depositing it all back in the drawer.

When Noah emerged a moment later, she was standing by the window, a glass of water in her hand and her back to him. Silently he walked over, slipping a hand inside the gown and closing it around one breast, his lips on her neck. She closed her eyes and groaned lightly, pushing her body back against the length of his, nuzzling into his touch. If he did feel the quickened thud of her heart against his palm, he would put it down to sexual excitement. Nothing more.

Chapter Fourteen

'We have a big problem.' Flora was pacing the tiny office, having waited all day for New York to wake up and then – thanks to a golfing day with clients at the Maidstone in East Hampton – for Angus to actually get near a Wi-Fi connection. It was Sunday but she had come straight from the airport and it was getting dark outside now. She was feeling almost hysterical at the thought of a shower, a meal and a sleep, and Angus's candy-pink golfing jumper wasn't helping matters.

Angus kept his poker face on. 'I'm listening.' This was what he always said when he meant, *'You're scaring me.'*

She took a deep breath. 'You know the portrait I found in the downstairs apartment?'

There was a pause. 'The untitled, unsigned – ergo worthless – one?' he asked after a moment, visibly relaxing that it wasn't anything to do with the Renoir and leaning on his nine iron.

'Exactly.'

He arched an eyebrow. 'What about it?'

'I've got an artist's name and a title for it.'

Angus looked baffled and Flora could see he was trying to link why she was telling him about this when she had travelled out to investigate the Renoir. 'Uh . . . OK. So?'

175

'No. The question you have to ask me is, how? How do I know all this?'

'OK, Flora, how do you know all this?'

'Noah Haas told me . . . The woman in the painting is his great-aunt.'

There was a silence. 'You're kidding?'

She shook her head.

'Well, that's a bit of a big fucking coincidence,' he exclaimed.

She took a deep breath again. 'Yes and no.'

Angus looked back at her suspiciously. 'What do you mean?'

'It's a big coincidence that I happened to end up in the apartment of the great-nephew of the woman whose portrait we currently have warehoused in Paris. Less so when you learn that it was sold to a certain dealer in 1943.'

Angus's face fell instantly. 'Oh Jesus, don't tell me—'

'Franz Von Taschelt. Yes, I'm afraid so,' she finished for him.

'Shit!' he hissed, getting up from his chair and beginning to pace too. He disappeared out of sight briefly but she sat still, knowing he'd reappear shortly. 'So that's two paintings, now, in the Vermeils' apartment that were sold to Von Taschelt?'

'Two that we know about but there could be more. Once we start researching the other paintings, it could be more of the same. Hell, the entire consignment could have been bought from him! A job-lot deal, nice and cheap in the middle of the war.'

Angus was quiet for a long time and Flora knew he was fretting about losing out on his juicy commission that would come from successfully getting these to sale; the

Vermeils weren't going to auction anything from the apartment if this was the backstory. 'Fuck.' He ran his hands through his hair, pulling so tight at the roots he gave himself a momentary facelift.

But Flora didn't laugh at the funny sight. She felt hollow inside. Last night – all of it – felt like a bad dream now. She didn't recognize the person she'd become out there: deceitful, reckless, bitter, manipulative. That wasn't who she was. What was happening to her?

'Does Haas know we've got it? The portrait, I mean?'

Flora shook her head. 'No, of course not.'

'Good. The last thing we need is for him to make some sort of claim on it.'

'He's got a copy of the receipt showing his family sold it to Von Taschelt. It was a pretty good price too, so it would be hard for him to argue it wasn't legit. But he *does* want to buy it back. He's been trying to trace it, but obviously the trail runs cold with V.T.'

'Jesus, we have got to establish why that Nazi's paintings are in our client's property.'

'I think for the obvious reason,' she said quietly. 'Because they bought them from him. He was their dealer.'

'No. I won't accept that until we've got the paperwork to support it,' he said stubbornly. He thought for a moment. 'There's still a very plausible chance that Von Taschelt sold the requisition to another party who then sold the lot, in its entirety possibly, to the Vermeils.'

Flora blinked back at him. A job lot sold not once, but twice, within a year? His hypothesis was a stretch of credibility to say the least. 'It's a tiny chance, Angus. I think we need to be prepared for the worst-case scenario that the family basically bought from him direct and profited from the Third Reich.' She shrugged. 'Hell, maybe that's why Jacques' father shut up the apartment. Maybe it was a deliberate plan. Lie low, let the dust settle . . .'

Angus closed his eyes as if in pain. 'Holy crap, don't even say that, *please*, Flora. You don't understand the potential gravity of this. The Vermeils are Jewish. If this was to get out to the press, the public consequences for them could be huge. They stood behind the President on Memorial Day last year. I can't . . . I can't even begin to think about breaking this to them.'

Flora fell quiet, looking helplessly round her tiny office. The room felt even smaller at night, as though the darkness outside was pushing against the walls, contracting the space. There were no curtains or blinds to keep it out, either, and she felt conspicuous in the all-white light, as though her first-floor office had become a stage.

'We need to see what it says in Von Taschelt's own ledgers – I don't care if it's a receipt, bill of sale, whatever. We need that final link in the chain to put a bit of space between him and them. It all keeps coming back to that,' Angus said finally. 'Tell me you've heard back from the gallery in Saint-Paul?'

'Not yet. I'll chase them again.'

'You said that before you went to Vienna.'

'Yes. And I went straight to Vienna!' she replied, frustrated. 'And then I came straight back here. I've been busy, Angus. I'm not dragging my feet! And do I need to remind you it's Sunday – supposedly a day of rest? They won't be working, even if I am!'

'No, you're right. Sorry. Sorry.' He raked his hands through his hair again. 'It's just, this is beginning to bother me. We're not making any progress. If anything, we're becoming more mired in problems.'

She didn't reply. He was right. They were stuck. Far from distancing their clients from one of the most disgraced names in the history of fine art, they were only finding ever more links between them. Carry on like this and they were going to uncover a full-scale collusion between both parties.

'Well, I'm afraid that's not all,' she sighed heavily. He might as well know everything. 'There's something else. The night before I went to Vienna, I discovered some photos of the Vermeils' apartment have been posted on the internet.'

'What do you mean? *How?*' His voice rose three octaves. 'Mother of God, have we been hacked?'

'No. They're not our photos at all, that's the problem. They're on some "urban explorers" website –' she made speech marks in the air with her fingers – 'and before you ask, it's some underground cult tribe thing. People go round exploring abandoned buildings and posting the photos on these websites.'

'And who posted these?'

She shrugged. 'Don't know. They're all anonymous – they'd be busted for trespass otherwise.'

'Oh Christ!' He rubbed his face in his hands. 'You're telling me there are photos of that entire art haul for just anyone to see?'

'No,' she corrected him quickly. 'No, the photos aren't of Apartment Eight – it's Apartment Six.'

'The empty one?' Angus brightened up immediately. 'Well, that's OK then! There was nothing in there of interest.'

'Except for the portrait! That's what I'm saying – Noah Haas could see this.'

Angus paused. 'Well, there's a chance, of course, but it's hardly the same disaster scenario as the haul upstairs being leaked. Can you *imagine* if people were to find out about that? The press would be all over it. It would be the Munich case – damn, what was his name?'

'Cornelius Gurlitt,' she muttered.

'Yes, him. It would be him all over again – that and then some! The Vermeils are a big deal. No, no, this is all fine – it's just a painting on a bed in an empty apartment. Why should anyone be interested in that? Let these explorers have their fun. We've got bigger fish to fry.'

Flora bit her thumbnail.

'Stop looking so worried, Flora. It's fine,' he laughed.

She was worried, though. 'I'm just . . . uneasy,' she said, trying to find the right words. 'The more I think about it, the more I think Travers lied to me about which apartment was discovered. He said it was Number Eight but you went in there with me, Angus – it was clear *no one* had been in before us. And then there's the whole issue of Natascha being given the wrong keys – again, by an office junior who's out of the loop.'

'What are you saying?'

'I don't think the family was supposed to know about the apartment downstairs. I think Travers deliberately handed over the wrong keys – the ones for Number Eight – to prevent them from knowing about it.'

'But why? There's nothing in the apartment downstairs, except for the painting on the bed. Why keep that a secret from them?'

'I know,' she winced, shaking her head. 'I don't get it either. But I just know something's not right. There's too many things that are . . . off.'

180

'And do you believe Elvis is still alive too? And that Marilyn was murdered?' he quipped, stretching his arms out wide, distorting the diamonds on the front of his jumper. 'I never would have had you down as a conspiracy theorist, Flora,' he tutted. 'Look, you said yourself papers have gone missing from the drawers in Apartment Eight. That means someone else *was* in there besides us. That means there *were* two sets of intruders – the explorer guys downstairs, and the others upstairs. I know it's bad luck but let's look on the bright side here – we're bloody lucky they didn't nick the art!'

She exhaled, feeling like a dog chasing its own tail. 'Perhaps you're right.'

'I know I am. Look, it's late over there and you look like you haven't slept in days. Go home, chill out and if you do nothing else tomorrow, get hold of that bloody gallery in Saint-Paul. Fly down there and storm the damned archives yourself if you have to. We've waited long enough. The answers we need are in those vaults, I know it. This isn't as complicated as we're making it.'

We? Or her? Was he passing the buck here?

He saw her concern and looked away guiltily. 'Look, you should know I spoke to Lilian yesterday. I know you're leading this project and I wasn't stepping on your toes, but you were in Vienna and she couldn't get hold of you.'

'Just say it, Angus.'

'She's insistent the painting goes into the Christie's sale.'

'Well, it can't,' Flora shrugged, nonplussed. 'Not until we've sorted this out.'

'That's the problem – we're out of time. The deadline was last night . . . and I've already done it.'

Flora's expression changed. They'd only talked about it

on Friday night. There had been no mention of the deadline being twenty-four hours later. 'But . . .' The penny dropped. Suddenly she understood why he had booked her on the first flight to Vienna, rushing to get her out of Paris and keep her out of the way whilst he negotiated with the family over her head to submit the painting. This hadn't come from Lilian at all. Angus was thinking about one thing only – that overdraft.

'Its fine, Flora,' he said, seeing her understand and holding up his hands. 'It's all going to be fine. But that's why I need you to get a shift on with the gallery, OK?'

Flora couldn't believe what she was hearing. To save his sorry arse, he'd submitted the Renoir for sale in the splashiest and most important Impressionist auction of the year, in spite of the fact that its high-profile Jewish-benefactor owners couldn't prove their ownership, only their business dealings with the Third Reich? Did the family even know how this was risking their reputation? She shook her head, knowing they couldn't; there was no way they would have sanctioned it. No, Angus was flying solo on this, hoping everything would work out OK and in time.

The man was mad! Or desperate.

'We need it to sell, Flora,' he said, reading her mind. 'The bank's getting shirty.'

'Oh Jesus, Angus!' she whispered.

'Look, the answer's in Saint-Paul, I know it is. It's always in the most obvious place. Speak to them in the morning and then go to the house at four p.m. Now the Renoir's in the sale, Lilian's requested a full update. She'll be expecting to celebrate.'

Flora's eyes widened. 'But what if I *don't* get anything out of the gallery? What am I supposed to tell them then? That their father did business with the Nazis?'

'Look, that's not going to happen. Why would that happen? If the Getty Index says the records are in Saint-Paul, then they're in Saint-Paul. It's fine.'

'And if they still haven't located them for me by four p.m.?' she pushed. 'What then?'

'*If* the gallery still can't get its arse into gear, then . . . then think of something. Tell them his father bought those paintings from a little old lady who fed the birds in winter and left her house to the city's orphans . . . I don't care! Tell them anything, anything *but* the story we've got right now. It's the truth but not the whole truth. There's more to come, I can feel it.'

The night felt thick, stilled by the weight of the heat, the trees drooping as though nodding in sleep, and as she stepped outside the office, she felt thunder in the air. She had a sense of worlds colliding, of there being just *too much* in the atmosphere – the very air she breathed overly full.

Traffic had thinned to a midnight trickle and though taxis drove past at regular intervals, she didn't raise her arm for a quick ride home. She needed to clear her head and try to think straight – so she walked. She walked past the parked cars and dark apartments, the shut boutiques with their bright windows, the cliques of students queuing to get into the clubs, the tourists falling out of restaurants, the deserted streets where graffiti littered the walls.

She walked down streets she didn't know, through areas she didn't recognize, oblivious to the sound of her own feet on the pavements, the commentary of what she was going to tell the Vermeils the next day running in a loop through her mind. Only when she heard the sound of glass breaking and a sudden shout coming from a narrow side street just ahead did she stop, suddenly aware of her recklessness. She turned on her heel uncertainly.

'Do you need a ride?'

Flora glanced over at the scooter dawdling beside her, wondering who could think she'd be enough of an idiot to get on a bike with a complete stranger.

Xavier Vermeil was looking back at her, sitting astride the bike. He wasn't smiling, but he wasn't scowling either and for a moment – only one – she forgot that they hated each other.

'No,' she said, suspiciously. What did *he* want? 'I don't need a ride.'

He looked down briefly, raised his black eyes to her again. 'You sure? It can get pretty dangerous around here this late.' He glanced towards the end of the street where the raised voices – several of them now – were yelling, a scuffle breaking out.

She took in the sight of his gypsy-dark hair falling wild around his face, no helmet on, naturally. In the dim light, she couldn't read the expression in his eyes – nothing new there – but she could make out the defiant jut of his lips. It seemed odd that he should be offering her help and yet appearing so reluctant to do so in the same breath; he had the resentful look of a toddler forced to share his sweets. 'You seriously expect me to accept help from *you*?' She was quite sure it would feel a lot more dangerous sitting on the back of that bike with him, than it would walking down a dark street alone. 'I'll take my chances, thanks.'

She turned and began walking again.

She waited for the sound of the engine to ignite, the

throttle to flare up, the inevitable roar of the tiny engine as he accelerated away from her – but it didn't come.

For several minutes, she didn't dare look back – she didn't want him to see her wondering about him – but curiosity finally won out and when she turned, she was astonished to see him 'straddle-walking' the bike a few metres behind her.

She stopped and stared, waiting for him to explain himself, but he simply stared back with that inscrutable, diffident expression that managed to be both defiant and louche at once.

'What are you doing? What are you doing *here*?' she cried, throwing her arms in the air, exasperated and uncertain whether his trailing her like this meant he was friend or foe. Was he trying to intimidate her, was that it?

'I'm on my way home. And you shouldn't be here on your own. You're crazy to be out here like this. This is a bad area at night.'

She blinked, dumbfounded that she was supposed to believe he supposedly, suddenly, cared whether or not she was safe in the dark. 'What do you care?'

But he made no effort to reply this time and after a minute in which neither of them spoke – as Paris slept and the sky thickened – she turned away and resumed walking. To hell with him, then. If he wouldn't speak, neither would she.

She walked faster, feeling the sweat prickle her skin but swinging her arms more defiantly nonetheless. She tried to concentrate on other things besides him – speaking to the gallery tomorrow, getting hold of Freddie to apologize for upsetting him on Saturday – but the knowledge that Xavier was kerb-crawling behind her buzzed in her brain like an angry bee, his eyes burning into her back, daring her to turn round again, to check whether he was still there. Occasionally she could glimpse his reflection in a shop window if there was a street light shining outside but she wouldn't give him the satisfaction of appearing to search. Whatever game he had going on here, she wouldn't play.

As she turned onto the next street, a flash suddenly opened up the sky and she jumped to a halt, whimpering before she could stop herself – she'd never liked being out in the lightning. Her body tensed, looking for somewhere to hide, fearing another break of the heavens. Instinctively she turned to him – the only other person around; he stared back at her, one eyebrow arched ever so slightly, as though mocking her refusal of his help, as if to say, 'See?'

Moments later, the thunder rolled across the sky like a bowling ball down an alley, bursting the overloaded storm clouds that had been building into wobbly towers and sending their floods down in a torrent. The rain fell as hard as hail, stinging her skin and soaking her clothes in moments. Her hair clung to her cheeks and she gasped as she tried to dodge the moon-silvered barbs.

Xavier laughed. At her.

He was drenched too but he appeared not to care in the least, his grey T-shirt as wet as if he'd swum in it.

'Are you sure you don't need a ride?' he drawled.

Flora glared at him hatefully, quite convinced he'd speed off if she did move to accept. 'Perfectly,' she snapped, spinning on her heel and marching away from him again. Even faster now.

Her pretty cotton-dotted Chloé dress was clinging to her legs, her scalloped ballet flats almost collapsing on themselves, the leather saturated, but there was no point in running. Wet was wet. She couldn't get any wetter than she now was, she thought, as she furiously raked her hair back from her face, her cheeks pink from where the front strands flicked her cheeks like tiny whips. More than that, though, she wouldn't run from him. She wouldn't allow him to think he'd harried her away, intimidated her. Won, in some way.

And so they wove through the sodden city in their peculiar dance, him a ruptured shadow behind her, swerving around the outsides of the parked cars as she resolutely ignored him. Well, ignored him, but she couldn't forget him – his silence filled her head, his will a wall she had to scale, and her breath came fast as she walked, her hands pulling into tense fists.

She was on Ines's road when her phone rang, her hand flying to her bag to get it, desperate for something to do, something to show him she wasn't alone out here with him.

'Yes?' she asked, glancing over her shoulder. Xavier was crawling behind, eyes on her but slightly closer than he had been, as she had slowed to answer the call. 'Oh, Noah, hi.' Her heart dived. She should never have answered it! A late-night call? Who else would it be but a lover? But she had been rash, reckless, desperate to do something to divert her attention away from *him*. 'How are you? . . . Yes, it was great, thanks. On time . . . Yes, just left . . . a crazy day . . . I know, on a Sunday too!' She realized she was almost at Ines's courtyard gate and she slowed down again, coming to a stop outside it. 'Oh? . . . I see . . .' Xavier rolled up, stopping in front of her now, his coal-black eyes burning with . . . what? What did he want? 'Y-yes, of course, that would be lovely . . .'

He turned on the ignition suddenly, revving the throttle

like some petrol-head teenager, over and over again so that she couldn't hear what Noah was saying. But it didn't matter. She suddenly understood that what mattered was what *she* said. 'Yes, I'm sure,' she said, holding Xavier's stare, refusing to concede so much as a blink. 'I'd love that.'

Chapter Fifteen

It was late when she awoke. She had forgotten to set her alarm and slept well for once, falling into a deep and dreamless oblivion, her sodden clothes still in a heap on the floor by the foot of the bed. She could tell by the breeze that fluttered in through the open window that last night's thunderstorms had cleared yesterday's oppressive humidity and from the silence that hummed through the apartment, she deduced she was alone.

She lay there awhile, feeling strangely optimistic. The sky was a celestial blue, airy tendrils spinning through it, and she had a sense of having transitioned from the past few weeks' state of chaos to one of calm. Today would be the day everything would get better. Today would be the day they'd get their answers. She thought of Freddie – today was the day for truth to win.

She grabbed her phone and fired off a text to Ines, asking her to brunch.

Ines's reply came back in seconds. She was on!

Flora threw back the duvet and climbed into the shower, feeling the water wash her clean and rinse away the grime of Vienna.

Vienna –

She remembered Noah's phone call last night, his

invitation, another date. She closed her eyes and let the water run over her face; she would need to call him back and set him straight. There was no point in wasting each other's time. She never would have said yes if it hadn't been for Xavier Vermeil *harassing* her.

Ines was already at the café by the time Flora ran up, her hair freshly dried, her dress catching the wind. Ines were stretched out in the plastic-wicker chair as though it were a sunlounger, her bare legs tanned and long in cut-off denims, a cigarette pinched between her fingers as her arm dangled out limply, hair splayed as though there'd been a small explosion.

'Hey,' Flora said brightly, pulling out her chair.

Ines lazily opened an eye and grinned. 'Hey, yourself,' she said, pulling herself into a slightly more upright position, tucking her legs in so that Flora could get to the table. 'You look perky.'

'Thank you. I slept well.'

'You slept *long*. I wasn't sure whether to wake you.'

'I'm glad you didn't. I needed the rest. Angus was right – I've been running on empty for too long.'

'Angus? Huh. And how is he?'

Flora knew Ines found Angus uptight and almost colonial in his Britishness, rarely ever moving beyond his 'network' of old school chums for work and play. As someone who had cast off her own privileged tribe for a bold new set as well as mindset, she was barely tolerant of his sort.

'Stressed. What's new?' she said lightly, catching the eye of the *serveur* and ordering two espressos, some croissants and orange juice.

'What's he got to be so stressed about? You're riding high, aren't you, thanks to the mighty Vermeils?' Ines took a final drag from her cigarette and stubbed it out in the ash-tray, blowing smoke from the corner of her mouth. Her fingers were adorned with multiple delicate gold rings – one shaped like an arrow, one bent to spell *amour* in looping, unbroken script, another a triple-stacked style with a central spine that ran down the back of her finger – and enormous gold triangle earrings winked in her hair.

'Oh, you know Angus, he isn't happy unless there's a drama to fuss about. He'll always find something.' Her tone was deliberately dismissive; she wasn't going to fret about their overdraft. Today was the day everything got better.

She looked down the street, watching the pedestrians clustering together by the traffic lights, shirtsleeves rolled up, sunglasses on; her eyes followed the cyclists meandering lazily down the road, baskets on their bikes and the wind lifting their hair. The whole city seemed in love with summer today.

Ines watched her watching them. 'So how was Vienna?'

Flora brought her attention back to her friend. She smiled. 'Fine. *Not* dull.'

'Did you get what you needed?'

'Oh, yes.' Flora's tone gave away the innuendo and Ines – a moment later – gave a sudden gasp.

'Oh my God, what did you do?' she asked with delight, clutching Flora's forearm.

Flora shrugged. 'I slept with him.'

Ines's jaw dropped open. 'With Xavier?'

Flora's jaw dropped open too. 'W . . . *what*? No! Why would you say *that*? Why would you think I'd—' she blustered, so furious and indignant and flabbergasted all at once that she could scarcely take a breath.

'OK, sorry, sorry. I just thought . . .' Ines shrugged and tailed off. 'So who then?'

'The guy I travelled out to meet in Vienna!' Flora said crossly, as though Ines should have known this.

'You slept with a client?' Ines asked, looking even more shocked.

'He's not a client,' Flora corrected her quickly. And now he never will be, she thought to herself, remembering her last view of the Renoir hanging in the bedroom as she lay in the bed. 'We were just following up a lead for the provenance.'

'Even so, that is not like you.'

'Yes, well, maybe I'm tired of . . . being me. It hasn't been much fun lately.'

'And was he? Fun, I mean?' Ines asked, leaning right in on the table, her head resting in one hand.

'Well, I'm not sure "fun" is the word I'd use for him. He's older, but . . .'

'It was good, yes?'

Flora smiled, giving a tactful shrug.

Ines looked delighted. 'Do you like him?'

'Well, I went to bed with him, didn't I?'

Ines hooked an eyebrow. 'Got a photo?'

'Of course not!' Flora burst out laughing. 'I didn't take a selfie of us in bed together!'

'Why not?' Ines laughed back, arms in the air questioningly. 'Are you going to see him again?'

'No. He called me, actually – last night.' Xavier Vermeil shot through her mind again. She pushed him straight back out. 'He's flying in this week and wants me to join him at the *Concours d'Élégance* at Chantilly but –' she shook her head, exhaled slowly – 'I'm going to call him later and say I can't make it.'

'But *why*?' Ines gasped.

'Because there's no future in it. He's in Vienna and I'm here, for one thing. And when we're not, he's in New York and I'm in London.'

'So? You just said he's flying in. If you li—'

Flora stopped her by placing a firm hand on her arm. 'Ines, I know what you're about to say, but it's not going to happen between us. He's very nice, I had a great time. But it just was what it was. Nothing more.'

Ines groaned, dropping her head onto her outstretched arm so that her face was almost touching the table. 'When will it ever be anything more with you?'

Flora didn't reply. The waiter had brought over their coffees.

Ines looked up at Flora, her head still resting on her arm. 'I just don't get it. You're twenty-seven years old, completely gorgeous. All these men everywhere are falling madly in love with you – and you never want to know!'

'Excuse me! It's not my fault if there isn't a connection there,' Flora protested.

Ines sat up straighter. 'You know Stefan's still mad about you, right? Bruno says he's always talking about you.'

Flora shot her a sideways look, rolling her lips inwards. 'Look, Stefan's a great guy. But what do you want me to say? He's just a *friend*.'

'But they're always just friends with you. How can you be this old and never have been in love? I just don't get it!'

'Clearly,' Flora muttered. 'And for the record, I'm not *that* old.'

'It's odd, that's what I'm saying. Most people have been in love by now. Most people have had their hearts broken.'

'Oh, well then, I'm gutted to have made it this far unscathed,' Flora replied, her voice heavy with sarcasm.

'Contrary to every love song out there, heartbreak is good for you. It makes you grow.' Ines jabbed a finger thoughtfully at her. 'You know, perhaps your expectations of what love actually is are unrealistic.'

'I don't think so.'

'It's not about rooms full of roses.'

'I'm fully aware of that.'

'It isn't always convenient either. Or maybe that person isn't who you imagined you'd fall for. And it's *very* rarely the love-at-first-sight thing. I didn't even notice Bruno the first few times I met him and look at us now.'

'Impossible not to,' Flora quipped.

'What I'm saying is, perhaps you might find a connection with this guy if you gave him half a chance. You obviously liked him enough to jump into bed with him.'

Flora didn't answer. It had been circumstance that had pushed her into bed with him – not chemistry, not connection. She'd been lonely and upset and far away from home. She'd been pushed to the point of exhaustion and was weary of being upset. She'd wanted a little comfort, a little release. That was all.

Ines slid another cigarette from the packet and lit it. Flora reached for her coffee.

'That's a nasty bruise,' Ines murmured, her eyes on the inside of Flora's arm.

'What is?' Flora asked, checking her tricep and finding four brown oval imprints on her skin. 'Oh. I wonder when that happened.'

'Vienna?' Ines asked lightly, arching an eyebrow craftily.

But the bruise was too old for that. Flora felt her stomach tighten as she remembered Xavier's strong grip outside the town house when he stopped her from falling down the steps. 'Yes, maybe,' she murmured, Xavier Vermeil back in her head. Again.

She looked at Ines. 'Tell me – why did you think I'd slept with Xavier Vermeil?'

Ines glanced at her. Then shrugged. 'I don't know,' she said after a pause. 'I really don't . . . it was just the first thought that came to me.'

'Odd thought given that I barely know the man.'

'Well, you barely knew the other guy, to be fair,' Ines winked at her.

'Yes, but I haven't had a stand-up blazing row with him.'

'That is true – another reason why you should *definitely* see him again,' Ines giggled, ducking out of the way of the sugar cube that Flora aimed at her head.

Flora was at her desk half an hour later, a green juice untouched beside her and splitting into watery layers of sediment like a pond-water sample as the ringtone beeped in her ear.

'*Attlee et Bergurren,*' a woman said in a quiet, clipped voice.

'Hello. Is this Attlee and Bergurren Gallery?'

There was a slight pause, possibly at the idiocy of the question. 'Yes. How may I help you?'

'Hello, yes. My name's Flora Sykes. I'm a fine-art adviser working in Paris for a client. I wrote to you last week re-questing information from the archives you hold for the former Von Taschelt Gallery in Paris?'

'. . . Yes.'

'So I was wondering if you had any information for me yet? It really is quite urgent now.'

There was a pause. 'Just a moment, please.'

She waited as the woman put the phone down on the desk, her footsteps sounding hollow as she walked away over a stone floor.

Flora bit her lip and twiddled her pen, waiting.

Eventually, the footsteps came back.

'Hello?'

'Hi. Hi, yes,' Flora said, sitting to attention.

'I am afraid we could not find what you were looking for, *madame*,' the woman said briskly, getting straight to the point.

'. . . What?' Flora asked, her voice scooped out and hollow.

'Your letter requested all sales after 1943. We have nothing after 1942.'

'But I thought you had the sales ledgers?' Flora blustered. 'It says on the Getty site . . .'

'Only up until 1942. There is nothing after. No papers at all.'

Flora fell silent, the sound of rushing blood hammering in her ears. This couldn't be right. 'All the papers were lost?'

'It was the war, *madame*. Very much was lost during the bombings.'

'I see. Yes . . .'

How the hell was she supposed to break this to Angus? It was a disaster, the last hope gone. The chain was incomplete, the evidence they needed lost after all; they couldn't prove that the Vermeils were the legal and rightful owners of the painting, merely that they were in possession of it. Would the French legal system recognize the old adage of possession being nine-tenths of the law?

'I'm sorry?' she asked, realizing the woman was still talking. 'Could you repeat that?'

'I said, you could perhaps enquire with the estate's notaries. There's a chance they may have some further information. Sometimes they have some paperwork in historical cases like this.'

'Oh. Yes,' Flora replied, without enthusiasm but picking up the pen again anyway.

'The number is 1 44 49 65 20. Travers et Fils. Ask for Lionel Travers – he is the senior partner.'

The pen dropped from Flora's hand.

'Lionel Travers is the notary for the Von Taschelt estate?' she croaked.

'Yes, *madame*. Is there a problem?'

But Flora had already hung up, her hands in her hair as she paced the tiny office, leaning against the walls and pushing herself off again as though she was bouncing on them.

She closed her eyes, trying to still her mind, trying to find rational answers to the questions it instantly raised – this, another unwelcome link between the Vermeils and Von Taschelt.

There was no doubting now that they had known each other, but the question was, how well? Had they been in a fully disclosed alliance with one another, Von Taschelt buying cheap and selling low to François Vermeil? How far-reaching was the business relationship, how many paintings involved? She squeezed her eyes shut at the memory of the hundreds of artworks stacked in the apartment. Oh God, how many of them were going to throw up this tainted connection? How many families – fleeing, desperate – had been involved?

She stared with laser-beam intensity at a hairline crack in the opposite wall, her brain in overdrive as she allowed the revelation to settle. So Lionel Travers's father had been the notary for both Franz Von Taschelt and François Vermeil. Was it really such a huge coincidence? Two rich, influential men; one rich, powerful lawyer? Of course not. The circles these people moved in were necessarily small, elite and exclusive and they shared more than just lawyers, always hiring the same party planners or valets from the same agencies. In fact, it might have been more unusual if they *hadn't* known each other.

But that didn't mean she wasn't troubled by Travers's dual involvement in this. His behaviour at their meeting had snagged with her at the time – his obstructive guardedness, his intimidating silences punctuated only by even more intimidating sarcasms. Little wonder he'd been so cagey! Had he guessed it was only a matter of time before she linked these two clients – one now nefarious, the other highly esteemed – together? Wouldn't it just have been easier for him to disclose to her there and then that his father's two clients had been in business together? How much longer had he thought he could keep it a secr—?

And then it hit her.

The empty drawers . . . the missing papers on the desk . . . the evidence that would have proved the shady deals. Travers had taken them! Of course he had. It was why he had blocked her in that meeting at every turn. Von Taschelt's reputation was in ruins, any connection with him now toxic whilst the Vermeils, society darlings, were the big-ticket clients that kept Travers et Fils at the top. It stood to reason that Lionel Travers would get rid of anything that could tie the two names together, even if it rendered a priceless art fortune worthless at a stroke.

Reeling from the realization, she went back to the computer and quickly brought up the photos of the apartments she'd taken in the first twenty-four hours. She may not have the paperwork to prove her theory but she was sure she remembered seeing it there. Hadn't she photographed it when she'd first walked in? Oh, but why hadn't she looked properly when she'd had the chance? Why had she allowed herself to be so distracted by the art when the backup material she needed for them had been staring her in the face? She would surely never find it now. If Travers was trying to protect his company's reputation then at the very least he'd have hidden any incriminating paperwork, if not destroyed it altogether. She felt sickened as she remembered his disingenuous question that day in his office. *'We are on the same side, are we not?'* But they weren't. He'd been working against her since she'd arrived, interfering with her investigations to safeguard his own interests. She'd never be able to complete the paper chain now. The Renoir would have to be withdrawn from sale and the agency's overdraft would continue to grow.

She tabbed down the photos quickly, knowing it was pointless. Even if she had unwittingly captured an image of some of the paperwork on the study desk, it was highly unlikely it would be clear enough for the writing to be legible, much less pass as evidence of provenance.

She came to the photos of the study and blinked as the proof that she wasn't wrong beamed back at her in high-definition colour – papers in chaotic piles were clearly visible, strewn across the top of the desk. She scrutinized them in turn, squinting to see if any of them could be magnified, blown up times ten, times a hundred . . . but she was out of luck. Her attention had been anywhere but the desktop, instead focusing on the expensive leather books, the decaying curtains . . . Success had been within her grasp but she hadn't realized the game that was being played as she tiptoed through the dust. Angrily, she jabbed the 'down' key hard, watching as the pictures flew past in a blur.

Flora sighed, dropping her head in her hands and staring desperately at the screen. It had stopped at one of the bedrooms in the apartment downstairs, showing a close-up of the bed, the painting and the large crate it had come in.

Natalya Spiegel's beautiful face stared impassively back at her, revealing none of the horrors of dealing with a double-crossing Nazi who had sent her to her death. Why had he kept this picture down here? Why just this one?

Of all the paintings they'd found in the apartment, it had been the one worth the least had it gone to market – an unknown subject captured by an unknown artist – and yet ironically it now stood the most chance of retaining some worth, trading not on name or prestige but beauty alone. Certainly, for Flora, it was the one treasure which had bewitched her. Had Natalya been even more beguiling in the flesh, she wondered. Had Von Taschelt been in love with her, was that it? Had she rejected him, and he'd thrown her into the path of the SS, keeping the portrait for himself as some sort of memento?

She stared at the photo of the crate it had arrived in – levered open, wooden splinters on the floor, the crowbar on the bed. An A5 sheet of paper was stapled to the inside of the crate, the contents invisible from this distance except for the distinctive red oval at the top which always ringed that dreaded name, Franz Von Taschelt. It was stamped on the outside of the crate too, in big black letters: *F.V.T.* – loud and proud to be officially sanctioned, an authorized dealer for the Third Reich.

She frowned, then cocked her head.

Caught her breath.

Held very still as a thought – an outrageous, improbable, unthinkable thought – grew from bud to bloom in her mind. Had she got this all wrong? Been looking at it the wrong way round from the very beginning?

She had been quick to accept the facts as they were pre-sented to her, but if she was to rewind events, would the story be the same? She frowned hard, pulling apart the given narrative and going back to just the facts: everything had been kicked off by those urban explorers finding Apart-ment 6 and sending a letter to Travers et Fils. The pro-forma docket stapled to the inside of that crate gave them a name, and one quick internet search would have revealed that Travers et Fils were the notaries for the Von Taschelt estate. So far, so logical. Why, then, had that letter been forwarded to the *Vermeils*? That docket showed only that the painting belonged to Von Taschelt, yet the unsuspecting junior clerk had forwarded the letter to the family, leading them to assume that the entire apartment and its contents were theirs.

But what if they were wrong, working on a false assump-tion? What if the office junior had made a colossal error and, tracking back through the archives for this historic client, had pulled out Vermeil instead of Von Taschelt? After all, in an alphabetical filing system, they would likely be next to one another. Human error: it happened. But given that the docket showed the painting had been sold to Von Taschelt, wasn't it more logical to assume that the apartment belonged to him too? Wouldn't it make more sense of the fact that every painting they'd investigated so far was registered to him?

She shook her head frustratedly. No, that didn't make sense. Travers would have picked up such a huge mistake immediately. As he'd told her himself, he had returned early from holiday to take over the situation, even scanning the very envelope the letter had come in. He wouldn't have let his most important clients linger in the mistaken belief that the apartment and its contents was theirs.

So then, *why* were the Vermeils still involved? And why was Travers in possession of a codicil that stated the apartment – that very one – should not be opened until after François and Magda's deaths?

Magda. Flora was suddenly struck by the incongruity of the name. Certainly, it wasn't French. Dutch perhaps? German?

The codicil had been written in German. Not German German. Not Swiss German . . . But Austrian German, perhaps?

Austria . . . ?

Flora's terrible theory took shape. Breath held, she entered another search into the computer, but even as her fingers flew over the keyboard, the clues were beginning to download in her brain: Blumka Von Taschelt 1934–1938, the Anschluss 1938; Travers et Fils; the empty drawers . . .

'So Flora, what have you got for me?' Angus asked cheerily, throwing his feet up on the desk as he plunged his sterling silver 'office' fork into a superfood breakfast pot.

'Travers's father was Von Taschelt's notary.'

She might as well have just shot him. Angus immediately spluttered, coughing on a pomegranate seed. He opened his mouth to protest but she held up a hand to stop him.

'And before you say it – no, it's not a coincidence.'

'It's not?' he croaked hoarsely, thumping himself several times on the chest to dislodge it.

'It would be if there ever had been a man called François Vermeil. But I've just searched the death records in the national archive and no one called François Vermeil, married to a woman called Magda, with a son called Jacques, died in Paris in 1943.'

There was a very long silence, Angus's face completely devoid of colour. 'What are you saying, Flora?'

She held up the fingers of one hand and began counting them off. 'I'm saying that if we looked in the national archives of Austria, we'd find a marriage licence between a woman called Magda and Franz Von Taschelt.'

Angus burst out laughing but there was no mirth in his eyes. In fact, he looked scared. 'Maybe we would. Maybe it's a common name there. But why would we look in Austria?'

Flora held up her second finger. 'Because before Galerie Von Taschelt opened in Paris in 1938, it operated in Vienna as Blumka Von Taschelt. It closed when they fled Vienna the year of the Anschluss, and reopened as Galerie Von Taschelt when they settled in Paris. You may recall the codicil was in German. Well it was actually Austrian German. Odd, for a Frenchman, don't you think?'

She held up a third finger. 'After his death in 1943, the gallery reopened in the South of France as Attlee and Bergurren. Bergurren is Magda's sister's married name. It's on a letter I found in the apartment.' She couldn't believe she hadn't made that connection before now, the letter forgotten and still in her jeans pocket.

She held up a fourth finger. 'The initials. F.V.T. and F.V. Hardly a world away. She just . . . *Frenched* his name. It's easier to keep a lie if you keep it as close as possible to the truth.'

Angus looked as though he was going to pass out and she felt genuinely relieved that he was already sitting down. 'Flora, I don't . . . ' he mumbled, his voice barely coherent.

'Angus, listen to me,' she said, knowing she had to spell it out. 'There's no birth *or* death record of a François Vermeil, and this French family's will is written in German, not French. The business is now in Magda's sister's name in the South of France, ten miles from where Magda is still alive and well and living in Antibes. You know what I'm telling you here. François Vermeil didn't deal with a Nazi. He *was* the Nazi. He's Franz Von Taschelt.'

Chapter Sixteen

Flora stood on the steps of the town house, looking up at the tall silvered windows that reflected the neighbouring buildings back to themselves, the lives it contained and the secrets they owned safely hidden behind the glass. How was she supposed to say what had to be said to these people? Why did it have to come down to her to reveal that their elite social standing was built on corruption and ruination? That there was blood on their hands? That they would be damned to hell once this got out? And it would. If *she* could find it out, anyone with an agenda against them would cleave it wide open in half the time it had taken her.

But there was no one else to do it. Even Angus, never slow to cross the Atlantic in a single bound, couldn't get here in time for this meeting.

The butler had already opened the door and was standing inside, the hole like a yawning black chasm in the grand Haussmann frontage. Slowly, she walked up the steps and into the mirrored hall. She had been here several times now in the past couple of weeks but familiarity with the surroundings didn't make them any less imposing and she found she couldn't meet her own eye in the many reflections winking back at her. How was this a home? There was more heart in the Louvre.

She walked with her face down, anticipating the butler taking her to the formal salon where Lilian and Jacques received most of their guests, so she was surprised when he headed right instead and led her down a wide pale-grey corridor along which ornamental pear trees were dotted. They entered a room that wasn't a room, more a holding chamber lined with a hand-painted silk Chinese garden scene and a large round table in the middle, adorned with tumbling white orchids. Behind it, on the opposite side, was a glossy chestnut-coloured door, firmly shut.

Flora looked at the butler. 'Here?'

'*Suivez-moi, s'il vous plaît,*' he intoned, leading her to the door.

Flora swallowed nervously, just able to make out Jacques Vermeil's languid drawl on the other side of it.

She rolled her lips together, took a deep breath and squeezed her eyes shut. When she opened them again, the door was open – and the entire Vermeil family, along with Lionel Travers, was staring at her.

Her stomach plunged.

'*Entrez*, please,' Lilian entreated warmly, motioning for her to enter as Flora found her feet wouldn't move. The sight of Natascha and Xavier – both of them sprawled on the sofa like teenagers at an Xbox – made her feel ambushed. Why were *they* here? Why today, at this meeting? All the courage she'd been trying to build up in the cab on the way over deserted her as she walked in, a weak smile plastered on her face.

The room was no less grand than any of the others she had seen but there were no mirrors in here; there were more photographs, the fabrics heavy-duty linens rather than brocaded silks, the colour palette a more contemporary graphite and white, thick plumes of white hydrangeas sitting like giant snowballs in their vases. It wasn't 'cosy', per se, but it was a vastly more private, intimate space than the formal salon and she realized she had been admitted to the inner sanctum. They considered her, if not a friend now, certainly an ally, someone on their side. She could almost cry from the irony alone.

Natascha, sitting huddled and sideways on the sofa, burrowing her bare feet into the cushions, watched her suspiciously, one eyebrow arched disdainfully as she took in Flora's conservative clothes. (Flora would like to know what she'd wear for a meeting with her mother, in the same circumstances.) By comparison, Natascha was wearing ripped-at-the-knee skinny jeans and a thin vest – no bra of course – threaded bracelets stacked up her arms, her fingernails painted olive green, her long hair piled on her head in a messy topknot.

Xavier, beside her, was no better. In jeans and a linen shirt so crumpled that it looked as though he'd driven over it on his bike, one ankle thrown over the opposite knee, his arms spread over the back of the sofa, he seemed to take up half the space – if not all the air – in the room, watching her cross the floor and take her seat, the way a lion watches an antelope.

'Don't look so scared, Flora,' Lilian laughed as she and Jacques rose to shake her hand. 'When I spoke to Angus the other day, he said we had made the deadline for the Christie's sale so we thought it would be good to share this happy news with Xavier and Natascha. They have been so interested in the discovery, wanting to know all about it, as you know –' she smiled, somewhat apologetically, Flora thought – 'so we thought it would be better if they heard what you have to report directly.'

'Of course,' Flora nodded, trying to smile, her mouth suddenly so dry that her tongue felt it would stick to the roof of her mouth. 'Yes. Uh, do you mind if I . . . ?' she asked, indicating the jug of iced water and glasses on the coffee table. There was a bottle of Laurent-Perrier champagne in an ice bucket next to it but Flora couldn't even bear to look at it. They wouldn't be opening that today, that was for sure.

Quickly she poured herself some water, aware of a bemused expression on Jacques Vermeil's face as she drank it down in great gulps. She replaced her glass and pressed the back of her hand to her wet lips and waited a moment, knowing from the expectant silence that they were all waiting for her to begin her presentation. Had they noticed she was empty-handed? Did they suspect her lack of props indicated that something was amiss?

She looked over at Travers for help, guidance, *something*, but he held her gaze for only a moment before turning away and a shot of anger arrowed through her. It gave her courage.

She sat in the only remaining armchair, back straight, ankles together, like a Victorian schoolmistress. 'Does the name Franz Von Taschelt mean anything to you?' she began, keeping her gaze squarely on the senior Vermeils but noticing in her peripheral vision how Lionel Travers's head whipped round at the sound of that name.

Both Jacques and Lilian shook their heads, faces blank but curiosity piqued. '*Non.* Who is he?' Jacques asked, his brown eyes alight.

'He was an Austrian art dealer who left Vienna after the Anschluss in 1938 and relocated to Paris.'

Jacques shrugged. 'I have never heard of him.'

'Well, his name kept coming up in our preliminary searches – the Renoir, the Faucheux, the more minor Picasso and Matisse sketches . . . he was the last-known, proven owner of the paintings.'

'Proven?' Lilian squinted, clearly not liking the sound of the word, nor the way Flora placed a stress on it.

'Proven in that there was no further paperwork showing that he had sold the paintings *on*,' she explained hesitantly.

Frowns buckled every brow.

'I know, we couldn't understand it either. It didn't quite add up,' Flora said hastily, sliding an accusing stare in Travers's direction. She swallowed hard. 'Until we made another discovery this morning.'

No one said anything but Flora could see that the lawyer was now as alert as a gundog on the peg. She could well imagine his terror at being found out for having deceived them all for so long. But she didn't care about him or his self-serving interests.

'The . . . uh . . . discrepancies that we found prompted me to make some enquiries outside the usual realms we deal with.' It was true that she had never had cause to check the veracity of the identity of her client before. 'I'm afraid there's no easy way to say this.'

She stopped and took a breath. Once she dismantled this seventy-three-year-old lie, would it break up the family it had been supposed to bond together?

'. . . There is no record, that we can find, of a man called François Vermeil.'

There followed an astounded silence, one so deafening

she swore she could hear the woodworm turning in the joists, the roosting pigeons on the sills ruffling their feathers.

'I . . . I know that is a truly shocking thing to say,' she said quickly, holding her hands up for calm as she saw each and every person's jaw begin to drop open as the words hit home. She looked straight at Jacques. 'But I'm afraid everything is pointing to the fact that the man – your father – known as François Vermeil, was in fact Franz Von Taschelt.'

Another rolling silence and then:

'Why?' a voice thundered. 'Why would he do that?'

It was Natascha, already on her feet, already in attack mode.

Flora flinched. 'I believe it must have been done for personal safety.' She looked back at Jacques. 'Your parents had already fled the Nazis once, leaving Vienna to settle in Paris. Your mother managed to make it to safety but when Franz, François . . .' she stammered. 'When he died, I believe your grandmother changed her name to try to escape attention.'

'What kind of attention?' Lilian demanded, her voice diamond-hard. 'If she was already safe . . . ?'

Flora felt herself quail as the high emotions charged the room. 'Franz Von Taschelt is acknowledged as a known dealer for the Third Reich.'

The sound of laughter, as sudden as it was booming, made them all turn in shock. Jacques Vermeil, still sitting in his chair, was slapping his thigh, his head thrown back.

'I . . .' Flora didn't know what to say. She stared at her hands. 'I'm sorry.'

'Mam'selle Sykes! Flora!' Jacques chuckled. 'I have never in my life heard anything so funny. My father with a different name? My father *a Nazi*? Do you know who we are, the work we do?'

She swallowed. 'Yes.'

'She's a liar!' Natascha roared, advancing towards her with an open hand, but Xavier caught her by the elbow and pulled her back onto the sofa.

'Don't,' he murmured, his voice perversely soft in the circumstances, his eyes like black stars upon Flora, directing a calm anger towards her that was more terrifying than any of Natascha's flailing and screaming histrionics. If he did believe what she was saying, then he hated her more than ever for saying it, for being the one to break this to them.

'But you know she's making it up!' Natascha protested, trying to wriggle free. 'She's trying to discredit us! Humiliate us! There's no—'

'Natascha!' Lilian screeched, shaking her head in despair, her face drooping with anguish. 'Just for once, control yourself, you wretched girl!'

'It's true.'

They all turned in astonishment to find Travers standing in his corner of the room, his calm a counterpoint to the passions raging around him. Flora stared at him in surprise. She hadn't expected him to admit it.

'It is why your mother was so desperate that you *not* enter the apartment,' he said quietly and with exceptional understatement. 'Everything she did was done – as Mam'selle Sykes has said – for your personal safety.' He gestured a hand towards Flora as though she was his collaborator, an ally working with him.

Jacques' expression changed completely. Flora's theory he could dismiss as fantasy, the well-intentioned but misguided mistake of a young, naive stranger. But his lawyer?

The man who had spent his entire career – like his father before him – working for and protecting his family?

'Leo,' Jacques protested, his skin paling to ash grey. 'What are you saying? You cannot mean that—'

'She is right, yes.' Travers looked directly at Flora. 'That day in my office, *mam'selle* – you were also correct about the missing papers. *I* had to remove them from the desk after you had left the apartment. The letter sent to our company from the intruders addressed the owners as Von Taschelt so I had to assume there was paperwork in the study from my father which identified us all. Naturally, I was under instruction to ensure that did not happen.'

Flora stared at him, having guessed as much, but she was still stunned – and suspicious – to hear him admit it. 'So then why didn't you just remove the paperwork *before* we went in?'

'My hand had been forced, *mam'selle*. The letter was forwarded to the family by a junior who did not know of the existence of the codicil, much less the specifics within it. By the time I knew what had happened, the family knew too and you had already been called. There was no time. I had to hope that you would be so distracted by the collection you found there that you wouldn't think to open the drawers. Or at least, not immediately anyway.'

Flora stared at him, trying to suss his game. He was saying everything she had painstakingly worked out herself as she separated the truth from his lies; he was confirming her hunches, playing the ally again, but she wouldn't be fooled a second time.

'I'm afraid I don't believe you,' she replied coolly. 'If the intruders saw from the papers that the owners were Von Taschelt and sent the note on to you, how did a junior, who you say supposedly knew nothing about the will or codicil, know to forward it here to a family of an entirely different name?'

It was the very question, the red thread, that had led to her unravelling the secret just a few short hours ago. He would have needed Vermeil's real name to be kept hidden at all costs; he could not possibly have afforded for anyone else to have known.

Travers shrugged.'Because it is on our computer system.'

'Your system?' Lilian repeated, shocked. 'You mean the information was just sitting there? Just *anyone* could see that the estate belonging to Franz Von Taschelt now belonged to François Vermeil?'

'No. Only those associates working directly with me had access to those files, *madame*. In total, two people.'

'But if they saw the name—'

'It means nothing to them, *madame*. Why should it? Estates pass through different names in the same family – via marriage – all the time, and the associate in question here is a twenty-three-year-old law graduate. The name of a Nazi art dealer from the Second World War means nothing to him and it shall remain that way. There is no reason why it should be recognized by anyone outside the sphere of art history, a small and closed world indeed.'

Travers looked back at Flora. 'It was not my intention to deceive you, *mam'selle*, only to act according to the strict and very clear wishes of our client.' Then he turned back to Jacques. 'Jacques, I am sorry. I had no choice.'

Jacques, by now leaning forward with his head in his hands, let out a small groan. 'No. No.'

Lilian rose in a fluid movement, and smoothing her narrow skirt distractedly, began to pace, wringing her hands.

'How can this be? How can this be? You are telling me we . . . we are not Vermeils, but Von . . . Von . . . ?'

'Von Taschelt,' Travers finished for her.

A sob escaped her and she slapped a slim hand over her mouth, eyes pressed shut. 'Is it legal, our name?' she asked finally. 'Who have I married? Are my children living with names that are not recognized in law?'

'Lilian, it was the war. Hundreds of thousands of people were displaced, emigrated, changed their names, tried to start afresh – nearly all of them Jewish families.'

'But I don't understand!' she cried. 'How can it be so easy to just . . . change your name like that, change your entire identity?'

'It was not easy. What Jacques' father had to do to secure that liberty for his family. He . . . he . . .'

Jacques looked up, then stood. 'He what? Say it, man. How did he save his family, when so many others couldn't?'

Travers swallowed, looking down. 'He cooperated.'

'Cooperated,' Jacques nodded, agitatedly, his hands planted aggressively on his hips. 'You mean he worked with them? He worked for them! He was one of them!'

'No—'

'No? Do you think I am a fool, Leo? Do you think I don't know what happened to those poor families? She's just told us he was a known dealer. He . . . he would have . . . *robbed* them. For his own profit!'

'For his own protection,' Travers said quickly. '*Your* protection.'

'No!' Jacques shouted. 'He got rich, made this fortune robbing those people of their assets whilst saving his own skin, knowing they were the only bartering tools they would have had – knowing he was trapping them in a country without any means of escape. No negotiation, no deals, just a one-way train ticket to the labour camps!' he cried, his voice breaking. 'My God, he was one of them.'

He dropped back into the chair as though he'd been cut at the knees, his face hidden in his hands, his huge shoulders heaving. Lilian came and perched on the seat beside him, her bony knees pressed against his thighs as she gently rubbed his back.

'How many people know about this?' she asked quietly, her own composure recovered in the face of her husband's distress.

'No one but us,' Flora said. 'And Angus, of course. I told him just before I left to come here.'

'Leo?' Lilian asked.

'Just me. My father entrusted me alone with the knowledge when I graduated into the company.'

She nodded and stared at a spot on the wall for a few moments. 'Then that is how it shall stay. We withdraw the Renoir from the sale. We don't sell a single thing – not so much as a button – from that apartment.' She enunciated every word with crystalline clarity. 'We just close it up again and continue as before.'

'How can we?' Natascha cried. 'Everything's changed!'

'Nothing has changed,' her mother replied, even more quietly. 'We are the same people we were an hour ago. Your father doesn't remember his father. Why should he bear the burden of his mistakes?'

No one said a word. It was true – but naive, surely, to think they could continue as before?

Flora glanced over at Xavier, wondering why he didn't say anything. He never said anything. He was the only person in the room who hadn't reacted. Was he made of stone? Was he still there?

He was standing by the window, his back to them, hands thrust in his jeans pockets and his head bent. The sunlight caught his profile and for a moment – just one – she saw something different in him: not the taunting arrogance or defiant anger or mocking haughtiness of their previous encounters, but something pale and unvoiced. A vulnerability.

'Xavier.'

He lifted his head at the sound of his mother's voice, his eyes catching on Flora's as he turned, and she glimpsed again what had shimmered between them last night in that split second before she had decided his agenda was capricious, when he'd asked the simple question, 'Do you need a ride?'

He blinked, looked away, walked over to Lilian. 'Yes?'

'You are to go to Antibes. I want you to speak to your grandmother.'

'Mother—'

'Listen to me, Xavier, you are the only one. You are close to her, she will talk to you.'

'What about me?' Natascha demanded, her body tense as she sat forward. 'Why don't you ask me to go?'

Lilian glanced at her for a beat, before looking back to Xavier. 'It is clear now why she has been so determined we were not to go to the apartment. She never wanted to be the one to tell your father the truth. She is ashamed.'

'Which is why it is between them. She owes Father the truth.'

'She will never do that. She would never hurt him. Your father is her only child, her obsession. We all know she barely tolerates me for taking him away from her.' She allowed a half-smile to stretch her lips as she reached for his hand. 'I need you to speak to her, find out what happened before it is too late. She is old and her health is not good – we must have answers.' She squeezed his hand. 'Tell me you'll go?'

Xavier stared down at her, the pulse visible in his neck. He nodded, barely.

Natascha sank back in the cushions as though she'd been pushed, her jaw thrust forward as she began to pick at her nail polish.

'What would you like me to do with the collection?' Flora asked quietly, into the silence.

Lilian looked over at her, as though surprised to find her still there. 'You must continue researching it. If we cannot sell it, we at least need to know exactly what it is that we now possess – whether we like it or not.'

'Of course,' Flora replied, feeling faintly nauseous at the thought of discovering the individual horror stories of these appropriated works. To whom had they belonged? In what circumstances had they been sold? She remembered Angus's expression again, as the realization had hit – the entire col-lection had become worthless at a stroke; they couldn't even donate pieces to any museums, not without the provenance being established all over again. If this secret was going to stay in the family, the collection would need to stay hidden.

'It is imperative that the information we've been given today never leaves this room,' Lilian said briskly. 'Do you understand?'

Flora and Travers nodded.

'Natascha?' her mother enquired in a firm voice when the girl remained silent. '*Do you understand?* This is not something for you to gossip about with your friends, do you hear me?'

Natascha rolled her eyes, which her mother seemed to take as a yes.

'Come.' Lilian helped Jacques to stand. 'This has been a great shock.' She looked across at Flora. 'Excuse us, we need some time alone to process this.'

'I understand,' Flora said, standing too and stepping back slightly to allow them to pass, noticing the beads of condensation slipping down the neck of the unopened champagne bottle.

Something seemed suddenly to occur to Lilian and she stopped walking and looked over at Flora. 'I want you to take the collection to Antibes. Work on it down there.'

Flora's eyebrows shot up. 'W-what? All of it?'

'Yes.'

Flora swallowed. 'But why there?'

'I want my mother-in-law to see it, I want her to *trip* over her past . . .' She paused, lost in thought. 'I want her to face up to what she's done. Whatever they did, they did it together.'

And she turned and led her husband away, Travers following almost on their heels.

Flora found herself alone in the room with Natascha and Xavier, a curl already on Natascha's lip. But before she could say a word, throw an insult or a cushion, Xavier spoke first.

'Go.'

Flora looked between the two of them. 'I'm . . . I'm so sorry.'

'Are you?' he asked, a scathing note in his voice matching the curl of his lip. She heard the blame, saw the shame in his eyes.

'You heard my brother,' Natascha hissed. 'Get out of our house. Or isn't this sufficient for you?'

Flora dropped her head and hurried out. It didn't matter what she said. Words weren't ever going to be enough.

Chapter Seventeen

'So, is this business or pleasure?' she asked as Noah stopped in front of her, looking fine in a cream suit and panama, one hand in his trouser pocket. 'Because I need to know whether I'm off-duty or not.'

He smiled, the corners of his blue eyes crinkling gently. 'Well, now that depends. You see, I need both a car *and* a lunch date, and you struck me as the perfect person for both.'

Flora laughed. 'I can't say that classic cars are my area of expertise. If you're serious about buying today, you'd have been better off with Angus.'

'Oh, I sincerely doubt *that*,' he quipped, giving her a blatant once-over in her lemons-and-oranges printed D&G dress that answered her question quite definitively. 'I think we'll just go with whatever looks best with you sitting in it,' he said, placing a hand lightly on the small of her back as they began to walk.

She chuckled, the very suggestion amusing. He was joking – right?

It was a crisp day, the clear sky foreshortening their shadows on the ground. Flora thought there was probably no more magical setting to enjoy the classic car market than here in the grand gardens of the Chantilly estate, where pleached trees were planted in long avenues and the frothy fancies of the baroque architecture were so beautiful as to be rendered not just once, but twice, reflected perfectly in the marble-still moats. What car could possibly be more appropriate to crunch over this gravel than a Bugatti or Bentley?

She herself had come by limo. Noah had travelled here straight from the airport but had sent a car to collect her in Paris and it was as well he had; the showdown with the Vermeils yesterday had overwritten everything else in her mind and she'd not only forgotten to cancel the date, she'd also forgotten all about the date until the driver had knocked early that morning, robbing her of another much-needed lie-in.

She glanced at him as they dawdled through the displays, feeling like a fraud for being here at all. She wasn't interested in him; he'd just been in the right place at the right time in Vienna, he'd called at the right time in the rain . . . She was here *with* him, but she wasn't here *because* of him; his presence was incidental to her.

And yet, it wasn't a chore to be in his company. He was funny, good-looking, attentive, intelligent; all the things her mother would be buying a new hat for. What could she say? She liked him, only liked him. It was the same old story.

The crowd was moving in a vaguely one-way system around the parked classic cars, people – mainly men – peering closer to read the detailed histories of each one, hands hovering longingly over the don't-touch, polished paintwork, eyes narrowing in appreciation of the hand-stitched leathers. She and Noah allowed themselves to be swept up in the drift, meandering, almost lazily, around the *concours*, her scuffing at the grass with her feet as they talked, Noah making witty wisecracks that prompted her to touch his arm as she laughed. They began to relax, Noah leaning in to her, their fingers brushing as they examined a brake light or steering wheel or brightly polished alloy.

It was another day of steaming temperatures and she took off her shoes after a while, allowing her bare feet to sink into the lawn as Noah lingered over the Bentley R-Type Continental with Mulliner Park Ward coachwork, imploring her to stand by the Jaguar XK120 with closed-in wheels for a photograph as she, giggling, protested. He won in the end, but only after she stole his hat and peered out from under the brim with a coy smile.

They walked some more, the sun beating in a constant pulse, and she stood still as he applied sun lotion to her shoulders, a kindness that felt strangely intimate amidst the milling crowds, every person there from the same tribe – scented and silken in expensive creams, low-key in clothes that started in the early thousands.

'It's hot. What do you think? A drink to cool us down before the auction begins?' he asked, jerking his chin in the direction of the chateau.

'Lovely.'

They walked towards the dramatically sweeping steps that had once been trodden by ladies in satin shoes and pompadour dresses and were today dotted with the well heeled sitting with their catalogues and engaging in laughing conversations. Champagne bars were set out along the terrace, Bonhams banners flickering in the breeze, all the shaded tables already taken.

'Try and find somewhere for us to sit,' Noah said. 'I'll bring the drinks over.'

Flora smiled and turned to find a spot, just as she heard her name called. She looked up to see Max St John, head of

Vintage and Prestige Car sales at Bonhams and a former associate of her father's, walking towards her. She went to call Noah back – this would be a worthwhile introduction for them both – but he had already disappeared into the crowd.

'Flora Sykes, what a delightful surprise,' he boomed. 'Had I known you were coming I'd have arranged special passes for you.'

'Well, I'm here in more of a personal capacity today,' she replied as he kissed her enthusiastically on both cheeks.

'Even so, you should always let me know. How's your pater? Retirement suiting him?'

She pulled a face. 'So-so. I think he misses the hubbub of the salesroom.'

'I quite understand. He's only a few years advanced of me and I can't . . .' He looked out at the champagne-quaffing, silken throngs. 'Well, I can't imagine not being a part of all this.'

'I can't imagine it either. You've done such an amazing job. What a coup! The setting's just perfect, and the calibre of the cars you've attracted. You even booked the weather . . .' She shrugged as a sleek brunette with glossed limbs wearing a jade-green silk dress and black Dior straw hat glided past. 'It couldn't be more perfect.'

'Have you seen anything you like?' he asked, waving an arm to encompass the exhibition of cars arranged on the lawns below them.

'Me personally? Plenty,' she smiled. 'But it's not going to be happening any time soon. I think I'll still be bombing about in my Mini for a while yet.'

He laughed, leaning in to her more closely. 'I say though,

fine art's your bag – what do you make of all this Von Taschelt business, eh? There's a turn-up for the books!'

Flora felt her blood freeze in her veins, the world spin a little more slowly, at the very mention of that name. 'Sorry, Max, I . . . I don't follow.'

St John lowered his head, and his voice. 'The *Vanity Fair* piece. Haven't you seen it?'

Flora slapped a hand to her mouth, not sure she wasn't going to throw up. No, she hadn't seen it but she immediately knew what had happened: Stefan. The filler article. The Urban Explorers . . . What had he done?

'Oh, don't worry, you're not behind the curve. It only hit the stands this morning.'

'What did it say?' she asked.

'Have a read for yourself. They've got some copies behind that hospitality stand over there. Don't get too excited – it's not a big piece, only a page or so, but it's going to make a splash here today, I should wager.'

A man, passing by, laid a friendly hand on Max's shoulder and he turned. 'Oh, hello, Rick. How are you? Do you know—'

Flora took her opportunity to escape. 'Hello,' she nodded quickly, before smiling and kissing Max goodbye. 'I'd better go and check out that thing we were talking about . . .'

'Absolutely! Lovely to see you! Let me know you're coming next time!' he called after her as she skittered away and over to the pale-blue tented stand.

Flora found several copies fanned on a wicker coffee table. She grabbed one, flicking through the pages, her breath coming fast and shallow. She needed to know what they'd said.

It didn't take long to find the article. They had used an

old paparazzi picture of the family at a society event, taken a couple of years back judging by the length of Natascha's hair. They were all in black tie, Lilian shimmering in pale Armani, Natascha in a skin-tight Balmain dress with heavily kohl'd eyes, Jacques like a retired Hollywood actor with his crinkled suavity, Xavier like a panther in his narrow-cut black jacket as he stared up from beneath his heavy brows. God, did he *ever* smile?

They looked very rich and very unhappy, Flora thought. There were other smaller photos too – of Lilian and the President's wife, photographed together at Roland-Garros; Natascha dishevelled and head down as she stumbled out of a club, flashing her knickers (at least she was wearing some); Xavier flipping the bird from his scooter – no helmet again – a beautiful brunette riding pilion; Jacques crossing the road with a woman who wasn't Lilian, her hand looped through his arm, a small red Cartier bag in his hand.

But it was the headline that made her gasp: *The Hypocritic Oath!* She hadn't noticed it at first, her eye instantly drawn to the pictures of this photogenic, broken family, but it was unambiguous. She scanned the text quickly. *How?* How could they have known all this? They knew more than she did!

Her hands shaking, she delved into her bag and retrieved her phone, finding Stefan's number.

He picked up after one ring.

'*Salut?*'

'Stefan?'

'Yeah? . . . Flora!' His panic and the ensuing silence – loud as a gunshot – confirmed her hunch. Her anger exploded as she felt his shock reverberate down the line.

'You bastard! How could you do this to me?'

'Listen—'

'No! You used me! You took information that was confidential, information that was shared between friends, and you used it for your own selfish ends! Fuck it if I lose my job, right?'

'You don't understand.'

'I understand it fine! I understand perfectly! You had an opportunity to hit back at a guy you considered to have slighted you and you took it – to hell with anyone else if they get in the way. What do they call that? Collateral damage, yeah? You *knew* how big this project is for me. I trusted you!'

'Look, I didn't plan it like this, OK? I thought it was just going to be a case of name-dropping the Vermeils. When you said the apartment belonged to a client of yours, I guessed that was who you meant; you had already told me you were working for them so it was just something to put their names in there and make the article look better. I was desperate. But you know what our legal team's like, Flora. Our researchers are on steroids! Nothing goes through till every fact has been checked and checked again.'

Flora didn't reply. She rubbed her temples. She had the beginnings of a headache coming on.

'We had the pictures of the apartment but we had to double-check who owned it; families like the Vermeils sue for smaller mistakes than that. But when it came back with Von Taschelt's name on the deeds . . . what could I do?'

Flora closed her eyes, able to see how they'd worked it out: like her, they'd discovered there was no François Vermeil and never had been, the two men's histories converging at the date when the apartment was closed up, one man appearing on the face of the earth just as suddenly as the other was wiped from it. 'Come on! It's a fucking sensation, Flora! I had to do my job. They are hypocrites! The public has a right to know.'

She didn't say anything. She couldn't. She felt literally mute with rage.

'Look, you're my friend and I like you, Flora. A lot. You *know* I do.' The stress in his words told her exactly how he liked her. 'But I'm a journalist. We would have got there with or without your help. We *were* getting there. We already had the photos . . . Please, I wasn't trying to hurt *you—*'

'It's not just about me, you fool! You've got no idea of what you've done,' she said, her voice like a whipcrack down the line. 'Not just to their reputation but to the charities they support, all the good they do. Everyone will turn their backs now. They'll have to or be accused of hypocrisy.'

There was a half-pause.

'I'm sorry about that. But all I have done is tell the truth.'

'Oh, yeah? And what good has it done? No one benefits from this, Stefan! No one but you and your fucking magazine sales! I could lose my job over this. I only found it out myself yesterday! I only told *them* yesterday. They'll know it came from me.'

'But it didn't,' he argued.

'It did and it didn't. Are you going to reveal your sources to them? Are you going to tell them it *wasn't* me that told you?'

There was a long pause this time. 'No.'

She gave a contemptuous snort.

'Flora, I'm sorry. Tell me how I can make it up to you.'

'Fuck you, Stefan!'

She hung up and leaned against the wall, her limbs tremulous from the adrenalin. She was screwed and the family was damned. The secret was out now in the most terrible of ways, printed and distributed around the world and they wouldn't be able to take out an injunction against it or sue, because it was all true – every single word. Lilian had been right about everything but one – the sins of the father *will* be visited on the children.

Noah was standing at the top of the steps, a champagne bucket under one arm, two flutes in the opposite hand, scouring the crowds for her when she walked back over.

'There you are, I was—' He stopped, taking in her pallor. 'Hey, are you feeling all right?'

'Uh, I'm not . . . No, I don't think I am, to be honest.' She wanted to get out of here. She couldn't stand to be here any more.

'Perhaps you've had too much sun?' he asked, taking her gently by the elbow and leading her towards the nearest table. Without hesitation, he approached the couple sitting there. 'I'm sorry, my friend's feeling unwell. Would you mind if we—'

He didn't need to finish the sentence; they were up and offering their seats in a flash.

'Thank you,' Flora smiled wanly, not sure if she might throw up.

A shrill laugh made her look up. A group of twenty-somethings were racing across the lawns, bare legs flashing as the girls tucked their skirts in their knickers and ran barefoot, the guys' shirt tails untucked as they chased after them. Flora looked away, feeling too miserable to cope with them right n—

Oh God, no!

She looked up again as she realized who she'd seen, her stomach lurching so violently at the sight of Xavier and Natascha Vermeil that she actually heaved forwards, slapping a hand over her mouth.

'Jesus, Flora, I think we should get you lying down somewhere. You really don't look well.'

But she barely heard him. She couldn't take her eyes off the rowdy group now, watching as a couple of wardens held their arms out to stop their stampede towards the lakes and herded them towards the steps instead, away from the cars. The *concours* was about to begin.

They dropped out of her sight below the steps for a moment but Flora could still hear them – the dominating laughter, bitchy comments – and then they were back in view, a muster of brightly coloured peacocks on the top steps. They spotted an older couple sitting at one of the larger tables, 'saving places' most likely, and plonked themselves down without asking, so that the older couple were effectively hustled off. The guys sat slouched in the chairs, legs spread, as the girls got out their phones and started taking selfies. Natascha Vermeil had her back to Flora's table but Xavier was sitting in profile to her, one arm outstretched on the table as he silently surveyed the cars being reversed off the lawns.

The whine of a tannoy whistled around the park, making everyone stop in their tracks – although seemingly, most of them had been stopped by the clique of socialites anyway – as Max St John took to a small podium on the lawn, opposite the steps.

'Ladies and gentlemen,' he began in flawless French, in his element as he addressed the crowd . . .

'Could I wear your hat? I'm . . . I think I have caught too much sun,' she said quickly, knowing she needed to remain out of sight.

'Of course,' Noah said, rushing to help, eager to be of assistance in any way he could. (God, her mother would just love him.)

Flora put on the hat and kept the brim dipped low. She couldn't cope with the thought of the Vermeils seeing her here. Did they know? They must know! Surely people in their circle must know by now . . . phones would be ringing . . .

But then again, if they *did* know, surely they wouldn't come somewhere like this? They wouldn't be laughing and braying and bringing attention to themselves, hijacking the sale as though it was their own private party, even if it was patently clear they could afford every lot here.

No, they didn't know. Not yet.

Flora closed her eyes, wondering how the hell she could get past without them noticing. The only way back to the car park was via the steps and she couldn't bear to think of how Natascha, in particular, would react, here in public with her friends, her clique – although she could well imagine.

The guttural thunder of a V8 rolling up the gravel drive drew shouts of admiration as the *Concours d'Élégance* began, each of the cars up for grabs doing the automotive equivalent of a beauty parade, showing off its curves and moves for the cheering crowd.

Noah, looking anxiously between her and the catwalking cars, laid a hand over hers on the table. 'Do you want to get out of here? We don't need to stay.'

'No, it's fine. You said you liked the pale blue Bugatti.'

He'd already told her he'd been waiting nine years for one of this model to come to sale. 'You've got to bid.'

He shrugged. 'I still can. I can register my top bid and they can notify me later. I'm more concerned about getting you somewhere you can rest.'

The Vermeils' group gave a roar of laughter at something one of them had said. Even Xavier, sitting in profile to her, was smiling. The sight of it was arresting. It changed his face completely. She had almost begun to believe it wasn't physically possible.

But he wouldn't be smiling if he saw her . . . She looked back at Noah, feeling ever more desperate. 'Well, if you're sure you don't mind . . .'

Noah patted her hand. 'I'll be right back. Don't go anywhere.'

Flora sat back in the seat, her chin down, trying to hide even as she strained to hear what it was on that table that they were all finding so amusing.

The bidding had begun and Flora listened with interest as the numbers rose in steady increments. It wasn't the same level as the art market – even the rarest car was never going to break into that league, but there was parity with the wine market perhaps, another solid returns portfolio for the serious investor.

The Vermeils' crowd were throwing their bids into the ring of course. Flora wouldn't be surprised if they were just bidding to drive up the prices for a laugh.

Flora watched them – well, him – from under her brim. She couldn't make him out. He seemed somehow on the outside of the circle, smiling at the jokes but not appearing to make any, everyone directing the conversation to him even though he barely said anything, his concentration more on the actual sales action than the girl to his right who kept looking over at him and rubbing his thigh. Flora watched, unable not to. She couldn't remember – was that the girl who'd run into her on the steps? His girlfriend, the passionate one he kept breaking up – and then making up – with?

An oxblood Aston Martin DB2/4 Mark 1 that Noah had admired earlier came to a stop at the podium and Max began to sell, using the same mix of humour and clubby, inclusive tone that had always been her father's trademark. She looked around for Noah, desperate to get away from here, but her arm caught her champagne glass as she twisted round and it shattered on the limestone flags.

Flora froze as everyone turned to see what had happened. Mortified, she moved to try to pick up the larger shards but waiters were by her side with brushes and pans within moments, ushering her back into her chair, worrying she might cut herself.

She apologized, glancing up in embarrassment – and found he had seen her. She sank back into her chair, unable to look away, feeling the blood draining from her as what she knew that he did not ran through her mind again; she knew how much blacker that look was going to become.

'Sorry about that. Tedious paperwork, took longer than I thought,' Noah said, rejoining her, one hand on her shoulder, sweeping up to cup her neck. 'Oh, what happened here?'

The waiters finished sweeping up and said they would bring a replacement glass over.

Noah sat down, grasping her hand and holding it in his. 'How are you feeling now?'

Flora, wrenching her gaze away from Xavier, looked back at him. '. . . Sorry?'

'You're still very pale.'

'Yes, I . . . uh . . .' She looked across to Xavier again. He was still staring and she felt her mouth dry up again, her stomach plunge, as though her world was made of paper and he was punching a hole through it.

What? She wanted to scream at him. *What do you want from me?*

He looked away, raising his arm in the same moment, jaw thrust forward.

'Thank you!' Max cried delightedly from the podium. 'A new bidder, ladies and gentlemen! Do I have two three thirty?'

Flora blinked at Xavier's sudden action. What was he doing? Did he actually want that car? Did he even know which car he was bidding on?

She watched as he raised his hand again. And then again.

'That price is getting toppy,' Noah murmured, watching interestedly as the bids were batted back and forth like a tennis ball over a net.

Flora couldn't speak. She just watched as Xavier raised his hand again and again. She recognized the body language – auctions were her lifeblood, she knew exactly how to read the players in them and he wasn't going to back down, she knew. This wasn't about buying. It was about winning.

But winning what? She didn't think it was that car.

When the gavel finally did come down, the Vermeils' party were on their feet, cheering, Xavier himself completely still as they all smacked him on the back, tousled his hair, the girl on his right leaning in to nuzzle his cheek.

'A new world record, ladies and gentlemen!' Max cried, more excited than anyone.

'Well, he'd better hold on to it for a while,' Noah said, unimpressed. 'I don't see it appreciating beyond that price for quite some time. He must have really wanted it to pay that.' He looked at Flora. 'Your colour's a bit better.'

'Is it?' She realized she'd been holding her breath.

'Still want to go?'

She glanced at Xavier's table again. A man was walking towards them, something in his hand. She felt her jaw drop open as he approached.

No, wait . . .

'Congratulations!' the man said loudly. 'That's quite a bidding arm you've got there.'

Xavier, still seated, nodded back at him. He looked wary.

The man gave a laugh, thrust one hand into his trouser pocket. 'Yes. We were all just saying you had your hand up so many times, it was practically a Nazi salute.' He paused. 'But then again, you'd know all about that, wouldn't you?'

A hush descended as the man's unfriendly tone broke through his passive demeanour.

'Sorry, what?' Xavier asked, his back straightening as he woke up to what was happening here.

'After all, I guess you've got to spend that stolen fortune somehow.'

Xavier was on his feet in a flash. 'What did you say?'

'You heard me,' the man said, chest puffed as though squaring up to get physical.

'You'd better watch your mouth! You don't know what you're talking about.'

'Don't I?' the man asked, throwing a battered hospitality copy of *Vanity Fair* onto the table. 'Well, they certainly seem to.' He turned to go.

'Hey! What the hell is this?' Xavier demanded, angry now, grabbing the man by his arm; but the stranger jerked it away, shrugging his jacket back on neatly.

'Why don't you read it and find out?' the man sneered. He jerked his chin towards their table. 'You think you're something special? You're not. You should be ashamed of yourselves. You disgust me. You disgust us all. Why don't you just do us all a favour and get out of here. Your sort isn't welcome here.'

Xavier's fight dissipated as he glanced down and saw the title on the magazine's open page. He looked back up again, saw that everyone was staring now, even Max, several feet below on his podium on the grass. There was a buzz of conversation as people broke into titillated groups, all discussing the contretemps, heads shaking in disapproval as they looked back and forth between Xavier and his sister. Word was getting round.

'Awkward,' Noah murmured with a wry smile, clearly bemused by the fracas.

Flora felt a sudden urge to slap him. She reached for her bag on the table. 'We should go before they start on the next lot,' she said stiffly. She needed to get down those steps and out of here before he read that article.

'Sure,' Noah said, quickly downing his drink. 'Stay there just a minute. I'll run ahead and bring the car round.'

Flora bit her lip as he sauntered past the Vermeils' table and ran down the steps, his linen jacket flying open behind him.

She looked back at Xavier. He was reading the article now, sinking in slow motion into the chair as he began to take in the detail, both hands pulled into fists on the table.

She could scarcely bear to watch, to see the way his Adam's apple bobbed in his throat as he swallowed down the ugly truths, the slight parting of his lips as dismay spread through him like a poison, the growing hunch of his shoulders as his head began to droop, shame and humiliation diminishing him before her very eyes; all the hard, angry swagger and flash braggadocio of only a few moments before had gone and he suddenly seemed very young.

She couldn't look any more. Snatching her purse and tipping the hat low, she skirted the tables, taking the long way round to the steps in an effort to avoid having to walk right past him.

She half-walked, half-ran over the grass towards the yew hedge, which had an opening onto the beech-lined avenue and led to where the visitors' cars were parked. Noah would surely be coming up any moment.

But she wasn't through the hedge when she felt a hand close around her wrist, swinging her back round so that she was face to face with those fierce black eyes again.

'You did this,' he hissed, his touch scorching her.

She shook her head, felt her arm shake. 'No.'

'Yes,' he snapped. 'How else could they know? *We* did not even know till yesterday. You were the only one!'

'I—' Her eyes filled with tears. He was right. It was absolutely her fault. Unwittingly or not, she had given Stefan just enough information to run with this and make his career. 'You don't understand.'

'No, I don't. You are supposed to be working for my family, not against it.'

'I'm not! I swear. I had no idea about the article. I was as shocked as you.'

'I doubt that.' His face darkened as the public pillorying he had just endured flashed through both their minds and she couldn't help it; a tear slid down her cheek as she saw the muscle ball in his jaw, felt the fire in his hands. Something . . . something else passed between them; like a blip of interference between radio stations she saw a change in his eyes as he bore down on her, anger transposed with frustration. He wiped away the tear with his thumb, pressure on her cheek. 'What the hell are you doing to me, Flora?' he whispered, his voice grained with despair.

'To you?' she echoed, confused.

Her words made him blink, as though he hadn't expected to hear them out loud. The channel changed again; he took his hand from her face. 'To my family. What are you doing to my family?'

'Hey! Is there a problem here?'

They both jumped in surprise to find that a sleek black Mercedes had pulled up beside them, Noah leaning through the open window in the back, one arm slung casually over the side – but there was war in his eyes as he saw Flora caught in Xavier's grip.

Xavier stared at him with chilling stillness, dropping Flora's arm as Noah pointedly looked at his hold on her.

Normal service resumed; the sneer climbed back onto Xavier's proud mouth. 'No problem, man. I was just helping your girlfriend. She slipped.' Bitter sarcasm clung to every word.

Flora opened her mouth to protest – although she wasn't sure which to protest against first. To Noah, that she hadn't slipped? Or to Xavier, that she wasn't Noah's girlfriend?

The driver got out and opened the car door for her. Noah climbed out too, showing off his size; he wasn't quite as tall as Xavier but he was older, broader and easily withstood the hostility in Xavier's glare. 'You OK?' he asked her, but with his stare still on Xavier.

'Yes,' she said quickly, walking towards him, the car. 'Let's just go.'

She went to duck into the car but for the second time she felt her wrist grasped and in the next instant, Noah kissed her on the mouth; she tried to pull back as she felt his tongue push her lips apart but his hand clasped the back of her head and she couldn't move.

He was the one who pulled back, a moment later, his point made. He didn't even bother to shoot Xavier a victorious look; he just gestured for her to get in the car. 'Ladies first,' he said, patting her lightly on the bottom.

The driver shut the door behind her but she kept her eyes down, the back of her hand pressed to her mouth; there was nowhere to hide, the window was still open from where Noah had sat and she blushed, feeling humiliated.

The seconds felt like minutes as they waited for Noah to saunter slowly round to the other side. He wouldn't be rushed.

'Enjoy your new car,' she heard him say to Xavier, the sarcasm his this time.

Flora kept her head lowered as finally the passenger door opened and he slid in beside her, one hand immediately on her knee. But she couldn't keep it up and as the limo began to pull away, her eyes betrayed her, flashing up to Xavier one last time. Their gazes linked for only a fraction of a second but it was long enough. *What the hell are you doing to me, Flora?*

Correction. What the hell was he doing to her?

Chapter Eighteen

Antibes

'And these are your quarters. Madame thought it would be easier for you here, away from the distractions in the main house.'

The housekeeper stepped back from the door, allowing Flora to pass through first. The dimness took a moment to get used to, coming straight in from the dazzling light outside, but as her eyes adjusted, she looked about her in wonderment. Everything was white – the floors, walls, ceilings, curtains, flowers even – and punctuated with vast plumped ikat-printed sofas in peach and mango and melon that broke up the room like pastel colour-bombs. A large bowl of fruit scented the space and she could just see a hand-worked lace coverlet on the bed in the room off the far left corner. A small but chic kitchen was in the back right corner.

'Oh, my goodness,' Flora murmured, mainly to herself. And this was just the cottage. The main house wasn't a chateau so to speak, but rather a tall sandstone villa with dust-blue shutters that looked like something Coco Chanel or Wallis Simpson would have lived in.

She turned back to the housekeeper – Genevieve, if she remembered correctly. 'Thank you. This is beautiful.'

Genevieve nodded and handed her a set of keys, one for here, one for the main house where her temporary workshop had been set up in the old flower-cutting room.

Genevieve retreated and Flora set her bag down, wandering – awestruck – through the dreamy space. The white plantation shutters outside had been left closed, keeping the cottage cool in the fierce August heat, and she walked over and through the striped shadows thrown over the floors and walls, her hand trailing over the blanket on the sofa (cashmere linen), lingering to smell the hibiscus flowers on the coffee table.

She stopped in the doorway of the bedroom (an en-suite colonial-style bathroom led off on the right) and saw that notionally it was simple and restrained: a bed, a rug, a wardrobe – only the rug was plush alpaca fur, the wardrobe covered in shagreen and the walls decorated with several bold James Whistler pastels.

Flora walked back through to the living area, opening the fridge to find it was stocked full of fresh groceries, a magnum of champagne and a box of truffles beside the coffee machine. She went and sat on the sofa that was opposite the still-open front door, letting the breeze lift her hair and tickle her face. Directly outside, the turquoise pool glittered as it caught the light, swallows intermittently swooping low to skim the water's surface.

She wondered how she dared to sit on this sofa or drink from those cups or sleep in that bed, knowing that – intentionally or not – this was her fault. The Vermeils were still unaware of her part in it all, Xavier notwithstanding. But for all his accusations, he knew nothing of her (former) friendship with Stefan, nor ever would he. One phone call by Travers had confirmed the magazine was asserting its right to protect its sources. *Her.*

The family was in no mood to put up a fight. The resulting furore had been everything they'd feared. In the three days since the issue had hit the news stands, the stain of a Nazi past blotting the illustrious Vermeil family's name had made for compelling reading throughout France and it had hit the front page of *Le Monde* the very next day. Lilian had been forced to cancel attending a Unicef fundraiser, Jacques' private offices had been daubed with *Nazi Scum* in red paint and, as feared, several of the major charities supported by the Vermeil charitable foundation had issued public statements saying they were 'reviewing their links' with the family. Photographers had camped out on the streets outside the town house so that no one could come in or out without being blinded by camera flashes – treacherous on those steps – and after several days' confinement, whilst Flora had packed and relocated the now-notorious art collection across the country, the family had made the decision to relocate to the Antibes estate too, until things died down.

Flora closed her eyes at the irony of their misplaced sense of security as they sought refuge behind their high walls and CCTV-protected grounds when she, the very person behind the leak, was living in the cottage at the bottom of the garden. Angus had been the first to suggest that the leak must have come from the website Flora had shown him of where the urban explorers' photos had surfaced, getting on the phone to the family himself and commiserating that they'd all been naive to think that the intruders had been satisfied with merely notifying the family of the apartment's existence, like some band of crusading architectural evangelists. This must have been their plan all along, he'd bemoaned and Flora had quietly agreed, too scared of losing her job to come clean and admit how this had all really played out.

It wasn't for want of trying to leave that she was still here. She had desperately tried to plead her escape – now that they were involved in full provenance research, she had tried convincing Angus that Bridget – their lead research analyst, based in the London office – should fly in and take over; it was her area of interest, after all. But Angus had been adamant: the family wanted her; they'd been badly hurt by events and felt they needed someone they could trust. It was to be her and no one else.

The flower room made for a perfect workshop – large and bright, with high ceilings, full-length windows and deep wooden counters running round the walls, there was plenty of space for her to set out the artworks and begin to get some sort of order established. Now that the time pressure of getting everything ready for auction had been taken away, she could get on with simply identifying and archiving the rest of the collection. The Renoir – still being professionally cleaned in Paris – at least had a full provenance now and should the family choose to sell it at some point in the future, the new owner would buy it in full knowledge of where it had come from and through whose hands it had passed.

She made good progress throughout the day, hanging many of the paintings on the small hooks that had once been pinned into the wall for binding wall-climbers, taking them down one at a time and starting on her condition and evaluation reports.

Her iPad rang on the counter – FaceTime calling – and she picked it up, walking over to the open French door and leaning against it, her eyes on the sweep of velvet lawn before her. She had taken her shoes off in the heat and rubbed a bare foot against her leg.

'Hey.'

Ines's throaty voice made her smile. 'Hey back.'

'How's it going down there? Shabby?'

'You have no idea,' Flora smiled, half-expecting a peacock to strut past and shake a tail feather. She turned the iPad around and gave her friend a quick 180-degree view of the gardens. 'I shouldn't be expected to live like this. It's criminal.'

'I bet.' Ines laughed, a reassuring sound. 'And how are you? Feeling better? You look better.'

Flora dropped her head. 'I feel so guilty.'

'It wasn't your fault. How many times do I have to tell you that? Stefan did this. Not you.'

'But I never should have said a word. I knew he was a journalist. Worse than that – he was a journo looking for a story!'

'You were among friends. You shouldn't have to act like you're a fucking spy! You know we're never going to speak to him again, right? I told Bruno, him or me. He has to choose.'

'Ines, don't feel you have to—'

'It's already done,' Ines said stubbornly. Loyally.

Flora shrugged, taking the iPad over to the bench as her arms tired from holding it up and out. She propped it up against the window and leaned over the bench, her head cupped in her hand.

'Anyway, look, it's already beginning to die down. They're yesterday's news.' Ines was ever the optimist. 'Did you hear about the Minister of the Interior? He's been shagging the Vice-President's daughter.'

Flora spluttered with laughter and dropped her head. 'Oh, my God! Are you kidding?'

Ines grinned, nosily scanning the room behind Flora. 'See? It'll be OK.' She whistled. 'Phew! Is that all the stuff you've got to organize?'

'Yeah.' Flora glanced at the decorative objects arranged in classified groupings on the far bench, the easel for photographing the paintings and sketches over her right shoulder. 'It's not as bad as it looks. Terrible as it might sound, everything's a lot easier to follow up, provenance-wise, now that we know where our end point is. I felt like I was banging my head against a brick wall before, trying to get past Von Taschelt to François Vermeil.'

Ines tutted, before changing the subject. 'So listen, we might come down for a few days. Bruno's got a promo to do in Nice so we'd only be half an hour away from you.'

'Oh, that would be amazing.' She lowered her voice. 'I could do with seeing a friendly face round here.'

'Things bad, huh?'

'Well, I'm not exactly surrounded by friends.'

'Have you seen the Son and Daughter of Darkness yet?'

'Don't call them that,' she said quietly, wincing.

'Why not?' Ines chuckled devilishly. 'They are, aren't they? Or do you know something I don't?'

'No, but . . .' She trailed off, not sure why she'd defended them. Perhaps because even they didn't deserve the vitriol being meted out to them at the moment.

'Well? Have you seen them?' Ines repeated impatiently.

'No. I mean . . . I've heard Natascha getting out of the car, I think.'

Ines rolled her eyes. 'Of course you have. And what about Xav? Glimpsed him in his swimming shorts yet?' She shrugged her eyebrows naughtily.

Flora frowned. '*What?*'

Ines shrieked with laughter. 'He might be a brat but he's a gorgeous brat. Go on – admit it.'

'No.' Yes.

Ines leaned in to the screen. 'Personally, I'm worried for your safety.' For a moment, her face was perfectly serious before she broke up into laughter. 'Well, your virtue more like!'

Flora shook her head, looking away. The truth was, she was desperate to avoid him. Their encounter at Chantilly – and this was within the context of *none* of their encounters having been positive – had left her shaken. They'd only ever spoken to argue, she had yet to find one redeeming quality about the man and yet . . . and yet . . . he kept creeping into her mind, unbidden. Just the thought of him made her feel restless, agitated, nervy, rattled.

So every day she managed down here without seeing him would be a good day. She had her plan worked out already – meals in the cottage, cloistering herself in the flower room all day. If she was careful, there was every hope she might get through these next few weeks without actually having to come into contact with either him or his sister.

'Heard from Noah?'

'Huh?'

Ines snapped her fingers. 'Noah. The rich handsome American guy with a Renoir and a Bugatti and the hots for you?'

'Oh.' She shook her head and tutted. 'No. I told him not to call me again.'

'*Why?*'

Flora remembered the tense car ride back into the city – how she'd angrily brushed his hand off her thigh and refused to look at him, fuming at his presumptuous behaviour and the way he'd practically taken ownership of her in front of Xavier, like a dog peeing to mark its patch. He'd sent fifty yellow roses to the office the next day, a flamboyant apology that had failed to move her; she couldn't be bought, nor would she be owned, and she'd repeated her request that he not contact her again in a brusque text. Since then, silence. 'We're not compatible.'

'Compatible? Huh,' Ines snorted with a 'why am I not surprised?' roll of her eyes.

Flora changed the subject. 'So look, let me know if you're coming down then.'

Ines sighed. 'Sure. I think it'll probably be Thursday. Bruno's getting his schedule today so I'll text you later.'

'Cool.'

They hung up, Flora inhaling deeply as she looked around the ordered space. The scent of roses lingered in the air and the countertops were stained where petals or stems had been crushed, dark circles from buckets sunken into the grain.

She went back to work on the small Dalí sketch she'd pulled down before Ines had rung. It was only ten inches high, pencil on paper. She turned the frame over and saw the remnants of an old oval sticker on the back. She squinted, peering at it closely, trying to make out the faint type. But '. . . NNA' was all that was clear.

Anna? Vienna? She photographed the sticker close up and measured it, knowing she'd need to cross-check it against copies that would hopefully be held at the Attlee & Bergurren Gallery in Saint-Paul. That the sticker was oval should make it easier to match to others – if she was lucky, other more complete stickers – in which the type was clearly visible.

A polite cough made her turn. Jacques Vermeil was standing by the door.

'*Pardon*, I did not wish to disturb you.'

She rose to standing. 'Oh, no. It's quite all right.'

'Do you mind if I come in?'

'Please do,' she smiled, motioning towards the artworks arranged around the room.

Jacques walked in, a polite but hesitant smile on his face as he scanned the multitudes of paintings that now stretched up to the ceiling and over every wall. 'Good grief. There are . . . so many.'

'Yes,' Flora replied, feeling uncomfortable. They both understood the subtext to his words. So many paintings, so many families . . .

'It shouldn't be a surprise. You gave that presentation the day after we unlocked the door. You flicked through all the pictures with us and yet . . .' He blew out his cheeks. 'To actually see them all. *Here*. It feels more. It feels worse.'

'Monsieur Vermeil—'

He turned round to her. 'Jacques, please. We have been through this . . . this ordeal together. We are friends now, are we not?'

Flora gulped. Oh God. Like she wasn't feeling guilty enough. 'Jacques,' she said quietly, trying to smile. 'I just wanted to say how sorry I am. I wish we had never—'

He shook his head, beginning to pace. 'The truth had to come out some day.' He nodded, stopping to look up at a fine Canet mountain scene, high on the opposite wall, his hands folded behind his back. 'Who knows? Perhaps it will turn out to be for the best this way. I never saw a picture of my father before this weekend. Can you imagine?'

She shook her head. She definitely couldn't imagine that.

'It goes without saying I wish he had not been what he . . . was. But, speaking as a child, wanting to know about his father . . . ?' He shrugged. 'My mother would shut down whenever I even raised his name. She said it was too pain-ful for her to think of the past.' He raised his eyebrows and shared with her a doubting look. 'But my mother is still alive and she does not need to lie to me any more. There's still time. I can finally ask my questions and learn the truth about my father from the person who knew him best.'

Flora didn't hold out much hope that it would be a happy story. Notwithstanding his links to the Third Reich, he'd been a poor husband too, she thought, thinking back to the letter she'd found – Jacques' aunt's advice that his mother stick with Franz, ignore his philanderings, have a child. Have Jacques.

'Has she . . . has she said anything to you yet?' Flora enquired, hesitant.

He gave a bemused smile. 'No. God, no. Not yet. My mother is a strong woman, Flora, but this has shaken her profoundly. I do not think she ever thought she would have to look me in the eye and tell me the truth about what my father was. She wanted me to be proud of him, to *respect* him.' He fell silent for a minute, as though the effort of speaking was simply too much, his feet shuffling over the floor in tiny steps as he looked at the multitude of paintings that had been other people's joys, had been stolen from them or sold under duress, the threat of the labour camps hanging above their heads like a swinging scythe.

She watched him, saw how his eyes flitted over the paintings with evident pain.

'I don't doubt that everything she did, changing our name, breaking from my father and his past – she did it to protect me. She wanted there to be no darkness in my life, no shadows. I suppose that is the legacy of a war, is it not? The survivors reach for the light.'

Flora thought of all the mirrors in the Paris town house – there was no hiding there. In that home, you had to look at yourself, from every angle.

'And maybe she was right. Maybe it was better not knowing. If I could step back into last week and change events, I would. But I never dreamed this was what lay in my history. For all these years I wanted more – I wanted more knowledge, I wanted him. I resented my mother for not being him, for being there when he was not. I was her only child and she herself a grieving, young widow – she poured all her love and hopes into me and I, in turn, found her love for me a burden.'

He looked at the floor.

'I perhaps have not been the son she deserved. Not kind enough. Not here enough. I escaped to Paris at my first opportunity.' He shrugged. 'But I am here now and the truth is with us. It is here in this room.' He held out his hands. 'Every one of these paintings has a story, a history. And my father is the one that binds them all. He is the dark thread that links them together.' He turned to face Flora. 'So my mother *will* talk to me, she *will* answer my questions. Maybe not today, or tomorrow, but one day soon I will learn the full truth and I will face it with the courage my father lacked.'

'I want to help you in any way I can, Jacques.'

He smiled, turning to face her square on. 'Good. Because I have decided what to do. Will you join us for drinks in the study at seven o'clock this evening? I have asked my family to make sure they are all in. There is something important I would like to say.'

'O-of course.' Oh God, no. Not another family meeting . . . 'Actually, I haven't met your mother yet. I feel I should introduce myself. It's strange being here in her house, not having met her.'

'And you shall, this evening. My mother is not so steady on her legs any more. She spends most of her days in her bedroom now.'

'Of course.'

'I'm pleased you will join us,' he smiled, turning to leave. 'But I should warn you, my mother is from a different generation, rather formal. We tend to dress up for dinner.'

'Oh, yes. Right. No problem,' she nodded. 'Sh-should I wear anything in particular?'

'With that face?' he smiled, tapping the door frame with one hand. 'Just a pretty dress.'

Chapter Nineteen

Flora stood by the cottage door and stared up at the house, feeling weak with nerves. It looked almost more imposing in the dark, its vast shadow pooling over the lawn, the pin lights on the balconies at every window throwing up plumes of light like an opera stage set. She had heard the car doors slamming earlier as everyone had come home in staggered arrivals – Lilian first, her high voice carrying as she was greeted by two small pugs on the drive, then Xavier (she guessed) silent apart from his heavy tread on the gravel. Finally Natascha, on her phone and laughing as she almost fell from the car, lurching precariously across the gravel in heels.

Flora had slipped away from the flower room, and the main house, at 6 p.m. when the ground floor had fallen silent, taking her opportunity to race barefoot across the lawn, back to the relative safety of the pool cottage when everyone was upstairs.

But now, now she had to go back up there. She had to meet Magda, Jacques' formidable mother – his word, even scarier in a French accent – and she had to endure Natascha's stares, Xavier's silences. It would be the first time she'd seen them since she'd put a bomb under their family's history.

With trepidation, she walked up the lawn, past the spotlit cypress and eucalyptus trees, her shoes in her hand again. All she had to do was listen to Jacques' announcement, a drink in her hand, and then she could go again. She wasn't staying for dinner. She could be back in the cottage in half an hour with any luck.

She walked onto the terrace and through a set of open French doors which gave onto the wide hallway decked with marble statues. No one was around. Every door leading off it was shut and she had no idea which one was the kitchen, the drawing room, even the front door.

Remembering that her shoes were still in her hand, she balanced herself against the door frame, and put them on. She was fiddling with the ankle strap when a door halfway down opened and Natascha walked out.

Natascha didn't notice her. She was walking in the opposite direction towards the stairs but Flora froze at the sight of her nonetheless, not least because Natascha was not in what anyone would call formal dress. In fact, she was wearing a white onesie.

Flora looked down at her own outfit in horror – a black-and-white gingham dress with a low, square neck and cinched waist. Alone it was just a sundress, but she had taken it up several notches by pairing it with her red suede heels and red lipstick for some old-school Bardot glamour. It wasn't a grand look by any means but then she hadn't packed for grand. She'd packed for work, and hopefully some downtime in the sun.

She looked down the length of the lawn . . . She could still race back to the cottage and change again. There was still time. A few minutes wouldn't hurt. She could blame the traffic. Ha!

No.

Oh God. What cou—?

'*Ah! Elle est ici, monsieur,*' Genevieve said, stepping out of the same room and catching sight of Flora frozen in the French doors. She smiled and beckoned for her to come forward.

Flora listened to the sound of her own footsteps echoing on the black-and-white marble floor as she walked. Her entrance may as well have been announced with a trumpet fanfare. Naturally, everyone was looking straight at her as she rounded the door.

Jacques was standing by a fireplace in a cream dinner jacket, Lilian and a tiny but very stout woman sitting opposite each other in blue silk occasional chairs, a small dog in the older woman's lap, another at her feet. Both women were wearing tights and had had their hair done. Flora, with her bare legs and girlish gingham, felt almost beachy by comparison.

Where was Xavier? Still upstairs? Her eyes searched for him but he was nowhere that she could see as she walked into the room under the fearsome appraisal of Magda Vermeil (or rather, Von Taschelt).

'Flora, I would like you to meet my mother, Magda,' Jacques said, walking forwards and pressing his cheek to hers, once on each side. Could he feel her trembling, she wondered?

'*Enchantée, madame,*' Flora said, having to resist the urge to curtsey. This woman might have been married to a Nazi – or at the very least, a Nazi sympathizer – but she had an air about her that was almost regal. Jacques had been right – formidable was the word. She was old but not weak, not

diminished and Flora knew she was being intensely scrutinized.

There was a sudden commotion behind her and Flora
turned to see Natascha flouncing back in, wearing a Saint
Laurent smoking and heels, no shirt underneath – little
wonder she'd changed so quickly. She stopped dead at the
sight of Flora, before pointedly looking over at her father.
'Better?'

'Barely,' he murmured with a tut.

It was then that Flora noticed Xavier standing at the back
of the room. He was pouring himself a drink from a bar in
the recess – no wonder she hadn't seen him. He was dressed
fairly similarly to his sister in a black dinner suit, although
he *had* remembered his shirt, which a tiny voice in her head
somewhere, treacherously, thought was a shame. He made
no move to suggest he was aware of her presence, or if he
was, that he much cared. She looked away again, her attention back on his sister.

'Well, Granny, I see you've met Flora,' Natascha said,
managing to place a stress on Flora's name that conveyed
her feelings perfectly, as she sauntered into the room and
perched on the arm of her grandmother's chair.

'We were just about to become acquainted,' Magda
replied, her small black eyes – like currants in a doughy face
– never leaving Flora.

'We are very fortunate to have someone of Flora's calibre
working on the collection for us,' Lilian said, addressing her
comment to Magda as though she was slightly deaf. 'And
Flora's father was the chief auctioneer at Christie's London
– he brought the hammer down on the *Sunflowers*, didn't
he?'

'That's right,' Flora smiled, grateful as Jacques placed a glass of champagne in her hand.

'So art is your family business,' Magda said in a chilly voice. 'Like ours.'

Flora stared at her, knowing what she was doing. Magda wanted Flora to call her out – to say no, her family were *nothing* like theirs. She wanted to see the judgement in Flora's eyes, to finally encounter the contempt that she knew was her due.

Instead Flora just smiled. Whatever Franz had done, Jacques wasn't his father, that much was clear to her. He was a good man, a doctor.

Jacques walked round to the fireplace again and picked up his tumbler that he'd left on the mantel. 'I'm glad that we're all here. I wanted to talk to you about what I've decided to do.'

'About what, Papa?' Natascha asked, lying back on the arm of the chair, her jacket gaping dangerously open.

'Our next steps as a family.'

'Then why's *she* here?' Natascha demanded, sitting bolt upright – jacket crisis immediately averted – and stabbing an accusing finger towards Flora, who in reply, took a step back.

'Because Flora is central to my plans.' Jacques replied calmly. 'Won't you sit down, Flora?' he smiled, indicating the sofa opposite.

Flora hesitantly took her seat, painfully aware that Xavier had now come further into the room and was standing right behind her, his drink in his hand.

'It would be no exaggeration to say that these past few days have been the worst of my life,' he began haltingly. 'The shame I feel is like a weight pressing on my chest, crushing me. Crushing us all. Ever since we learned the terrible truth, I have asked myself repeatedly – how did we not know? How did *I* not suspect for all those years the darkness in our past? Is it who we are? You?' He looked at his son. 'You?' He looked at his daughter. 'It has made me sick to my stomach to see the way you have all been treated, as though it was *you* who signed those papers, or stood over those poor people with a gun in your hands.' He closed his eyes, falling silent for a moment. Flora slid her gaze round the room, noticing how Lilian was staring up at her husband with genuine concern; even Natascha's customary scowl had melted away, her eyes round and sad when they weren't slitted with scorn. Magda's eyes, on the other hand, were clamped firmly shut, her chin thrust forwards and her hands stroking the snoring dog in her lap.

'I wish this truth were a lie. I would do anything to make it different, but what happened back then, we cannot change. I know that. Our knowing the truth, finally, of our own family's role in those dark years, doesn't change what happened. But it does change us, our focus, because there is something we can do now. We can repent, openly, for the world to see. We can join with their dismay, let them know we share it too.'

Lilian looked anxious. 'But how, Jacques?'

'We give the paintings back.'

'We *what*?' Natascha spluttered. 'No!' But there followed a silence and stare from her father, so severe that she sat back again and lowered her gaze.

Flora was feeling a panic of her own, but for very different reasons. Tracing all those heirs, to give the paintings back? She'd be here for years!

'Flora, this is why we need you. You have already shown us how diligent you are in your work, how determined you are to do the right thing—'

Magda harrumphed.

Flora scanned his face, looking for sarcasm, but there was none. Just calm appeal.

'This is why I want no one else working on this but you. Those transactions were never made in true faith. They were made in fear, terror, desperation, false hope. I want no part in it.'

'Jacques,' she began. 'I'm flattered. And this is a noble idea. I have so much respect for you for even considering it, but it's not going to be as easy as simply finding the previous owners and handing the pieces back. The Germans were meticulous in their paperwork, they went over and above to ensure that everything looked like a legal sale – it will be almost impossible for us to ascertain which deals were made under duress and which weren't.' She blinked. 'But even if we can establish which were the forged deals – those that were effectively armed robbery by the SS, as you say – tracing the heirs will be a mammoth task. So many of the people who sold these paintings will have died in the camps, and divesting their estates were last-ditch attempts at trading assets for freedom. Those that did make it would have moved city, moved country, changed their names . . . Unless a sale is disputed or an artwork registered with the Art Loss Register, finding those heirs will be like pointing at stars in the sky.'

Jacques nodded, listening to her with due consideration. 'I hear what you're saying and I have a proposal for stream-lining the process. We draw a line from 1938, the time of the

Austrian Anschluss. As you say, after that date, we have no way of knowing whether a brokered sale was genuine or made under pressure, as part of a flee bargain. Anything that was sold to my father before 1938 I think we can more safely consider to be a deal that was made with free will on both sides. Those items I want to sell at auction.

'The others – everything sold to my father after 1938 – I want us to try to trace the names of the previous owners where possible, return the items to their heirs. Where we can't, we will have to take the provenance at face value – that the sale to my father was undertaken freely – and sell them at auction too.' He raised his hand for silence as Natascha opened her mouth to speak (or rather, complain). 'Once your commission, Flora, and that of the sales house has been deducted from the final value, I want all the monies to be put towards a new fund that we will set up to benefit the children of refugees.'

An astonished silence inflated in the room.

'They will call it blood money,' Magda said, her bitterness piercing her voice. 'They will not take it.'

Her every word was thrown like a stone on the ground.

'I disagree. We will show France that we are not monsters, we were as ignorant of the facts as anyone. We cannot change what happened, but we can show our regret and humility and our desire to atone for what my father has done. Because what was done may have been done with our name, but not in it. We are not Von Taschelt. *I* am not *him*.'

Magda looked away, long before Jacques turned his head and looked at Flora. 'Will you help us? I have already placed an advert in the LAPADA bulletin, asking people who believe they may be the rightful heirs to contact us.'

Flora swallowed, her mouth feeling dry. She felt she was being sucked into the marrow of this family. What had started as a cursory inventory and valuation was now turning into a full-blown forensic search across Europe (and perhaps further afield) for heirs to victims of Nazi-looted art. She looked at the faces waiting for her response – Jacques, anxious to atone; Lilian, like her own mother, merely anxious; Magda and Natascha, bristling with hostility and resentment. Xavier – well, she didn't need to turn round to know the look that would be on his face right now. She could feel the heat of his glare just on her neck.

Half the family terrified her, openly pouring scorn on her, while the other half was beseeching, asking for her help, trying to scrabble out of this tabloid world they'd been thrown into because of *her* indiscretion. She wasn't the ally they presumed her to be, she thought miserably. Wasn't this the very least she could do? The least she owed them?

'Of course I will,' she replied. 'It would be an honour to work on this project and help you restitute the artworks to the rightful owners.'

Lilian clapped her hands and got up, coming over to kiss Flora on the cheek. 'We are so grateful,' she said, her hands on Flora's shoulders.

'There is one more thing,' Jacques said as Lilian took her seat again. 'Our name is Vermeil, not Von Taschelt. We know the truth of our past – we can't pretend we don't – but we can turn our back on it. From this moment forwards, I do not want to hear my father's name ever mentioned. Not in this house, not anywhere.' He looked at his mother, his children. 'Is that clear?'

Flora couldn't see Xavier's response of course but she saw Natascha nod, meek for once.

'So then I propose a toast,' Jacques said, holding his glass aloft. 'To new beginnings.'

'New beginnings,' Lilian trilled, just as Genevieve came back into the room.

'A visitor for you and Madame,' she said.

Jacques looked surprised. 'Thank you, Genevieve. Excuse us a moment.'

Flora watched in dismay as Jacques and Lilian left the room, leaving her alone with Magda, Natascha and Xavier. It would have been safer swimming in a tank of sharks.

Flora took a sip of her drink, not entirely sure what to do, a silence filling up as the atmosphere in the room changed. 'Well, I should probably get going,' she said, placing her drink on the table and rising to stand. 'It was a pleasure t—'

'You are the one who started all this trouble,' Magda said, cutting over her, her hand still stroking the dog as she looked at Flora with chilling calm.

Flora shook her head. 'No,' she protested, feeling her mouth go dry again.

'You did this. Everything was fine until you started digging, like a little weasel.'

Natascha gave a choked laugh at the sudden insult.

Magda sat forward in her chair, the dog giving a small squeal as it was squashed by her stomach and jumping onto the floor. 'Why did you not leave it alone?' The old woman's hands were pulled into fists, her mouth grimly set in a straight line. 'You only had to work on some paintings. Not *destroy our lives*.' The last words came out as a hiss.

'I . . . I wasn't trying to cause trouble.'

'No? Then what were you doing, *hein*?' Magda slapped her palm on the arm of the chair. Flora jumped. Behind her, she heard Xavier move. God, what was he going to do? Put her in a headlock? She turned slightly so that she could see him on her right.

'I was trying to be thorough. To understand,' she said, as calmly as she could, but her voice clearly wavered and the old woman smiled at the sound of her fear.

'Don't be fooled by this act. She's a troublemaker, Granny,' Natascha chimed in with a cruel sneer. 'Did you know she hit me? Did Papa tell you?'

Flora's mouth dropped open. 'What? No, it wasn't like that,' she protested, feeling tears gather in her eyes at the growing attack, the outright lies. She was outnumbered in here and they all knew it.

'No? What was it like then? You saw, Xavier, didn't you? You walked in and found her attacking me because she didn't like something I'd said or done, or . . . *whatever.*'

Xavier didn't reply.

Natascha arched an eyebrow, surprised by her brother's silence. 'Xav? Tell Granny what you saw. Tell her exactly what this bitch is really lik—'

'That's enough!' Xavier snapped.

An astonished pause ricocheted off the walls.

'What did you say?' Natascha whispered, so utterly stunned it was as though she'd been punched.

'I said that's enough,' Xavier repeated more quietly.

Natascha's mouth opened in shock, her eyes narrowing to slits. For several moments, she literally couldn't speak. 'You're taking her side?'

'No. I'm not taking—'

But Natascha wouldn't be denied. 'You are. You are! But you hate her. You told me so yourself.'

'I . . . No, I . . .' He glanced at Flora. 'I just don't think anything's going to be achieved by acting like this. Papa's right. What's done is done. What matters now is how we move forward.'

But rationale found no home with Natascha. 'Have you slept with her, is that what it is?' she cried, on her feet now. 'Has she got in your head?'

'What? No!' he sneered, almost recoiling from the suggestion.

Flora felt it like a slap but Natascha whirled her attention onto Flora again, giving her no time to breathe. 'Is that your game – divide and conquer? You think you can come between *us*? You think your Little Miss Perfect routine's going to work on him like it has my father?' She gave a brittle laugh. 'I'll give you some advice right now. Don't. Even. Try.'

'You've got this all wrong,' Xavier said, advancing towards his sister. 'Nothing has happened between us. She's . . .'

'She's what?' Natascha asked, as he failed to finish the sentence. Slowly, she walked towards her brother, holding his gaze in hers. 'What is she, Xav?'

He looked down at her, not answering. Flora felt herself trembling as she – they – awaited his verdict.

'What is she, Xav?' Natascha prompted. 'Tell me.'

He shrugged. 'She's nothing.'

Flora couldn't help it, a gasp escaped her, her humiliation complete – a 'little weasel', a 'bitch', a 'nothing' – and she ran from the room before they could see her tears, Natascha's victorious laugh ringing in her ears.

'Wait!' she heard Xavier call, but he didn't follow, didn't apologize and within minutes she was back in the cottage, sobbing on the sofa, the front door firmly locked.

Chapter Twenty

She kept the door locked to the flower room now too. She explained to Genevieve the next morning, as she asked for the key, that it was a precaution – that until the appraisals were complete and valuation estimates made, insurance couldn't be arranged. But it kept *them* out: Magda, Natascha, Xavier . . .

The French doors onto the garden were open, of course – the daytime temperatures in there would have been untenable otherwise – but either no one thought to seek entry that way, or they weren't stupid enough to try, and for the past two days, she had been able to work in splendid isolation, letting herself into her workshop at 7.30 a.m., long before anyone else was up, and running back to the cottage at 6.30 p.m., when the family seemed to disappear upstairs to get ready for drinks and dinner.

She was keeping her days intentionally long. Not only did it mean she didn't have to see anyone – the only time she was ever at risk of that was during her occasional furtive sprints across the lawn for lunch and even then she was careful to check the coast was clear before making a dash for it – but it was also clear that the sooner she did this, the sooner she could be out of here and back in London with her own family, where she was needed.

Her iPad FaceTime rang out and she picked up. 'Hey, Angus,' she said over her shoulder, walking to the far wall and unhooking a Pissarro that was next on her list.

'How's it going? Or do I even need to ask? It looks terrible over there. Another day of rain, I see.'

She walked back to the bench and, laying the painting down on the counter, began removing the fixings on the back. 'Ha! You can talk. Where are you now? The Hamptons again?'

'Working!' he protested. 'This is where the market is in the summer. There's not a living soul left in Manhattan.'

'Not a rich one, anyway,' she smiled, expertly popping the painting carefully from its gilded frame so that she could examine the sides of the canvas.

'How's it going there? I was getting concerned I hadn't heard from you.'

She glanced up at him. 'It's all fine. Just putting my head down and trying to make some progress on this lot.'

He watched as she squinted at the brushworking around the artist's signature. 'Amazing that they want to sell after all,' he said.

'I guess there's no reason not to now,' she murmured. 'Everyone knows the truth anyway.'

'Well, I got your email. It's a great idea, giving the money to charity. Very philanthropic.'

Flora stopped what she was doing and smiled. 'You think it's a great idea because *we* still get our commission, regardless of where the profits go.'

Angus shrugged happily. 'Tomayto, tomahto. So what's the latest?'

She sighed and put down the canvas. 'Well, I'm working my way down from the top – so orange dots first, then yellow, green, blue. For the orange, everything's now inventoried and photographed and I'm pretty much done on the condition reports. So next up's provenance—'

'Your specialist subject.'

She rolled her eyes. 'Yes.'

'Found anything so far?'

'I haven't even started although Jacques is hoping that placing that ad will mean we herd the heirs to us. I'm not so sure. I have a nasty feeling we're only going to end up trying to weed out chancers and hoaxers. Angus, it's going to be a nightmare. You do realize I'm going to have to go into the *catalogue raisonné* of every single artist to get the title and date and start from there?'

Angus thought for a moment. 'Or you could go straight to the Von Taschelt ledgers. You said they're kept at a gallery in Saint-Paul anyway, right? What's that? Half an hour from there?'

'About that. But they've only got papers from before 1942.'

'Great. That could still net a haul. Go there and see what info they have first. They might have photos or descriptions of the pieces he bought – that would save you having to individually consult the *cat rais* of every single artist and then trace it outwards from the beginning.'

'That's a good idea, actually.'

'I have been known to have them once in a while,' Angus smiled. He paused. 'And everything else OK over there? Clients behaving themselves?'

'They're fine.' Even she could hear the change in her voice.

He paused a beat. 'Look, I know it can't be easy for you living in the grounds with them. You're doing a great job,' he pressed. 'They're not exactly the easiest family to rub along with at the best of times and things are obviously pretty intense at the moment. Are the press laying off?'

'A little,' she shrugged. 'Listen, don't worry. I'm keeping a low profile and just getting on with the job. I think they've mostly forgotten I'm here, to be honest.'

'You reckon?' he chortled, the smile fading away as he saw her expression. 'Well, look, just let me know if you have any trouble off them. I know Jacques is aware of what his kids are like and he wants to keep you happy.'

She swallowed and kept her eyes down, reliving her character assassination in the study. 'I'm fine,' she mumbled. 'How are you getting on with the Faucheux? Any progress?'

'It's in with your chap at the Courtauld at the moment. They're examining the paint.'

'Good luck.'

'I think we're going to need it. I'm drawing blanks on it left, right and centre. There's no mention of it in the *cat rais*, so I've put a request in with the Wildenstein Institute to gain access to their records. Apparently they've got his diaries. I'm hoping there might be something in there that alludes to paintings he was working on.'

Flora didn't reply. He didn't need her to point out how minuscule those chances were. 'Oh, by the way,' she said, walking over to the coffee machine that had been installed especially for her and popping in a cap. 'I'm taking this afternoon off if that's all right.'

'Sure. I don't think anyone can point the finger at you for shirking off recently. Doing anything nice?'

'My friends are down from Paris for a few days. I'm just going to hang with them for a bit, try to relax.' She pressed the button for the coffee, steam billowing in clouds around her. She walked back to the bench with it.

'Good, that's good,' he frowned. 'I've been worried about you. You've been looking very stressed recently.'

'I'm fine,' she sighed.

'So you keep telling me. You're sure there's nothing else you want to tell me?'

'I'm sure,' she replied, rolling her eyes and trying to smile. 'Bye, Angus,' she said, disconnecting the line.

She walked to the open doors and sat on the step, her coffee in hand, looking out at the immaculate garden. It had a parkland feel to it, with large, mature trees dotting the grass, orange and white flowers framing the borders.

The sound of a splash made her look up. Someone was in the pool. From the high-pitched shriek that followed, seemingly owing to the temperature, it was a girl. Natascha?

Another person – Xavier surely – was standing on the side in slim black swimming shorts, looking down into the water. They were talking. Flora watched, feeling sick at the sight of them both, as Xavier raised his arms above his head and dived in – easily, elegantly, no big show.

It was too far away for Flora to make them out clearly but the buzz of their conversation drifted on the breeze that swept in from the ocean, only two roads from here. There was a lilt to their voices – happy, excited. From her vantage point, the water droplets caught the sunlight as they became airborne, glinting like shattered glass over their heads. Bitterly, Flora wished it was.

'Hey.'

The voice made her jump. She jumped again when she saw that it was Xavier standing on the lawn just a few feet away. He was wearing jeans cut off at the knees and another of his signature bleached linen shirts that always seemed to be trying to fall off him.

He blinked at her, as calm as she was unsettled, and she had to look over to the pool again to check there was still someone in there with Natascha. Who was it then, if not him? Her latest boyfriend? Today's love interest?

He followed her gaze, looking back at her questioningly.

'What do you want?' she asked, but her voice sounded thick with emotion. She looked away quickly. 'Actually, whatever it is, I don't care what you want. I want you to go.'

She turned away, dismissing him, and walked back into the room, over to the sink where she ran cold water over her wrists; but when she turned back, she saw he had come in too, one hand on the counter as he watched her. He wasn't a big man – not like Noah, not like his father – but he was tall and although lean, finely muscled. He seemed to fill the space, squeezing the oxygen out. She caught her breath. Was he trying to intimidate her? 'I said—'

'You're right to hate me.'

What? She swallowed, trying to work out his game. Was this some sort of trick? 'Damn right I am. You've been a bastard to me from the moment we met.'

His fingers tensed, pressing down into the wooden surface. 'That was my intention, yes.'

His words had a brutality to them that took her breath away. It was his *intention*? Did he know what he was saying? Perhaps his English lacked the subtlety of a native speaker's – but no, what other possible interpretation could there be?

She looked back at him, feeling herself tremble with a

wildness she hadn't felt before – rage and fury and indignation welling up in her that he not only felt entitled to behave
badly but then casually admitted it too. A taunt.

He looked away, perhaps seeing the storm build up in
her, his eyes alighting instead on the paintings that surrounded them, their silent witnesses – and she saw him
flinch as the sheer scale of the stories and histories bore
down on him. His reaction was similar to his father's: his
shoulders slumped a little, his mouth slackened.

But she didn't care.

'Just get out.' Her voice was low, almost a growl. She
hated him. She hated him with an intensity she'd never felt
for anyone before. She couldn't even stand to look at him, to
be in the same room as him.

She went to walk out into the garden but he sidestepped
into her path, blocking her way. 'How dare you!' she hissed,
feeling the emotion begin to erupt now. She wouldn't toler-
ate this. Him. She wouldn't. 'I am working here. You have
no right to come in and—'

'You're not nothing.' The words hung in the air like fireworks, leaving their glorious impression long after the
bang. 'Things with Natascha are . . . complicated. She's not
what you think.'

'Oh, really?' she asked sarcastically, folding her arms
over her chest and staring right up at him, refusing to let
him think he intimidated her in any way at all. 'And *you*
know what I think about her, do you?'

'I can guess.'

She gave a derisive snort, refusing to look away, back
down.

'And what about you?' she asked with a sneer. 'Are you
what I think too?'

He looked taken aback by the question and for the first time, she saw storm clouds pass through his eyes. 'Yes.'

'Really?' She laughed contemptuously, quite sure his own high opinion of himself precluded the possibility of realizing how very low her opinion of him really was. 'So – the drugs, the cars, the women . . . ?'

'Yes.'

His unflinching honesty wrongfooted her. She upped the ante. 'And you don't care that other people regard you as spoilt and vain and shallow? An expensive waste of space? A loser playboy with more money than is good for you?'

'No.'

She watched him closely, his body completely still, betraying nothing, but she had seen that look in his eyes a moment ago, his answers just that bit too quick . . . He wasn't as comfortable with this line of questioning as he wanted to suggest.

'Or maybe you're lying. Perhaps you do care,' she suggested, determined to fight him, to find the crack in his armour, dismantle his arrogance . . .

'Why should I lie?'

She shrugged. 'I really don't know.'

Scorn furrowed his brow but as he stared down at her, she felt it again – that imperceptible shift, his black eyes pulling at her like quicksand, making the ground fall away beneath her feet. She felt her breath catch and he looked away quickly. Had he noticed it too?

She stared at his profile, seeing now the tension in his jaw – his entire body, in fact – as though he was holding himself in check.

'Why have you really come here?' she asked.

He stepped away, his eyes back on the canvases on the

counter again. Did he find it easier to be confronted with his family's shame than to stare at her? 'It was wrong what happened the other day, that is all. You did not deserve it.'

'Didn't I? But I thought you said it was all my fault. *I* put your family through this.' Her words were pushing him now, she could see. Suddenly she had him on the retreat. The air between them had become tight, thin.

He looked back at her. 'I don't know what you did or didn't do, but my father trusts you.'

'But *you* don't.' Her words snapped at the heels of his, her temper thin. He was playing games, trying to be oblique, vague with her, avoiding her even though he had sought her out.

'It doesn't matter what I think.'

'Doesn't it? Don't you count? Is everything in your family always about your sister?'

'Don't!' In an instant, he was bearing down on her, his hands on her arms, pinning them to her sides.

She gasped, having to bend back for some space, his face just inches away, and as those angry eyes burned on hers again, his body as tensed as a boxer waiting for the first punch, she suddenly understood exactly how good his English really was, why he'd even needed to have an 'intention': in a flash she remembered the way he'd held her on the steps as his girlfriend stormed past, his face in the rain as she'd rejected his kindness, why he'd bid in Chantilly as Noah stroked her hair . . . *'What the hell are you doing to me, Flora?'*

She saw the fight in his eyes, could tell from the pulse in his jaw that he didn't want to want her.

'Xav—'

'Don't,' he repeated. The word was a wall, stopping her

in her tracks, and after another airless silence, he turned and walked away, crossing the room in three strides, out of sight in six.

Flora watched him go, her heart pounding. She had never felt more confused. She wanted to hate him . . . hated to want him. He was more trouble than she could handle, she knew that, and yet to her shock, her surprise, her horror, she *wanted* him to be the stereotype, the man in the headlines, the one Ines kept warning her about. He might be no good for her, he might be the biggest mistake she'd ever make, he might be fire . . .

But she still wanted to play.

Ines had bagged the best sunloungers, white-and-gold-striped ones on the jetty which, for the hire price, got you valet parking too. They jutted out from the beach over the shallow sea, away from the hubbub on the sand. It was a perfect day. The water was like bottle-bottom glass and every so often, she could see shoals of tiny silver fish shimmy underneath the decks.

It was an intense scene, not one for naturists or peace-seekers. All around them, with not more than a foot between the beds, were bodies, beautiful ones admittedly – tanned and slim, decked with Melissa Odabash bikinis and water-proof Rolexes. Flora shifted position and stretched out, admiring the delicate silver-and-turquoise anklet Ines had brought her as a surprise gift and wondering where she could get a pedicure around here that wouldn't require a mortgage. Bruno was off SUP-boarding somewhere but Ines was lying on her tummy beside her, reading her book. She was wearing the purple crochet Kiini Bea bikini that had been sold out since March, her skin bronzing before Flora's eyes.

Flora sighed, fiddling with her sunhat and idly watching the masses converged on the thin gold crescent of Garoupe Bay. The private beaches were demarcated by coloured umbrellas – blue-and-white stripes, red, yellow, gold and white – and on the small patch of public beach, every inch of sand was staked and claimed.

It was a privileged bubble to be floating in, she knew. As the nearest beach to the Cap – where the Vermeils' estate was situated – it attracted a wealthy, international crowd. It had to – just a Coke here cost 12 euros. But the people-watching alone was fabulous and she was sure that if she were to hand out her business cards on this beach (admittedly impossible to keep anywhere in her scanty aqua Eres bikini) she'd probably get a 40 per cent call-back rate.

She changed position again, wondering what Freds was up to, knowing he'd hate it here. 'Posers,' he'd groan, scoffing at the Rolexes and diamond toe rings and children with £200 haircuts. This was exactly the kind of scene he had in mind when he teased her about being 'so jet-set' these days. His idea of a beach holiday had a sand dune with a golf course behind it and grey whales in the water; there wouldn't be another person in sight – beyond Aggie, of course (Flora didn't care what he said – she knew they still loved each other) – and they'd have a portable BBQ tray for cooking up sausages, and a cricket set.

Flora smiled at the thought of it – it reminded her of their family holidays in the Highlands, growing up – before realizing she was smiling and promptly wiping the grin from her face. How could she daydream when his life was a waking nightmare? How could she even lie here, lazing above the water, watching the social elite at play, when he was potentially counting down the days he had left of freedom? How could she call herself a good sister, basking in the sun whilst knowing that his days had never been darker?

She shifted position again, feeling guilty.

'Oh, what is wrong with you?' Ines demanded, looking up from her book and squinting into the sun at her.

'. . . Nothing.'

'Really? Because you've been jumping around on that bed like it's got bugs in it.'

Flora cleared her throat, knowing she was still nervy from this morning's showdown with Xavier. 'Sorry. Just a bit restless.'

'Well, why don't you go for a swim or do something then?'

'No, I'm fine. I'll just . . . lie here. You read.'

Ines arched an eyebrow.

'Really. Read.'

Ines sighed and went back to her book.

Flora stared up at the roofs that peered out through the dense vegetation on the Cap, jigging her leg in the air. Privacy certainly wasn't an issue for the residents here – between the high walls and the pine trees, it was a wonder they had any ocean view at all. There had clearly been a lot of new developments built in the last few years, with contemporary glass-cube apartments cutting into the rocks, but many of the larger villas were in the old-school colonial style of the Vermeils' place: tall and blocky, with louvred shutters and painted in ice-cream colours of mint, strawberry pink, vanilla.

Ines's family place was set back one street from the sea. It was modest compared to most of the places around here – a mere six bedrooms – but Ines had been coming here all her life; every summer had been spent on this beach, and she was recognized and accepted by the locals as one of them. Useful, when trying to find a parking spot.

Not that she imagined the area's VIPs ever had to worry about that. Natascha and Xavier Vermeil probably got a Mexican wave from the crowds on the beach every time they came down here; they'd probably be allowed to land a helicopter on a lilo if they wanted (actually, she didn't know whether the family owned a helicopter but she was quite sure that if they did, they could – that was her point).

She frowned, realizing she was thinking about Xavier again. She shifted onto her side—

'Oh my God, really?' Ines demanded crossly.

'Sorry!' Flora squeaked, hands held up defensively.

'You just don't know how to relax, you know that?'

'Like your boyfriend, you mean?' Flora smiled, trying to make Ines smile too.

But she didn't. 'Seriously. You work too hard. You've forgotten how to chill.'

Flora closed her eyes and took a deep breath. She could chill. She could relax. She could—

Xavier drifted into her mind again. The way he'd leaned over her in the flower room, how his hands had felt on her skin, how his words had told her one thing and his eyes another . . .

She swung her legs off the bed and stood up in one fluid motion. Ines gawped up at her as though she were mad. 'Ice cream?' Her voice was high and shaky and she knew she was perilously close to betraying herself; she needed to move, do something, get away from Ines before she dragged the truth from her.

'Sure,' Ines said with a shake of her head and baffled expression that implied she would go along with whatever it was that would calm Flora down.

'I'll choose?' Flora asked rhetorically, sliding her feet into her flip-flops. She went to retrieve her kaftan – only to find Ines hadn't put the cap back on her suntan lotion properly and sticky cream had oozed all over it in a gooey blob. She let it fall back in a heap. It was too hot for layers anyway.

'Why not,' Ines said, in that same 'let's keep the ship steady' voice.

'Bruno?'

'No. He could be hours.'

Grabbing her tiny cross-body Marcie bag and slinging it on over her bikini, not losing a moment, Flora strode along the jetty, the decking boards rattling as she walked. She felt much the same herself, rattled. It just wouldn't go out of her head – that damned moment, the sheer perversity of it – her chasing him, for God's sake! Him practically running from her! Wasn't he supposed to be the bad boy?

She climbed the steps and walked over to the café where Ines usually bought the ice creams. There was no queue. Her heart sank. She'd be back sitting down and stuck on that lounger again in three minutes flat and her nerves would still be jangling.

She looked up and down the pavement. It was set up above the beach, a small hill rising above it and leading back to the shaded residential streets, but she knew there was a grocery shop on the corner, just opposite Christie's Real Estate at the top.

An idea came to her. Flora walked over to the valet who

had parked Ines's car earlier. He had flirted a little with her as they'd got out and given him the keys.

He straightened up as he saw her approach. 'Hi,' she smiled. 'How are you?'

'Good,' he replied. 'You?'

'Yeah, great.' She fanned herself with one hand, blew out lightly through her lips. 'Hot.'

'Yeah.'

'Listen, I want to get some ice creams from the shop up there. Can I borrow your bike?'

'My bike?'

She smiled and nodded, indicating the battered black bicycle propped against the wall behind him. 'I'll bring it back, I promise. You've still got our keys, right?'

He shrugged. '. . . Sure.'

'Thanks,' she said, flashing him a beam as he wheeled it over, looking perplexed that a girl who had arrived in a Porsche should be leaving on a pushbike.

She pedalled away, feeling the breeze quicken and lift her hair, grateful for the chance to expend some energy and burn off this restlessness that was making it impossible for her to sit. Xavier Vermeil had managed to boil her blood and then just left her to simmer but she wasn't going to sit around, brooding on him; she had far bigger things to worry about. She loved her brother and she needed to place all her emotional energy in him.

She took the long way round, not in any hurry to go back to lying down and having nothing to do but think. Instead she pedalled hard up the hill and turned into the Cap itself, trying to lose herself in the winding, shaded lanes that were banked on every side by high walls and staffed gates, Rolls-Royces and Bentleys purring softly as they passed by. She had no idea where she was but nor did she want to either, preferring to hide from her own shadow and enjoy the feeling of her thigh muscles burning and her breath coming fast.

She stood out of the saddle on the hills, sitting back and freewheeling on the other sides, dodging the pine cones that lay where they fell, no pedestrians, no pavements. She meandered lazily in and out of the roads, feeling heady as the balmy air kissed her exposed body as she darted from searing sunspots to the dappled shade of giant plane and eucalyptus trees. She wondered about the families who had once lived here, as well as the families that lived here now; the biggest estates were owned almost entirely by Russians, and in fact Abramovich's yacht *Eclipse* was currently moored just off the Cap, eliciting a roll of the eyes from Bruno, who had remained resolutely unimpressed.

By the time she pulled up at the corner store thirty-five minutes later, she was puffing and pink-cheeked from her exertions – fatigued but not worn out, shadows still creeping through her mind – shivering as the air conditioning chilled her skin when she paid for the ice creams.

She hopped on the bike again and glided down the hill, back towards Garoupe. The valet was still standing at his post and she could see Ines with him. Flora waved, the plastic bag with the ice creams inside dangling from her wrist.

A lime-green Mini Moke – roofless, barely ten inches off the road – was coming up the road in the opposite direction to her. Flora barely noticed. She could tell from Ines's body language that she had questions she wanted answers to.

It was only as she passed the car that she saw the dark hair of the driver flash by, the darker eyes. Xavier stared back at her and Flora felt time become elastic again; she felt as though she was in slow motion, life on a go-slo filter as everything that hadn't happened between them stretched out, there again, not going anywhere, his eyes locked on hers, unable to look away . . .

Then he was behind her. Out of sight again, out of reach—

The sharp scraping of metal on metal, the sudden squeal of tyres, startled her, the bike wobbling precariously side to side as she pressed the brakes and tried to stop without going over the handlebars on the slope. But by the time she was able to look round, he was gone, the bright green paint from his car now scaped along a street light, the only evidence he'd ever been there.

She didn't allow herself the luxury of pondering his evident surprise or why he might have been distracted to the point of crashing. She wheeled off again quickly, staying busy-busy-busy, dismounting the bike in silence as she arrived at the valet's stand thirty seconds later. He took the bicycle from her, as slack-jawed as Ines. Flora reached into the bag and triumphantly held out the ice cream for her friend, ignoring both their gawping expressions.

'What?'

Chapter Twenty-One

The very air was lavender-scented up here. Grasse, the world's capital of the lavender industry, was just behind the ridge of hills that the car was slowly climbing and as they moved away from the blinding glitter of the Côte d'Azur to the dense green lushness of the wooded mountains, the very tenor of the land changed. They had only been travelling for twenty minutes but the glitz and flash of the promenade, where bikinis were worn with wedges and Pagani supercars sat at the lights with Vespas, had given way to a humbler, more crumbly aesthetic with rough stone walls and gnarled centuries-old olive trees, giant pines shedding their coats on the pass, the houses painted in spice colours of saffron, cumin and turmeric.

The hills folded in undulating ribbons, pleating back inland before jutting out again, steep sand-coloured escarpments boldly bare as they rose above the forests. Away from the oligarchs' domination of the coastline, the more modest homes of the merely rich colonized the flatter land in the high valleys amidst the vineyards, with orange and lemon groves landscaped as gardens, and pools winking up at the mountain road that folded around in ripples.

Flora could already see Saint-Paul-de-Vence ahead of them. It clung to an outcrop of rocks like a giant barnacle,

the square, unsentimental church tower like a finger pointing up to God, as though boldly betraying his hiding place.
The grey stone ramparts seemed to meld invisibly with the
cliffs, the clay-tiled roofs of the medieval houses ridged and
rippling downwards in steps, the towns in the Provençal
foothills beyond indistinct in the midsummer haze.

The cab pulled to a stop in the centre of town, outside a
café, its tables shaded with a rattan sunroof, ivy creeping
over the walls in sticky tendrils and a giant watermill wheel
set into the side of the building. Flora paid and jumped out,
allowing herself to be swept along with the tide of tourists
all heading down a narrow street, past the old covered
flower market where an elderly woman was sitting on a
deckchair, fruit laid out on trays before her. Opposite was a
large pedestrianized square where several games of *pétanque*
were being played, surrounded on three sides by cafés, their
tables full thanks to the blistering heat, and people sitting
and resting on the low wall.

Flora drifted past. She wasn't exactly sure where she was
going, only that the gallery was somewhere in the old town.
The town walls were impossible to miss, rising ten metres
above the streets, the ground itself becoming cobbled, the
rounded stones polished but highly uneven under her
Hermès H slides. She trod more carefully as she and the rest
of the crowd were funnelled up a ramp leading into the
ramparts. The sun was momentarily eclipsed from sight
and she was grateful to be back in the shade, unwittingly
smiling at the horde of already-hot children jostling by the
public water fountain beneath a giant plane tree.

But if everything seemed oversized outside the town
walls – the trees, the view, the walls themselves – stepping
through the gate was like stepping into Lilliput: everything

seemed scaled down and tiny, the streets so narrow she felt she could brush both sides with her outstretched arms. The lanes were stepped in parts, rising sharply before levelling out again, the shops' wares hanging on the outer walls and doorways like in a bazaar. There were ice-cream parlours and sunglasses boutiques, dress shops selling boho cheesecloth dresses, homewares boutiques boasting local cold-pressed olive oils and the region's famous lavender essential oils. And art galleries. Hundreds of them.

She well knew, of course, that the area had been a mecca for some of the biggest names in the French modernist art scene – just 100 metres away sat the famous Colombe d'Or hotel where Picasso and Dalí and Braque had paid for their lodgings with works of art which, even now, graced the cracked, unpainted walls of the otherwise modest establishment. She knew too that both the art world and the film world had converged here in the 1950s to create a sort of golden age for the town that rivalled the glamour of nearby Cannes for attracting big star names. But she hadn't counted on the sheer number of studios and ateliers still in operation here.

Of course, much of it was tourist tat, feeding the artistic appetites of the hordes attracted to the town's distinguished heritage, but there was some true quality as well and several times she stood with her face pressed to glass windows, hands cupping her head as she tried to see more, stepping inside to get artist details. She even found herself looking in the windows of an estate agent, intrigued to find out how much an apartment went for here – a lot, it transpired.

Mostly, though, she was propelled along by the crowd, her gaze switching left and right, glancing at every shop name as she looked for Attlee & Bergurren, Jacques' aunt's gallery and her reason for being here – but half an hour after stepping through the arch, she was thoroughly lost. She had no idea where she was in the walled town, only that she had turned left twice and right three times, climbing a total of four separate stepped alleys, and was now staring at a street sign, a hand-painted rock affixed to the wall by iron hooks, that read *Rue de Derrière l'Église*. So at least she knew she was behind the church then. That was something.

She turned on the spot, not sure she could even retrace her steps. All the winding, labyrinthine lanes looked so much the same to her eye. She had moved into a more residential area where the people who dawdled past her had their faces either upturned to admire the profuse window boxes, or else they were looking for street signs, or, with their sights on the ground, tracing the daisy designs set into the stones and trying to get back to the shopping streets. There was no sign of any locals, anyone who looked as if they knew where they were going.

A magnificent white jasmine tree was in full flower further along the street and she walked over to it, sheltering in the shadows again and reaching for the small bottle of water in her bag. She leaned against the wall, pleased to catch her breath, and watched as people slipped past her, oblivious to her presence. Unlike the look-at-me preening of the coastal towns – St Tropez, Cannes, Juan-les-Pins and Antibes – where the scene was all about people-watching, here it felt as though the buildings were the main event, history oozing through the walls and imbuing the place with a rare sense of permanence. It was almost as though the town wasn't a man-made settlement at all but had been hewn from the mountain itself.

After a few minutes, she began walking again, taking sips of her water every few metres. Ines had said it was forecast to be the hottest day of the year so far and based on the scorching temperatures even at this tender time in the morning, she didn't doubt it. Heat radiated back at her from the dark cobbles underfoot, the warm walls . . .

She rounded a corner and saw a narrow lane leading downhill to her right. She was sure she could see a flash of white, a shop window at the bottom, and there was a small tavern halfway down, two large oak barrels standing either side of an arch, clearly to attract the shoppers' attention. She decided to try her luck down there, her sandals slapping against the stones as she skipped lightly over the steps.

She wasn't ten metres away when a figure emerged quickly from the arch and headed off in the same direction in front of her, stopping her in her tracks. She would recognize him anywhere now. His head was low, a battered straw panama pulled over his dark hair, but she knew from the way his shirt was barely buttoned up – and the fact that even when it was, it was buttoned incorrectly – and the way he wore his car shoes with the backs pressed down, that it was Xavier.

What was *he* doing here? In a flash, yesterday became alive again and she found herself unable to move. Had he turned around he would have seen her staring after him, open-mouthed, but he didn't and within moments he was almost out of sight.

She bit her lip, willing her heart to calm down. It didn't matter that she'd seen him, that her head was full of questions – Why was he here? Had *he* followed *her*? – she was here to work, she just had to find the—

The gallery! Like her, he must have come to see his grandfather's records. She ran down the cobbles and got to the bottom, looking in both directions.

She had been right. She was back on the shopping streets, but the crowds had multiplied in number threefold, and all she could see were shuffling backs and anonymous faces.

The hat! She saw it and began pushing her way through the hordes, ducking and slipping past all the people between her and him, trying to make up the distance. He was walking with his head down, as though he didn't want to be recognized; he was walking like a local too, seemingly knowing exactly where he was going.

The street was climbing again, rising uphill, and it hooked left further ahead. He disappeared out of view. She tried breaking into a run but it was almost impossible with these crowds and shoes and this heat. By the time she had rounded the bend, he was gone again.

She stood, breathless in the street, her hands on her hips as she tried to work out where he might have gone. She could see straight down the lane from this aspect and there was no sign of his hat in the crowds; there were no lanes shooting off at tangents here.

Then her eyes took in where she was. She didn't even need to raise her sights to the elegant gilded font on the boutique sign to see the words *Attlee & Bergurren*. The paintings, set on easels in the window, were enough (hell, even the quality of the display lighting was a world apart) – they were of an entirely different calibre from the pulp catering to the day-tripping crowds; this was the rarefied level of art she was trained to recognize, evaluate and sell to serious collectors. She pushed her way through the crowd over to the windows, recognizing a Marcel Canet in the right-hand one. She reached for the door handle and she pushed –

The door didn't budge.

She pushed harder. Nothing.

She frowned and stepped back, only now noticing the handwritten note: *Open at eleven.*

Eleven? Who opened at eleven?

She pressed her face to the glass and looked into the office at the back of the gallery. Had they closed up the gallery at Xavier's behest? Was he having a private appointment in there? It was owned by his grandmother, after all.

She rapped her knuckles hard against the glass, her breath obscuring the view, but no one replied. All the lights were off – save for the window display – and after a few minutes, she stood back in the street, wondering what to do.

It was 10.25 a.m. now, not worth going anywhere else. She looked around for a café and spotted one just a short way further up the street. Tiny square slatted tables were pushed against the walls, director's chairs with famous Hollywood names emblazoned across the back. Flora hesitated. She would most likely spend much of her time ducking the elbows of passers-by but at least she would have a clear view of the gallery – and Xavier when he emerged.

She ordered a frappé and sat down, sneakily pushing out a potted hibiscus that was positioned against the wall, forcing the passing pedestrians to swerve around it and away from her. She sat and waited, feeling restless, her eyes on the still, dark gallery, waiting for the opportunity to see him again.

Listlessly, she looked around. There was a clothes boutique on one side of the café and a puppet shop on the other, both attracting lots of browsers. Across the street there was another gallery. She couldn't see what was in it thanks to all the moving bodies shuffling past the windows but she could make out from the sign – *Galerie Noir*, written, ironically, in red on a white background – that it was small, a single unit only.

She sighed impatiently, drinking her coffee too quickly, looking away, looking down the street, looking up it, looking at her watch, looking at her emails. Then she looked across again, her eyes drawn to the ombré effect of the peach-coloured render blackened in parts, an old wisteria hugging the walls. Her eyes came back to street level.

A rare break in the crowd suddenly afforded her a view of the display in the gallery window opposite and she immediately leaned forward in her seat, trying to get a better look. The quality shone! From what she could see, a giant verdigris bronze ball had been fashioned with two lovers standing atop it, except their feet spread like tree roots over the top of the globe, their arms – as they kissed – held over their heads and spreading into the canopy of an olive tree. The overall effect was whirling and euphoric, a sense of 'rising' lifting off it, the two tones of the bronze and verdigris highlighting each other.

Bodies blocked her view again. Dammit! Without thinking, she got up and wove her way over to the window, oblivious to the shouts behind her. It took a tall American man to tap her on the shoulder and say, 'I think he means you,' before she realized she had left without paying and she turned to find the waiter, furious, trying to push through the crowds towards her.

'*Pardon!*' she cried, fishing in her purse for 5 euros, trying to explain, but he simply snatched the note from her with a scowl and pushed his way back to the café again, picking up her cup and saucer and taking them inside.

Flora sighed and turned back to the window. The sculpture was even more impressive up close – the globe wonderfully textured like stippled oil in a painting, the twisted bodies of the couple so perfectly redolent of the striated trunk of an olive tree. Simply put, she'd never seen anything like it. Sculpture and decorative art weren't in her area of expertise – Lydia in the New York office specialized in that – but she knew what she liked, her eye told her what was good even if she didn't know the nuances of the market and she pushed the door open, determined to get more details to pass on to the team. They were always looking for fresh talent and new blood as future investments for their clients.

The sound of the bell alerted an elderly man to her arrival; he wandered into the space several moments after she'd closed the door, wiping his hands on a black apron that fell to his shins.

'*Bonjour,*' she smiled, lapsing into the language which had long since become second nature. 'I'm interested in the piece in the window.'

He walked over to it, his expression softening as he took in the texture, evidence of the care and time taken with it. 'It is striking, no? We get a lot of enquiries about it but I am afraid it is not for sale.' He gave a *comme ci, comme ça* shrug.

Flora was surprised. 'Then why is it in your window?'

'The artist is a friend of mine. He allows me to display it as a way to bring customers into the gallery.' He had the grace to look sheepish.

'That's rather unfair, don't you think?'

He nodded. 'Yes. I could have sold this piece a thousand times over but he does not sell his work. But if you'd like to take a look at some of my other artists—'

Flora smiled and crossed her arms. 'You know, I've found in the past when someone's told me something's not for sale, what they really mean is that it's not for sale until we get to the right price,' she smiled, well used to haggling for her clients. 'What can you tell me about it?'

The old man looked bemused by her directness. 'It is called *Love Three.*'

She smiled. Of course it was. It shouted that from the rooftops.

'It took the artist five months to make this model. Do you see how the feet are not riveted or bolted on here, but formed from the one piece? He is an artist of talent *and* patience.' The old man chuckled.

'And what's his name?'

'Yves Desmarais.'

'I'd love to know more about him and to see more of his work.' She reached into her bag and handed him a business card. 'I assure you I'm very serious. I have a lot of clients that I know for a fact would be interested in this.'

The old man stared at the card and then at her, his small brown eyes staring at her deeply before he nodded. 'Well, in fact he is here . . . Would you like to meet him?'

'Yes, I would,' Flora replied with pleasant surprise.

'Wait here, please. He's in the workshop at the back.'

'He works here?'

'Sometimes.'

Flora felt her heart quicken again. If she could get a pre-view of any of his other work, she could distribute it to the team and get first dibs on the pieces, maybe before they were even made. 'I can't wait to make his acquaintance,' she smiled.

The old man nodded. 'I shall bring him through.'

Flora rubbed her hands together as the owner disappeared into the back of the unit, scuffing her feet as she walked slowly around the rest of the space. There were other pieces by an artist working with driftwood, creating organic representations of horses and other wildlife, but whilst they were accomplished, they in no way touched the vision or expertise of the bronze artist. She stopped to admire a rendering of a bull – this one worked without any of the same texturizing. The angles were rounder and more contoured, in the school of Barbara Hepworth.

A sound made her start and she turned expectantly.

The old man was back in the doorway, but he was alone. 'My apologies,' he said with an awkward smile. 'But the artist is currently working and cannot be disturbed. It was wrong of me to offer an introduction without checking he was free, first.'

'Did you tell him I . . .' Her voice faded away as she caught sight of something behind him on a hook.

A battered hat.

She looked up and saw a CCTV camera on the wall, realized she was standing centre stage for it.

All became clear.

'Well, that's quite all right,' she said, feeling her cheeks burn, the rejection sting. She reached for the handle and pulled the door open too hard, the bells jangling noisily, for too long. 'Goodbye.'

She flung the door closed behind her and strode down

the street, trying to get out of sight of the gallery and its cameras as fast as she could. Attlee & Bergurren was finally open – the lights inside telling her so – and she dived in, grateful for the refuge, aware of the irony that although she was the one running, she wasn't the one hiding.

Bruno was heavily involved in a serious game of *pétanque* with a seventy-year-old local when she finally met up with her friends at the café. Flora was relieved to see they were sitting in the shade, Ines chatting away merrily with the people at the next table.

Flora plonked her bag down and threw herself into the chair, sitting slumped as she watched Bruno throw the *boule*.

'You look cross,' Ines said, disentangling herself from the neighbouring conversation and pulling her chair round to face Flora.

'Me? No,' Flora said, pulling a nonplussed face, watching as the ball landed heavily on the ground, sending up a dust cloud. 'I'm not cross.

'Stressed then.'

Flora shook her head. 'No.'

There was a short pause, Ines lighting up a cigarette and watching her friend suspiciously. 'So how did you get on?'

The waiter came over and took her order for a glass of rosé.

'So-so. I've got copies of all the acquisitions Von Taschelt made between 1938 and 1942. It doesn't help me much for anything he bought after then, which is probably when he acquired most of what we've found in the apartment, but it's something to work with. I'll cross-reference the descriptions against my own inventory and see if I get any hits. It'll be quicker than going to the *cat rais* of every-single-different-artist,' she said, bouncing those lost words with a groan.

Ines looked back at her blankly. 'Sorry, you've lost me. The *cat* what?'

'Never mind,' Flora said, shaking her head irritably, her eyes still on the game.

'Well, so long as it wasn't a wasted morning, because I *wish* you'd been with me earlier. I bought the most amazing dress in a boutique in Cannes. You'd have loved it.'

Flora doubted that. She wasn't interested in shopping right now. She sighed. 'Let me see.'

Ines reached down and pulled out a long white silk jersey dress with a red abstract apple print and draped shoulders.

'Gorgeous,' Flora said listlessly, reaching out to touch the fabric. 'I can totally see you in it.'

'Yeah?' Ines grinned as she folded it back into the bag. 'What about you? See anything you liked? There's a lot of rubbish in there, no?'

'Yes, but there was some quality stuff as well.'

'That is the thing – it's either tourist rubbish or high, high-end for the Russians.'

'Give me that,' Flora said, reaching out for the cigarette suddenly.

Ines looked back in surprise. 'But you don't—'

'Just – give,' Flora demanded bossily, brooking no argument.

Ines handed it over, looking back at her in open bewilderment now. Flora took a drag, not even having to suppress the urge to cough; she was so keyed up, even her body was toeing the line. She was quiet for a few moments, knowing she'd aroused Ines's suspicions now with her uncharacteristic behaviour. 'Have you ever heard of a sculptor called Yves Desmarais?'

She watched Ines's features carefully for signs of recognition. Thanks to her family's old-school connections and her crossover status in Paris's cool bohemian-hipster scene, she knew everyone and everything.

'No. Never heard of him.'

'No? He's good. Excellent, in fact.' Every word was like a staccato point.

Ines shrugged, not sure where Flora was going with this. 'OK. Do you want to introduce me?'

'Actually, you already know him.'

'I do?' Ines knew there was no point in reminding her she'd just said she'd never heard of him.

Flora cast her a sidelong glance. 'It's Xavier Vermeil.'

Ines's mouth dropped open and Flora watched as incredulity morphed into bemusement. 'Xavier Vermeil – work? Do me a favour!' she laughed, smacking the table with her hand.

'It's true. I saw his hat in the gallery.'

There was a beat. 'His hat? You recognized his hat?'

'He was ahead of me in the crowd when I was on my way to his grandmother's gallery. I assumed he was going there too.'

Ines snorted again, reaching for her cigarettes. Flora went to offer hers back but Ines shook her head. 'Keep it. Looks like you need it.'

She lit up again and watched Flora closely, Flora keeping her attention on Bruno's match; he was being thoroughly whipped by the older man. 'So when you say you saw

Xavier in the crowd, you didn't try to walk with him? Have a chat, be friendly with your client's son . . .'

'No, he was ahead of me.'

'You just followed him.'

'Yeah.' Flora didn't need to look at Ines to know she had the devil's imp on her shoulder.

'Well, that's a normal thing to do.'

Flora took another drag, ignored her friend's sarcasm, pushed the information out with minimal emotional output, maximum efficiency. 'I saw his work in the window of another gallery. Didn't know it was his. The owner invited me to meet him but he refused to come out and speak to me.'

Ines leaned in, her elbows splayed on the table. 'He actually refused?'

'Hid in the back,' Flora said, taking another deep drag and jerking her chin in the air.

There was a pause as Ines mulled it over. 'Well, perhaps he's pissed because you made him crash his car.'

'I didn't make him do anything.'

'You cycled past him in a bikini. He crashed his car. Go figure.' Ines threw her head back and laughed, stabbing her cigarette in the air. 'I knew it! I knew something was off between you. I saw it that night at the Hermès party.'

'Saw what?'

'His face. He looked like he didn't know whether to throw you off the roof or slam you against the wall and ravish you.'

Flora looked away, her heart pounding.

'Say it,' Ines said, watching her closely. 'He's gorgeous.'

Flora didn't pause. 'He's gorgeous.'

'Oh, shit!' said Ines, panicking now that her bluff had

been called. 'Listen to me, I've told you from the start, he's trouble. Not right for you at all. He's chaos and danger and darkness, and you're calm and light and serenity. You are completely wrong for each other. He is everything you've ever said you *don't* want. The further you stay away from him, the better.'

'Don't worry, I fully intend to,' Flora said, viciously grinding the cigarette into the ashtray and scanning the menu, hating the way her stomach twisted at the thought of following her friend's kindly advice. She changed the subject. 'D'you recommend anything in particular here?'

Ines watched her for a long moment before answering. '. . . Go for the *moules*. Amazing.' Her family had been coming to the town for generations. It went without saying that she knew all the best places to eat.

Bruno came over, kissing his girlfriend square on the lips and ruffling Flora's hair as he sat down. 'Have you ordered yet? I'm starving.'

'You're just in time, baby,' Ines smiled. 'Were you humiliated?'

'Completely,' he grinned back. 'Don't mess with these old boys.' He picked up one of the menus, saw that it had burgers and dropped it down on the table again. 'Did you hear the town ball's on tonight?'

'Yeah. It's always fun.'

Bruno tore off a hunk of bread from the bread basket. 'Fancy it?' he asked Flora. 'You can both be my dates and I get to look like a player.'

'Ha! You wish!' Ines snorted at the suggestion.

'No, thanks, Bruno,' Flora muttered.

'Why not?'

'Flora would make a very sour gooseberry at the moment, isn't that right?'

Flora narrowed her eyes in warning. She wasn't in the mood for being teased right now.

Bruno shook his head, not understanding. 'Listen, you'd like it. It's not grand – why do you think *I'm* going? It's open to everyone – you just eat wherever you want at long benches and the dancing is some old folk dances and a disco.'

Flora pulled a sarcastic face. 'Love to but I've got nothing to wear.'

Ines reached over for some bread too. 'That's OK. We'll go back to that boutique. I already saw a dress that would be great on you.'

'Ines, I'm not going,' Flora said sharply.

'Flora! Yes, you are!' Ines grinned, matching her tone. 'You're being a cow. If you're not going to get laid, you need to get dancing. Your choice, *mon amie*.'

Chapter Twenty-Two

A note had been slipped under the cottage door by the time Bruno and Ines dropped her back. She picked it up and read it, leaning with her back against the door.

> *Dear Flora,*
>   *We have our first heir! He is coming tomorrow at 11 a.m. Would you join us in the library? Your expertise shall be much appreciated.*
>   *Yours,*
>   *Jacques*

An heir? That was quick, she thought, dropping the note on the coffee table and padding over to the kitchen to make a cup of tea. She switched the kettle on, then wandered through to the bathroom, stripping off and turning on the shower, deploring Ines's obstinacy.

She was about to step in when her phone rang in her bag and she had to make a dash to get to it before it switched to voicemail.

'Hello?' she asked breathlessly.

'Floss, it's me.'

Her stomach tightened. 'Freds! How are you?' She sank onto the side of the sofa, her eyes falling to the tight stretch of water in the pool outside, just visible through the shutter's slats. There wasn't so much as a breath of breeze to ruck the surface today and the temptation to dive in was almost overwhelming. She loved swimming naked but clearly that wasn't going to be an option with the number of CCTV cameras on the estate.

'Well, the CPS is pushing on with it. They've set a date for the preliminary hearing at the Crown Court,' he said tightly.

Oh God. She closed her eyes, devastated and berating herself for even being surprised. She had set herself up for this fall; by the time of that weekend at Little Foxes, he had already been held and questioned, charged, hauled in front of the Magistrate for a first hearing and bailed – but something in her had dared to hope it would all still go away.

She took a deep breath, as though bracing herself for a body blow. 'When?'

'September the twenty-sixth.'

Five weeks from now. Shit! She rubbed her temples, feeling the pressure building up in her. '. . . Are you OK?'

'Bearing up.'

Flora doubted that. 'And you've spoken to Mum and Dad, obviously.'

'Obviously.'

'Are they still in London?'

'Just gone back to Little Foxes – the pavements here are bad for Bolly's arthritis.'

'I wish you'd go back to Little Foxes too.'

'No. I think it's probably better if I stay here. They need a rest from looking after me before the trial. Mum's going to run herself into the ground and even Dad's reached his limit on shepherd's pies at the Antelope. There's only so many fatherly chats he can give – he's run out of ways to put an optimistic spin on it. It just is what it is.'

She looked around the plush cottage. What the hell was she doing here? 'Freds, I'll catch the next flight home. We should all be together at a time like this.'

'No,' he said, a little too quickly. '. . . Sorry, Bats. I just mean, it's actually easier for me this way. There's no point in us huddling around and crying. It won't change any-thing. This is still happening.'

Yes, it was. The flatness in his voice told her that.

'Look, I'm gonna go. Talking . . . sucks. I just wanted to let you know.'

'Sure,' she said quietly.

'I'll give you a call in a few days, OK? Honestly, don't worry about me. I'll be fine.'

He kept saying that.

He hung up, Flora sliding sideways off the arm onto the sofa, her body inert. Had anyone walked into the room just then, they would have thought her catatonic, but inside, she was a maelstrom, despair and fury whirling and roiling inside her like an electrical storm.

She'd never been one to 'make a fuss'. Her entire family was famously understated, even her mother – when Freddie had fallen out of the crab-apple tree behind the kitchen, she had calmly rounded off the phone conversation she'd been having with the line, 'Must go, Jill. Freddie's broken his arm.' Flora was cut from the same cloth, always calm in a crisis, even when she didn't feel it, even when others called her a 'cold fish' for not showing more panic / angst / vulner-ability (delete as appropriate). But there was no handbook on how to get through a situation like this. What were you supposed to do when lies tore through your life like flames, reducing your world to ashes? Just watch? Let it happen?

He had been right that day on the roof. It was as though a bomb had been dropped on their small square of green-carpeted England, leaving a crater where their home had once stood, obliterating in an instant all the carefully chosen antiques and worn-in decors, the unshowy vintage sports cars and dusty fine wines that had defined who they were and presented their family's game face to the world.

Instead, they were stripped back, raw and vulnerable in the face of the accusation, bitter, white-cold winds of shock and disbelief howling around them. In an instant they were reduced to nothing but this lie and although she knew that was what it was, other people wouldn't; they couldn't be certain the way that she could, they'd say there was 'no smoke without fire'. This would always follow him, it would be on his records, it would be the added whisper after every introduction when he turned his back.

It had fallen to her to tell the rest of the family. Freddie couldn't meet their eyes, he could barely stand up. It had taken almost all his reserves to gather them there without provoking suspicion – not entirely successful – to pretend that life was normal, to hold on, even if only for a few hours, to the illusion that their perfect family and the idyllic life they shared was still intact, pristine, untouched.

But the story was already half-told, anyway. They had all instinctively known that there was something devastating behind the dramatic weight loss, something that even Freddie's louche poses, lazy wit and easy smiles couldn't mask. Who was it who'd told her that animals could sense fear? Smell it, even? They'd all done the same, tapping into something feral and broken in him. But even so, when her words had clapped like thunderclouds over the room, her father had dropped his drink (Austrian ice wine, the lemon mascarpone cheesecake called for it) and her mother, who for so long had worried about such small things, had buckled at the knees as she stood nervously by the fireplace.

Flora quickly fired off a text before she could stop herself. There was no longer any reason not to. Her family had spent the past few weeks fearing this day was coming and now, finally, it was. Soon everyone would know their dark secret – not just Freddie's employers and friends and friends of friends, their collective acquaintances and old family friends, godparents and former colleagues; but complete strangers, people reading the newspapers on their way to work, office workers scanning the Sidebar of Shame for something scandalous to gossip over at the water cooler.

They were all going to read about Freddie Sykes.

Her brother, the rapist.

Chapter Twenty-Three

'Ball' was a loose term for the event, Flora decided unkindly as she and Bruno and Ines walked towards the heaving crowds. A stage and dance floor had been set up at the foot of the outer town walls, the countryside falling away beyond them towards the distant sea.

The outdoor space looked beautiful, the huge plane and eucalyptus trees so densely threaded with lights it was as though their canopies had been bleached white, and miniature French flags – threaded as bunting – looped between the trees that encircled and defined the space. Long tables flanked the dance floor on three sides and a small guitar trio was providing the background music to the surging chatter.

The crowd was a riotous mix of ages and backgrounds. Many of the local elders were in attendance, already occupying the tables nearest the stage, but there were young children too – some only toddlers – playing on the currently empty dance floor as their parents chatted and drank wine from the carafes dotted along the tables. Clearly, some of the teenagers from the ritzy villas in the high valleys had come along, the girls showing off their tans in second-skin bandage dresses and wedge heels, the boys looking moody in jeans and Lacoste shirts. And she thought she could tell the Antibes crowd by their low-key, stealth-wealth style: the watches gave them away and the Dinh Van jewellery, their coconut-oil glossed hair and skinny Paris-by-winter limbs. They were well heeled and well connected, their links with the town stretching back generations, no doubt.

Certainly, Ines moved through the crowd with the ease of someone who felt at home. She knew the mayor and his wife – apparently their daughter had once babysat her as a child – and fell into immediate conversation with a woman with candyfloss hair set so hard, it would have cracked teeth. Flora wanted to smile at the odd couple they made – the older woman in Escada, Ines in her Grecian maxi dress and flip-flops. Flora hoped her own dress wasn't *de trop*: a Missoni special, it was lilac gazar and embroidered with tiny flowers. The skirt fell to the floor and was swoopingly full, counterbalanced by a simple bodice with a high T-shirt neck and long sleeves that puffed slightly at the wrists. Apart from a nude slip underneath, it was entirely sheer, with daisies embroidered in a tumbling fashion. It had been the dress Ines had winkled out for her and there was no doubt it had the 'wow' factor, but was it too much for tonight? There didn't seem to be a cohesive dress code. Some people were in glitter and sequins, others in white jeans and heels. At least she'd brought the dress 'down' by teaming it with nude scalloped Chloé flats and pulling her hair into a simple ponytail, barely any make-up.

Not that she cared about how she looked. She was here to drink. She wanted to get so drunk tonight she couldn't stand, much less dance.

'Come on,' Bruno said, used to his girlfriend's social-butterfly status and taking Flora by the arm, steering her towards a gap in the crowd, near one of the tables. He poured them each a hearty glass of local red wine, chinking the glasses together. '*Santé.*'

'I hate this bit. All the talking – y'know? Who do you know? Where are you from . . . ?' he said, leaning in slightly to her, his eyes on the crowd as though he was standing outside of it. It struck her how much more natural and relaxed he looked twisting on a board three metres in the air, than here, in a pressed shirt and trousers. It wasn't lost on either of them that Ines was smack bang in the centre of everyone, her head thrown back in laughter and her white, perfect teeth an indicator of her pedigree and belonging. She could literally fit in anywhere, any crowd.

Flora drank the wine down in big gulps. Bruno laughed in surprise but refilled her glass without comment.

'You mustn't worry. She really loves you, you know,' Flora said, jogging him gently with her elbow as she began on the second glassful. 'You're all she wants.'

Bruno glanced at her before looking back at his girlfriend. 'Yeah.' But his tone was sceptical.

'What, you don't believe me?'

'No, I do. I do, but . . .'

'But what?'

'Will I always be what she wants, I guess? I dunno . . .' He narrowed his eyes, watching with concentration as another woman joined Ines's conversation – huge aquamarines sparkling at her ears, a Chanel Timeless bag dangling from her wrist. 'I guess I feel like I'm on borrowed time with her. I mean, four years on and I still can't believe she fell for me. *Me!* I'm no one.' He looked at Flora and shrugged apologetically. 'You know?'

'No, I don't know. You're a total catch. Talented and funny and gorgeous. Why wouldn't she have fallen for you?' she asked, slapping his arm playfully and taking another glug of wine. 'Enough of this nonsense.'

'You know what I'm saying, though. I'm never going to be part of that world. I can't give her that life – and I don't want to. It's alien to me.'

'Listen, Ines knows that world, she grew up in it. It holds no mystique or glamour for her. If she wanted it to still define her everyday existence, she'd be with someone else, you can be sure of that. She chose you. She's with you because she wants to be.'

He looked hesitant. 'Yeah? You think?'

'I know! Honestly, she drives me bonkers banging on all the time about true love and following your destiny, like I'm just being difficult not doing it too. She has no idea that what you and she have got is exceptionally rare. Contrary to popular opinion, it's actually not that easy to fall in love.'

Bruno turned to face her, his interest seemingly piqued. 'No?'

She shook her head, taking another swig of the wine. 'Nope.'

'Who were you last in love with, then? You've not been serious with anyone in all the time I've known you.'

'Actually, I've never been in love.'

Bruno almost dropped his glass. 'What, never? Oh, come on! You're kidding, right?'

'Nope. God's truth. I am twenty-seven years old and I have *never* been in love.' She gave a sudden nervous laugh.

'But Ines says you've gone out with lots of guys.'

She shrugged. 'I have. But I just haven't fallen for them. Not really hard, anyway. I mean, I've had my obsessions but . . .' She sighed. 'It's just never more than that. I don't miss them if they go away, I don't fret if they don't call . . .' Her voice faded and she pressed the glass to her lips.

Bruno shook his head, watching her. 'Poor Stefan. He never stood a chance with you, did he?'

Flora held up a warning finger. 'Don't even mention his name to me. He is not poor Stefan. He is a ruthless bastard who screwed me over to advance his career and score a point against a bloke who probably doesn't even remember he exists.'

Bruno held his hands up as though she was pointing a gun at him. 'Hey, look – I'm not defending the guy. What he did was shitty. I've ignored *all* his calls for the past week. I'm too scared of you and Ines not to!' He hugged her by the shoulders, grinning wildly. 'But don't think I feel any sympathy for that Vermeil scum either. What they did?' He tutted loudly.

Flora stared into the distance. 'Yeah,' she murmured. She wouldn't defend them tonight, none of them. She didn't care if Jacques was opening a foundation for refugees, she didn't care if Lilian had lost her friendship with the President's wife, she didn't care if Natascha was gossiped about in the tabloids, Xavier heckled in public. They weren't her problem. Her problems were bigger than anything even they were dealing with right now.

'Tell me about your new sponsorship deal,' she said, eager to change the subject. How had they ended up talking about Xavier Vermeil, anyway? Couldn't she have even a moment's peace from the guy? She took another slug of wine. Why wasn't she drunk yet? 'You must be so stoked.'

'I am. It's my dream, you know, being able to make a living off the board? I've just got to try and win as many trophies as possible and appear at any exhibitions or events they sponsor.' He shrugged. 'Happy days . . . Flora? You OK?'

'Sorry, what did you say?' she asked, tuning back in.

He put a hand on her shoulder. 'Is everything all right?'

'Absolutely. Tickety-boo. Just peachy.'

Ines sauntered over. 'They want us to sit, food's ready,' she smiled, sweetly taking Bruno's glass from his hand and emptying it. 'Thanks, baby.'

They found three free places at a table mainly occupied, it seemed, by a group of merry widows. Bruno, sitting opposite Flora, looked terrified and more in need of his skateboard than ever. Ines, of course, immediately launched into conversation as though she'd known them her whole life. Flora was seated next to Sylvie, a seventy-six-year-old woman with the skin of a baby who proceeded to regale Flora with merry tales of her widowhood and, in particular, her current torrid affair with the butcher.

The food was delicious but rustic, bowls of ratatouille passed down the benches from the waitress who stood at the far end, dishing them out from a giant tray. Flora took a look down at her dress and hoped for the best. One spot of tomato sauce and it would be ruined.

More wine was served and as the women around him talked, Bruno occupied himself intently with either eating or drinking; it meant he didn't have to make small talk. He took it upon himself, as the only man on the table, to keep everyone's glass full at all times – so that soon Flora had lost count of how many she'd had, which was rather the point for her tonight. She wanted to let loose. She wanted oblivion; she wanted to give up the pretence of being in control of her own life when in fact she was anything but; it had run away without her. What was the point in even trying? One lie and an entire life could fall. Why did anyone even try to keep it together? Chaos had its own gravitational pull; sooner or later, they all had to succumb.

The mayor got up to make a speech, everyone clapping and calling as he took to the stage. Flora shifted slightly in her seat to get a better look. A band behind him was already warming up, the guitarist strumming quietly by the speakers.

Beyond the stage, Provence twinkled below them, the vividity of the azure-blue sea dimmed for the night. Sylvie had told her there was a fireworks display due to go off at 10.30 p.m. – it would still be too light before then – and she could only imagine how much more spectacular the setting would become as colours were scribbled in the night sky, gathering the entire region under the umbrella of their celebrations.

She looked around at the crowd as the mayor spoke, intrigued by this madly diverse, eclectic group of people gathered together to eat, drink and dance by the foot of the town walls: rich and poor, young and old, local and foreign, families and dignitaries, lovers and enem—

And then she heard her. She heard Natascha before she saw her – that sharp laugh that always made Flora catch her breath, breaking through the respectful silence accorded to the mayor during his speech. Several heads turned, frowns settled on foreheads as the culprit was identified. Bruno caught her eye but he didn't need to say a word. She knew as well as he did that where Natascha led, Xavier was usually sure to follow.

She dropped her head suddenly, knowing that he was here and he had seen her; now that she had broken off from her polite conversation, she felt the weight of his stare as surely as if he'd been kneeling on her chest.

Natascha laughed again, like a hyena in the savannah, the sound warning others of her presence. In spite of herself, Flora looked up. Natascha was sitting three tables along; Xavier five people down from her. He was pouring some wine, a blonde – different from the one who'd knocked her flying in Paris – talking intently on his left. But as he put the carafe back down, his eyes rose to hers again with a certainty that he'd find her, as though he'd only left off from looking at her for a moment.

She looked away before he could lock her in a gaze. She remembered his snub this morning; and the one yesterday afternoon; and the way he'd called her nothing in front of his family; and . . . no. She was *done* with him, his games. She only had energy for Freddie now. She was on emotional lockdown.

And yet she didn't hear a word of what the mayor said. She didn't notice that everyone was clapping. She could only think of him, a man she didn't want to want.

She sat out the dances, steadfastly refusing to get up as she saw the locals arrange themselves into intricate positions. 'Categorically not,' she said bluntly every time Bruno tried to get her to join him and Ines, all the while belligerently, drunkenly watching Xavier dance with the blonde. He was an accomplished, if not enthusiastic, dancer.

'Come on, Flora, you're going to love this one,' Bruno said, breaking her reverie and snapping his fingers in front of her face.

'No, I won't,' she said.

'Too bad. I'm not taking "no" as an answer this time. This is the last of the folk dances.'

'Bruno, I told you—'

'I don't care. Up.'

Oblivious to her protests this time, he pulled her up by the wrist and led her over to the dance floor where Ines was already standing, arranging people into correct places. Everyone had divided into five pairs of lines that each spanned the length of the dance floor, men on one side of the pair, women on the other.

Flora watched as the MC – a portly man in a red braided jacket that looked more like a lion-tamer's suit – demonstrated the dance with his wife and two others on stage. It vaguely reminded her of some reeling lessons she'd once had as a teenager – linking opposite arms to turn, twirling on the spot . . . Bruno was right, not so hard.

She could see Xavier further up their line but there were at least fifteen people between them and she pointedly ignored him as the music started and the first couple in their 'set' began to dance.

Everyone started clapping in time, Flora too, as the first pairs in every eight couples moved towards each other and, linking arms, turned on the spot. She watched closely, concentrating hard and finding the pattern as the woman moved down the line, repeating the turning sequence with each man before rejoining her partner in the middle. At the end of the set, when the couple had danced with all of the seven other pairs, they then rejoined each other in the middle for a flamboyant twirling extravaganza (Flora was immediately worried for Sylvie – she'd mentioned something about a dodgy hip at dinner) before moving down the line to the next set of dancers.

Even feeling as tipsy as she did, Flora was pretty sure she'd got it: twirl your partner, link arms with Man 2, twirl your partner, link arms with Man 3 and so on until Man 8, then back to your partner who will twirl you like mad for sixteen bars. But . . . Flora felt her nerves spike as she thought it through more fully. Didn't this mean those at the top of the line would end up dancing with those at the bottom? I.e. everyone would dance with everyone?

Sociable it might be, but she could already see that it was Xavier's turn to move down the set and he was eight couples closer than he had been four minutes ago. The blonde was his partner, her hair snapping like a whip as he spun and flung her with careless ease, the girl laughing delightedly as he passed her to one man and himself turned another woman.

Desperately, she counted the number of couples between them. Five, six, seven . . . Had he seen her here? Did he know they were in the same set? She looked around, trying to find an escape route off the dance floor but Ines had positioned them slap bang in the middle, with two dancing sets either side of them. She couldn't walk between them without causing havoc – there was a very high chance of getting hit by an outflung arm or leg if she tried that – and she certainly couldn't run down the middle between the twirling pairs.

It was academic anyway. He was already here, turning Ines who was standing to her right and had clocked her dance partner too late. But Xavier wasn't looking at Ines; his eyes were on Flora – as he linked arms with Ines, as he twirled the blonde again – and then suddenly it was her turn, his arm pressed against hers for a whole revolution. She saw nothing but his face, the lights and colours and festivity around them smeared into bright streaks that flashed past in the periphery.

It was a moment before she realized he was supposed to have let her go by now. He was supposed to be back dancing with his partner in the middle of the line – Flora could see the girl standing alone, gesticulating wildly at the two of them – but Xavier was either oblivious or just didn't care, his arm as clamped to hers as if they'd been shaped from a single sheet of bronze: not riveted together, not bolted, but made as one. She felt her hair flying upwards, their bodies spinning in time, and when the music suddenly stopped and he twirled her into a dip, her body twisted round his as she stared into those black eyes that betrayed none of his secrets, none of his thoughts. Just his desire.

Slowly, he brought her back to standing, the two of them breathless in the middle of the line as everyone clapped and called for another dance.

Flora couldn't look away. What was he doing to her? He had been a bastard to her by intention, he had walked away from her, snubbed her – and then he danced with her like *that*?

The blonde came over, pulling Xavier by the shoulder, but he didn't stir. He didn't seem perturbed to be found staring down so brazenly at another woman. It was Ines who broke them up, yanking Flora away by the wrist and walking her off the dance floor and straight over to the bar.

'No!' she said, wagging a finger in her face. 'No, no, no!'

Flora inhaled, went to speak, to protest that *she* hadn't done anything—

'No!'

Bruno joined them, looking too scared to speak.

'Bruno?' Ines commanded, demanding backup.

Bruno looked at Flora, jerked his thumb towards his girlfriend. 'What she says.'

Flora sighed and looked away, back towards the dance floor. Xavier was still standing there, staring after her, oblivious to the blonde standing with her hands on her hips and calling him out. She realized why the music had stopped now; everyone was looking heavenwards, children (those still awake, anyway) sitting on their parents' shoulders as the fireworks display began.

Ines hooked her finger under Flora's chin and made her look back at her. 'I said no! You know what he is.'

A sudden bang split the sky, making them all jump and look up. A brilliant shower of golden beads was cascading towards earth. Flora looked up at the stonework in the walls, now picked out by the dramatic pink-and-blue spotlighting. She looked back at the dance floor again; she couldn't help it. He was still watching her, observing how her body language changed, how her friends had closed ranks around her.

And then he was coming over.

Another crack of the heavens; this time blue screamers, tearing up the sky.

'Oh God,' she said in panic, making both Ines and Bruno whip round to follow her eyeline.

'Give us a minute,' Xavier said to Bruno and Ines, but looking at neither. His eyes wouldn't leave Flora.

'What? And leave her alone with you? I don't think so,' Ines said fiercely, standing in front of Flora and crossing her arms over her chest for good measure.

He glanced at them both then, Bruno looking mainly embarrassed that his girlfriend was slightly overreacting to the situation. After all, what had the guy done apart from dance with her?

Xavier looked back at Flora again, seemingly instant-aneously forgetting the two of them were there. 'You look beautiful.'

Flora couldn't have been more surprised. A compliment? From him? It stunned her more than a double-punch.

'Right, that's it,' Ines said, bossily. 'Bruno, get my bag. We're leaving.'

'Ines, wait—' Flora protested as Ines caught her by the elbow and began to pull her away. 'This is ridiculous.'

'Oh, it's ridiculous, is it? Protecting you from making a huge mistake with a guy who has pretty much slept his way through Paris, treats you like dirt—'

The sky above them was coloured purple and green, a crescendo of 'oooh's coming from the crowds.

'Don't fall for it. Have some self-respect.'

Xavier's head whipped round, his eyes scornful on Ines. 'You don't know me.'

She looked up at him, fearless. 'No, but I know all about you.'

'And that means it's the truth, does it? The gossip you pick up at parties?'

'Friends. Friends of friends. Reliable sources. They can't all be wrong,' she replied defiantly.

Xavier turned back to Flora, dismissing Ines with the gesture. 'I want to talk to you. Just to talk.'

'Ha! Not based on what just happened out there, you don't,' Ines laughed, refusing to be cold-shouldered. 'Your girlfriend's not looking too happy about this, by the way.'

Xavier didn't turn to look, his eyes on Flora alone. Flora tried to read him – she didn't understand why he was so hot and cold with her; snubbing her one moment, chasing her down the next. But there was something there, between them. It might not be logical or rational but the air between them was always charged; neither one of them could deny it.

The sky flashed white, the explosion like a thunderclap. And as the night was suddenly lit up, she saw something over his shoulder.

A couple was walking towards a parked car – only the woman wasn't walking so much as being led. Or . . . or dragged. Flora squinted, trying to see better. The sky was jet again and although dramatic lights were being thrown up the walls, the ground beneath seemed to be drenched in blackness by comparison. But she caught a glint of sequins – gold hot pants, the lambent flash of long, long legs that were far too much on display.

Another flash and the sky lit up. The scene became more real, more vivid. She could see now what was happening. The girl was crying, shaking her head, leaning back on her heels. 'Oh my God,' Flora gasped, as the couple arrived at the car and the man tried to push the girl in, though she was locking her arms straight against the door frame and resisting. 'Xavier, it's Natascha!'

He spun on his heel and with the next whipcrack of light, saw what she'd seen – the couple struggling in the shadows. His face drained of colour. In not even half a moment, he was sprinting across the dance floor, over the grass, sending people flying as he roughly barged them out of the way. People stared after him in the commotion – tutting loudly, hissing insults, his family's disgraced Austrian name audible in the crowd – as they briefly turned to watch him race towards the parking area, arms pumping, the tails of his shirt untucking as he ran, before they turned back to the celestial display.

The sky brightened. Crack! Flora's hands flew to her mouth as she saw the man slap Natascha hard round the face, hard enough to make her hands leap to her cheeks, and he pushed her into the car, slamming the door on her and running round to the driver's side.

Flora watched in horror as Xavier raced over the grass. He wasn't going to make it! The car had started, it was pulling away, a spray of gravel shooting out from behind the back wheels.

Xavier dived forward, straight into the path of the car, landing on the bonnet. Flora screamed as the driver braked hard and Xavier rolled off, landing heavily on the gravel. People turned at the sounds, gasps spreading as the show on the ground began to outshine the one in the sky.

Xavier was already getting up. The car windscreen was cracked, the bonnet heavily dented, and it was clear he'd taken a hard hit. His head drooped as he got unsteadily to his feet, swaying. He looked up and saw the driver's door was already open, the man beginning to sprint as fast as he could away from the scene.

Adrenalin kicked in. Fight or flight. Xavier ran, his long legs catching up the smaller man easily and he dived again, rugby-tackling him to the ground. The crowd gasped as one – rapt now – as they saw his arm rise up and then dive down on the prostrate man in a ferocious punch. Flora heard someone calling for the police.

Everyone had begun to move, the crowd surging forwards.

'Oh my God,' Flora cried, beginning to push through the people in her way.

'Flora, don't.' It was Bruno, holding her arm, holding her back. 'Leave it.'

'But he's hurt!' Flora cried.

'Someone will have called an ambulance. Look.' He gestured to the crowd clamouring towards the scene by the car which was now hidden from sight. 'You can't help right now.'

'But—' Flora protested, every instinct in her body telling her to run to him.

'Bruno's right. You can't do anything. It's not like Natascha is going to thank you, let's be honest.'

Flora felt herself deflate. They were right. Knowing Natascha, she'd scream at Flora for kicking up a fuss and making everybody stare.

'Let's just go,' Ines murmured, watching as the crowd splintered – the older people and families with young children hurrying back to the tables, away from the violence, the rest surging onto the grass. 'I think it's going to be a while before they get this party back on track.'

Flora didn't reply as they guided her away from the commotion – she was searching for Xavier in the crowds but he was gone from sight; gone from her; that moment that had nearly been something, gone.

Chapter Twenty-Four

Flora gripped her hand tighter round her Evian, the glass chilled against her palm as her legs kicked lightly in the water. She was sitting at the end of the pool in just her bra and knickers – even at this time of night it was too hot for clothes – but she wasn't worried about being seen. The pool lights weren't on; they had gone off at midnight, along with the automatic lights spotlighting the gardens an hour ago. But even if they had been on, she didn't much care any more.

Everyone was in bed, the house in darkness. She'd heard the sound of wheels crunching over the gravel in the drive telling her when Xavier and Natascha had come back and she had stood in her doorway, desperate to hear something, to know what had happened after her discreet exit. Their voices had sounded so altered from usual – Natascha, not raucous, but weeping quietly, whimpering almost; Xavier's voice beseeching, low, tender. They had stood out there, talking like that for several minutes, Xavier trying to calm his sister before they entered the house. Flora hadn't been able to see the front door of the house from the cottage – she was side on to it – but she had seen the cone of light pool on the drive as they'd opened the door; seen it snap off a few seconds later as it closed behind them for the night.

She had tried going to bed, lain there wide awake with the moonlight playing on her sheets, her head running through scenarios that would never be, *should* never be, but the air conditioning was about as effective as a toddler blowing on her and beads of sweat prickled her skin as she lay awake, the sheets getting hotter beneath her, her heart skittish and racing . . . So she had got up and made herself a cold drink, stepping out into the night.

It had been strange at first seeing the house and grounds without their 'make-up', so to speak; the spotlights were precisely positioned to highlight everything to its best possible advantage but as she adapted to the darkness, she found there was something charming about seeing the garden minimized and stripped back, bare in the moonlight, the trees more navy than green, the grass bleached a ghostly grey in the lunar beams. She thought she was seeing it now as it was supposed to be seen, stripped of artifice, of pretence and posturing; back to nature. Behind her, somewhere in the shadows, she heard crickets scratch in the shrubs, an owl calling from a faraway tree . . . The crush of dewy grass underfoot.

She didn't need to turn to know it was him, she didn't turn even when he came and sat beside her, his thigh unapologetically pressing against hers, his feet dangling in the cool water, the hems of his trousers becoming instantly soaked and clinging to his calves. She didn't feel exposed or embarrassed to be found sitting here in her underwear. (How different was it from a bikini anyway, and he'd already seen that?)

Wordlessly, she offered him her water bottle. He took it and as he did, she saw the bandage wrapped around the knuckles of his left hand. She gasped, looking up at him

319

finally, but he simply shook his head imperceptibly. It was nothing.

He handed her back the bottle and she set it down on the grass, keeping hold of his left hand in hers. Slowly, she raised it to her lips, kissing the bandage lightly, her eyes closed in tenderness.

When she opened them again, he was staring at her with a look of wonderment. His hand grazed her cheek, his eyes exploring her face, his fingers brushing her lips. She had anticipated the savage passion Ines had predicted – clothes-ripping, back-slamming lust, the practised ladykiller working his moves on her. Instead, she lifted her legs out of the water and swung one over him, straddling him on her knees, cupping his head between her hands.

She gazed down at him, knowing this was a mistake. They hadn't ever had a proper conversation, only argu-ments; she didn't know him, didn't know his middle names or his birthday or what he liked to eat, and yet instinct was overruling consciousness, convention, caution . . .

She bent her head, her lips softly, finally, crushing his, and the world was swept out from beneath her. She felt awake, alive, for the first time in her life. She was in free fall in his arms. She was Flora Sykes, twenty-seven years old, and she was falling in love.

She sat on the side of the bath, watching as he got up from the bed, majestically, unabashedly naked, the moon greedily kissing his skin just as she had done. He moved like a cat, silent and sinuous, and already she craved the touch of him again as he threw her a glance, his eyes rapacious before he passed out of sight into the kitchen.

She tested the water temperature and swirled the bath

cream, feeling uprooted by so much emotion. She had never wanted a man the way she'd wanted him. Was it because he gave her so little? Had the tables been turned – her famous emotional reserve now played back on her?

A moment later he reappeared, two glasses of water in his – still-bandaged – hands. It wasn't just his knuckles that had been bloodied. His shoulder was badly bruised from where he'd hit the windscreen, his arms and back and chest scratched and pitted from the gravel. She had kissed every wound, revelling in the way he flinched and then relaxed under her touch, trusting her, succumbing to her.

And yet still, they'd barely spoken, their moans saying all that had to be said, binding them to one another more closely than a shared secret or past.

She turned off the taps and climbed into the bath, pushing herself against the back, creating room for him between her legs. He groaned with discomfort as he leaned back, his battered body protesting at the movement, but he took her legs by the ankles and wrapped them around his hips; she sighed as she felt his skin against hers again, his back pressed against her breasts, his hair against her neck as they sank back together into the water. She kissed his ear, her hands lightly squeezing the flannel over his chest.

'Is Natascha OK?' she asked quietly, almost reluctant to pierce the silence, the protective seal that enabled them to exist in this vacuum.

'She will be.' He paused. 'What you did for her . . . she's so grateful.'

Flora doubted that but instead said, 'She doesn't need to be grateful to me. You're the one who saved her. I just looked up at the right time.' She soaked the flannel again, wishing they didn't have to talk. Ever. It felt like walking barefoot and blindfolded through a minefield. She didn't know where the danger was, where the safety.

He shifted his head so that his cheek rested against her shoulder, his face in profile to her, as though he was trying to see her. 'Yes, but most people would have let her get in that car. They think that's all she's worth.'

Flora was shocked, her hand falling still above his chest. 'No—'

'Yes. She's the tabloid's favourite party girl. She's cheap, nothing, just a headline. She *deserved* to be thrown into that car.'

Flora didn't know what to say. The bitterness in his words was reinforced by the sudden tension in his body, his muscles hard again, that ball pulsing in his jaw as she knew now it did, when he was stressed. Soaking the flannel again, she laid it flat against his chest. He relaxed.

'No one ever asks why does she party so hard?' he said more quietly. 'No one. Not the papers. Not our friends . . . Not our parents.'

Flora held her breath. His parents?

He shifted his head, turned to face the far wall again. 'I am not the only one to know. But I am the only one who will remember.' She felt the tension build up in him again, like he was instantly ready to fight, and she knew his body was still coming down from the adrenalin surge earlier. When he did finally sleep tonight, she knew, he would crash into oblivion. She placed her hand on his forehead and kissed his ear, his temple.

'Don't think about it now,' she whispered. 'You've had a rough night. You need to rest.'

He shifted in her arms. 'But don't you want to know why she is the way she is?' The words were a challenge. 'Surely you cannot accept why she behaves the way she does to you?'

Flora hesitated. 'Maybe I don't think it's any of my business,' she said carefully.

'She is my sister,' he said abruptly. 'If you are with me, then it is your business.'

Am I with you? she wanted to ask. In all reality, would they have anything beyond this night? Surely whatever passion had brought them to this point would now be sated, extinguished. Done. They'd be free of it.

'Do you think she would want me to know?' she asked, choosing her words.

'She wants the whole world to know!' he laughed bitterly, hoisting himself forwards and standing up suddenly, the water sloshing over the sides of the bath. 'But no one will listen, that is the problem.'

Flora knew then. Or at least, she could guess. She watched as he grabbed a towel and tied it round his hips – the bruise on his shoulder already blooming – his hands planted on them defiantly, and she saw that same combat in his eyes that was always there, staring at her as though she was the enemy.

Her mouth parted in dismay. He was at war with the world, a fighter. There would always be passion, yes, but there would never be any peace with him.

'Flora,' he said, slumping suddenly as he saw how she retracted under his stare. He rushed over and pulled her up out of the water, throwing his arms around her, his face nestled in her neck.

She let him hold her; his arms were so tight she was sure her ribs would crack under the pressure, sensing he'd be the one to crack without it. Even aside from Natascha's history, the stresses on his family were intense; they were vilified, their fall from social grace catastrophic. The media hadn't let up in days and weathering the storm from behind the villa walls could only do so much – people still stared, whispered, pointed at them whenever they set foot outside. They couldn't stay sequestered in here for ever.

She waited until his grip loosened, his need lessening. 'Xavier, I want to help. I want to help *you*,' she said, leaning back and taking his face in her hands. '. . . Tell me what happened to Natascha.'

He stared at her and sighed, anguish a mask that he wore – she saw now – all the time. Only in the throes of his desire had he cast it off, swapping conscious pain for enveloping pleasure, his mouth upturned in a smile as he'd kissed her, mischief and playfulness in his eyes.

He sank onto the side of the bath, his head dropped. 'When she was fourteen, she was attacked,' he said to the floor.

'. . . Attacked?' She swallowed, feeling her anxiety rise.

He looked up and his dark eyes blinked at her, growing hard again. 'Raped.'

Oh God. Her hands flew to her mouth. It was as she'd feared, the worst-case scenario that had jumped into her head as Xavier had started on the subject, but still, she'd hoped to be wrong, exaggerating, a needless worrier like her mother after all. She stepped out of the bath and sat beside him, oblivious to the coldness of the porcelain on her bare skin, her hand squeezing his upper arm lightly.

'Do . . . do you know who?'

'Yes.' He turned to look at her, his eyes as diamond-hard as if she'd been the perpetrator. 'Jean-Luc Desanyoux.'

Flora blinked in surprise, her eyes wide. She knew that

name. He was a former racing driver, now a big name on the corporate-speech circuit, talking about what it takes to drive at 300 mph and not touch the brakes, how to take risks, work at your limits.

'Do you know him?' He was as still as a stone, watching her, assessing her reaction.

'Yes.' Her mind was whirring. He had a significant collection of classic cars and she had seen him at a photography sale in Los Angeles a few years ago.

'Then you know he is surrounded by powerful people. As he told her – and she, me – she cannot prove it so who would believe her word over his?' He shrugged as if the logic was indisputable.

'But surely, there would have been evidence? DNA? I mean, she reported it . . . didn't she?'

He slid his jaw to the side, his eyes on a distant spot on the bathroom floor. 'What do you think? She was fourteen and he was on the cover of *Time* magazine.'

Flora felt sickened. 'How did it happen?'

'She was friends with his daughter. They'd been at a party and gone back to her house afterwards. They were both drunk. It wasn't Natascha's first time but it was *one* of the first times she'd been drinking. You know that age – beginning to experiment.' He played with his fingers, his voice slurring into a murmur.

'Were you there?'

'No, I was at uni.' He dropped his head down, his hands on his shoulders, his elbows up by his ears like a child trying to hide, and she felt a lurch of devastation as she realized he felt guilty for not having been there, as though he could have – should have – stopped it. She watched, helpless. What words could assuage the horror of this?

He let his hands fall, leaning heavily on his legs. 'She was thirsty in the middle of the night and went down to the kitchen to get some water. He was in there, saw the state she was in and insisted on making her some coffee. He was nice, she said, told her to sit down with him, chat, tell him about herself.'

His hands on his thighs balled into fists, the bandages spreading tighter over the knuckles, and he stood up as suddenly as if he'd been launched. Flora jumped at both the suddenness and the vehemence of the action. 'But then when she tried to leave, he . . . he told her to show him what was under her T-shirt. She refused but he got nasty, said she'd been teasing him, leading him on, that she'd come down – half-naked as he put it – with the intention of seducing him.' He looked back at her. 'She was in a Hello Kitty nightdress and bedsocks, for fuck's sake!'

Flora stared up at him, feeling helpless, distressed by his pain.

'Our parents move in similar circles to him. He threatened to tell them that she had seduced him, that no one would believe her – she was a troublemaker and a liar. A fantasist.' He bit his lip. 'She'd been getting into trouble a bit anyway – skipping school, smoking – and she had been arrested for shoplifting shortly before. It was a dare, apparently, but you can imagine – my parents were furious. They thought she was going off the rails.'

'But they would have believed her if she'd told them what happened, surely?'

'By the time they found out, her behaviour had . . . escalated. She had become what he'd said she was. She believed him, she truly thinks she's nothing.'

That word again. The ultimate insult, the one Natascha

had been so desperate to see deflected away from her for once, defining someone else.

'She didn't tell *me* for seven months and we're . . . well, we're close. We have always had a bond, you know?' He looked at her and she nodded, knowing what he was also telling her here – that he was part of a package; to be with him was to be with Natascha also. 'She had told no one for all that time? Of course her behaviour deteriorated! She believed him when he called her a whore and a liar and a fucked-up little bitch.'

Flora's face fell. 'He said those things?'

'While he was raping her.' His voice was so distant it sounded boxed.

Flora felt pummelled, barely able to take it in. A fourteen-year-old child, violently assaulted, her self-esteem shattered, her trust in the world obsolete.

They were quiet for a long time, Flora feeling increasingly sick and sickened at how this universal act – cruel and vicious and devastating and total – had cleaved both their families; she felt buckled by the irony of how difficult it must have been for Natascha to tell the truth, how easy it had been for Milly, Freddie's alleged victim, to lie. Flora had remembered her vaguely from some group jaunts to The Phene in Chelsea, a satellite contact of Aggie's from university who had never quite made her way into the crowd . . .

'But your parents must have understood,' she said quietly. 'When she told them, they must have understood why she was acting up? I mean, surely?'

'Yes. They did.'

A 'but' hovered between them.

Xavier's expression changed again – the raw anger receding behind that mask he wore so well, a closing-down of the light in his eyes. 'They explained that it was a delicate situation. Time had passed. There was no physical proof by then and with her reputation being what it was . . . it would be his word against hers.' He shrugged. 'They said that if she tried to pursue a conviction, yes, his career and reputation would be in ruins – but in all reality it would be harder for her to go through the trial by media. She would be victimized all over again and there'd be no guarantee of justice at the end of it.'

Flora covered her mouth with her hand. 'And it almost happened again tonight . . .' she whispered.

He looked away, sadness and exasperation intermingling in his features. 'Sometimes I think it's like a death wish. She's deliberately reckless, provocative, pushing too hard all the time, almost like she's trying to make it happen again – only this time she'll do it right and they'll catch the bastard. I try to keep my eye on her, I stay with her when we go out but I can't be by her side twenty-four hours a day.'

'Of course you can't.' She remembered the sight of him, alone in the crowd in Saint-Paul this morning, and she looked at his bandaged hands again. Was it really those hands that had sculpted such beauty? She knew the lightness, the deftness of touch in them, she'd felt it for herself now, his hands expert on her body as though she were a map he knew by heart. But what about the soul that had crafted such an ethereal vision of love? Was that the man he would have been if he hadn't been forced to become his sister's minder? Was it the man he might still be? 'Can I ask you something?'

He looked at her, still lost, his eyes hard at first but softening as they took in her face. 'Anything.'

'Why wouldn't you see me earlier, in the studio?'

It took him a moment to catch up, realign his thoughts. He gave a careless shrug. 'You were too close.'

She was confused. 'To what?'

'To me.' He blinked, unknowable to her. 'I'm not looking for *this*, for you. It's not what I do.'

What I *do*? She swallowed, feeling as though she'd been slapped. Of course. The playboy.

He saw her expression and shifted his position, his hands on his knees, his back long. 'I made a vow a long time ago that I'd never leave her alone again. I'm all she has.' He looked across at her. 'But you . . . it's like you haunt me. Everywhere I look, you're there – in my parents' home, in the street, Chantilly. Even when I close my eyes at night and you're *not* there, I still see you.' He looked away, his jaw squeezed tight again. '. . . But at the studio? Even Natascha doesn't know what I do – no one does apart from Laurent, the old guy you met . . . It's the only thing that's truly mine but even there you found me . . . I feel like you see every part of me. I can't pretend with you. I don't know how to keep you out.'

They fell silent, Xavier getting up, walking over to the basin, his head bowed low as he leaned on the counter. Flora watched him – handsome, fearsome, fierce, wounded. She'd learned more about him in the past half-hour than she had in the past month, none of it easy to hear.

'So you're saying you don't want me close to you,' she said quietly.

He came back over, pulling her up to standing again so that she was almost on tiptoes, his hands on her upper arms, their bodies pressed together. 'I'm saying I don't want to want you. But being close to you is all I want.' His eyes roamed her face as he grazed a finger over her cheekbone. 'You're different to the rest, Flora.'

She swallowed, sure he could feel her heart thumping against her chest, against his – knocking to be let in. 'How do you know? Maybe I'm not. We don't know anything about each other. You don't know me. Not really.'

'I know you're not in awe of my family – I know you stood up to Natascha and me. I know you're independent, that you've got a great career.' He grinned. 'And you're sexy as hell when you whistle . . .'

Her mouth opened in surprise. So it *had* been him at the window, that day in Paris! But she had no time to object, as he bent down to kiss her again, a lingering kiss that drew their bodies tighter, closer, stirring up all the hunger she felt for him.

'Why are you even letting me do this to you?' he murmured, raking his hands in her hair, pulling it back slightly so that she lifted her chin.

'Because I want you to.'

'But you could have anyone.'

'I want you.'

He kissed her again. His towel dropped to the floor and he picked her up, her legs wrapping around his hips as he carried her into the bedroom and threw her down on the bed. She laughed, delighted.

He knelt over her, kissing her tummy, before looking up at her. 'Wait – what happened to that guy? The one at Chantilly?'

'Noah?' She shrugged, folding her hands behind her head. 'I dumped him in the car on the way back to Paris.'

He didn't reply but she could tell from his smile that he was pleased – and relieved. He began kissing her tummy again but she put her hands on his head, making him look at her.

'And your girlfriend? Or should I say *girlfriends*?' How many different women had she seen him with in the past few weeks? Three?

He shook his head dismissively. 'They were just distractions.'

'Distractions from what?'

'*You.* You've been driving me out of my mind.' He kissed her stomach again, making her sigh, her arms thrown back over her head as she sank into the pillows. He inched his way up her, his lips like feathers on her skin, raising goosebumps and making her wriggle. He lay atop her on his elbows, a hand on either side of her head, gazing down at her. He stroked her hair away from her face. 'I never did anything so good to deserve you.'

'That's not true.'

'It is . . . I'm no angel, Flora.'

'Who said I want you to be?' she asked. 'I'm not looking for whatever *this* is, either. I don't want a white knight, thanks.'

'Good, because I can't be that.'

She looked up at him. 'You always do that.'

'Do what?'

'It's like you're determined to lower people's expectations of you.'

His dark eyes flickered and she knew she was getting too close again. 'But you don't fool me any more. I know you're not what you want people to believe. That's just a mask you wear to keep everyone away, so it's just you and Natascha. It's how you think you'll keep her safe.'

He didn't reply.

'I get it. You're an amazing brother to her.' He went to demur but she reached up and kissed him, stopping the words. 'Don't argue. You are.'

He smiled. 'Do you have any brothers? Sisters?'

'One big brother, God help me.' She rolled her eyes, as she always did when asked this question. Her stock comic response.

'And is he protective of you? What I mean is, will he beat me to death for falling for his sister?' He grinned.

It was a moment before Flora could reply. He'd fallen for her?

'Freddie? Oh, well . . . h-he's so relaxed he's practically horizontal.'

Xavier watched her. 'And you are close to him.'

She nodded. 'Very. There's only two years between us.'

'So then I need to get Freddie onside. He's the one who can convince the rest of your family to like me.'

Her hands cupped his cheeks. 'They will love you.'

He stared down at her and a moment full of an unspoken, unspeakable truth passed between them. It was too soon to say it, to even think it.

And then in the next instant, it was erased altogether. 'No. Being with me is . . .' He looked away, shame flooding his face, but she grabbed his shoulders, holding him in place.

'Xavier, listen to me. You are not accountable for what your grandfather did. You are not him. Your father's taking every step open to him to make amends.' But still he wouldn't look at her. She put her hands either side of his face. 'Listen to me. I am *not* ashamed to be with you – I couldn't be prouder.' She hesitated. 'You're not the only family to have lies written about you, you know.'

He looked back at her sceptically. 'Oh, really? And which lies have been written about your family in the national papers then?'

He meant it ironically but she felt the tension set in her bones. He'd shared so much with her tonight, he was laid bare: his family's humiliation, his sister's attack . . . How could she not respond in kind? She couldn't avoid it anyway; the trial was just a few weeks away now and it would be her family's turn to grace the tabloids. How could she not tell him she understood him better than he could possibly know?

'There's . . . there's something you should know. It's about Freddie.'

'My ally?'

'Yes. Because he *is* nice – he's the kindest, sweetest, gentlest guy you'll ever meet.'

Xavier shrugged, tracing a finger down her nose, clearly not taking her seriously. 'OK.'

'The thing is, he's . . .' She didn't want to say the words, didn't want to give them shape, put flesh on the bones of this lie. 'He's . . .'

'What is he, Flora?' he murmured, bending down to kiss her again, his mind clearly moving on to other matters.

'He's been charged with a crime he didn't commit.'

He chuckled again. 'You sound like the voiceover person on a film.'

When she didn't reply, he pulled back and looked at her. 'OK, sorry. What's he been charged with?'

'. . . Rape.'

A silence as loud as a thunderclap shook the room. Xavier's body changed completely, his languid weightiness

333

suddenly transformed with a rigidity that almost lifted him off her, as though he were levitating.

'Xavier, it was a one-night stand, they were drunk – but it was consensual. The girl who's doing this, she's angry because he rejected her. He had a girlfriend he loves very much. It was all just a horrid mistake that's been twisted into this *lie*.'

It was true. His crime wasn't even that he'd cheated, but that he'd scorned. Just the way he'd recounted the events to her – 'I freaked . . . told her it was a mistake . . . high-tailed it out of there' – had told her exactly why lust had turned into revenge.

Flora herself had realized how often she'd catch Milly's gaze on Freds on the few times they'd all been out together. She'd thought it sweet, if anything, but it required no stretch of the imagination at all to know that Milly had seized her chance when she'd bumped into Freddie out with the boys, Aggie away for a hen weekend.

But the truth wasn't going to save her brother. It was telling the truth that had brought him to his knees: telling Milly, the morning after, that it had been a mistake; confessing to Aggie before she'd heard it from someone else; admitting to the police that they'd slept together when they first hauled him in. He hadn't thought to protect himself with lies, too lacking in guile to think that anything other than honesty was the best policy.

The prosecution's entire case rested on the text he'd drunkenly sent her in the club: *Where are you???* Separated, Freddie told her he'd sent it trying to find her *and the others*. But Milly's barrister claimed it proved premeditation, his client desperately trying to escape him as he 'hunted' her down.

It was a joke. The only person hunted in any of this had been Freddie, Milly even coming to his flat the night after when she heard Aggie had dumped him, trying to jump-start things between them and only succeeding in forcing him to reject her again. But there was no proof of that, even though they'd been over it a thousand times – she'd been too clever to leave any digital trace of her harassment, there were no telltale texts or phone messages from her; she'd even been astute enough to keep her face covered from the street cameras as she'd climbed out of her cab. Her brother had been no match for this woman scorned.

She brought her thoughts back to the present and saw that Xavier was standing, staring down at her with an expression more devastating than a slap. It wasn't anger or contempt – the glares she was accustomed to him throwing her way – but the worst of all: disgust.

She scrambled to her knees, watching in horror as he turned and picked up his still-wet trousers from the floor. 'Xavier, did you hear what I said? It's not true. I promise you. If you'd met Freddie you'd know I'm telling the truth.'

'Yeah, it's funny that,' Xavier said, zipping his fly. 'Rapists never look like you think rapists will look, do they? Monsters are masters of disguise. Most of France thinks Desanyoux's a top guy too.'

Flora felt a chill of fear spread through her blood. 'No, it's . . . it's not the same thing. Freddie didn't . . . he couldn't hurt anyone. He's nothing like Desanyoux.'

'Do you have any idea what that crime has done to my family? That monster, masquerading as a family man, a liberal? He's completely destroyed my sister's life! Every day, she lives with the horror and the shame of what he did to her, every day she wakes up believing she's nothing and she goes to bed thinking the same. She spends her every waking moment being what he told her he was, because she doesn't – she *can't* – believe she's worth more than that. Because of what *he* did. What *he* said. And now you're telling me your brother's the same?'

'But he's not!' she cried, growing angry now.

'You're his sister! Of course you would say that!'

Flora stared at him, open-mouthed, scarcely able to believe this was happening. 'You're Natascha's brother! Why can't you believe me the way I believed you? I'm telling you, he's innocent! If you met him, you'd know it too.'

He grabbed his shirt off the floor, throwing it on, violently shrugging his arms through the sleeves, wincing as he remembered too late his injured shoulder. 'You're deluding yourself,' he sneered, fastening the middle buttons incorrectly, striding into the sitting room and picking up his shoes.

Flora jumped off the bed and ran after him. He was heading for the door. 'I can't believe this,' she cried. Tears were beginning to slide down her cheeks but she rubbed them away furiously. 'You're the *only* person I've told. The only one I trusted! I was trying to show you that I understand the devastation it's caused you. I thought you'd understand – Freddie's the victim too.'

'No!' Xavier whirled on the spot in the open doorway, one finger pointed at her and stopping her dead in her tracks. '*He* is not the victim.'

She stared after him as he strode outside, back into the blackness of the garden. 'Xavier!' she called. 'Where are you going? You can't go like this!'

He turned, ten metres up the lawn but already a hundred

miles from her. 'I can't make my parents fire you, Flora, so I'll leave. I'll leave here tomorrow.' He blinked at her, that black look back. 'I don't ever want to see you again.'

Chapter Twenty-Five

The moon was still in the sky as she let herself into the flower room, long shadows stretched out over the floor, the riot of colours bearing down from the walls muted and subdued in the pale light. She switched the desk lamp on and opened up her laptop, firing off the email:

> Angus, I'm sorry but I can't work on this project any more. Things are too difficult with the family. I'll be flying back to London tonight. I understand if you decide to fire me. Regards, Flora.

She watched it send, aware of a weight lifting off her at the prospect of freeing herself from this gilded cage and this once-illustrious family.

She got up and made herself a coffee, the roiling of the kettle sounding amplified in the stillness of the house. Her hands clasped the steaming mug – she had no intention whatsoever of drinking it but she couldn't stop shivering – as she sat on the back step by the French doors and looked out again into the garden. Dawn was just a breath away, the first chink of light beginning to bleed up from the horizon like a curtain that was about to be lifted above a stage.

Only, the players had well and truly left this theatre now.

Xavier would be in Paris in a few hours, she would be home in London and this night – its exquisite pleasures and drubbing pain – would be nothing more than an aberration, something she'd forget soon enough, just as she always did. What was it Freddie always said about her? Teflon-coated. Nothing and no one stuck to her!

She pressed her hands to her eyes again, stemming the tears that had been falling as silently and endlessly as snow since he'd left. It had been three hours and forty-two minutes now but it would get better soon, she knew that. Her anger was beginning to settle and harden already. This wasn't heartbreak, there was no point in being hysterical about it. Just look at the facts – she barely knew the man, not really. Sharing a few dark secrets didn't make them soulmates; just because they were heavy in subject matter didn't make them more significant than the myriad tiny humdrum details that define people's lives, the ones you really have to know to know a man truly – like how he took his coffee or where he bought his socks, the name of his best friend and his first pet.

No. This wasn't heartbreak. Someone couldn't break your heart unless you placed it in their hands first, and she hadn't done that. What she'd thought was a primal connection between them had been nothing more than a thrilling game of chicken. Who would look away first? Who would run?

She put down the mug and lay on the floor, curling herself up as tight as a shell. No. This wasn't heartbreak. She was Flora Sykes, twenty-seven years old. And she'd never been in love.

The splash in the pool awoke her and she moved with a groan, at first confused as to why she was asleep in the doorway which opened onto the garden. A cool breeze must have been blowing over her as she slept for her neck felt stiff when she lifted her head, trying to see who was in the water, instinctively trying to get out of their sight. Was it Xavier? She blinked several times, trying to focus, but she knew he wouldn't be so stupid as to swim metres from her door when his last words to her had been that he never wanted to see her again.

Natascha then? The prospect didn't repel her as once it had. Not now. She felt nothing but compassion and tenderness for the girl, all her ugliness explained away – but how could she ever express that? Flora sensed Natascha would see her brother's revelation as an indiscretion, a betrayal.

To her surprise, as she haltingly pulled herself up to sitting, she saw it was Jacques ploughing up and down the pool, almost as driven as his son as he furrowed deeper and deeper tracks in the water.

Her hand touched the cold cup of coffee on the floor beside her; it was remarkable that she hadn't knocked it in her sleep and she realized that she mustn't have moved. Her body stiff and sore, she slowly stood up and took the coffee cup to the sink, rinsing it and leaving it to dry on a tea towel on the counter, before splashing her face with cold water. Her eyes – she was thankful to note she'd stopped crying at least – were puffy and swollen, the feel of her lids, one upon the other as she blinked, thick and leaded.

She stared around at the room – there was still so much work to do, this collection's histories as hidden now as they had been a month ago, but she would never know them now. She was done, here. The Vermeils' past was none of her business any more, much like their future.

Beyond the locked door into the house, she could hear

activity in the hall and she knew the family were up – or some of them anyway. Her eyes closed again in despair at the thought of going out there and telling them she was leaving, but it was unavoidable. Though she had done everything in her power to avoid running into Magda or Natascha or Xavier whilst working here, Lilian and Jacques deserved to be told to their faces that she was leaving. And if she were to see Natascha, she knew she would be able to let the barbs slide right off her now: let the girl be heard; let her be right even if she was wrong. She deserved that at the very least.

With trepidation, Flora unlocked the door and stepped out into the hall. The French doors through to the garden were open, the breeze tickling the flowers frothing from the urns. Her footsteps were silent on the floor and she realized, as she stepped into the kitchen, she was still barefoot, still naked beneath the loose Ba&sh dress she had slipped over her head before lurching up the lawn in the dead of night to send that email and begin her escape.

Her hands flew to her hair, smoothing it quickly, but she was too late – they were in there. At least, Xavier and Natascha were, Genevieve standing by the oven as she poured pancake mixture into a pan.

Natascha was sitting with her feet up on the chair beside her so that her bare knees peeped over the top of the table, a bowl of chopped fruit uneaten before her, her fingers swiping listlessly on an iPad.

Xavier was sitting beside her and staring down at the table, one arm flopped over it as though it was broken, his fingers loosely pinching the handle of a mug of espresso – short, black, strong; she supposed that was one more detail she could add to the tally of things she knew about him. Pointless now, though.

The bandages on his hands were grubby, loosened from their bath together; tiny bloodstains had seeped through marking them like stigmata, outward testament to his devotion to his sister. His hair was wild, like Flora's, and the rings around his eyes were so dark he looked as though he'd been punched in both. Well, he damn well should've been, she thought angrily. After what he'd said and done last night, he deserved it!

She watched him for a moment, feeling that familiar rush of longing and confusion that she got any time she saw him. What a fool she'd been to think that sex – even sex as good as theirs – had brought her closer to him than any of his other women, and it was all her own fault; he'd warned her himself he was no angel. She'd allowed herself to believe she was different from the rest, that he was a better man than he made out, but they weren't, either one of them. They were both totally and utterly ordinary.

'Oh, Mam'selle Flora!' Genevieve said in surprise, turning and spotting her standing frozen in the doorway. She frowned. '. . . Are you OK?'

'Oh . . .' Flora felt herself panic as both Xavier and Natascha looked up, Xavier visibly jolting at the sight of her. She remembered his last words to her and unwittingly took a step back, half in, half out of the kitchen, as though trying to obey. 'I'm just looking for—'

But she didn't get a chance to finish. In the next moment, Natascha had flown across the kitchen in a tawny streak and was throwing her arms tightly round Flora's neck. 'Thank you,' she repeated over and over.

Flora stood agape, her gaze as stuck on Xavier's as if

bolted in place. She saw the disgust in his eyes for what he considered her hypocrisy, her treachery.

'Really, I didn't do anything,' Flora said quietly as Natascha put her down.

'But you did. Do you know how many people ignored what was happening? They pretended they didn't notice. I *saw* them – they turned away.'

Flora looked back, appalled. She didn't know what to say; how could she say anything without revealing that she knew the full truth? 'Then shame on them,' she whispered as Natascha hugged her again, her arms tight around the girl's slight shoulders.

'I was wrong about you,' Natascha said, tears in her eyes as they pulled apart. 'I've been such a witch to you. Can you forgive me?'

'There's nothing to forgive.'

Natascha smiled then and for a moment, Flora was struck by the flash of youth in her face, the world-weary cynicism that she usually wore replaced by an almost winsome innocence. Was this the girl she might have been? Was she now what Freddie would soon become? 'Have you eaten? Will you have breakfast with us?'

She took Flora's hand and tried to tug her towards the table but absolutely nothing would make Flora take a step closer to him. 'Actually, I was just looking for your parents. I think your father's swimming but . . . is your mother around? I'm afraid it's urgent.' She felt Xavier's eyes alight on her inquisitively at the words.

'Sure. I think she's in the library.'

'OK, great. Th-thanks.' She turned to leave.

'Hey listen, we should go shopping sometime. Maybe.' The raised inflection in her voice turned it into a question and behind the breezy demeanour, Flora could see the fear of rejection in her eyes. 'How's tomorrow?'

Flora opened her mouth to reply, hesitating that she was going to have to confess her plans, here, in front of him. 'I . . . I'd have loved to, Natascha, really I would. But I'm afraid I won't be here.'

Xavier's eyes narrowed upon her.

'You're leaving?' Natascha looked dismayed.

She nodded, keeping her gaze on the floor. 'I'm afraid so.'

'You're going back to Paris?'

'London.'

'But who's going to finish the work? I thought there was months' worth to do? Granny was making such a fuss about not having the flower room for weeks on end, wasn't she, Xav?'

Natascha glanced back at her brother but he was staring at his coffee.

'The agency have decided to send out a provenance specialist instead. It's not my area of expertise.'

'That's such a shame,' Natascha said, squeezing her hand. 'Mum and Dad are crazy about you. I know it was you they wanted.'

'It's better for them this way.' Flora bit her lip, stoppering the words as she felt another rush of tears threaten; her bottom lip wobbled but she would not cry in front of him. She wouldn't. 'I'll just see if I can catch your mother.'

She extricated her hand quickly, stumbling back into the hall, her heart like a battering ram at the sight of Xavier so far away from her, further than he'd ever been. She made her way back into the hall and hid in a doorway, pressing her hands to her eyes as the tears began to flow again, last night's new, wholly alien feeling of hollowness opening up in her as suddenly as a sinkhole, threatening to pull her down, bury her, crush her.

But it was OK, she told herself. It wasn't heartbreak. It would pass. She was fine.

Even so, it was a few minutes before she moved, a few minutes before her breathing was steady enough to attempt a conversation. A few minutes before she felt steeled enough to get to the library.

The door was ajar but she knocked anyway.

She waited.

Nothing.

She knocked again – a little louder.

Still nothing.

'Hello? Lilian?' she enquired softly.

When there was, again, no reply, she put her head round the door and peered in. In comparison to the wash of sunlight rushing up the marble hall, the room was dim. Unlike the eastern aspect of the house – the side where the kitchen and flower room were situated, amongst others – the southern aspect was still in shade, and unlined linen curtains in grass green hung, half drawn, at the tall windows.

Flora stepped in and turned in wonder. Books, books, everywhere.

Unlike the more traditional dark mahogany or cherry-wood that she'd been expecting to find, the woodwork in the room was white – all the ladders and balustrading and shelving that spanned the four-metre height of every single wall. In the centre of the room were a couple of chairs, a large round table and on it, another bowl profuse with lime hydrangea balls and white peonies – Magda really did need that flower room, Flora thought to herself. Some of the shelving on the left wall had been cut around a nook, inside which an ivory linen sofa had been pushed.

'Lilian?' she asked again, turning slowly on the spot, her eyes scanning the walkway on the upper levels. But she was alone.

She was about to leave when her eyes fell to an old cardboard box beside the sofa. *Vienna / Paris* had been written on the side in black marker pen and the taped seal sliced open, a silver letter opener still on one of the cardboard leaves, an orange suede album, it seemed, set on its side and peeping out of the top. Flora walked over and picked it up. Was this what she thought it was? She remembered how Lilian had told her there were no old family photographs from before the war: no wedding photographs, no photographs of Jacques' father. But that had simply been Magda's lies as she tried to keep their shameful past a secret. Only a few days ago, Jacques had stood in the flower room and confided his bittersweet optimism that he would finally see an image of his father's face.

The edges of the album were grubby, the peached skin flattened from use, and as she flicked it open quickly, she saw it was filled with old black-and-white photographs that were gently yellowing. The first one was a wedding photo – the bride in a long-sleeved, rather unflattering satin dress and limp full-length veil, an extravagant bouquet of dark flowers in her hands that tapered to a point around her knees. The groom was smartly dressed in a dark suit and tie, his shoes so brightly polished they shone. Their heads were inclined towards each other; neither one of them was tall and they both looked middle-aged in the picture, even though Flora knew they were nothing of the sort – for the bride was clearly Magda, her raisin-dark eyes unchanged, although here they glittered with love and not resentment.

Flora sank into the sofa, her weight perched on the front as she brought the album onto her lap for a closer look. So then, this was Franz Von Taschelt. She stared at the man's face, looking for traces of the monster: his hair was thick – unusually so – and very dark but with salt-and-pepper sprinkles at the temples already. He had what her mother would call a 'strong' nose and, if she was being mean, a slightly receding chin.

She looked harder. There was little in his appearance or demeanour to indicate his greed, his callous disregard for humanity. Maybe the intense shine of his shoes betrayed his ambition? Perhaps that wasn't love for Magda she saw in his eyes, his hands doubly clasping hers, but a love of money, of power? Or maybe he really was just a plain man, looking proud and happy on his wedding day.

She sighed, not knowing anything any more, her instincts shot to hell as she remembered Xavier's words all too clearly: *'Monsters are masters of disguise.'*

She glanced at the cover. 'Vienna and Paris' had been blind-embossed on the orange suede cover. She turned the page after the wedding picture. Another photo showed Magda sitting on a picnic blanket, a small hamper by her knees as she squinted up at the camera, her hand shading her eyes; a tiny blur at the side of the shot indicated that the photographer (Franz?) had left his finger over the aperture. In the photo beside it, the two of them were leaning against a wall, both wearing hand-knitted cardigans, the wind catching their hair.

She turned the page: Magda sitting in a small white sports car – Freddie would recognize it in a flash, he was such a petrol head – her hair covered with a silk scarf; Another at a castle or chateau with Magda in a coat leaning against a crenelated wall, an ancient forest in the background. In all the photos, she appeared somehow slightly dissatisfied, a hint of a frown on her brow, impatience in her smile.

Flora kept turning the pages. Magda sitting outdoors at a café with two women – Flora peered closer, picking up a resemblance between Magda and one of them. Her sister? The other woman caught her attention too, though she couldn't make out why; she didn't think she could have seen her before.

One of Franz standing outside a shop with another man, his hands folded behind his back, his chest puffed out proudly. Flora's eyes picked out the bottoms of the words, framed in an oval, just visible in the top of the frame. If she hadn't known what to look for, she couldn't have deciphered it, but she did know; she had seen it replicated in the old stickers on the backs of the paintings and heading the ledgers still kept in the gallery in Saint-Paul: Blumka Von Taschelt, the gallery Franz had run in Vienna before the Anschluss, dating this photograph between 1934 and 1938. So then, was the other man in the photo Blumka?

She turned the pages more quickly, noticing how their circumstances began to change: Franz filled out, his cheeks became rounder, the weight adding strength to his features. Something in his demeanour changed too, his chin pushed up, his eyes stared back at the camera with, if not quite superiority, then something like it. Was it pride? That first taste of success? Power suited him.

Certainly his suits fitted better, his shoes shone brighter, Magda had her hair cut fashionably short, started wearing showy jewellery. Flora stopped towards the back of the album at a photo taken of both Franz and Magda at a formal event. They were standing on the steps of some-where grand – an opera house perhaps? – Franz in tails and a hat, Magda in a pale satin dress with pleats, a fox fur over one shoulder and a feather in her hair.

There was no doubt they had moved up in the world, but their body language had changed too. Where Magda had dominated the early snaps with her beady eyes and passive-aggressive agitation, now Franz had eclipsed her – laughing easily in the frames, his hands more often louchely stuffed in his pockets than holding his wife's. They stood together but apart.

Flora stared at him, willing herself to see his monstrous-ness now. He was well on his way – making money, hitting the big time. But at worst that only made him a vain, selfish man.

Then she turned the page and saw it: proof in the boldest terms of what he was capable of. They were sitting in a formal drawing room with another couple – Flora recog-nized the other woman from the café snap.

It was clear they were all great friends, well matched in their lifestyles – all were in evening dress, low-ball drinks in their hands, jewel-coloured Tiffany glass lamps on the tables and fringed silk shawls draped over the sofas. Magda stared straight to camera, somehow dissonant from the little group, but Franz was centrally positioned, one hand on the other man's shoulder as the two of them stood behind their seated wives, the other woman half-turned in Franz's direction and laughing at something he must have said.

Which made his betrayal all the greater, his monstrosity

laid as bare, with hindsight, as if he'd been standing there with two heads. Flora couldn't take her eyes off the paintings on the back wall – the Renoirs, that portrait; even in black and white, she could detect the richness of tone in the peacock-blue dress, the ruby a rich drop of blood red on the woman's hand.

Suddenly she knew why the woman seemed familiar to her. She had seen her before, in another photo still kept in Vienna, in a portrait that had been found in Paris. She even knew her name: Natalya Spiegel. And her husband, Noah had told her, was Juls. They had been friends!

Flora stared at their faces, all of them having a good time, full of vitality and high spirits, no sense yet of the horrors that were to come their way; no sense yet that the camaraderie was a sham, the friendship an illusion. That only the paintings, ergo the money, mattered.

Flora stared at Franz, drinking his friend's Scotch and no doubt flirting with his wife, the man who would one day soon turn them over to the Nazis and pocket his commission. The traitor in their midst.

When had they realized, she wondered, that he had betrayed them? When they'd signed the contract he pushed before them? When they'd answered the door to those SS soldiers? As they'd been hustled onto the train, still thinking they were heading for the border? Or maybe they had never known his role in it. Perhaps he had got away with it and they had gone to their deaths thinking him the good friend he'd always been. Had that thought sustained him? Reputation was all to men of power, was it not? Hadn't the Nazis – Hitler and Göring themselves – even as they plundered Europe of its greatest cultural treasures, tried to present themselves to the world as aesthetes and not thieves? Art was the only currency with any value for them. They had wanted to be remembered as men of taste, of supreme civilization. The master race.

The thought stopped her. Reputation is legacy . . .

An idea came to her. She punched the number in her phone and dialled.

'It's me,' she said quickly, before he could reply. 'If I mean anything to you at all, then you'll do exactly as I ask.

Chapter Twenty-Six

'Oh, Flora, there you are!' The voice broke through Flora's immersion in the pictures and she looked up in surprise to see Lilian coming into the library. 'Natascha said you were looking for me.'

Hurriedly, Flora snapped the album shut but it was pointless trying to pretend she hadn't been snooping. 'I'm sorry, I—'

'Fascinating, isn't it? You know Jacques had never even seen a picture of his father until two days ago?' she said quietly, coming to sit beside Flora on the sofa and opening up the Vienna album again. 'Of course, he hasn't looked at any of these other photos. He took one long look at his father in the wedding picture and then walked out . . . He's devastated.' She shook her head mournfully and Flora had to resist the urge to clasp her hand. Lilian was her client, that was all – not the mother of the man who'd shared her bed last night, not the wife of a good man paying for the sins of his father; not the mother of a daughter broken against the wheel of social politics.

She closed her eyes for a moment, knowing now how right she was in leaving here. She'd been getting too close, blurring the boundaries. This family, this troubled, beleaguered, powerful family, was not her concern.

'Are you OK, Flora? Genevieve said you really don't look well and I have to say I agree with her. '

'Oh, no, really, I'm fine. Just tired.' She thought Lilian looked little better than she did, to be honest. What on earth had happened to the two of them, she wondered, remembering their poise and polish in the early meetings. Not even a month later and they were shadows of their former selves.

'Is it the cottage? Is the air conditioning OK? It can play up a bit sometimes and I know that can be just havoc on *my* sleep.'

'Oh,' Flora tried to smile. 'No, it's not . . . no.' She stared at her hands, summoning her courage. 'Uh, Lilian, I'm sorry to have to say I'm going to be returning to London tonight.'

'London?' Lilian gasped, as though she'd said the North Pole.

'Yes. But don't worry. Angus is sending over an expert in provenance research. Her name's Bridget Plaidstow. She's like a modern-day Miss Marple – honestly, she can uncover anything.'

'I thought *you'd* done rather well at that, to be honest.'

Flora glanced at Lilian to find she was smiling. 'Well, it's not my strength. Things will move a lot more quickly with Bridget. The project is so huge you'll really be better off with a specialist.'

There was a brief pause, Lilian watching her intensely, taking in her dishevelled appearance. Flora hoped she hadn't noticed that her son looked almost exactly the same. 'Is that really the reason?'

'I'm sorry?'

'Well, the past few weeks haven't been without event,' she said with characteristic understatement. 'And I'm under no illusions as to how prickly my family can be. Plus I heard about what happened last night . . .'

Flora felt the world rock. What? Had Xavier announced he was leaving? Had he told . . . ?

'What you did for Natascha.'

Oh. 'But I really didn't—'

'Yes, she said you'd say that.' Lilian hesitated, taking a deep breath. 'I don't know if you know anything about Natascha's past—'

'I do,' Flora said quickly, not wanting to make her say the words, not wanting to face the hypocrisy of sitting here sympathetically, even as she led the rally cries for her brother in the other camp. That what he was accused of was lies, scarcely seemed to matter. Was it any wonder Xavier couldn't bear to look at her? 'I do. And I'm so sorry. For what it's worth, I think she's a lovely young woman. I hope she'll believe that one day too.'

At her words, Lilian's face crumpled suddenly, all her elegant composure gone in a flash, and she covered her face with her hands as her shoulders began to heave.

'Oh, Lilian,' Flora gasped, horrified to have made her cry, to have made things worse yet again, when all she'd wanted was to make them better. She shuffled closer to her and put an arm hesitantly around her. To her astonishment, Lilian reached back with both arms, grasping her and holding on to her firmly as she sobbed, as though she was a life-raft in storm waters.

They sat there like that for several minutes, were still sitting like that when the library door suddenly opened and Xavier walked in. He stopped in his tracks at the sight of Flora holding his weeping mother. Had she been doing a life-drawing of her in the nude, he couldn't have looked more shocked, and Flora half-wondered whether he'd ever actually seen his mother cry before.

'What have you done?' he asked her coldly, striding over.

Lilian looked up at the sound of his voice, instantly remembering herself as she inhaled sharply and patted her cheeks dry, pushing her index fingers against her lower lashes and removing the mascara stains. 'Killing me with kindness, darling,' Lilian said, managing a smile and, looking over at Flora, patting her knee. 'Thank you. Please don't leave without saying goodbye, will you?'

'Of course not.' She didn't dare meet Xavier's eyes.

'What is it, darling?' Lilian asked her son as she rose to her feet, her voice shaky but perfectly in control again.

'Father's looking for you. He wants to talk to you before the meeting.'

Lilian looked back at Flora. 'Oh, you will still come to that, won't you, Flora? We will need your help. I'm afraid we wouldn't know the first thing about how to prove if this claim is genuine or not and I suppose this advert is going to attract a number of hoaxers.'

'Of course,' Flora nodded, trying to smile. 'My flight's not till this afternoon.'

She felt Xavier's eyes on her and she wondered if he would stay, now that she was the one falling on her sword?

Lilian reached out for him, her hand patting his shoulder. 'You're my good boy,' she murmured affectionately.

Flora – and Lilian – saw him wince.

'Oh, darling, your poor shoulder.'

'It's fine.'

'Are you sure you shouldn't get it X-rayed?'

'It's fine, Mother. Just bruised.'

'You should have a hot bath to bring it out.'

355

Xavier instinctively looked across at Flora again – flashes of the tenderness, the intimacy they had shared for just a few precious hours, racing through both their minds. But then of course too, the secrets shared, the darkness in the centre of both their lives, spilled like blood on the floor, separating them once again.

'I already have,' he said quietly, offering his mother his arm and escorting her out of the room.

Flora watched as the door clicked shut. Was that the last time she'd ever see him? Tears rushed at the thought as she stared at the closed door, seeing nothing, trying to feel nothing, to ignore the sudden sense that without *him* she was nothing.

But the door didn't open. He wasn't coming back.

The sun was already moving round the house, peeping in at the windows like a playful child. She knew she needed to get back to the cottage and get dressed. If she was going to go to this meeting, she couldn't turn up looking as though she'd slept in the bushes. And yet . . . Her feet wouldn't move. She didn't care that she was pale, her eyes puffy; she didn't care that her hair was still tousled from playing in bed.

Her eyes scanned the room, saying goodbye. In a few hours she would be gone from here and back to the real world, running home to the faded, cluttered, shabby decor of Little Foxes where the strips of wallpaper in the family bathroom remained, twenty-seven years after Freddie had torn them as a toddler, and their heights on each birthday were all painted inside the door on the cupboard under the stairs. The only marble in their house was on the chess board and her father's taste in antiques ran to the Regency period rather than the Greco-Roman antiquities that Magda clearly favoured.

Lilian had left the album lying open on the sofa and automatically Flora went to close it, wondering whether Jacques would ever get past the first page. He didn't have to forgive his father, but surely he would want to at least see his story? Didn't everyone have an innate need to know the stock from which they came? Their tribe?

She replaced the album in the box, but as she went to close the flaps, she glimpsed a slip of ballet-pink satin down the side. She slid her hand in and pulled out a thin bundle of letters tied in ribbon, the envelopes so delicate and aged as to be friable, thumbprints visible on the paper from multiple readings.

Magda Von Taschelt was the name written on the envelopes, but the address was neither Vienna, Paris nor Antibes. It was Geneva.

Switzerland? So that was where Magda had escaped to? Because of Franz's collaboration with the Germans?

She pulled on the ribbon, knowing this was beyond her remit – she had quit and this wasn't her concern any more – but she was too far in not to know.

The bow gave easily, the letters weighty in her hands. She pulled the first letter from its envelope and began to read.

Paris 75010
12th October 1942

Magda, my darling,
Your letter brought me great joy. You cannot imagine my relief to know everything went as planned. There is so much uncertainty in

this world we find ourselves in, it gladdens my heart to know you are safe. Forgive me that I am not there by your side.

I miss you so very much but am remaining busy. It helps no one if I dwell on my doubts and besides, there is much to do. Every day, there are more people, more deals and if it is not me, then who? You will be pleased to hear the Miró consignment was shipped safely, docking in New York two days ago. Things are very different there – the sun continues to shine, the world continues to spin, the markets continue to prosper. You could be forgiven for forgetting, on those shores, that the rest of the world is at war.

I have been finalizing plans for a delivery to Copenhagen next week. God willing, all will be well. The situation is worsening in the city, here – hundreds are leaving, paranoia grows, I cannot trust anyone. I suspect I am being watched. Old friends have become new enemies. My heart breaks a thousand times a day and is only put together again at the thought that you are not here to see it.

Bring me more happiness in your next letter. Write to me and tell me about the mountains. Has the snow come? Are the night skies silent from bombs?

I shall write again soon, my darling.

Your loving husband,

Franz

Flora folded the letter and took a moment to consider it, feeling conflicted about the discrepancies in it – sympathizing with the Jews' suffering on the one hand and then speculating on the upbeat art market in the US on the other. He lamented the breakdown of friendships – yet would go on, she knew, to betray his own. And in contrast to Magda's sister's letter, he was seemingly a devoted husband.

She opened the next letter with a sigh. What the hell did she know?

Paris 75010
18th November 1942

My darling wife,

Forgive my long silence. Things have become more difficult in recent weeks and I have been working almost every hour of the day. Just last week I was flown to Austria – twice – Amsterdam and Berlin, which is to say nothing of the work that must be done here in the capital.

I fear, my love, you would not recognize our home. The bombs fall like rain and the nights are as bright as day with all the fires. The 14ème was evacuated two nights ago when the raids were very heavy, but not everyone got out in time. The end of a block was destroyed, with a family inside at the time, sleeping – father, mother, six children. I offer thanks that they would not have known anything of it. God rest their souls.

On a happier note, I have made two more successful deliveries to America in the intervening period since my last letter. They cannot get enough of our European modernism and for that I am eternally grateful. It might be the only good thing to come from this war.

I saw Juls and Natalya in Vienna last week. They are bearing up well, all things considered, although their change in circumstances is severe, particularly on the children. They asked after you and kindly send you their regards.

Send more cheer from the mountains, my love. Your letters sustain me more than you will ever know. Sleep well, knowing we shall be together again soon.

Your loving husband,
Franz

She didn't bother to slip this letter back into the envelope, instead impatiently pulling out the next.

Paris 75010
2nd December 1942

Magda, my beauty,
There is little time to act and none to explain. Be at the border at
05h00 on 5th.
Take delivery of the consignment, batch code 01196ESR /FVT.
Cargo valuable beyond measure.
God speed.
Your loving husband,
Franz

Flora swallowed as she reread the note, taking in the hastiness, the cautious, almost paranoid tone. So they had been in it together. Magda – safe in the Swiss Alps – smuggling stolen art, building their fortunes as Paris burned.

Hurriedly, she picked up the next letter. The penultimate one.

Paris 75010
31st December 1942

Magda, my darling,
Herewith the final day of the most terrible year. These past few
months without you have been an agony I have scarcely been able to
endure. In my blackest moments, I crave your presence in the dark
beside me. Forgive me. I am a terrible husband to ever wish that you
be here with me, in this, and I am only lifted by the knowledge that
you are safe in the light.
As we turn the page on 1942, I want to believe the future is
coming. I try to sense bright new horizons where we will all be
reunited, to live as one family again. This is the hope that feeds me.

I think of you constantly and wonder what you are doing. Are you settled? Are you safe? My arms ache to hold you. It has become hard to sleep these nights. I fear God will judge me for my sins and the mistakes I have made on this path. Can any of us right the wrongs done in the name of freedom?

I fear I am suspected. Or that my usefulness is coming to an end. Or perhaps that is the paranoia speaking? People here are afraid of their own shadows, as thin as them too. I see the looks they give me as I walk past, fattened like a pig on the spoils denied to them. My sweet darling, have I the strength to continue on? Sometimes I think the deception is more wearing than the fear, but then I only have to look at what is being done to our people, and I know I must continue on. There is no other way.

Sending glad tidings to my little family for 1943,
Your loving husband,
Franz

Flora closed the letter, barely aware that she was breathing more quickly, her fingers fumbling with the envelopes in her haste. She opened the final letter.

Paris 75010
21st January 1943

Darling Magda,
They know.
You may not be safe. Move, disguise yourselves. Do not write to me here. Contact Travers, he knows what to do.
God speed to you and little Jacques.
Your devoted husband,
Franz

Flora closed the letter, her hands shaking. What had happened to him? Where had they gone? Flora knew Franz had died in 1943 but when exactly? January or later? Was his death connected to the event in this letter? And how long before Magda had known that he wasn't coming back?

Flora didn't like the woman, could scarcely believe she could feel sympathy for a couple who had profited so shamelessly from the war and yet . . . his fear had jumped from the page. Whatever he'd done, he'd suffered for it at least.

The library door opened and she looked up, startled, her hands trying to obscure the fan of letters on her lap.

It was Genevieve. 'Mam'selle Flora, they are waiting for you in the study.'

'Oh.' Flora was surprised. How long had she been in here? 'Yes, right. Of course. I'll be right there. I'll just . . .' She shuffled the letters back into a pile and retied the ribbon. 'Research,' she mumbled.

Genevieve disappeared and Flora got to her feet, trying to calm herself down, reminding herself that this family's history was none of her business. All that she had left to do for them was sit through this meeting. If the paper trail added up, they could all be out of it in twenty minutes.

She automatically smoothed her dress, remembering again what she was wearing – or rather, wasn't. No shoes, no underwear. She froze. Could she really go into a meeting looking like this? She barely went into her own bathroom looking like this.

She sighed. Attitude and proficiency were going to have to count for more. She was halfway to gone from here anyway. Who the hell cared what she looked like?

She walked towards the study and knocked on the door.

'*Entrez*,' Jacques' voice said from behind the door.

Flora walked in – and froze.

'Hi, Flora,' said Noah, a cold smile on his face. 'I thought I might see you here.'

Chapter Twenty-Seven

'Oh, you know each other?' Jacques asked in surprise, his gaze moving between them.

'Well, socially really, although we first became acquainted through a professional enquiry,' Noah said, his eyes never leaving Flora. From his quizzical expression, she could see he was wondering what was going on for her to walk in barefoot, hair unbrushed and with no make-up. She was a far cry from the poised, self-possessed young woman he'd met that day in Vienna and he arched an unimpressed eyebrow before looking directly at Jacques.

'Flora was researching the provenance of a Renoir which is the companion to one already in my collection and which my family "sold" –' he made speech marks with his fingers to convey he was using the word loosely – 'during the war.'

'A Renoir? Really?' Jacques looked back at Flora, clearly ill at ease with the unexpected direction the conversation had taken. It wasn't the painting under discussion today.

'Yes. In fact, if you are the client she was representing –' he smiled, coldly – 'and I do entirely believe you are, then I will be chasing restitution of that artwork too. I told Flora at the time I would be interested in making you an offer for it.'

'I see.'

'But clearly circumstances have changed since then.' Noah's gaze was hard.

'Indeed.'

'What makes you so sure Jacques is my client with the Renoir?' Flora asked briskly, sitting straighter and trying to exert a little authority. She had come in on the back (bare) foot. 'I have many clients, Mr Haas.'

'Oh, I'm sure you do,' he replied, his eyes glittering with the shared understanding of why he himself had not become one of them. 'Well, let's see – you told me your clients were based in Paris.' He gesticulated a hand towards Jacques. 'And that Von Taschelt was the last-known owner you could trace.' Another hand movement, this time made with greater irony. 'Not to mention your very special interest in the painting behind you which has brought me here today.' Flora turned to see the portrait of Noah's great-aunt on an easel behind her. She'd been so shocked to find *him* here, she'd missed it altogether but the woman's presence felt as physical in the room as if she'd been sitting in the next chair.

Noah watched her. 'Stunning in real life, isn't it? The colours really are something else. You can imagine how disappointed I was to learn of its actual whereabouts – given that I'd confided to you that I'd been searching for it.'

'I'm afraid client confidentiality meant I wasn't in a position to divulge the information at that time,' she said primly, looking back at him and straightening up again.

'Even after I'd told you what had been done to my family by that man?' Noah's sudden anger was chilling and even Jacques shifted in his chair, picking up on the animosity vibrating across the table, knowing 'that man' was his father. 'You still chose to keep quiet?'

Flora swallowed. 'I had no choice. At that point, *no one*

knew the truth about Von Taschelt's real identity. I was simply searching for proof of another sale between Von Taschelt and the man we believed to be Jacques' father, François Vermeil. That was my focus. We believed the sale to be genuine, we had no idea they were . . .' Her voice trailed off.

'One and the same man?' Noah finished for her, glancing at Jacques who had dipped his head and was staring at the table.

'As *soon* as the truth became known, Jacques took proactive steps to ensure he made what amends he could,' Flora said protectively. 'You're absolutely right, it's exactly why you're sitting here today. We're not trying to hide anything. The advert in LAPADA is going to bring in thousands of potential claimants.'

Noah sat back in the chair, looking for all the world as though this study was his and they his guests. He shrugged. 'Well, I haven't seen any ad in LAPADA. *I'm* here because when I saw the headlines about this family, I worked out what was going on. I told you in Vienna you weren't the only one who'd hit a wall with Von Taschelt's paper trail, so those headlines were a God-given gift! Finally, everything made sense – a long-lost apartment with all those paintings in it and then suddenly you're on my doorstep representing clients with the Renoir my family once owned, *snooping* around my great-aunt's portrait . . . ?'

His choice of words left her in no doubt that he'd uncovered her error in putting back the file incorrectly when she'd crept from his bed in the middle of the night to read it, and she wondered how long he had known, or at least suspected her hidden intentions. God, had he known at Chantilly? Was it why he'd been so bilious to Xavier, why he'd made such a show of 'claiming' her? Or had that just been male pride, plain and simple? Was that what was happening here now – her two-word text – *'Please, don't'* – after he'd sent the yellow roses to the office the final rejection that had curdled his feelings for her into something darker? There was no doubt he was enjoying this revenge scenario on more than one level – restitution of his family's property and one-upmanship over her.

'Mr Haas, however it was you came to find us, I am very glad that you did. I don't want to keep anything that my father stole from your or anyone else's family,' Jacques said strongly. 'Rest assured, I know quite well that it amounted to theft and it sickens me.'

Noah looked surprised – and, Flora thought, almost a little disappointed – by this response. 'Good. Well, this should be simple then,' he said after a moment, reaching into his suitcase and pulling out the file with all the original paperwork for the painting. 'I have photographs too, showing the portrait hanging in my great-grandparents' house in 1911, 1917. And then in 1926, 1933 . . . Well, you get the picture.'

He tossed it over to them as Flora shot him a look, unamused by his pithy pun, but knowing he was telling the truth. She had proof of the painting in his family's possession too – she'd just been looking at the orange photo album in the next room.

Jacques skimmed the paperwork, then passed it over to Flora: a receipt from the artist Gustav Huber to Natalya's husband Juls – a wedding gift perhaps? – and then the recognizable oval logo on the Von Taschelt receipt, acknowledging Franz's purchase from his friend, Noah's great-uncle, Juls Haas. She had seen all this before, naturally, but she took her time to study it anew; last time she'd looked, she hadn't been looking at it with an eye as to its authenticity and – although highly unlikely – it wasn't beyond the realms of possibility that these papers had been faked. It was amazing what you could achieve with tea-stained paper and a grudge.

'We would need to get these verified by an independent expert,' Flora said, handing them back to him.

Noah looked surprised. He had assumed his self-righteous sleuthing was a slam-dunk. 'You're going to do that with every single one of the claimants, are you?'

'We'll have to. This sort of approach tends to attract opportunists, people willing to give it a go.'

His eyes narrowed. 'Is that what you think I am?'

'No,' she said briskly. 'But we need to be thorough. I'm sure you can appreciate that.'

There was a small pause. They both knew she was being unnecessarily officious, her own petty retaliation. 'Well,' he said, 'I suppose it's not like you can go anywhere with it. Your secret is out now. Everyone knows who you are. There's no hiding behind fake names any more.' He was looking defiantly at Jacques, who didn't try to dignify the barb with a comment, but Flora wanted to smack Noah on his behalf. She understood why Noah harboured such bitterness towards Jacques' father – he was thoroughly entitled to despise him – but Jacques wasn't Franz! Why was that so hard for people to see?

'Well, I don't think there's anything mo—'

The study door opened and Lilian walked in.

'Gentlemen, Flora,' she said, serenely breezing into the room and heading straight for Noah. She stood before him in a cloud of Estée Lauder Linen and he automatically rose in greeting. *'Enchantée,'* she said, shaking his hand. 'I hope I am not too late?'

The tilt of her head – though her eyes remained on their guest – suggested the question was directed at Flora.

'We've discussed preliminary evidence but that's all that can be established at this stage until we get independent verification. But certainly everything is looking positive,' Flora said evenly.

'Good, I'm glad. There was something I wanted to add.' She turned to her husband who was looking ashen and standing stooped. 'Jacques, darling, I thought it would be beneficial for all concerned if your mother were to meet some of the claimants.'

Jacques' face dropped but Lilian didn't see; she was already looking back at Noah. 'I hope you don't mind but I think it's important to try to get some formal closure on this once and for all.'

'Actually, I do mind! I think that's in very poor taste,' Noah said brusquely, his colour heightening. 'Are you aware of the number of people sent to their deaths by your father-in-law's actions? He put greed above humanity. He chose to save himself by condemning others. He blocked their passage for flight from the regime. He double-crossed them in deals where as soon as they had signed on the dotted line, they were stripped of everything and sent in cattle-trains to the labour camps. People like my family.'

Contempt dripped from every word, Jacques almost bent double from the accusations. Noah's breath was coming hard but he couldn't – wouldn't – be stopped.

'I am sorry if this is distressing for you to hear, Monsieur Vermeil, but make no mistake – *your* family profited from *my* family's extermination. You have this house because my family were robbed of theirs. Why on God's earth would you think I would want to meet the woman married to *him*?'

Just at that moment, Genevieve came into the room holding Magda by one arm, Xavier holding her by the other as she walked unsteadily in pigeon steps, her cane swinging on her forearm, her face a picture of studied concentration as she stared at the floor. The dogs scurried at her feet, running in circles.

Flora found herself holding her breath as the old woman stopped before their group. Talk about timing . . .

Noah and Xavier saw each other first, their eyes narrowing in recognition before they both looked across at Flora. Instinctively, her eyes met Xavier's – her eyes would always look for, find, him first – but she swung her gaze away quickly to Noah, watching as she saw him register what no one else had: that they both wore devastation on their faces, their sleepless night as visible as a rash on their skins.

His eyes narrowed and she knew he knew. Or maybe he'd already known – even before them. That day at Chantilly, when three had been a crowd . . . Had he sensed what surged between them, though neither of them wanted it?

Magda looked up, at least a foot shorter than them all, and the energy in the room shifted.

'Magda,' Lilian said graciously, determined not to be denied, in spite of Noah's vehement protest. Charm would always blunt rudeness. 'This gentleman is Noah Haas.'

'. . . *Haas*?' Magda repeated, her voice a croak, but it wasn't Noah she was looking at. Her gaze had fallen to the painting on the easel behind him – that sublime rendition of femininity captured so perfectly in a blur of brushstrokes. Her jaw dropped down, the colour from her face drained and in the next instant, her knees gave out from beneath her.

Xavier had gone behind the armchair, propping his grandmother's walking stick against it and crossing the room to pour her a drink, but Genevieve, who was still holding her lightly under the arm, almost toppled as the old woman's weight pulled her downwards, and she only just stopped Magda from falling to the floor.

'Help me to get her lying down!' Jacques shouted to Noah, who – after a moment's hesitation – helped take Magda under the arms and carry her to the sofa. 'Genevieve, water, now.'

Genevieve darted out as Lilian retrieved a decorative antique fan from the wall and began wafting air over her mother-in-law. She was revived a few moments later but her colour was still peaky, though she insisted, via a series of irritable slaps on any arms that tried to keep her lying down, on moving to a seated position.

'Mother, I think we should get you up to bed,' Jacques was saying, looking not much better himself.

'Absolutely not.'

'. . . I should go,' Noah said to Jacques. 'Clearly your mother needs to rest. I'll wait to hear, but please – don't test my patience.'

Magda turned to look at Noah, hearing the arrogance in his voice. 'Haas.' The name, a question before, was like a bark now, and she stared at Noah with the sharp-eyed scrutiny Flora herself had had the misfortune to endure. She stared at him for minutes, her eyes examining every part of him – his hair, his eyes, his brow, his nose, his hands, his feet, his stance, his build . . . 'I knew Natalya.'

Noah stiffened, his briefcase held in front of him as

though it was bulletproof. 'My great-aunt. Yes. I know.' He was polite, just.

'And her husband Juls.'

'Yes.'

'You look like her father. Same profile.'

Noah looked surprised by the observation. 'Thank you. I didn't know that.'

She settled her hands upon her lap. 'They were our best friends. Did you know *that*?' Her eyes were challenging him, just as they'd challenged Flora, daring him to say it – put voice to the horrors meted out by her husband.

But Noah, as cocky as he'd been with Jacques, didn't take the bait. 'I knew you were acquainted.'

She snorted derisively at the word. 'How?'

'Photographs.'

Magda nodded, looking away for a moment. 'And you believe my husband betrayed your family.'

'I *know* he did.' Noah's voice was flinty, his tolerance for the elderly woman clearly paper thin.

'You know nothing,' Magda spat, undiminished by age and staring at Noah so hard, Flora was amazed he wasn't beginning to melt. 'They were our closest friends. Franz didn't betray your family, he helped them.'

'No.' Noah's rebuttal was absolute. 'He double-crossed them – robbed them and then served them up on a platter to the SS who were waiting for them.'

Magda stared at him with withering disgust. '"Art is the lie that tells the truth" – so Picasso said anyway,' she spat. 'But you see nothing.'

There was another silence as Lilian tried to calm her down, Noah clearly refusing to be drawn into an argument.

It wasn't dignified to quarrel with a ninety-nine-year-old, for one thing, even if she had been married to a Nazi.

'What does it even matter any more? I am an old woman,' Magda said, stating the obvious. 'I will be dead soon enough. I did what I had to do and we're all safe.' She looked at her son, taking his limp hand in hers and fiddling with the signet ring on his little finger, like a pilgrim with prayer beads. 'I kept you safe.'

Flora jolted as Magda's words chimed an echo from the letter she'd just read – Franz's orders for them to flee, to hide, to keep safe. But from what? If Magda and Jacques were already in Geneva by then, they were safe already, surely? It was Franz who had been in danger. She remembered his paranoia in the letters that the SS were having him watched. He couldn't trust anyone. *Hundreds are leaving* . . .

Something shifted in her brain, like a jammed cog suddenly lurching forward. The wheels weren't spinning yet but something had been dislodged, freed . . .

They know.

What had the SS known? Why were they watching him? And where? Like every *cinéma noir* film she'd ever seen, she imagined their spies on the streets outside the apartment, recording his movements in and out of the—

She blinked. Of course! From the street, anyone seeing him going in and out of the building would naturally assume that he was travelling to and from his own apartment, Number 8. But . . . but if he had two apartments, if he wanted to hide something, in the apartment below, who would ever know?

Flora gasped as it suddenly became clear why he'd had both apartments in the same building. Apartment Number 6 wasn't Von Taschelt's overflow storeroom – it was his secret. He *had* been double-crossing the Nazis! But what could he have been hiding from them back then that still needed to remain hidden, over seventy years later? Why the codicil?

She thought of Travers, the keeper of these secrets. He had lied when he'd told her the explorers had broken into Number 8. She knew that – the photos on the web proved they'd found the apartment downstairs, not the one upstairs. So why divert the family by handing over the keys to Apartment 8? It had made life inordinately more difficult for him exposing that apartment to the family's collective gaze – he'd already admitted to having to sneak in after she and Angus left, in order to remove all the paperwork in the apartment that would link Von Taschelt to the Vermeils. It had been a hell of a gamble. He'd had to hope that they would be so distracted by the art haul that they would focus on the artworks and not the paperwork – and they had been. But why go to all that trouble if not to avoid a greater risk? Something greater even than exposing Von Taschelt's true identity? What was in Apartment 6 that Travers – following instructions – had to hide above all else? There had been nothing in there apart from the portrait facing them all now.

'We're done here.' Noah looked at Jacques. 'Call me when the test results are in.' He began to walk across the room.

Flora didn't hear him. She was deep in her own thoughts, mentally retracing her route through the apartment. Why did a secret need to be kept for over seventy years?

In her mind's eye, she conjured the empty rooms, the bed, the crate, the painting. And something else . . . Suddenly she remembered what she'd found on the floor by the crate. Something so small and innocuous and covered with dust . . .

Over seventy years . . .

Noah's hand was on the door when Flora gasped, her head jerking up to find Magda already staring at her, the alarm in her face confirming Flora's hunch. Flora's gaze fell to the old woman's hand – or rather, the hand she held. The signet ring on Jacques' finger had been turned inwards, the stamped seal now palm-side so that it looked like an ordinary wedding band.

'It was never about the paintings,' she whispered, feeling the floor rock beneath her.

Noah turned.

'That's why there were so many in there.'

Magda stared back at her, defiant in her silence but quivering with rage as Flora shone a ray of light onto the darkest corners of her past, the suspicions hardening into facts one by one. She knew she was right.

'Franz *didn't* betray them – it's like you said,' Flora said quietly. 'Were those paintings just the ones the Nazis didn't want? The ones they allowed him to keep for himself?' she needled. 'And sell on for his own profit?'

'He couldn't even bear to look at them!' Magda spat, provoked. 'He never would have sold them!'

Noah came further into the room and as Magda's eyes slid between him and the portrait, something in her slackened. Jacques saw it too, covering his mother's hand more closely again and unwittingly bringing the ring into the light.

Magda watched as Flora's eyes fell to it again and she knew the game was up. She had run out of time, lived too long to outrun her past. She was quiet for a long time then, but nobody spoke to or harried her along, sensing somehow that the truth was finally pushing its way to the surface.

'What else could he do?' she said in a barely audible voice. 'He had to disguise himself as one of them in order to help his own – getting them the best price he could without attracting attention, negotiating border passes for art.' She gripped Jacques' fingers tightly. 'Do you know what it took for him to do that, right under their noses? The constant fear, the paranoia, the agony of the pretence? He couldn't sleep at night. He had to endure the disgust of people who had once been his friends, his blood. He was a Jew himself! Art was the only thing that kept him alive – his expertise was the only power he had. It was the only way he could help, even if those people he was helping despised and cursed and condemned him as he did it.' Her eyes blackened as she pinned a look on Noah. 'And still do.'

Noah swallowed, looking uncharacteristically uncertain. 'My grandfather told me he betrayed them.'

'Then he was wrong. He bought the act,' Magda sneered. 'Franz did everything he could to try to save your family. He sold what he could for them in exchange for those border passes. He tried to help make them look obedient to the Reich, *compliant*, but there was a limit to his influence. They already suspected him. He had tried to help too many others, that was his downfall.'

Jacques fell to his knees beside his mother's chair. 'Why did you never say this?' he cried. 'How could you let us – let the whole world – think that he was a traitor?'

Magda raised a hand to his cheek. 'To keep you safe, my boy. Let them tell lies. I would have weathered anything to keep you with me.'

'But the war ended years ago.'

Magda shook her head. 'Not for me.' She fell silent, her eyes as gentle on her son's as they had been hard on Flora and Noah.

No one said a word. Both Xavier and Noah had moved back to the centre of the room, standing, almost side by side, in front of Magda's chair. But Flora didn't see them – the only person in her sights was Magda, still hiding the full truth.

'Tell him.'

Magda glared at her. 'I have! His father was a hero. What more do you want?'

'I want you to tell him the reason why you've kept that a secret for all these years. Why you've remained silent and let your husband's good name – and the reputation of your family – be vilified. What could be worse than what you've endured?'

Magda said nothing, just gave a careless, dismissive shrug.

'I know what.'

'You know nothing!'

Slowly Flora raised her arm and pointed at the portrait. 'There's a very good reason why you collapsed when you saw this here. It tells the truth even if you stay silent. You've done everything you can since you came into this room to keep attention off that painting and on you.'

Jacques' expression changed as her words settled, his body stiffening as he stared at the woman in greater detail. Unthinking, he withdrew his hand from his mother's, pulling a gasp of anguish from Magda.

'You should never have gone in there!' she cried, directing

her fury at Flora all over again, her voice as splintered as wood breaking beneath a great weight. 'Never!'

The old woman began to sob.

Lilian looked over at her. 'Flora? What's going on?'

Flora's voice was quiet. 'The ring, Lilian. Look at her ring.'

She watched as the facts lined up like a slot-machine win in their minds, the reason why that particular woman had always seemed so familiar to her suddenly now so clear. She knew exactly what Von Taschelt, and latterly Travers, had been trying to protect – and it had been smuggled out of the house in that big crate with the painting inside. It was the reason it had been found set apart from the others, all alone in Apartment 6 – the secret room where the Nazis wouldn't have known, or even thought, to look.

The room swelled with silence.

Jacques, who looked ashen, stared at the painting with dawning incredulity before looking down at his own hand. '. . . She's my *mother*?'

'No! I am!' Magda cried, grabbing his hand again and clutching it so tight that her knuckles blanched, the ring hidden from view again. '*I* kept you safe, *I* raised you. You're mine. My boy. *My* boy.'

But Jacques couldn't take his eyes off the woman in the painting, the woman with the same ring, the same eyes.

Magda slumped, the fight trickling out of her as she saw the truth settle on her son's face, a truth she had hoped never to live to see.

'He *stole* me?' Jacques cried, sounding stricken.

'He *saved* you. And many more besides! He worked for the OSE, don't you see? He used his consignments to smuggle children to Switzerland and America. He had the perfect cover story – packing every crate himself, giving the child a sedative that would make them sleep through the journey, accompanying them every step of the train journey and sitting in the cargo departments with the crates in case they woke up or cried. And all the while, he was pretending he was safeguarding valuables of the Reich, lying to the faces of the Blackshirts.'

OSE? Flora had heard of it, of course. The Oeuvre de Secours aux Enfants, or the 'Children's Aid Society' had been a French-Jewish humanitarian movement that worked with the Resistance, going underground in the early forties. But to learn that Franz had been one of their number? She swallowed, feeling disorientated by the revelation. Where was terra firma with this family? What was real and what wasn't? Who was good and who bad? She looked across at Jacques and Lilian but it was clear they didn't know the answer either.

'But you, my darling? We couldn't let you go to strangers. When he learned your parents – our dearest friends – were being set up, it was all he could offer. I was already in Switzerland.' Her voice was thin. 'Your two brothers and your sister were too big . . . they had been seen, *counted*, on the first visit. But you weren't in the room, you were sleeping, not yet two . . . The Germans didn't know you were there.' Magda's face crumpled, pleating into deep folds like an origami puppet and she covered her face with her hands. 'They were such beautiful children,' she sobbed, her voice shredded now. 'But the house was being watched. There was no other way to get you out. You were the only one he could save. The only one.'

Flora felt her own tears come, her hands at her mouth as she watched Jacques fold in half as the loss of his family was laid bare – his beautiful mother, his father, his older siblings whose only crime was to be Jewish, whose fate was sealed by their age and size. It was that simple and that tragic. He sobbed, heavy retching sounds that came from a primal source, Lilian wrapping herself over him like an exoskeleton and weeping too at the sight of her broken husband, Magda like a prisoner in the dock, awaiting the judge's verdict.

Noah sank into the opposite fireside chair, looking thunderstruck. Jacques was his cousin? 'I . . . I'm so sorry.' He looked sick.

Flora went and sat beside him, feeling a certain sympathy for him. He'd been so self-righteous in his loss, so certain he was the only victim. How could he possibly have known the truth? He looked at her, guilt ringed with devastation. 'Flora, I didn't know.'

'No,' she said sadly, watching Jacques and Lilian huddle together like wounded animals, a look of desolation on Xavier's face, Magda as alone and silent in her suffering as she'd ever been; after all, she'd had seventy-three years of practice. 'No, you didn't. That was the point.'

Chapter Twenty-Eight

The cloudburst was fierce, hurling down stinging rain in torrents, but Flora was glad of it. The thought of walking into that courtroom on a bright, shiny day would seem perverse, to be surrounded by office workers in shirtsleeves on their way to have lunch in the park, women trying to tan their legs in their lunch hour, whilst her family were cloistered in an airless, sunless room being torn apart by lies.

Flora turned away from the window as she heard someone come into the kitchen. Her father was opening his briefcase and shuffling through the papers inside, a fixedly impassive expression on his face.

'Goddammit!' He slammed the lid down hard, a fist pressed to his forehead. 'Where the hell is it?' he said to himself.

'Where's what?'

He looked up, surprised to see her curled on the windowsill, her knees tucked up by her chest.

'My BlackBerry. I can't find it anywhere. I swear I had it last—'

'It's in the fridge.'

Her father looked dumbfounded. 'F . . . ?' He couldn't get the word out.

'I know. I thought it was weird too,' she shrugged. 'But I

381

didn't know if it was some techno thing you do – you know, to improve battery life or whatever.'

'No. No,' he mumbled, baffled and walking over to the fridge to see for himself. 'It's not some—' He lifted it out, looking worried.

'Don't worry about it,' she said gently. 'There's a lot going on.'

'Yes, but there's being busy and there's being *mad*, Floss. I may be getting on but I am not so doddery that I put my own BlackBerry in the fridge.'

She rested her head against the cold glass of the window and smiled kindly. 'If you say so. Is Mummy ready yet?'

'Drying her hair,' he mumbled, still staring at the chilled phone. He looked up at her.

'Any sign of him?'

She shook her head, biting her lip as she looked back out at the dreary street scene. Freds's street was always quiet during the weekdays. Parking was residents only, and the right-turn-only sign at one end meant it wasn't used as a rat run by taxi-drivers trying to get to the river.

'He should be back by now,' her father murmured, checking his watch. 'He's been gone – what? Nearly two hours now?'

'I know but . . .' Her voice trailed off; she understood exactly why he'd needed to be alone. He was due for the preliminary hearing at the Crown Court in an hour, and the dismantling of his life would begin. The press – entitled to be there – would, with minimal digging, soon realize he was tabloid gold: the son of the man who brought down the hammer on the *Sunflowers*, an arrogant posh boy not used to being told 'no'. His name would be splashed everywhere, there were no rights to anonymity for him. 'He'll be here.'

'But the car's coming in twenty minutes.'

Actually, it was already parked outside – she'd watched it pull up a few minutes ago – but Flora kept that to herself. It wouldn't do for everyone to start getting fractious about Freds's whereabouts when they were, officially, ahead of time. 'Don't worry, Daddy. Freds knows what he's doing.'

'You don't think—'

'No,' she said quickly, knowing he was worrying that Freddie had done a runner. 'I really don't. He wouldn't do that. Freds will face up to this.'

They were quiet for a moment. 'Do you want a drink?' her father asked, desperation in his voice.

'No, thanks.'

'I think I need something more fortifying than tea.'

She watched as he wandered over to the kitchen cupboard and poured himself a finger of whisky, before opening the fridge and pulling out some ice from the ice tray, replacing the BlackBerry on the shelf below.

Flora bit her lip but didn't say anything. She could retrieve it for him in a minute, once he went to check on her mother. She went back to watching the rain smear the windows. London was obscured – its stone buildings and rushing river just a smudge of grey – and she felt as though they were all in a bubble: dry, safe, together, sealed off from the outside world.

This was how the Vermeils must have felt, she knew, as shame and humiliation had snapped at their heels; how they'd been driven to hide behind their high walls all summer, only those wall-mounted CCTV cameras every ten metres the unblinking eyes that dared to look out.

No. She took a deep breath and forced them – him – back

out of her mind. She wouldn't waste any emotional energy on him. Not today.

'Oh! I think I see him!' she said suddenly, sitting arrow-straight as she saw a forlorn, lanky figure round the corner and trudge its way up the glistening street. He was still in his jeans and Vans – no jacket – and was soaked through. In another minute he'd be alongside the car sitting idle by the kerb, ready to whisk him to court.

Flora jumped down from the sill. Freds was going to need to change into his suit in double-quick time. 'I'll get the door for him,' she said, running across the flat and flinging open the door. 'Oh, hey, Troy!' she said as she almost collided with him in the communal hall.

'Hey.' Troy was clad head to toe in black Lycra, a high-vis fluorescent vest on over his jacket, his eyes protected behind clear plastic goggles, some mud spatters dried around the rims. This wasn't an unusual look. In fact, Flora wasn't sure she'd ever seen her brother's neighbour in 'civvies'. He was a serious cyclist, choosing to ride the North Downs every Saturday morning – whatever the weather – before breakfast, and every holiday he took involved two wheels and an Alp.

'Just going out?' she asked politely, her eyes flicking to the communal door, knowing that any minute now she'd hear Freds's key in the lock

'Yeah.' He double-locked his front door and snapped closed the chin strap for his helmet.

Flora stepped around him quickly to open the door onto the street. Freddie was already halfway up the steps.

'Hey,' she smiled brightly. 'I saw you from the window. Thought I'd save you the bother of getting your keys out.'

'Oh. Right. Thanks,' Fred replied flatly. He saw Troy and

stepped aside to let him pass. He tried to rally, keep up appearances. 'Hey, man, how's it going?'

Troy nodded. 'Good, mate. Where've you been? I haven't seen you around in a while.'

'Working,' Freddie nodded, rolling his eyes.

Troy skipped down the short flight of steps and started fiddling with the high-tech lock on his bike. 'You given any more thought to coming out with me one weekend?'

'Uh, yeah . . . yeah . . . I'm definitely thinking about it.'

Flora bit her lip as she watched her brother stuff his hands into his pockets, nodding away chummily as though his own future was his to control. She thought her heart might break just to see him trying so hard to appear normal, not a man twenty minutes from being driven to court for a rape trial.

'Don't think, just do,' Troy replied, pocketing an Allen key in the back of his jacket and wheeling the carbon-fibre bike from its hiding spot behind the bins.

'Had any more problems with thieves lately?' Freddie asked, quickly changing the subject.

'Not recently. This lock's the nuts, although I reckon they know not to mess with me now.' He swung a leg over the bike and sat on the saddle, only then noticing the flat tyre on his front wheel. 'Agh! Motherfuckers!'

Flora tried to suppress a smile as he jumped off again, examining the wheel to find a slash mark as long as his thumb down the inner rim of the tyre. He swore violently under his breath before straightening up.

Freddie grimaced apologetically. 'Sorry, mate.'

'No, it's fine,' he panted, his hands on his hips, his cheeks pink with anger. 'They won't get away with this. I'll have their faces to show the police this time!' he said, his mouth drawn into a thin line.

'What do you mean? How?'

Troy pointed to his bay sash window. A small black camera was only just visible sitting on the sill inside. 'The police advised me to get it after the last bike went. We'll see who's got the last laugh now, shall we?'

Flora frowned. '. . . Troy, when did you get that?'

'What? The camera?'

She nodded.

'Earlier in the summer. July time, I guess.'

Flora felt her heart rate quicken as she glanced across at Freddie who was merely looking back at her, perplexed. 'Do you keep the footage?'

'Sure, it automatically uploads onto my Cloud every night. Why?'

Flora tried to stay calm. 'Would it have captured people coming up these steps?'

'It records every person, animal, goddam *thief*, that approaches the flats.'

Flora stared hard at Freddie with what he'd always called her 'plotting face', before looking back at Troy again. 'Hey, Troy, if you've got a spare tyre, we can hold your bike for you while you go and get it, if you like.' She smiled, trying to look helpful.

'Oh, that's decent. Thanks.' Troy nodded, falling for her smile and passing the bike into her care, climbing carefully up the steps in his cleats.

Flora waited for the door to close behind him before she allowed herself a gasp. 'Oh my God, Freddie, do you realize what this means?'

'Not really, no.' He looked back at her blankly.

'Freds, you said Milly came over to your flat the day after, right? When she heard about you and Aggs breaking up.'

Freddie blanched, as though reliving events. 'Yes, but I can't prove it. No one saw her come in and her flatmate's sticking to her story that she stayed in her room all evening, crying. And the street CCTV just shows someone in a hoody getting out of a cab. There's nothing to show it's her. We can't see her—' His eyes widened. 'We can't see her face!'

'But I bet Troy's camera can! And if you can show it's her, it begs the very big question of why, if she'd been attacked by you, she would have willingly travelled back to your flat the very next day?'

Freddie threw his head back suddenly and laughed, his arms outstretched as the rain continued to pelt down. 'Christ, Batty, you might just have blown a fucking great hole in her story!'

She propped the bike against the wall and cried, 'I know!', throwing her arms wide too and flinging them around his neck. He twirled her on the spot so fast her feet left the ground, both of them laughing and crying.

'You always were my favourite sister,' he beamed, hugging her tightly.

'Oh my God, we've got to tell your barrister,' she said, looking up at him, suddenly serious again.

'Yeah, you're right. I'll call him now. Oh, no, wait.' Freddie raked his hands through his hair. 'Oh shit, what's the time?'

She checked her watch and pulled a face. 'He'll already be at court. We need to leave right now. Quick, go get your suit on, the car's waiting. I'll try and see if I can find the footage on Troy's Cloud.'

At that moment, Troy reappeared, the new inner tube limp in his hand. 'Right,' he said with a sigh. 'Let's get—'

But Flora was already halfway up the steps, ushering him back into the building.

'Hey, what's going on?'

'No time to explain, Troy,' she said breathlessly, pushing on his back and urging him to move faster. 'I'll tell you everything, I promise, but this is massively urgent and we don't have a moment to lose.'

'But what about my bike?' Troy protested, frowning as Freddie sprinted past them, already pulling his sodden T-shirt over his head.

'You're a good man, Troy,' Freddie said, patting him on the shoulder. 'I owe you a pint or ten.'

Three minutes later, Flora was on her way back out with a flash drive in her hand and a smile on her face. Her parents were already in the car, Freddie locking and double-locking the front door nervously, his hands shaking. He turned to face Flora, looking more scared now than he had at any other point, as though hope was the most terrifying proposition of all. '. . . Did you find it?'

Flora smiled, reaching up to loosen his tie which he'd tightened as hard as a knuckle. 'Yep. We've got her, all right. It's over, Freds.'

Freddie slumped, a sob escaping him, and Flora threw her arms around him, rubbing his back as the stress of the past few months overcame him. Flora saw her parents' white faces looking up anxiously from behind the rain-smeared windows. But something else too.

It took a double-take for her to register the slight figure standing on the opposite pavement, her hands clasped protectively in front, her chin dipped in trepidation, that distinctive fiery hair ablaze in the rain.

Flora gasped. In spite of Freddie's stark warnings, she had texted Aggie several times, asking her to call, telling her it was urgent – but Aggie hadn't responded and in desperation yesterday, knowing she risked someone else overhearing (a new boyfriend, flatmate, the cleaner), Flora had left an angry message on her answerphone, explaining exactly what was happening to her ex-boyfriend and the reason why he'd been keeping a profile lower than the dead. Reckless? Yes. There had been every chance Freds would be true to his word and if he found out what she'd done, going behind his back . . .

But it wasn't going to come to that.

'What is it?' Freddie asked, feeling her straighten and pull back. His gaze followed hers and he fell still as he saw Aggie looking back at him, bedraggled and wretched. But here.

She was here.

Epilogue

The saleroom was packed, the buzz of conversation more akin to a cocktail party than a fine-art sale. Flora sat still in her seat, her paddle on her lap as she let the chatter fly around her head. She felt strangely serene in the babble, the swirling passions and torrents of the summer beginning to recede into memories that would one day not hurt any more, but just become vague facts with no emotion attached – a sleepless night in Antibes, a lie laid bare . . . That was all they would become: a string of words, a sequence of images turned down to mute, shed of all the anger and hurt, despair and confusion that had blared at her in surround sound this summer.

A hand squeezed her shoulder, the specialist in Asian Contemporary Art at Christie's grinning down at her. 'Thought I might see you here. Congratulations! What a project. I'd love to hear about it. Breakfast next week?'

'Sure,' she nodded.

Coolly, she watched a couple of women joyously greeting each other on the far side of the room, lipsticked lips never touching the other's cheeks. She looked away, unmoved by their excitement, and watched, instead, an older gentleman sitting alone and thumbing the catalogue with great interest, his brow furrow deepening on certain pages as he held them close to the end of his nose.

She hadn't bothered looking through the catalogue herself, of course; she knew the collection being sold tonight by heart. She found it deeply ironic to be bidding on a piece she herself had found – not just found but inventoried, researched, named, returned to the world. Of course, she was acting for different clients tonight. Angus had promised to be here to represent the Vermeils – as the sellers – and make sure everything ran smoothly. Naturally, his flight was delayed . . .

'Flora! Haven't seen you all summer. We must have lunch.'

She raised a smile and nodded back at the Bruton Street gallerist. 'Lovely. Absolutely.'

None of the family was here either. According to Angus, they had debated it long and hard; the response to the LAPADA advert had been favourably received and overwhelming, especially when it had come out in the press about Von Taschelt's true role in the war. Whilst he couldn't be hailed an outright hero – his estate had profited too much from his dealings with the Third Reich for that – his efforts to save the condemned and most notably, smuggle thirteen children to safety in crates, had gone a very long way in restoring his reputation and the family's name.

In the end, though, they had decided against making a personal appearance here, which could be construed as 'showy' or attention-seeking, instead settling for placing an open letter at the front of the sale catalogue, reiterating their wish to return the looted art in their collection to the rightful owners; and where that wasn't possible – as per this sale tonight – to raise funds for a foundation benefiting children of refugees.

'Flo! I hope you've asked for a pay rise! Coffee soon?' The vice president for Jewellery at Bonhams was en route to her seat, her eyebrows shrugged high.

'Love to.'

Ideally she wouldn't have been here either; whether the family was in the saleroom or not, the moment the first lot came out, they would be all around her again – memories swirling as she remembered their voices gabbling, eyes assessing her, scrutinizing her, dismantling her . . . She sniffed lightly and straightened her back, head held high.

It was fine. Just another sale. She'd only come for the Seurat – a mid-sized portrait of a Moorish woman, for an Ibizan villa belonging to a new German client. She'd flown there only last week in order to see and 'feel' the space herself, although she'd already been 80 per cent sure that the Seurat was the right fit. The guide price was £18,000–£20,000 but she was prepared to go to £27,250.

The shuffle of leather-soled shoes and a cloud of cologne announced the arrival of someone in the seat beside her, someone who wasn't Angus, for whom the seat was provisionally saved.

She turned to find Max St John, of Bonhams and the *Concours d'Élégance*, settling himself beside her. She didn't turn him away.

'Flora! How are you?' he purred in a low, silky voice, in his natural element as the room swarmed with familiar faces, people taking their seats as the clock ticked ever closer to eight.

'Very well, Max,' she replied. 'I wouldn't have expected to see you here tonight. Busman's holiday?'

He smiled. 'There's a small still-life pastel that Cynthia's keen on – bowl of pears.'

She nodded. 'Oh, yes. The Redon. It's lovely. Very charming. Great shadowing.'

'Of course, you're the real expert on it!' he laughed, nudging her in the waist.

'Well, I wouldn't say expert,' she demurred, looking back across the crowd. 'Close observer, perhaps.'

He looked at her attentively. 'It must have been some experience curating that collection, I bet.' Her name had been quoted extensively as the specialist in charge of the 'lost art' collection and Angus was tap-dancing daily as the new business rolled in. In fact, far from losing her job (Angus had shouted at her most about that when he'd read her email – *Are you mad? Stop bloody trying to quit!*) it had never been so secure, with a pay rise and an equity stake in the company to boot.

She was riding high. Sort of.

'It was indeed quite an experience,' she replied with understatement, remembering the town ball in Saint-Paul-de-Vence, the way Xavier had danced with her, refusing to give her up, that look in his eyes when he'd finally just *stopped* – stopped in the middle of the dance floor, stopped pretending, stopped pushing her away . . .

She bit her lip and looked down into her lap, taking only a moment's pause before she looked up again. It wasn't heartbreak. There was no point in being hysterical about it. She'd be absolutely fine soon.

Soonish.

'Well, I can't imagine what it must have been like for you working so closely with them in the midst of that scandal . . . Very stressful.' He tutted lightly. 'Mind you, the heat's well and truly off them now. The press has got itself a new whipping boy, what with the latest revelations about Jean-Luc Desanyoux. I take it you've heard?'

'Desanyoux?' she asked innocently.

'Before your time, probably. Retired F1 driver, won everything in the eighties before Schumacher and Ferrari got going; *Vanity Fair*'s rumours column alleged an *inappropriate liking* for young girls and now they're coming out of the woodwork. I can't say they tried too hard to disguise his identity, so they must have been pretty sure of their facts. Anyway, I understand his wife's left him.' He lowered his voice. 'I sold him a Porsche 959 once, but I have to say I never warmed to the fellow. Always considered him a rather shady chap.'

'Goodness,' she said primly, making a mental note to text Stefan afterwards. He was officially off her hit list.

The first lot was wheeled out, two white-gloved porters carrying a large ornament draped with a protective black cloth. Flora tried to guess what it was from memory. She tried to care. Once upon a time, these sales had set her pulse racing, the bloodlust up as she vied against the rich, the arrogant, the experienced, the entitled. That rush when she won used to sustain her for weeks; she had loved pitching her natural coolness against impatient passions, becoming as impassive as a high-stakes poker player as she'd pitted her strategic sense of timing and pressure against those with bigger wallets. But now? Since returning to London, she'd lost her hunger and thirst for these little battles. She did her job but with no enthusiasm or pride; she should be euphoric after the biggest project of her career but she felt numb.

The auctioneer took to the floor and the lighting changed,

funnelling everyone's attention onto the draped object on the podium. The hum of conversation broke up into speckled silence, people sitting to attention in their chairs.

Flora felt herself change too. The quiet intensity of the selling process made her taut as a quiver – all her attention focused on the 'what' and the 'who' on the stage. She knew how to scan the room without moving her head, when to introduce her first bid, drop out, then swoop back in for the final kill. *This* was her specialism – cool, clinical bidding where passion was the enemy. As in life, it came at too high a cost.

The dust cloth was whisked off the object on the podium and a vibrato of appreciation rippled through the room. Flora felt as though her bones had been shot through with steel rods, holding her upright and stiff . . . What?

On instinct, her heart rate immediately rocketing up to 104 bpm, she looked around the room – several clusters of people had their heads inclined together, their eyes on the prize, nodding, others hurriedly flicking through the catalogue to find it.

'Ladies and gentlemen, our first lot tonight – *Love Three*. A spectacular bronze rendering. Height one hundred and eleven centimetres, weighing in at four point three kilos—'

Flora's eyes continued their scrutiny of the crowd, persistently swinging back to the bronze globe as though it was magnetic north.

'. . . A unique opportunity to purchase tonight from the Vermeil family's private collection, a piece by Xavier Vermeil himself, hitherto working under the pseudonym Yves Desmarais. This piece is offered exclusively for tonight's sale with all proceeds going to the charitable foundation established in the family name.'

It was a nice touch, she could see that; a little more generosity, something for the family to give back to the world, another way to say 'sorry'.

'Who'll start me at seventeen thousand pounds?'

A hand shot up in the far-right corner and Flora almost jumped at the sight of it.

'Seventeen three?'

Another hand.

Flora felt her pulse spike, her mouth become dry as she watched the price spiral upwards. Within minutes, they had sailed past £25,000.

Flora stared at the beautiful sculpture, remembering the hands that had made it, held her. Under the singular beam of light, every notch and stipple of bronze was highlighted, the globe textured like clodded earth beneath the lovers' feet, their twisting sinuous bodies leaning in to one another, arms and hair upswept and fanning out euphorically—

'Twenty-seven six.'

The auctioneer nodded at her only briefly, his eyes swinging back in the next moment to a woman sitting three rows in front. Flora jolted as she realized she had moved.

More than moved. Raised her arm. Placed a bid.

What? No! She hadn't come here to buy this—

'Twenty-eight two.'

The auctioneer nodded at her again. Flora stared back at him in horror. It was as though she'd lost control of her own body.

She tried to concentrate, to calm down. She wasn't in this race. Just breathe, Flora.

She looked around, gathering her wits, her usual poise. The bidders had fallen back to two people – a new entry, a phoner (which she never liked – she couldn't see who she was up against) and the flushed woman just ahead of her, whose make-up was shining under the lights. The Christie's employee on the phone to the other bidder kept looking over at her, checking to see whether she was coming back into the game.

She forced herself to watch, even though she couldn't hear the numbers now above the roar of blood rushing in her head. She watched as the two bidders became more entrenched in their positions, a battle-hardened expression on the woman's face; but Flora could tell by the way her nostrils flared slightly at £29,000 – her face in profile as she surveyed the audience for further bidders – that she was approaching her limit. The phoner was going to win in the next couple of thousand.

She stared at the sculpture. At the very most, if she was advising a client, she wouldn't have gone beyond £25,000 on this. These bidders were already overpaying and getting carried away. It was stunning – but he was an unknown artist.

Then again, aside from his obvious skill, he came from a prominent family and there was rarity value.

She was surprised when the phoner dropped out at £33,800; she'd thought whoever it was had it in the bag (not that it was easy to tell anything when that person wasn't even in the room) but going by the woman's reactions alone, she was teetering on the very edge of being able to afford this.

The woman fell very still – she was within a hair's breadth of winning the piece now – as the auctioneer went back to the room, surveying the crowd as he checked for other bids, his palm covering the top of the gavel, ready to strike.

'Going for the final time at thirty-three thousand, eight hundred pou— Thank you, madam.'

His eyes were on her once more and Flora found to her horror that her hand had not only shot up again but was *still* thrust upright, her arm as straight as a pipe for all to see, as though she was answering a question in class. Mortified, she lowered her arm. What was wrong with her? She didn't want this piece.

She did. She wanted it desperately. It was the only thing she'd have of him.

No. She didn't. Why would she spend all that money just to be reminded of how it had felt to be in his arms, to bathe in his gaze, to be the one to make him sigh, smile, moan? Why would she spend all that money to relive how it had felt to watch him walk away, deserting her when she'd been there for him? Why would she want to remember that? Why would she pay for the honour? No, *over*pay for the honour. She'd have to be mad. She'd have to be—

Her hand shot up again. Oh, dear God.

Beside her, Max chuckled. 'You go for it, Flora,' he murmured. 'Just trust your instincts.'

'No!'

People in the vicinity turned to look but the sound of the word had brought her to her senses – her *instincts* had betrayed her before.

Max was looking surprised, even a little embarrassed, but she didn't feel the need to elaborate; she'd come back to herself.

The phone bidder had come back out to play again too but this time, when the auctioneer looked back at her, she kept her hands down (by sitting on them) and firmly shook her head. There would be no mistaking her withdrawal now, she thought as she tried to calm down.

'Bad luck,' Max murmured to her as the hammer came down and the phoner won it.

'Not at all. You've got to know when to quit,' she said briskly. 'It's a nice piece but I'm not prepared to lose my head over it.'

He nodded approvingly. 'True mark of a professional,' he cheered, but his eyes were questioning.

The audience politely clapped as the bronze was taken away by the white-gloved porters. Flora rose from her seat. She wasn't going to bother with the Seurat. Her nerves were shot. She just wanted to get out of here; it had been a mistake to think she could go through with this.

'Not staying to see the Faucheux?' Max asked in surprise, swinging his legs to the side to let her past.

'No. I've seen it before,' she smiled. 'Good luck with the Redon.'

'Thank you, yes. Big wedding anniversary coming up, thought I should make a proper effort before she sees what a fraud I really am and leaves me for the tennis coach.'

Flora laughed, patting his shoulder as she passed. 'See you, Max.'

'Regards to your father.'

'Sure thing,' she replied, walking up the aisle to the table at the back and handing in her paddle. Were people staring? She couldn't help but feel they somehow knew; as though her rash impetuousness had betrayed all her summer secrets.

'Not staying?' the coat girl asked, taking her ticket and rifling through the rails for her red double-faced cashmere coat.

'No.' The word came out almost as a sob, surprising them both.

She over-tipped and turned away, walking as quickly as she could towards the doors, desperate to feel fresh air on her face. She felt smothered suddenly, her lungs rigid and small, the room too hot, the past too close.

Through the doors she could see it was raining, umbrellas domed over people's heads as they scurried for shelter, and she burst through, desperate for the feel of it, as though her problems were an ink that could be washed away, him a stain she could rub out.

She stood at the top of the steps for a moment, wondering which way to go, the sound of car horns and the wet hiss of water sluicing off wheels an urban soundtrack in her ears. She wasn't due to meet Freddie and Aggs for another hour and she had no plans. Coffee, perhaps?

Vodka tonic more like. She felt shaken and—

She saw him.

He was getting out of a car – no doubt here to see what price his sculpture had fetched. The driver was holding up an umbrella, but he shook his head dismissively, fastening the button on his jacket. He looked good – different – in his slim black suit and white shirt, a far cry from the chaotic, barely dressed linens of the summer, that summer when they'd both so nearly come undone.

His head down, keeping out of the rain, he ran up the very steps she was standing on, looking a prince among men. She turned away on instinct, felt the rush of air as he sprinted past, caught a trace of the smell of him – and that was it, the memories flooded her, crashing down with devastating force.

Why did it have to be him who made her feel like this? Ines had told her that passion rarely follows the rules but the past few weeks had been the worst she'd ever known, trying to convince herself he was just a Mediterranean storm who'd barrelled into her life, thrown everything against the walls and barrelled out again; after a little clearing up, life would continue as it had before. Only it hadn't and she knew it never would. The sun had been pulled from her sky.

She didn't wait to hear the clatter of the doors being thrown open. She skipped down the steps quickly and turned the corner out of sight, tears blinding her path. The rain fell hard but she didn't care, didn't even notice; it was a good thing, camouflaging her as she stumbled through the crowd.

'Wait!'

His hand, her wrist. She was swung round in a dance that was becoming their tarantella, her eyes instantly locked on that extraordinary face that commanded spells over her.

'Flora,' he panted, flesh and blood and tanned and bergamot-scented and just inches away. She could see the rain in his hair, her face in his eyes.

'Leave me alone, Xavier!' she cried, angrily yanking her arm from his grip and attracting searching glances from the commuters hurrying past.

'I can't.'

'Too bad.' She was moving again, slipping through the crowd, away from him, escaping him.

His hand. Her wrist. Back there again.

'Listen to me—'

'No. I heard enough.' She went to claim her arm back but

he was holding harder this time. She couldn't fool him twice.

'Look, I got it wrong, OK? I let you down when you needed me.' Every word seemed cloaked in velvet, his accent a caress she could curl into.

'But I didn't need you,' she replied coolly, watching to see her words wound. 'The case was thrown out. She's been charged with perverting the course of justice. It was all lies, just like I said.' She looked up into those dark shimmering eyes, wanting to see the look that came into them when he saw he'd thrown her – them – away for nothing.

It was already there. 'I should have listened to you.'

'Damn right you should,' she said, her anger a white heat that radiated from her. 'But instead you left me to face it all on my own. *You*, who should have known better than anyone how lonely it is to be defined by lies! No one else could have understood it but you – and you didn't. You just couldn't see beyond your pain, your loss. No one else mattered. Not me. I didn't.'

He stared down at her, unbroken and resolute. 'You have to understand – it's been *years* of trauma that we've gone through with Natascha. It broke us all. She is not the only victim, you know. My mother does not eat, my father does not sleep. I haven't been free to live my life the way I want, where I want, doing what I want. Our entire lives are lived through the prism of her needs, Flora. How could I have explained to her what you meant to me and in the next breath, told her about your brother? She would have seen it as a betrayal. I had no choice!'

'No. And I guess you never will.' Flora blinked back at him, willing her anger to stay with her. She understood his dilemma even if she couldn't forgive it, but there was no point in either compassion or forgiveness. There would be no apology, no begging, for this was the bleak truth that would always separate them. Freddie had been the lucky one. He'd been able to get justice in time, but it was too late for Natascha now. Xavier was right; they had been living with the scars for too long and she was too damaged to ever let him go. He would never be there for her. Natascha would always come first. 'You're trapped, Xavier. But I'm not.'

Like a flash of light on a blade, she turned away and slipped into the crowd, her arm raised in the air to catch the first passing cab.

'Flora, wait!' he cried, catching up with her three seconds later, standing by her shoulder. 'You don't understand. That's why I'm here. Things have changed. The press at home – it's all come out about Desanyoux. Natascha has given a statement to the police about what he did. It's looking like they're going to prosecute. Don't you see? It's set her free. She can finally move forward with her life.'

A taxi had pulled to a stop by the kerb in front of her and Flora – who had reached to open the door – paused, feeling her heart quicken at the news.

People bustled past them, newspapers turned into make-shift rain covers over their heads as they ran for shelter, and Flora realized as she looked up at him that she – he – must be soaked too, although she wasn't aware of it. Rather, she was remembering the last time they'd stood in the rain; it had been the same then, too – wanting him, not understanding him.

'I really hope so,' Flora said sadly. 'She deserves it. You all do.'

She opened the taxi door but he stopped it mid-swing, with an outstretched arm.

'Where the hell are you going?' he cried. 'Didn't you hear what I just said? We can be together now.'

She shook her head. 'It's over, Xavier. I can't be with someone I don't trust – and I don't trust you not to throw me over again. I'm sorry but whatever you think's going on between us – it isn't enough.'

'It's everything!' he shouted above the rain. 'You know how I found you just now? I smelled your hair! In this city, with all these people, in the pouring rain, I could smell *you*. I turned round and there you were running in the opposite direction, even though I'd told them to keep you there till I arrived.'

A beat pulsed and the cabbie stuck his head out of the window.

'Look, love, you getting in or what?' he asked.

Before Flora could think to reply, Xavier hurriedly pulled a twenty from his pocket and told the driver to beat it.

She stared at him, open-mouthed.

He shrugged, a playful smile twitching on his lips. 'What? I'd pay anything if I thought it would get you back. Twenty pounds? Thirty? There's no limit!'

She half-laughed but not quite. To laugh was to let him in and she wouldn't – couldn't – do that again. Her shoulders slumped, wearied from the fight. 'Don't you get it, Xavier? We're no good for each other. All we are is a fucked-up mix of lust and confusion. I can't live like that. I don't know which way is up with you.'

He took a step closer. 'Good. Your life should be turned upside down when you fall in love.'

'L . . . *love?*' she spluttered. 'Are you completely mad?

How can you even use that word? This is the second-longest conversation we've ever had!'

'So? You had me at "Go to hell".'

She laughed this time in spite of herself, seeing the way his eyes softened at the sound.

It emboldened him and he took another step nearer, standing so close now their toes almost touched. 'Actually, it was before that. I fell for you the second I walked in and found you wrestling with the ostrich.' He paused for a second, mischief enlivening his eyes, making her heart skip. 'How did you know it was my fantasy?'

Flora laughed again, wrong-footed by his humour at a time like this, but she stopped soon enough as his fingers pushed her hair away from her face. She tried to read him, resist him, knew she could do neither. 'Her name's Gertie.'

'Gertie? The ostrich?'

She nodded, wishing he didn't smell so good, wishing his eyes didn't burn like that – desire and laughter and irreverence and fearlessness swirling in an intoxicating mix that made it hard for her to breathe.

His hold on her tightened. 'God, that was in the fantasy too,' he murmured, pulling another smile from her.

'Anything else in this fantasy of yours I should know about?'

There was a riot in his eyes now. 'Well, if you want to be faithful to the original version, you're naked.' He shrugged.

She laughed again, cross to be laughing, helpless against his charm assault. 'Oh, am I?'

He shrugged. 'Yes. You, me . . . Gertie.'

Her smile faded as she stared up at him, wondering how this enigma of a man had managed to change so much, doing so little. 'We don't know each other, Xavier.'

She felt his fingertips press against her. 'Yes, we do. In our souls we do. We've both known it from the beginning. The rest is just detail.'

'You call knowing the intricacies of someone's life a detail?'

'Yes. All that matters is the kiss. It's the kiss that reveals the heart,' he murmured, rubbing his thumb gently along her lower lip, triggering a flutter in her belly.

It was all over. Who was she trying to kid? Her head didn't believe a word of what he was saying but for the first time in her life, that was seemingly irrelevant; her heart wouldn't have it any other way. She'd take him however she could get him. 'You'd better kiss me then and show me yours.'

His eyes fell to her lips and she felt her longing for him surge. '. . . No.'

'No?'

He smiled wickedly, stepping back and taking her by the hand. 'First we talk.'

'Oh, *now* you want to talk?' she protested as he began to lead her up the street, his arm outstretched for his driver whom she could see now, parked a discreet distance away. 'I don't believe you! You're incorrigible. Is it always going to be like this?'

He stopped and whirled her into his arms, his fingers pushing back her hair as she stared up at him, the rain on her face: breathless, disoriented, his. 'Yes,' he whispered. 'It is.'

Acknowledgements

This story is based on the real-life discovery a few years ago of an abandoned Paris apartment, locked up since the Second World War. I vividly remember seeing the images online – do google it and you'll see – and feeling so fascinated by this dusty time capsule. I kept wondering not just about the people who had been forced to flee it, but why no one had ever come back. After all, it takes something to wilfully forget that you own an apartment in Paris!

So where does real life end and fiction begin? Well, Gertie the ostrich is real (although perhaps not called Gertie by anyone else!), but I've allowed my imagination to run away in almost every aspect – from the apartment's location and layout to its ownership and reasons for abandonment – and although I've used some real names, such as Auguste Renoir and Ambroise Vollard, others such as Faucheux and Huber are made up, as are all the paintings described. I really hope you enjoyed the story, but of course, its historical backdrop is rooted in painfully true events and I was very conscious of this in the telling of it. Even over seventy years later, it doesn't make for easy reading and nor should it.

I would like to thank my brilliant, indomitable, 'give me a bar chart' agent Amanda Preston for being so enthusiastic when I first mooted the idea of writing this story. I wasn't sure whether to proceed as the apartment's discovery had been widely covered in the media and I wasn't convinced I could take such an intriguing, high-profile prospect and do it justice. As ever, Amanda gave me the courage to have a go.

Also, the amazing team at Pan Macmillan who have embraced this book with gusto and big hearts, delivering a beautifully fresh cover look – thank you James Annal – and energetic marketing campaign – yes, I do mean you Jodie Mullish! I am indebted to my copy-editor, Mary Chamberlain, and proofreader, Amber Burlinson, who took a very dense plot and helped me simplify and streamline it; and to my editors Victoria Hughes-Williams and Caroline Hogg, who knew exactly how and when to crack the whip. To Anna Bond, Daniel Jenkins, Eloise Wood and Katie James, you shall all be hugged very hard next time I see you, so perhaps adopt the brace position?

For my parents, Malcolm and Mally, and my parents-in-law, Victor and Lynne, your love and support is invaluable. You had faith in me even before the first book was finished, and writing two books a year with a young family is only possible because of all your help with the children, the dogs, tea and cake, and fizz o'clock. I appreciate each one of your kindnesses and every effort.

To my beloved family, thank you for walking the entire Cap of Cap d'Antibes with me, just so that I could check out the big estates, and particularly to my husband Anders for tolerating spending fifteen euros on Cokes. Trekking all those Provençal miles – oh my goodness, Saint-Paul-de-Vence in 95-degree heat! – may have been done in the name of research, but you all made it such fun. If the journey is the destination, I never want ours to end.